VALANCOURT CLASSICS

SLEEPING WATERS

BY

John Trevena

Edited with a new introduction by
Gerald C. Monsman

Kansas City:
VALANCOURT BOOKS
2013

Sleeping Waters by John Trevena
First published London: Constable, 1913
First American edition, New York: Mitchell Kennerley, 1914
First Valancourt Books edition 2013

ISBN 978-1-939140-00-5 (*trade paper*)

All Valancourt Books publications are printed on acid free paper
that meets all ANSI standards for archival quality paper.

Design and typography by James D. Jenkins
Set in Dante MT 11/13.75

Published by Valancourt Books
Kansas City, Missouri
http://www.valancourtbooks.com

10 9 8 7 6 5 4 3 2 1

SLEEPING WATERS

ERNEST GEORGE HENHAM ("John Trevena") was born in England in 1870, and as a young man travelled to the New World, where his sojourn in the Canadian Northwest provided the inspiration for some of his early works. As Ernest G. Henham, he published *Menotah: A Tale of the Riel Rebellion* (1897), *God, Man & The Devil: A Novel* (1897), the weird Gothic horror novel *Tenebrae* (1898), *Bonanza: A Story of the Outside* (1901), *Scud: The Story of a Feud* (1902), *The Plowshare and the Sword: A Tale of Old Quebec* (1903), '*Krum*': *A Study of Consciousness* (1904), and *The Feast of Bacchus* (1907).

Suffering from ill health, he moved to Dartmoor around this time. In the words of a contemporary, "It is one of the strangest facts in literary history that a man, who had defined his place as a writer of fiction with nine novels or so, published under his own name, should have seen fit to begin his career afresh and write a long series of commercially unsuccessful novels under a pseudonym." However, this was what Henham did, publishing *A Pixy in Petticoats* anonymously in 1906 before adopting the pseudonym John Trevena in 1907 for *Furze the Cruel*, the first in a trilogy of novels focusing upon Dartmoor life, followed by *Heather* (1908) and *Granite* (1909). He continued to write prolifically, achieving widespread critical acclaim but little commercial success. His notable works include *Bracken* (1910), *Written in the Rain* (1910) (short stories), *Wintering Hay* (1912), which the *Los Angeles Times* ranked with the works of Turgenev and Dostoevsky, *Sleeping Waters* (1913), and *Moyle Church-Town* (1915). Trevena's life is so shrouded in obscurity that at the time of this printing even his date of death was not known, though he is believed to have died around 1946. Until the Valancourt edition of *Furze the Cruel* in 2010, all his works were out of print, despite the near-universal critical consensus during his lifetime that his works would live on among the classics of English fiction.

GERALD C. MONSMAN is Professor of English at the University of Arizona in Tucson. He is the author of *Pater's Portraits: Mythic Pattern in the Fiction of Walter Pater* (Johns Hopkins, 1967), *Walter Pater's Art of Autobiography* (Yale, 1980), *Confessions of a Prosaic Dreamer: Charles Lamb's Art of Autobiography* (Duke, 1984), *Olive Schreiner's Fiction: Landscape and Power* (Rutgers, 1991), *H. Rider Haggard on the Imperial Frontier* (ELT, 2006), and the editor of Haggard's *King Solomon's Mines* (Broadview, 2002). Recently, his work has focused on rediscovery of Trevena and the South African writers Bertram Mitford and Ernest Glanville, and he has prepared scholarly editions of six novels by Mitford and four by Trevena for Valancourt Books, as well as editions of Pater's *Marius the Epicurean* and Haggard's *Nada the Lily*.

By the Same Author

As Ernest G. Henham

Menotah: A Tale of the Riel Rebellion (1897)
God, Man & The Devil: A Novel (1897)
Tenebrae: A Novel (1898)*
Bonanza: A Story of the Outside (1901)
Scud: The Story of a Feud (1902)
The Plowshare and the Sword: A Tale of Old Quebec (1903)
'Krum': A Study of Consciousness (1904)
The Feast of Bacchus (1907)

As John Trevena

A Pixy in Petticoats (1906)*
Arminel of the West (1907)
Furze the Cruel (1907)*
Heather (1908)
Granite (1909)
The Dartmoor House that Jack Built (1909)
Bracken (1910)
Written in the Rain (1910)
The Reign of the Saints (1911)
Wintering Hay (1912)
Sleeping Waters (1913)*
No Place Like Home (1913)
Adventures among Wild Flowers (1914)
Moyle Church-Town (1915)
The Captain's Furniture (1916)
Raindrops (1920)
The Vanished Moor (1923)
The Custom of the Manor (1924)
Off the Beaten Track (1925)
Typet's Treasure (1927)

* Available from Valancourt Books

CONTENTS

INTRODUCTION[1]

JOHN TREVENA began his writing career under his own name, Ernest G. Henham, with fiction such as *Tenebrae: A Novel* (1898) in the Gothic style of E. A. Poe's "The Fall of the House of Usher." But he reinvented both his style and career at the time of his anonymously published *A Pixy in Petticoats* (1906), a narrative of romance and legend neither grotesque nor decadent which proved extremely popular in the United States as well as England. Thereafter, his novels were published under the pseudonym "John Trevena." And when *Furze the Cruel* appeared in 1907, *The Academy* hailed it as "a great book," while the *Dundee Advertiser* predicted that "it will rank in the forefront of modern fiction." A review of *Sleeping Waters* (1913) in the *New York Times* began:

> It would be difficult to find a novel more unusual or more original than this latest work of the author who chooses to be known as John Trevena. Allegory and realism, folk-lore and character-study, impressive pictures of a land strange and wild as that famous "misty mid-region of Weir," and, dominating all, a divided personality, a mind at once disordered and clairvoyant, seeing all things in unreal and twisted guises, yet sometimes penetrating to the ultimate truth, even to that truth of thought and motive which men refuse to admit to their own souls—it combines all these interests while remaining primarily a story wrought by a mystic, yet on the surface a tale susceptible of an entirely materialistic explanation.[2]

Trevena is currently classed as a British regional novelist whose work, set among the Dartmoor valleys and rocky hilltops, exhibits

---

1 As this Introduction reveals certain important elements of the plot, the reader may wish to return to it after finishing the novel.

2 "Fiction," *Academy*, 16 October 1907: 66-68; *Dundee Advertiser*, quoted in "Some Press Opinions," *Furze the Cruel*, Popular Edition (London: Rivers, 1913): ii; "New Year Fiction," *New York Times*, 10 January 1915: 53-55.

a strong feel for social customs and realistic dialogue. In this respect Thomas Hardy's Wessex novels have a close affinity to Trevena's writings—particularly Hardy's vision of nature's resistless power and cruelties. But Trevena's use of the land as a metaphor of its people, a place of the mind as well as a topography that is real, has an originality all its own. The *New York Times* reviewer concluded his estimate by declaring that the author of *Sleeping Waters* was "unquestionably one of the most notable of living writers."

How can such a writer be so neglected today? In the middle of the nineteenth century Bulwer-Lytton defined fiction of the "Intellectual School" as a genre requiring a longer attention span and a higher level of understanding owing to the development of character and plot through subtlety of form and content rather than primarily through direct action—an observation later fashionably reworked in Roland Barthes's *S/Z* (1970). From Bulwer's point of view, Trevena's accessible regionalism becomes an inclusive vehicle for underlying multiple layers of intellectual engagement. The *Times* reviewer had noted:

> "Sleeping Waters" is emphatically not a book for the intellectually lazy. It demands close attention and mental alertness from the reader who desires to follow its venturous attempt to portray—partly by means of symbolism—the complex relations of body and soul and brain in a man of "extraordinary psychological development," intensely nervous, more than a little morbid, exceptionally imaginative, who under the stress of change and shock, saw all things in strange aspects. That it is beautifully written, full of poetic passages, and contains many fascinating descriptions of the moor . . . will be regarded as a matter of course by those who have read any of the preceding books.

In his lifetime Trevena was popular with discriminating readers, but the mingled flow of perceptions, memories, scenes, and a poetic and philosophical style proved in later years too intellectual for mass market popularity. And, yet, how could anyone not admire his image in this novel of a nubile girl sitting on a rock, "her face detrimental to all philosophy." Or pity the celibate priest of his witticism, "A man who has never loved a woman can only half love his God." Or applaud his gracious recognition in light of Protestant and Catholic antagonism that "charity is too holy to need a creed." Or endorse the enlightened pragmatism of "Self-sacrifice is much the same as suicide." Or chuckle when his protagonist answers a lazy farmer's charge of trespass: "I am not damaging your crop of moss by trampling on it."

Trevena's late-Victorian and Edwardian-era novels may well be ideal candidates for reclamation. The time is right—ambitious though it may seem—to argue that he is no less significant a novelist than Hardy, although Trevena is the more recondite writer. The only previous book-length study of Trevena's work has been an able but limited-circulation dissertation some eighty years ago; however, in the meantime newer interpretive methodologies have been forged, better able to make sense of Trevena if carefully applied. As an opportunity for innovative canon revision, republication of *Sleeping Waters* in a contemporaneous edition analyzing the artistic handling of its thematic materials will add a new "intellectual classic" to the canon.

Very much as Trevena himself had been compelled for the sake of his lungs to seek the higher elevations of Dartmoor—"which is said to have brought health to its author as to John Anger"[1]—his protagonist (whose surname is an old Norman one, pronounced "Ahn-jer") is a young priest of the slums whose selfless and continuous exposure to the poverty and polluted atmosphere of London has left him physically exhausted and near death. For "Father Jack" Dartmoor's earth and sky becomes an awakening to a new life of the body and spirit: "a big rounded hill beside the village . . . healed me. It hung over my bed, breathing new life into me." When after four months his initial symptoms of exhaustion, pulmonary distress, and fever leave him, he is allowed to go out of doors. But later, after drinking the magic "sleeping waters" of the stream Nympha (the new River Lethe of forgetfulness), he becomes lost in a mist. The shock of exposure from mist on the moors seeming-

1 *New York Times*, 10 January 1915: 55.

ly renders Anger delirious, and from this point onwards he begins to move through a strange and wild world. Anger's fever filters objective reality through his unstable perceptions and subliminal ideational structures in which the initial baseline of daily reality is lost. He bizarrely correlates his naturopathic cure with that of his friend's Catholic ancestor in the time of Charles I. In Anger's present, with old political-religious animosities of the Civil War behind them, his Catholic and Protestant friends combined to rehabilitate "Father Jack." But although long gone, Hugh Billacott, a Royalist supporter of King Charles I in his struggle with Parliament, becomes part of Anger's present reality, a quickening prototype from ancestral history three hundred years previously whose doings phantasmagorically return in the present. The early seventeenth-century cavalier had been wounded, but after he drank from the healing waters of Nympha he was so fully cured that according to the Billacott family book he engaged in an affair with his wife's lady-help, Petronel Vigar.

In this fantastic dream world that amalgamates new and old, Anger and Hugh are part of the cycle of renewal that keeps modernity in touch with its past. In the mist Anger stumbles upon the shelter of the beautiful river nymph Petronel and her demented worshiper, the boy Whippety. Whippety's father is the lawyer Curgenven, a demonic and crafty dwarf; the violent and drunken mother, Judith, is also Petronel's adoptive parent. Curgenven, hidden by piles of books or behind his revolving *trompe-l'œil* bookcase, is not merely Anger's competitor for the prize of "Petronel" but also doubles the author's fallen self screened by the text. Anger's passion for Petronel, who is sometimes endearing but often cruel, culminates when, as a winter storm rages, she induces him to murder Judith with a hammer—a crime in the cellar of the dark house of Stiniel where all that is demented and guilty is concentrated. Spellbound by Petronel, Anger descends to this act of brute passion, experiencing a guilt never before known. Yet, like John Milton's Adam, he falls to rise—from seduction by the senses to a "far better" love and beauty. Anger gains his reward only after Charon has been paid and he awakens from the spell of the sleeping waters. He and Trevena are now alike, weighed by the shadows of experience and knowledge yet open to new life. As Petronel vanishes upon the moor, Anger finds in her place Mary Wiggaton, who had been his sisterly London companion-in-charity. Hitherto, Mary's love for the saintly "Father Jack" had remained necessarily unspoken, and he had refused to acknowledge even to himself his love for her. Mary Wiggaton embodies the creative powers of Petronel yet is herself an actual woman, reconciling in one person nature with grace, the tangible with the inexpressible infinite.

Trevena's novel appeared just before the beginning of the First World War, its London scenes foreshadowing post-War disillusionment and alienation as evinced in the Expressionist and Surrealist art that was to come. In *Sleeping Waters* Trevena explores the story of Anger's treatment and convalescence via the emerging generic possibilities of magical realism. Among aesthetic modes seeking to reinvest life with an intrinsic enchantment, magical realism opened up an in-between or hidden space within an early twentieth-century technology and consumerism that had lost its contact with the numinous. Although the phrase *magical realism* may have first originated with artistic Surrealism, the mode itself is typical of an earlier neo-romantic concern with the mind's subconscious or nonrational relationships to the external world, its merging of the marvelous with the ordinary. In 1913 Trevena's original readers assumed a narrative timeline or sequence that brought pattern to events and moved toward the protagonist's confronting his personal problems and their resolution. But Anger's escape into the unpredictable mythic events of Dartmoor is not as unequivocal as conventional mimesis which keeps a sharp narrative line drawn on the page between the marvelous and the logical. By combining dream with fact Trevena's novel problematizes the reader's understanding of Anger's situation: what is his dream, what is his reality? How magical or how real is this magical realism? And what is the generic difference between this aesthetic and fantasy or mysticism?

Trevena told Myrtle Henry that "mysticism has always been a part of my nature: I mean a feeling of contact with other lands unseen."[1] His word in *Sleeping Waters* for Anger's uncanny contact with the fantastic lurking within the ordinary is "enchantment," from the Old French *enchanter* and Latin *incantare*, to bewitch or cast a magical spell by song. Trevena begins with classical realism; but to redress limitations of the ordinary he employs strategies to subvert reality, presenting images and scenes in unfamiliar or uncanny ways to accent a latent and mysterious power within the flat, the jejune, the modern. This balance between magic and realism in which one ontological level supplements the other (present here more than a half century before Gabriel García Márquez's *One Hundred Years of Solitude*, 1967, the most celebrated work of magical realism) opens windows on unsuspected possibilities—not the possibility that the fantastic may be *literally* true, but the possibility that things as we assume them to be (and of which we often despair) might be somehow otherwise. The appeal of magical realism lies in its capacity for liberating readers from the "reality rut" of daily life, bringing them for a time into fruitful contact with emotion, imagination, and "the unknown" so that when they return to their trades and professions, they have a richer context for their lives' possibilities.

In a farsighted review of *Sleeping Waters*, Cornelia Van Pelt is able to appreciate the impact of this avant-garde narrative technique:

> Months in bed under careful nursing build up the priest's body, but his mind is still asleep. Flesh reigns and desires unknown before awaken. He finds the Water of Nympha and drinks thereof. What happens after that is told with a consummate art which we do not recognise at first. We feel irritation at the jerky, jumbled style of the narrative until the truth comes as a delicious shock, a decided sensation, and we see how artfully, or rather how artistically, the style fitted the impression to be made. We are as much at sea as is "Father Jack," and cry confused "what here is dream and what is waking?" Was Petronel, the sun-browned maiden, really only a figure in a dream, or was she the Spirit of Dartmoor revealed to a mortal for a time? . . . This is done not as seeking sensational effects but written with

---

1 Myrtle Henry, *John Trevena: A Study* (Philadelphia: Privately Printed, 1935): 3.

a virility that seems like the natural exuberance of an imagination controlled only by the limits of literary style.[1]

The power of *Sleeping Waters* is owing to just this merging of the subjective—the unconscious or intuitive side that cannot be adequately apprehended through empirical reason or sense—with the objective. When describing John Anger's search for the waters of Nympha, Trevena writes:

> "I grow wiser," declared Anger, as he found himself in a solitude which might have been unexplored territory, so entirely was it lacking in every sign of human occupation, and looked upon a region of furze and heather, shining bogs, and stony upland. . . . Being an imaginative man, he could not wander there alone and keep romance away. The tales he had listened to in childhood became retold; falsehood and truth were mingled together; history and myth kissed each other. The folklore, which Jonas the singer stubbornly believed in, the rites and mysteries of his own Church, the deed from the Abbot of Buckfast, the mystic powers of consecrated water, became to his mind the chapters of a story which his own life was to continue, a dream-like story to which he must add realities.

One senses Trevena is working within a modernist aesthetic, achieving some of the striking effects of modernism or post-modernism, whether they be the time-lapse of sleep in Virginia Woolf's *Orlando* (1928) or the delusions of Vladimir Nabokov's "Terra Incognita" (1931) in which the baseline of reality vanishes. But the closest affinity with Trevena's evocative imagery and innovative aesthetics may be Thomas Mann's philosophical masterwork, *The Magic Mountain* (1924), a novel of inner growth or a *bildungsroman*, as it is called in Germany, of Hans, an everyman figure, who spends seven years at an isolated tuberculosis sanatorium at Davos in the Swiss Alps. Is he truly sick or simply trapped by the magical rocks and snow? As a microcosm for European life just before the transformative catastrophe of World War I, Mann's retrospective

---

1 "Twelve Books of the Month," *The Bookman*, March 1915: 99.

setting allegorizes the spiritual and psychological illnesses of a pre-war society selling its soul to the devil. He pits ideologies of modern science and cultural progress against occult medievalism and mystical communism; and he explores the passage of time and its relationships with space, body, and mind, including Hans's awakening to a life of the senses with desire for *"das Ewig Weibliche."*

Sleeping Waters opens with the indictment that Exeter has destroyed its urban antiquities for the sake of commercialization, making money being more important than any touristic value inhering in tradition. At first Anger naively dismisses "old traditions" as "worth nothing" and impulsively exaggerates: "Modernity is unlawful in my church." The narrative uses "rasped" and "clashed" to describe the past's incompatibility with the present. This question whether the old is worth keeping especially relates to Curgenven's scheme to replace the quaint village of Youlstone with resort villas.[1] The year this novel was published, for example, the Okehampton Golf Club, self-described as "The jewel in the heart of Devon," was built in an ancient deer park on the banks of the West Okement river in Dartmoor. The farmers' connection to their land was the essence of their livelihoods, culture, and identity; but farms that not long before seemed of little outside value were now being sought by investors for real estate development—perhaps accompanied with new livelihood opportunities for the commoners (so called because, in addition to their farms, they have joint rights in Dartmoor's common moorland) but more likely only a net loss. As a young man Trevena for a time had clerked in a law firm until its senior partner discovered he wrote poetry. Before he was thereupon promptly fired, he likely enough had learned the facts of modern commercial land development and the fraud issues that *Sleeping Waters* spotlights. Curgenven the diabolic money-lender hustles loans to these naive commoners, who are unaware that they are losing their independence and selling their souls to the devil. It is not just "the silent moor mortgaged to

---

1 Trevena's place-names, which may exist somewhere in the West Country, are fictional for Dartmoor.

winter" or Petronel who is "in the power of a humpbacked dwarf."
Anger observes: "It seems to me the commoners of Youlstone
are children, taking pocket-money from their master, and never
dreaming of a day of settlement. . . . To accept a loan, knowing
it means the sacrifice of a home, is the act of a madman." But
the stubborn villagers, bound by ignorance and traditional pride,
refuse the help they so desperately need, even when Anger offers
them an opportunity.

When Anger first sets out for Dartmoor the only myths or
magic in his life are artificial and unimaginative clichés, though
kindly meant. His London friend Billacott informs him that he will
find "Buttercups and daisies instead of smuts and chimneys. A parish full of larks and butterflies in place of sweated seamstresses
and penny-toy merchants. That's the poetry of it, Father Jack—
and I shall visit you with sonnets in the summer." Trevena com-
pares such pastoral fantasy to real-life social concerns, the harsh
rural life that in *A Pixy in Petticoats* he had called "unutterably drab
and dirty in reality" and that in *Sleeping Waters* he presents as the
choking backwardness of Dartmoor from which "those who have
profited by education emigrate, while the old and the dull stay on;
and tradition dies hard with them." Although the commoners lead
grueling lives, their formidable ignorance nevertheless is cause for
satiric treatment. In *A Pixy in Petticoats*, Ann's milking stool emblematizes stubborn rustic tradition. Willum gives his mother's
reason why her cow is in the middle of the road: "'Mother milked
'en here, so did her mother, so did hers, and I be going to long
as I lives.'. . . Mrs. Cobbledick had always milked her cows in the
middle of the road, and she intended to persevere in that practice
so long as she might live. . . . For it had never occurred to her that it
would be easier to shift the stool than to place the cow beside it."[1]

Although the satiric authorial voice may polish up the narrative's factual fundamentals, the underlying bone structure of
Trevena's realism, as it were, is largely true to life. Like the bizarre
rocks of the moor and its flora, the whimsical or idiosyncratic
dwellers on it are seriously comic. Trevena's covert autobiography

---

1 Trevena, *A Pixy in Petticoats* (Kansas City: Valancourt, 2012): 28, 209.

is given an extra twist when one considers that the Anglican clergyman, Mr. Hanson, undoubtedly is a satiric pen-portrait of his
adoptive uncle. Even Trevena's personal political views on the currently seething conflict between labor and capital are included—
the "great unrest" with strikes upon a scale unique in British history, pronounced by the *London Times* to be "the greatest catastrophe that has threatened the country since the Spanish Armada."[1]
He indirectly criticizes "King Socialism" and the mass turmoil in
urban workplaces around the country, commenting on the primitive life-ways of Dartmoor where "within each parish communism
flourished"—only because the commoners do not know they are
practicing it. Until the illusion of representing reality is shattered
by a willful narrator there is nothing magical or mythic in satire of
political, business, religious, or educational issues.

In 1910 Trevena published a story, "By Violence," that one
might call a prologue to *Sleeping Waters*. Father Searall has not
found fulfillment in service to his Church. He retires early to seek
the meaning of his life in the peace and innocence of nature but
discovers he first must affirm death and violence as constituents
of the earth's ceaselessly interacting antinomies of generation and
decay: "[H]e awoke from the sleep of death and felt the spring.
The winter was over and past, the time of the opening of flowers
had come, and the voice of creation stirred upon the garden; and
the change had been wrought by violence."[2] In *Sleeping Waters* the
opening of the religious self to new life revolves around this inevitable violence. Although Victorian and Edwardian novels portray
numerous Anglican clergymen, not surprisingly Roman Catholic
priests are less in evidence, and few of these are fictional protago-
nists. The closest predecessor to Anger's vocation and transforma-
tion may be Prior Saint-Jean in Walter Pater's "Apollo in Picardy"
(1893).[3] In Pater's story, this medieval monk and his servant are
sent to the country "for the benefit of his body's health, a little

---

1 "The Coal Strike and the Public," *London Times*, 26 February 1912: 9.
2 Trevena, "By Violence," *Written in the Rain* (London: Mills & Boon, 1910): 28-29.
3 Pater, "Apollo in Picardy," *Harper's New Monthly Magazine*, 87 (November 1893):
949-957; republished in Pater, *Miscellaneous Studies* (1895).

impaired at last by long intellectual effort. . . . The Prior and his companion, were come in contact for the first time in their lives with the power of untutored natural impulse, of natural inspiration." Similarly on Dartmoor, where the Bronze Age quite literally meets the twentieth century, neolithic ruins and pagan beliefs co-exist with the living present.

The psychological transition of both the Prior and Anger portrays an escape from "overwrought spiritualities" into the "ancient life of the senses" with "some subtle reminiscence of older gods."[1] In Heinrich Heine's "The Gods in Exile" (1853) Pater found this fantasy of reincarnated Greek deities banished from Olympus by the advent of Christianity. It serves as an allegory of the pagan-Christian competition between sense and spirit for the protagonist's soul. Pater's Apollyon is "immersed in, or actually a part of, that irredeemable natural world" which the Prior dreads to encounter. His "unnatural magic," potentially "secret evil," and "heathen understanding with the dark realm of matter" flouts conventional neo-Platonism that feared contamination of the spirit by the lust of the eye. And just as the figure of Apollyon is "an embodiment of all those genial influences of earth and sky," so Trevena's classical river nymph Petronel (*nympha* means bride or water spirit, an elemental deity) becomes the mythological embodiment of Dartmoor's streams and rocky outcrops (her medieval name is the feminine of Peter, from L. *petra*, "rock"). With narrative richness Trevena invests the *dramatis personae* of *Sleeping Waters* with the elemental forces of the moor and the ancient myths of the seasonal cycles, fulfilling the novel's theme of "the death of an old life, the beginning of a new."

Petronel, the fairy-tale sleeping princess or "elf-maiden," is a twofold seasonal goddess of summer and winter personifying Demeter's daughters. In her summer phase Petronel is the nymph of the magic waters, a counterpart to Pater's Apollyon in "Apollo in Picardy" who at first is the Apollonian god of summer, comi-

---

1 Pater, "Poems by William Morris," *Westminster Review*, 34 n.s. (October, 1868): 307-308. This conceit was cited also in an anonymous source Trevena extensively drew upon, "The Pleasant Land of Devon," *Quarterly Review* (April 1894): 431.

cally exaggerated in Trevena's novel by Bobby Billacott, a bibulous incarnation of summertime life in the green sap. But autumn initiates her period of exile in the underworld, the provenance of Anger's troubled delusions. Apollyon in this latter phase "accidentally" kills the Prior's companion, Hyacinth, with a discus, figure of the seasonal cycle. Similarly, in winter Petronel becomes the violent and sorrowing princess of death. She is the cold land epitomized by her absent "drowned" brother, whom she may or may not have killed, who may or may not be buried in the crypt-like cellar of Stiniel. Petronel's controlling stepmother, the "dark witch," embodies winter's fierce madness. Curgenven is an elemental dwarf-god of the earth and of the dark unconscious, a Hades-like figure with Petronel in his power. Whippety is Petronel's wordless "familiar," son of Curgenven and the witch. And the novel's protagonist, Anger, aspires to be Petronel's reborn fraternal double, her sun-prince of springtime renewal. Possibly the vegetation myth closest to the turbulent John Anger-Petronel Vigar kinship is the Egyptian story of the twins Isis and Osiris as recounted by Plutarch. Brother and sister began their intimacy in the womb; in maturity Seth/Typhon kills Osiris and dismembers him; Isis then collects the fragments of Osiris's body that originally had been cast into a river. Because his "genital member" had been eaten by fish, his impotence emblematizes the sterility of winter. When Anger offers himself to Petronel as her reincarnated "brother" and divine consort, she resists owing to her self-division between vanished summer and tyrannical winter, as well as to his clerical celibacy and illness, like the debilitating sterility of Osiris who waits among the dead until the coming of spring when Isis resurrects him as her partner.

Sleeping Waters, like "Apollo in Picardy," belongs to Bulwer's "Intellectual School," given that in place of direct action its aim is portraiture, a revelation of character. Not only does it recast traditional plot in terms of sensations and forces, but sharply etched impressions are lifted above themselves as if in a nightmare. Trevena's literary style, unsurprisingly, is often similar to Pater's sensuously rich, deep, "harmonious murmur"—Apollyon *sings* (the root sense of enchantment) the monastic tithe-barn into existence. As in Pater's aestheticism, Trevena mastered the gem-like impression, fragmentary yet entire in itself: "A woman stood bare-headed, calm, but in an agony. A gaslight, placed behind a bottle of green liquid in a chemist's shop, made her face terrible. She stood and swayed; and following the direction of her gaze towards a newsvendor's across the way, Anger saw in that needless horror of green light the latest evening paper rumour; and a ship had been wrecked; and she was a widow who stood there staring." The accidental play of malefic light might be Walter Pater's; the absinthe hues surely leapt from the palette of Toulouse Lautrec. In Arthur Conan Doyle's "The Hound of the Baskervilles" (1902), based on the "West-Country legend" of a spectral whist hound on the moor, Holmes promises Lestrade that "we will take the London fog out of your throat by giving you a breath of the pure night air of Dartmoor."[1] But Doyle may come closer to anticipating Trevena's personifications of evil upon the night moor less in his terrorizing *tour de force* of "the enormous coal-black hound" with glowing eyes and fire in its mouth than he does with the Grimpen mire, a hidden destroyer that swallows ponies and people—a force of nature like Petronel, queen of the underworld, "who gathers all things mortal with cold immortal hands" (Swinburne).

Anger's psychopathology reflects his priestly iconology in subconscious fantasies and fragments from the darker side of his psyche—mythical figures, bewildering scenes, and ominous incidents—with perplexing flashbacks from his illusions to reality: "The sun in its course cast upon the ground the shadow of a point of rock, . . . the blot of black suggested a limbless trunk, a mighty pair of shoulders with a strong head midway." Trevena seemingly alludes to early psychological experiments where blots, leading to the Rorschach inkblot test in 1921, were used to assess subcon-

---

1 Doyle, "The Hound of the Baskervilles," Copyright Edition (Leipzig: Tauchnitz, 1902): 235. "The Pleasant Land of Devon" mentions the superstition about "the pack of 'wish' hounds who hunt the Moor by night, breathing out blue flames as they run."

scious obsessions, here the diabolic in the shape of Curgenven. By tapping into Nympha's dreams, Anger plunges into ancient mythic patterns and historical lives without the limitations of objective circumstances. Somewhat earlier, just before the turn of the century, the British physician, Neil Macleod, reported experiments in the *British Medical Journal* with bromide-induced narcosis, giving psychopharmacology one of its earliest successes in the form of deep sleep therapy. Trevena's plot seemingly substitutes Nympha's waters in the place of Macleod's pharmaceutical doses. The related idea of "medical dreams" used to identify "the maladies of the soul" dated back to the ancient Greek Aesculapius.[1] From ancient and medieval times febrile delirium had been described by Celsus, Hippocrates, Procopius, and others as a mix of intense insomnia and waking dreams, the patient exhibiting intervals of incipient lucidity between states of dreaming hallucination. Such observations of delusion culminated popularly in the work of Trevena's contemporary, Sigmund Freud, who observed that retreat into illusion and an alienation from reality is comparable to a waking dream or a psychosis in which the brain refuses to subordinate its neurotic dreams to what actually is. Parallels between delusion and dream suggested a new diagnostic category known as "the clouding of consciousness," symbolized in *Sleeping Waters* by Anger's confusion in the mist about his immediate surroundings. In such delusional dream states, actual stimuli are given additional, bizarre significance, often unfolding at a different tempo and in a sequence dissociated from actual cause and effect.

These subjectivities of time and space were ratified, even before Einsteinian relativity, by the new velocities of the railroad which expanded mobility in space and compressed travel times; while such avant-garde technology in the 1870s as the time-lapse photography of Eadweard Muybridge's running horses overturned the limits of reality and provided new insights into the enigma of the individual moment. Additionally, the new temporal and spatial scales of geology and biology combined with the unprecedented

---

1 Walter Pater, *Marius the Epicurean* [1885] (Kansas City: Valancourt Books, 2008): 22-23.

global spread of the British empire to "psychologize" the scope
and feel of things in which the baseline of daily reality seems lost.
Anger recalls sleep-lapse episodes in legends that collapsed or tele-
scoped time and place such as those of the monk Felix, so enchanted by the song of a bird that a hundred years passed seemingly in
a single hour, or of the sleeping Finn (a Celtic hero-legend) and of
"Thorn Rose," the Grimm Brothers' sleeping princess. Sleep, says
Lord Byron, is a boundary world in which dreams become

> A portion of ourselves, ...
> They make us what we were not.
> . . . . . . What are they?
> Creations of the mind?—
> . . . . . . in itself a thought,
> A slumbering thought, is capable of years,
> And curdles a long life into one hour.

Dreams become subjective mindscapes, perceptions driven by
instinct. Anger's is thus not the story of a man, but the story of
a man's mind—not events as they happened, but as a mad priest
imagines they occurred.

When authorial self-consciousness intrudes upon the fictional
presentation of life as it really is—*i.e.*, as literary conventions give
the illusion of "reality"—its representational veracity is shattered.
In *Furze the Cruel*, Trevena had described Boodles as caught in a
script that another consciousness seems to have written for her,
the outcome of which she cannot control. The author himself
steps in to overrule the "compositor-ogres" whose realistic story-
ending, he says, he will not endorse. A gentler authorial presence
in *Sleeping Waters* entangles Anger's personality in incidents and
psyches from earlier cultural texts, disrupting the stability of re-
alist narration by shifting among these frames or levels of reference. Trevena especially cites Shelley's tragedy, *The Cenci* (1819),
in which "Petronel played the tragic part of Beatrice," victim of
incestuous rape, and Anger plays Cenci's brutal "assassin." The
narrator also self-consciously incorporates direct quotations or literary echoes. When in *Pixy* Burrough described himself in love he

asked: "How many would confess to the initials they had carved on beech-trees?" Trevena's readers might recall Shakespeare's *As You Like It*, in which Orlando would "carve on every tree / The fair, the chaste, and unexpressive she" (3.2.9-10). At the end of *Sleeping Waters* Anger asserts, less grandiloquently than Prospero in *The Tempest*, "now that the enchantment has been removed things are changed. You must know, Mr. Billacott, I have been all my life a great reader of mystical romances. The stories which above all else have impressed themselves upon my fancy are those of the *Arabian Nights*." In Scheherazade's famous chain of never-ending tales, the imagination of the vizier's daughter keeps her alive telling stories in her "real" world—a self-conscious reference *in* the novel to the romantic irony *of* the novel.

Trevena's indefinite "ground situation" (as metaphysicians would call it) and his novel's multiple "planes of action" (as a literary critic might say) deny that a person lives solely in one experiential level of reality. In *Sleeping Waters* Anger's life-changing infatuation with the seasonal goddess Petronel recapitulates the *topos* of Lucius's transfiguration in Apuleius's *Golden Ass* afterwards re-embodied by the ass-headed Nick Bottom in *A Midsummer Night's Dream* ("The eye of man hath not heard, the ear of man hath not seen . . . what my dream was" [4.1]). But inasmuch as Bottom's speech has travestied 1 Corinthians 2:9 ("Eye hath not seen, nor ear heard . . ."), the affirmation of religious revelation from ancient Palestine has been turned by North African comical witchcraft and Renaissance clowning into twentieth-century Dartmoor's enchantment of a man delusively but chasteningly in love with a supernatural spirit. When the vanishing of Anger's hallucinations resets life within his original unenchanted reality, Trevena's readers, having been taken in by the realism of his delusions, are as likely disoriented as Anger himself. The dream has argued for its internal and surreal representations as a primary reality so convincingly that his return from those illusions to sanity is a shock. The Dartmoor dream-figures as previously encountered are now discovered to be nothing like Anger's anagogic personalities: toward the end of his dream Curgenven is killed, fittingly buried by Whippety in a collapse of earth and rock; yet after this dream dissolves, Curgenven in the outer "real" storyline frame is still alive in Riversmeet, no longer the devil, only an imperfect man. But most startling is that when Anger's delusions are remitted and his pre-morbid level of functioning returns, the original familiar urban life is not returned to its *sole* position of ontological primacy or dominance.

Because Anger's formerly unacknowledged desires and his new holistic vision have been experienced under the guise of real-time sensory stimuli, as if in a virtual world, the after-effects of this subversive vision carry back into his sane, rational personality as clairvoyance; and he adjusts his perceptions accordingly. This scandal—that the fantastic is not an empty echo but actually may fashion quotidian reality—had been used to good effect earlier in H. G. Wells's *The Time Machine* (1895) in which his time traveler returned from the future to Victorian London with Weena's actual flower petals. So effective was this device that in *Perelandra* (1943) C. S. Lewis copied it—with never a hint of his disapproval of Wells's scientific agnosticism—when his protagonist Ransom returned from Venus. Thus when Trevena's story resets to its primary frame of reality, Anger's previous dreams provide him insights very much like axiomatic and intuitive *gnosis,* knowledge of the personal secrets of Dartmoor's inhabitants previously hidden from everyone but God. In terms of Trevena's contemporary intellectual contexts, Anger's mountain sojourn has boldly challenged the premises of literary realism and naturalism that humans exist in one and only one sensory environment, their destiny delimited wholly by heredity and objective circumstance without a spiritual dimension. For Trevena the enchantment that underlies life pulls reality toward what he calls a "magnificent realism" that opens a "supernatural door" to "the spirit realm."[1]

GERALD C. MONSMAN
Tucson

July 12, 2012

---

[1] Trevena, "Matrimony," *Written in the Rain* (London: Mills & Boon, 1910): 340.

NOTE ON THE TEXT

Sleeping Waters was published by Constable of London in 1913. The first American edition was issued by Mitchell Kennerley of New York in late 1914 and was identical to the British edition except for the imprint on the title page. This edition follows the first edition verbatim with the exception of a couple of minor printer's errors in the original, which have been silently corrected.

SLEEPING WATERS

CONTENTS

SLEEPING WATERS

THE BREAK

"EXETER is a city of fools," declared Merchant Wiggaton. "As you are going west, you cannot altogether avoid the place; but, if you have any feeling of respect for my ancestors, you will keep your eyes shut as you go through."

"Yet you are a man of Devon; I have heard you often boast of it," replied Father John Anger hoarsely. He wore a muffler round his mouth, though the weather was not cold, and he coughed a good deal. His ungloved hands were thin and claw-like.

"And guilty of treason, you suppose. Not a bit of it, Father Jack. I speak as a patriot," said the merchant. "My family hails from Dartmoor, though I have hardly set foot on its peat; neither has friend Billacott. We are both from stock raised among the holly of South Wyld. The Wiggatons of Brimelford fought with the Billacotts of Gnatesburg from the Norman invasion to the Restoration, until by chance the heads of the two houses bumped together when intoxicated according to the genial custom of the time; and in that condition two foolish tongues swore a sensible friendship, which was afterwards secured by marriage and cemented by a partnership in business. Our names have been wiped off Dartmoor, I suppose, and if we returned to Wyld we should certainly be regarded as foreigners. You must send me an account of Dartmoor as it is: harrowed by civilisation, but not cultivated by it."

5

"When did I say I was going there?" gasped the young priest. His breath came with difficulty in the thick London atmosphere.

"The doctor has said, 'go west,' and that means in your case Dartmoor. Let me do the talking; you have been instructed to keep your mouth shut out of doors, and this Goswell Road does not suggest the pine woods. Friend Billacott will tell you that the men of Exeter are ever faithful to folly; but don't think we are wanting in loyalty. When we Wiggatons flourished in the west, Exeter was our glory. There was no London for the old Dartmoor squires, no city but old Exeter, and my ancestors rode their pack-horses to it with no little pride, I tell you. That was long before the birth of the simpletons who destroyed what had been handed down to them for preservation."

"There is a fine Anglican cathedral," murmured Father John.

"Which happens to survive because the city council could not pull it down and cover the close with convenient offices," went on the merchant. "We may leave the cathedral to the destructive zeal of its restorers. The ordinary Exonian does not swell with pride over his big church, but they are all mighty proud of their sewage-farm. I went to the city a few years ago, not because I love the place as it is but because I revere the memory of its past; and every other man I spoke to asked me if I had visited the sewage-farm. I mustn't make you laugh, Father Jack."

They halted until the young priest had his cough out, then went on towards the city where fog was thickening. Wiggaton took his companion's arm, disregarding a muffled protest, and helped him along.

"Not so very long ago Exeter was the finest mediæval city in the land. Neither York nor Chester could compare with it," continued the merchant. "The walls which surrounded the city not only remained, but were in good repair, while all the lunettes and towers existed intact. Of the six gates, the one on the north hill had been alone destroyed. That was done to make the roadway more commodious to passengers; but it was the wickedest precedent ever set, for when the spoilers had enjoyed the thrill of destruction there was no holding them; the sight of old stonework seemed to make them mad; wall-breakers were kept hard at it; down fell the ramparts to satisfy the lust for modernity. Hardly a sane voice was raised against the unholy work. A town councillor of those days could very easily win popularity by a promise to continue the demolition of his city. The heads of the citizens had become like their dumplings—a mass of thick pudding. There is a story my father used to tell of a certain burgess who was wont to convey his young son to school on horseback. One day the animal was discovered to be lame, so the father, anxious to spare the beast, had the boy strapped upon his shoulders while he sat himself in the saddle. There is another story concerning two strangers who were looking at the west window of the cathedral. One remarked that St. Peter was looking very sad. 'How can he help it?' replied the other. 'He reckons his cathedral will go next.'"

"You are destroying my illusions," murmured Father John.

"I am not sure that an illusion is worth keeping," replied the merchant. "You will find realities upon the Dart, and the substance of the past in many a place not cursed with a ruling body of trades-men. Not that I abuse them—I'm a tradesman myself—but surely it is madness to entrust the treasures of antiquity to a parcel of men who measure linen, and weigh cheese, and know as much concerning art as I do about the rubrics of your church. You would not appoint a butcher as curator of a museum; yet butchers, and drapers, and tallow-chandlers were appointed guardians of old Exeter; and now it is ruined, Father Jack. The walls of Athelstan have been wheeled to the rubbish-heap. Open any book which deals with Exeter, and you may find phrases such as: 'This is now taken down.' 'This has been irretrievably destroyed.' 'Every trace of this has been demolished.' One gate survived the others for a considerable number of years; some said it was allowed to remain because it showed hardly a sign of decay, although that argument was, of course, ridiculous; others declared the hand of the spoiler had passed it by because it was too strong to destroy. The truth of the matter was nobody had complained about it. One day, however, a farmer whose name is not recorded—let us call him Farmer Cobley—drove into the city with a load of potatoes. Upon

reaching this sole-surviving gate, it was discovered he had piled
his load too high so that the cart could not pass through. He had
to unload the precious vegetables and waste his time. A complaint
followed, and the mayor and corporation stood aghast. Farmer
Cobley hindered while bringing potatoes into the city! What
was the finest mediæval gateway in all Europe in comparison to
the great Cobley's farm produce? The gate must be destroyed at
once lest Farmer Cobley should be inconvenienced a second time.
Destroyed it was."

"Commercialism," murmured Father John.

"Anything but that," said the merchant sharply. "This did not
make for trade, but the ruination of it. A well-preserved mediæval
city, such as Exeter was before the wave of madness submerged
its inhabitants, has no need to advertise. Its walls and gateways are
capital which produce a large and steady income. What turns the
flood of traffic towards Chester? What brings thousands of visitors from across the sea to York? Their old walls give the answer.
I believe a few Americans do go to Exeter," added the merchant
drily. "Cultured Americans know far more English history than
we do ourselves, and they are anxious to see the walls of Athelstan
and the gates which held out against the Yorkists. The first question they ask upon getting outside the station is, 'Where are your
walls and gates?' Very promptly they receive the answer, 'We have
no walls and gates now; but that's the way to our sewage-farm.'
Never mind those poor people, Father Jack. You have to think less
of the destitute and more of yourself now."

The young priest had made a motion as if he would have crossed
towards one of those groups of poverty so common to London
streets—a diseased man grinding at an organ in the company of
a starving wife and shivering child. The merchant held on to him
saying, "You have given to the poor all your life. Now you must
spend upon your own necessities. Pity you haven't got a mother to
look after you; or, better still, a wife," he muttered. "This solitary
life is a curse on you young priests."

"I could never be lonely while there are people in need of help,"
murmured Father John.

"Self-sacrifice is much the same as suicide," said Wiggaton gruffly. "Hold on to me while we cross the road. There goes friend Billacott! He will bubble with delight when he hears you are going west."

An odd-looking little man, with nothing on his bald head and very shabby clothes about his body, had just run into the doorway of a wholesale house of business. Above the windows of the ground floor appeared a long board bearing the name of the firm, "Winnacott, Billacott, and Wiggaton, Importers of Natural Products." No Winnacotts remained; the senior partner Billacott remained a bachelor, while Wiggaton was blessed with a large family. Both partners lived together in one of the Bloomsbury squares, which was as near as they could get to their place of business; they would have lived above their offices had the space been less valuable, for they were old-fashioned and loved their Aldersgate. In a narrow house, dark externally but very bright inside, Billacott satisfied himself with two small rooms, joining the Wiggatons at meals, sharing with them in all pleasures, and regarded by the young folk as an uncle whose pockets contained great possibilities.

A fine spirit of friendship prevailed in that house, although neither Billacott nor Wiggaton had social inclinations, while the wife of the junior partner was more than satisfied to be removed from the obligations of suburban life. The senior partner was an over-grown boy, exceedingly fond of introducing happy incidents into the family life; he loved the Wiggatons and was godfather to half the young ones. It was he who had introduced Father John Anger, somewhat timidly because the Wiggatons were Protestants while the Billacotts had always been Catholics.

"I like the young man, but I don't want to force him upon you," he had said. "Regard him as the safe in which my conscience is deposited. I do not harm you by being a Catholic and I satisfy myself. A man of business may abuse the Church of Rome, but he cannot despise it, for it is one of the three really sound institutions of the world; the other two being the Bank of England, and 'Winnacott, Billacott, and Wiggaton.' The Church of Rome will not go into liquidation before either of the others; and I wouldn't sell my shares in it for the wealth of all three."

With that the humble shareholder presented his young spiritual director to the Wiggaton family, every member of which absorbed him immediately into his or her friendship, and soon came to regard him as one of themselves, calling him Father Jack, and giving him the right of entry at any time. The Church of the Resurrection, which claimed the young priest's services, was not far distant, and although only Mary of the Wiggatons had entered it, many were the gifts of food and clothing which had been sent into dark courts and byways by Mrs. Wiggaton and her husband, who knew that charity is too holy to need a creed.

"Take off that muffler," ordered Wiggaton, leading Father John into his office and playing the master. "The air is wholesome here; none better in the City. You may breathe the odours of Indian tea and all the spices of Ceylon. Ah, the youngster has discovered us!" he exclaimed, as a door upon the other side of the passage was flung open with a great deal of noise. "I saw the bald head bobbing up and down behind the glass. My boy! please observe the notice on my door," cried the merchant, as his partner came bounding in.

"Bother your privacy! What are you doing with my little priest?" replied laughing Billacott.

"He has received some worldly advice; and I am about to hammer it into his spirit."

"I know! I met the rector in the street, and he gossiped," said Billacott, his merry voice breaking a trifle. "I was always warning you, Father Jack—the machine would run down, the lamp would go out. Hang my oily metaphors! You must go, you shall go; if you protest, we will fasten you in a crate and send you west as frail goods. We shall miss you," he said jerkily. "The church will seem dark without our Father Jack. More than a few slum-women will weep when they hear the little priest has left them."

"My desire is to stay and fight on; and to die in harness if I must," said Anger, as clearly as he could with his increasing hoarseness.

"You, a boy, talking about dying in harness," said Wiggaton gruffly. "You are a colt. You have not been broken in yet."

"I am not very ill, Mr. Wiggaton; I am only run down."

"Attend to friend Wiggaton," implored the quaint Billacott. "If he hits the nail hard, he does at least hit it upon the head."

"You have been too gentle with him, youngster," said Wiggaton, addressing the senior partner with his customary lack of respect. "Warnings are no good to a man who is bent on killing himself; you must use force. My superior muscles brought Father Jack before the doctor. I had almost to drag him into the consulting-room."

"Quite right. Just what I should have done," declared Billacott.

"I told the doctor I had brought a stubborn patient, and the only way to root him out of London would be to frighten him."

"By a beastly bogey," added Billacott.

"The doctor examined him," continued Wiggaton, "and passed sentence——"

"Of death," whispered Anger half fiercely.

"No, no," cried Billacott piteously. "Doctors will be pessimists. When they pass sentence of death on a young man, he smiles and lives for ever. That's an invariable rule."

"Keep quiet, both of you," said Wiggaton, smiling. "Stop bouncing about, youngster, and sit down. Your priest will live to be eighty if he looks after himself."

"It is sentence of death to be taken from my work, sent into the country, told I must live in London no more," said the condemned man passionately.

"It is merely a break in existing conditions. The death of an old life, the beginning of a new."

"That's all it is," said Billacott. "Friend Wiggaton puts it more prosily than I should. Buttercups and daisies instead of smuts and chimneys. A parish full of larks and butterflies in place of sweated seamstresses and penny-toy merchants. That's the poetry of it, Father Jack—and I shall visit you with sonnets in the summer."

"I know nothing of the country. It will be a new world to me," said the young priest. "I was born in the town; my heart is here. I am frightened to think what may happen if I leave it."

"You will become well and strong," said Wiggaton.

"Fat and jolly; a sort of Friar Tuck," cried the irrepressible Billacott.

"Rest, pure air, and good food will restore you," Wiggaton went on. "The doctor felt sure of that. You ought never to have got into this condition, but by denying your body its necessities you have placed it at the mercy of the poor man's disease, which you have no right to."

"None at all. Ridiculous!" seconded Billacott.

"Therefore it is your duty to take the cure. I mentioned Dartmoor to the doctor, and he said at once it was just the place."

"South Wyld," cried the senior partner. "The parish of our ancestors, friend Wiggaton; where the holly-bushes grow, and the robins sing, and water-wagtails hop about the rocks."

"The doctor hinted that you might return," resumed Wiggaton, turning to the thin figure shivering like a shadow near the fire.

"I did not hear him," said Anger quickly.

"Not unless you make a good recovery, which he considered you ought to do."

"By not fretting; by resigning yourself, Father Jack," added Billacott. "You have done good to others; but you have sinned against yourself; therefore we sentence you to one year's imprisonment, without labour of any kind, upon the lonely moor."

"If I can be sure of health to go on with my work here, not to obey would be a sin," the priest murmured.

"What we chiefly require now is this month's Bradshaw," said Billacott. "The question we have to decide is not whether Father Jack will go or remain, but whether he will travel in a comfortable compartment with a rug round his knees or inside a crate with a 'W. B. and W.' label attached thereto."

"I will go quietly," said the young man, smiling in a miserable fashion.

"No time is to be lost. Every day in London means a gain to the enemy. Your housekeeper must pack this evening; to-morrow we see you off," said Wiggaton firmly.

"To Wyld," cried the senior partner. "A year will pass like sleep while you explore the lands of our ancestors, and discover the boundary stones against which the detestable Wiggatons flung the unoffending Billacotts for several centuries. You must know,

Father Jack, that during the Middle Ages we country gentlemen were wont to spend our whole time fighting against the enemies of the king and the immediate neighbours; our teeth for traitors, and our nails for neighbours. History relates that the Wiggatons of Brimelford were a quarrelsome, beggarly family, not worth a louse——"

"Take care, youngster!"

"It is written in my household book," cried Billacott gleefully. "Let me take you home, Father Jack." He put his head out of the office and told a clerk to whistle for a cab. "There I will entertain you with extracts from my wonderful volume. Friend Wiggaton would be glad to throw it on the fire; the spite and malevolence of his family are betrayed by it. Look at him now, with violence in his eyes! He calls himself a respectable London merchant, when he is nothing but a barbarous squire of the moor, lusting to destroy his hereditary enemy, the sole surviving representative of an honourable house, who is his senior partner and top-dog."

The friendly threats and laughter of the merchants, who understood each other very well, helped to arouse Anger from his distressful musing. He went with the odd and cheerful Billacott, and in a snug back-room, which overlooked more chimney-pots than could readily be numbered, allowed himself to be placed with grandmotherly attentions beside the fire. His companion then flung back the lid of a chest and produced his book.

"The diary of my ancestor, one Hugh Billacott, who lived through the tempestuous reign of Charles the First. It interests me vastly: you it may amuse," he explained, scanning the faded lines with tender eyes. "Look, Father Jack! See what a beautiful colour the ink has turned; a rich golden-brown like leaves in autumn. My ancestor, you must know, was a good cavalier; also, I fear, an unconscious humorist. He spent much of his money and a trifle of blood in the services of his unfortunate master, and all he got for his loyalty was the sequestration of his estate and the infliction of an enormous fine. Here is the entry: 'My selfe and sonne became bound to ye Protector Cromwell in 2000 lb. for my good abearing.' Between you and me, Father Jack, I suspect a strain of artfulness, as well as humour, in the Billacott character; I am fairly confident that much of this record was penned and carefully stored away in the family chest at Gnatesburg in the hope that some day the king, or his successor, might repay the money sacrificed upon the royal and hopeless cause."

"'Put not your trust in princes,'" murmured Anger abstractedly.

"Many of the gentry who supported our erratic Tudors and Stuarts must have found that quotation upon their lips; especially those who were repaid for their devotion by the stroke of the headsman's axe," continued Billacott. "Here is an example of the worthy Hugh's gay humour. It appears that he fought in person for the king's cause, and outside Plymouth had the misfortune to be wounded. I gather from his continued progress that the wound was a very slight one, but as you will see he made the most of it. The day after the skirmish which occasioned his wound, Squire Billacott proceeded to Plympton, and the entry occurs: 'Imprimis: from ye 5th of ffebruary to ye 10th at Plimpton—much hurt.' And upon the next page, 'Item: at Tauestock, where I lay hurt,' and again, 'I lay before Okehampton—hurt.' The next year I find the entry, 'Item: at home again—still hurt.' My word!" cried Billacott, placing the book upon a table in order that he might rub his hands. "It would never do to show that to friend Wiggaton."

"We have an idea the men of old were stronger and braver than ourselves merely because they lived more roughly," said Anger. "They were actually the same. When the fighting spirit rises it can be seen that civilisation has not softened our nature if it has changed our customs."

"You may be interested to know that in the year 1641 a good sword cost one shilling," said Billacott, returning to his household book. "Also the fees for a half-year's teaching of a young gentleman at a good academy amounted to no more than thirty shillings. You are to multiply by four to get the present equivalent of that money. There must have been a great demand for horses in Devonshire about that time, as my ancestor had to pay seven guineas for a five-year-old nag which he goes on to state, 'was marked with a star in ye further buttock.' Another point worth noting is the fact that lady-helps were not unknown in those days, as, 'my little cozen, Petronel Vigar, came to my wyf for 3 lb. wages. Item: a goodly wench.' I am afraid Mrs. Hugh soon had cause for complaint," laughed Billacott. "The entries close abruptly with one which is to me important: 'Item: paid what I layd out in London for my dame's gownd, £6 15s. 7d. Item: for Fiddle strings for Pet. Vigar, 3 shillings.' This is very interesting," went on the merchant. "There is a tradition that about this period a Billacott of Gnatesburg became a citizen and mercer of London, and lived at the Sign of the Unicorn in Cheapside. I suspect the writer of these lines was that individual; and if I could prove it I would certainly add to the name of the firm the announcement, 'founded in 1650.' It is clear my ancestor had lost the greater part of his fortune in the king's service; and then, as now, when a man wanted to better himself he would go to London. I have also a shrewd idea that the squire became enamoured of the lady-help, Mrs. Hugh got to know of it, and to appease her wrath he purchased her a new gown, and a sumptuous one it must have been. You perceive the sinner was unrepentant, since he insisted upon buying fiddle strings for the goodly wench. Does all this bore you, Father Jack?"

"Everything is a burden to me to-day," said Anger, as he shivered beside the fire. "I believe you have an object in bringing out this book," he added.

"I hoped to amuse you now, and to give you an interest in the life which is before you," said Billacott much more solemnly. "You will remember how constantly my ancestor was complaining of his hurt. After he returned home, I come across the entry, 'Drank ye waters of Nympha, claimed by Wyggaton, but not hys.' After that I find no mention of the hurt. Quite recently I discovered between the pages of a worthless book in this chest a tiny scrap of parchment which had been once part of a deed. It was so decayed that it broke in my hand, while the ink came away in flakes. This deed was the one, I believe, which conveyed the property at South Wyld from the Abbot of Buckfast to some remote ancestor of mine. I have transcribed what was engrossed upon the scrap of parchment. The fragment runs thus: 'From La Haven to

Gnatesburg, and so by the waters of Nympha, wch be good for sykenesse, ascending to Abbotsford, and so lineally to the head of Wester Walbrake until it falls into the Avon.'"

"Why do you tell me this?" asked Anger wearily.

"To interest you; to help you win back the joy of life," cried Billacott, his own odd self again. "You will gain health and strength by wandering about the moorland. I give you an object, something to walk for, to fill your days of leisure. I desire you to explore, to find the waters of Nympha, and drink of them. Then you may send me a supply in quart bottles."

"These old traditions are worth nothing," Anger muttered.

"I am persuaded there is virtue in this water. It cured my ancestor of his hurt; it may help to cure you. Seriously, I am curious to know whether it can still be traced. Look for the stream, Father Jack; find it, and let me also taste of the water which was reputed good for sickness many hundreds of years ago. Send none to friend Wiggaton, for he would pollute it with his whisky," said Billacott with his windy laugh.

Anger's response to the merriment meant to cheer him was a moan, while he leaned nearer the fire, unable to get too close; and muttered, "It is all so distant. This journey into the unknown looks like death."

"Because you have lived confined," said Billacott. "Like a fish in a pond swimming round in the same water. You have not given yourself to the world, but to a dozen poverty-stricken streets. These seem everything to you now, but it is not necessary to forget them, and when you get into the wild places they will not seem very far away. You will still hear the bell of the church, and your spirit will be with us in the Mass. Cheer up, dear Father Jack," implored the merchant with tears in his comical eyes. "You are going to have a sleep, a good long sleep; and when you awake you will be healed."

"When I awake," said Anger hoarsely. "I will not think of that time. I have not slept yet."

"Let us join the Wiggatons. We shall become sentimental if we stay here," Billacott mumbled.

The sick man suffered himself to be led into the drawing-room. Only Mary, the second daughter, was there; and she came forward at once with both hands extended, exclaiming in a passion of friendliness, "Oh, Father Jack! I know what this means to you, and to the Church. You will get well; I know you will—you must—but nobody can take your place."

"I wish you would learn to dissemble, Molly. You are not to make things hard for Father Jack," said Billacott as sharply as he could, for this girl's open nature was a thorn in his flesh.

"May I not be sorry? How can I help it, uncle? It is dreadful to think Father Jack is going, and to know that he must."

"Where is your mother?" asked the merchant quickly.

"She has gone out. I am not to tell you where."

"I can guess," said Anger, drawing near the fire. "She has gone to arrange for my departure with my housekeeper. She is a mother to me."

"I might say the same, although I am old enough to be my dear lady's father," said Billacott in his odd fashion. "Whenever I am ill I bear myself dutifully as her youngest child, and I am bound to confess she treats me as such. We priests and bachelors are in very good conceit of our loneliness while we are well; but when we are sick—ah, Mary, my dear, don't look at me with round eyes. Make them narrower, child, and let them shine less."

"I was wondering who is going to nurse Father Jack," she said.

"That's the sort of thing a man forgets, and a woman does not," murmured Billacott.

"I am not bed-ridden; I can look after myself very well," said Anger. "The doctor especially mentioned it is not nursing I require but rest and mountain air."

"Don't forget the food, Father Jack."

"Who is to tempt him to eat when he does not feel like it?" Mary flashed out.

"Bother the girl," said Billacott to himself. "All women think of the same old thing. Pity reflects the heart upon the face, makes it throb upon the tongue, and shine from the eyes. She believes she may play with what is impossible." He added aloud, "Father Jack is

weak, not ill. He is being punished for devoting himself to the poor
and homeless. That sounds harsh, but it's the way justice works."
Then remembering he had some business awaiting, he ran off and
left Anger huddled over the fire in the vain search for warmth, and
Mary standing apart, her hands clasped before her, watching the
young priest with pitiful eyes.

"You are sorry for the people," he said at last, adding quickly,
"I do not speak with conceit, but it is true I have given myself to
them, while my successor may feel it his duty to devote his energies elsewhere. Besides, he may not have the means to help them."

"I am not thinking of the people," she said, as if trying to
imitate his hoarseness.

"I cannot allow you to grieve for me."

"You cannot prevent it," she said. "I have a feeling you will not
come back."

"That I shall die?"

"That you will enter another life, and find it a better one than
this."

He did not turn to look at her, knowing every feature and line
of her face so well, but rested his forehead upon a shivering hand,
thinking of the words of Billacott, wondering if he should find
the waters of Nympha, and drink, and forget. He was going on a
long and lonely journey, and many a romantic picture would rise
between his eyes and the Church of the Resurrection, between
his mind and Mary's love. For he knew that the girl with her eyes
still shining loved him, not as a brother, not as a friend. She could
not dissemble. He had come into that house as a priest, and the
heart of Mary, conquering all sense of duty out of weakness, had
sought to make him a mere man. Religion with him came first,
and was at that period of his life strong enough to subdue all else;
therefore, he did not love her, he might not. Yet they had been
together far too much, had trifled in a social fashion, had gone
about in the streets, Mary holding a basket of good things for the
needy ones. Half in ignorance of the fire mixed up in them they
had shared each other's life, he supposing no temptation could be
possible, she fighting it down. But in moments of leisure, given by

him to his friends, they had laughed too much, chatted too easily, and made merry over trifles in the trusting way of lovers. All this was unlawful. Not being of Mary's world he should have refrained from it. She was a plain English maid, loving and desiring love; while he, though English-born, was an alien, made so by having embraced the creed of an alien Church. He was an exotic growth planted in London's garden; he should have bestowed his affections upon other exotics, and not have sought to fertilise a home-grown plant.

"Mr. Billacott tells me to regard this break in my life as a sleep. When I awake, I may return and continue my work as if only a night had passed," said Anger, sending the voice of hope from the attitude of despair.

"It may be a long night for your friends," she murmured.

"There is a tale I read once of a Finn who entered a cave after being wounded in the hunt. He fell asleep, and when he awoke his wound was healed; but the bow and arrows at his side were decayed, for three years had passed away."

"What were those years to his wife, if he had one?" asked Mary faintly.

"She at least had the use of those years. The man was to be pitied for losing them," said Anger. "You see I am feverish, Mary; my brain is excited, and I go on repeating that myth to myself, and my mind adds its allegory. I am about to go into solitude which to me is fearful. I am to lose myself in mountain mists—I, who as Mr. Billacott says truly, have spent my life in a dozen streets of crowded poverty. I know nothing of the country; I have not seen it except from the windows of trains carrying me from this crowd to another; and now that I am weak I fear it. The strength of the country may fight against me. These streets keep the one religion warm at my heart. The country suggests pantheism. I do not know what its temptations are."

"Think of happier things," begged Mary, coming near and placing a hand unsteadily upon his shivering shoulder. "It is your poor tired body that is frightened, not your soul. If you were not ill you would laugh at the idea of being terrified at this break. I would laugh for you if I could, but when I think of—of your poor people asking after Father Jack, wondering why he does not come to help them, I cannot."

"Keep your hand there, Mary. It helps to warm me," said the spiritual body, still playing with humanity. "I can no more kill my fear than check this shivering. The man of the world may think nothing of going away into the wilderness to heal himself; he knows the world, and his knowledge protects him. I know nothing but love for my people, and for you—don't take your hand away—for your relations and yourself, dear Mary, my sister and companion. The story of the Finn remains. I shall not sleep as he did—mine will be restless—but when I awake, and am healed of my wound, and look for the bow and arrows at my side—you know what I mean, Mary—the bow and arrows which protect my spiritual self—shall I find them lying ready; and if I find them will they be decayed?"

"What if they are?" she cried recklessly, hardly knowing what she said. "If your faith fails you, there is mine. If you awake a new man, you may turn to another life, not lower because more natural; filled with the same charity, and controlled by another creed which does not bid you pass through life in chains."

"Your faith!" Anger muttered, turning so that he could look at her.

"Think of my father and mother," she said hoarsely. "Are they not good enough?"

"Not because of Protestantism, but in spite of it."

"There is only one religion of the one God," she said bitterly, for she could not be tender, knowing how much he wanted her, how dear was that thin, spiritual face; and she was wild to think of the fetters some white-clad, peasant-born priest, daring to call himself the vicar of God, when sitting in a certain wooden chair, claiming inspiration from some craftsman's handiwork, had flung upon the bodies of so many millions of earnest creatures created to be men and fathers. "It is the religion of love."

Anger closed his eyes, and put out a hand weakly to find hers, but failed because she drew away from him, frightened herself, now that she frightened him. All things were in shadow to him then; but through the weakness of the body passed the strong arrow which has always hurt humanity, and he perceived that the comradeship, which had carried charity to others and had inspired him much, was on his side wholly selfish, and on hers self-offering. They had worked together in a labour of love, not spiritual, since it consisted often in feeding hungry children and buying garments to cover naked bodies; and Mary had now flashed her own needs upon him with her eyes and tongue. She too was in want of charity, she too was cold and hungry, and was calling him to feed and clothe her. While he was going, possibly for ever, going to his sleep in mistland, going to be taught in the school of elemental forces. He might not awake. Better so, perhaps; to sleep on, and learn no more.

"We must be silent, Mary. Speech has its dangers," he murmured, leaning over until he was in danger of falling upon the red-hot coals, colder to him then than the other heat which might not burn. "I shall remember you each time I turn over in my sleep."

CHAPTER II

NEW BLOOD FOR OLD

THE end of March Anger left London. Upon arriving at Wyld he found a lodging without difficulty, but after a doctor's visit upon the day following he was requested to leave; the local specialist pronounced him to be somewhat seriously ill, pulmonary disorder being complicated by fever dangerous to a body so neglected. Anger, who had always faced infection without a tremor, was repaid by rejection when he had become himself infected; which was his first warning that the moorland was harsher than the town. His medical attendant was able to procure a furnished cottage, and in one room of that the young priest lay from early spring until late in summer, attended by a woman, who took charge of domestic arrangements, and a ministering nurse.

Four months he lay awake while a death-like change worked in him. The bed was placed so that he looked out day and night upon a hill, its summit wild with broken rocks, and always lonely except when ponies became visible moving in search of food. The sick man beheld the hill in all its aspects: wreathed with mist, beaten black by rain, touched white with snow, tortured by wind, calm beneath moonlight, majestic in the sunshine. He saw the dawn flashing upon its bogs, he watched the evening creeping up to join the sky-line and make night; he beheld growth commencing, the grass losing its whiteness and becoming green; afterwards the drying up of water, the glorious early summer flash of furze, and at last the blush of pale-pink heather. As yet unconscious of the change in himself, he looked on and wondered why the hill grew softer every day, and why the vastness and solitude of it had no terror. For many weeks speech was denied him, but when permission was granted he turned to the nurse, who was a well-educated woman, and asked like a child, "Where does this air come from?"

"From the side of that hill, I suppose," she answered.

"Then it is the hill which has cured me."

"With rest and food," she added.

"It is the hill," he repeated. "At first it looked as if it might crush the life out of me; and now it is a god, healing and protecting. I long to be out, and to climb the slopes towards those rocks."

He fell into musing, and presently went on, "I called London my mother, but when I turned to her for nourishment she could not help me; she was weak and bloodless. So I was taken from her, and given to the mountain which has restored me to life. The memory of my natural mother grows dim already; my affection for her is less than it was."

"When you return to your friends they will not know you," said the nurse.

"The Wiggatons would know me; and good Billacott. Only my health has changed," he murmured.

"If you had a wife, she might not recognise you now," the nurse declared.

"Why not?"

"You are another man. You weighed scarcely nine stone when you came here. Now you are over thirteen," she said lightly.

"Give me a glass," cried Anger. "I must see what my foster-mother has done."

"Let me introduce you to yourself," laughed the nurse, as she brought a glass and held it near his face.

"Is this a magic mirror?" Anger murmured.

"You are the miracle."

"It is the work of the Creator walking on the mountainside. The raising of Lazarus was hardly more wonderful than this."

He had not looked into a mirror since leaving London. Then he had seen a small face marvellously thin, clean-shaven and much lined, with tired eyes and tight-lipped mouth; below, a shrunken chest and bony shoulders. Now he beheld a full bronzed counte-nance, bright eyes, a strong black beard as tough as heather, lips full of blood, and not a line worth noting; below, a manly chest and heaving shoulders. He gazed until he shuddered. This was not John Anger, priest of the slums, but a lusty countryman. The work of transfiguration had been too thorough, for not only had every trace of the sick man disappeared, but it seemed as if the priest had gone as well. No sign of the ascetic remained. This new face lacked high intellect, and spirituality had gone. Its blood was charged with elementary passion; the mouth looked no longer made for blessing but for the idle phrases of the world; and the eyes were careless.

"Take it away," he gasped, and lay back breathing quickly. He knew that if he could stand in Mary's presence, she might regard him as a stranger. Old Billacott would have glanced at him and murmured, "That's a jolly looking priest." His rector, seeing him in the vestry, would certainly have asked his name and business. He had come to the moorland to be nourished, and was now, with body fed and built up by strong air, transformed into the likeness of one of its own children, a son of the heather and rocks.

"I know of one other case similar to yours," said the doctor, when pressed to speak upon this miracle. "The man I have in mind was older than yourself, and had also spent the whole of his life up to the breakdown in an unhealthy district. He came under treatment as a mere shadow; when discharged he was a burly creature whom his own mother failed to recognise."

"His nature!" exclaimed Anger.

"A cure of this kind is something like a re-birth. When a man's whole body has been changed——"

"Can his mind remain the same?" broke in Anger.

"I was going to say, he may regard things from a different aspect."

Anger thought of these words while lying awake that night, hearing the careless wind, watching the outlines of the hill in ghastly moonlight. A barrier had been placed already between his body and the crowded streets; and its name was no longer illness but desire. Tired and punished in that London life, he had never once cried out, but had accepted all discomforts patiently. That old body had not asked for idleness and human pleasure. The mind surely was the same, turning with tenderness towards the small dark church and darker streets, leaning with love which lacked desire towards his helper; but where was the wish to play the priest again? This new body was in revolt against starvation, for the great act of transfusion had taken place, and the blood in his veins was no longer the weak fluid unable to find heat but the rich juice of Dartmoor's fierce vitality.

Moonlight in a mist and mad with wind; and the dark mountain tossing to the sky black clouds of rock. Heaviest things that night were all in motion, and were feminine. He, the young priest, seemed the one man cast from the world into this Venus-night. For the first time moonlight was not chaste, while its light seemed to fall upon shaded gardens of love and beauty deified, not as cold saints but as immortal wantons. He closed his eyes to hide the figures which would not go, being subjects of his mind; and while in struggles the door opened, and his nurse entered with a lighted candle.

"Did you call me?" she asked.

"I have not spoken," he answered.

"I heard you shouting."

"I was awake; I could not have been dreaming. What did I say?"

"I thought you called for Mary."

"I might have fancied myself at home. Perhaps I slept without knowing it. Leave the candle; the moonlight and wild wind disturb me."

"Yes, the night is wild," she said.

In the morning he was not so well, and could not take his accustomed ramble up and down the passage. The day was clear, and the moorland, washed by rain at break of day, looked pure and spiritual. The greater part of the morning Anger slept, and waking at noon pointed to some distant granite, showing white against dark heather, and asked what meant the ringing sound he heard, "like blacksmiths beating iron upon an anvil."

"Granite-breakers are there procuring stone," said his companion.

"Do men work so hard as to climb a rugged hill to bring down rocks? If that is so, how little I have done," he cried despairingly.

"It is hard work," she said. "Many a man gets mutilated; some lose a hand; few escape a hurt."

"To break the foundations of the world!" he murmured. "Are the rocks that I see yonder broken?"

"That, I think, is a hut-circle," she answered, looking where he pointed. "There are many on the side of that hill. Old dwelling-places," she went on, "where savages once took shelter."

"Was there ever a time when men and women herded there, with wind and moonlight beating full upon them?"

"There are upon the moor thousands of such huts," said the nurse. "They were made by men whom history does not mention. These circles are merely rough foundations; the superstructure, made probably of turves and wattles, would quickly disappear when the dwellings were abandoned. But to deal with Dartmoor's early history is to grope in darkness."

"This is new life indeed," cried Anger. "Modernity is unlawful in my church; here it must be impossible."

"When you walk out into the solitude, you will find yourself far away from modern life," she told him.

"Tell me more. I must know the life-story of the giant who has saved my life."

"I can only tell you what to look for. I can explain nothing," said the nurse, not wondering at her patient's natural eagerness. "You will discover pounds and enclosures; mysterious walls which look as if they could never have served a purpose, made of dry masonry, built probably before Rome had ever heard of Britain, or the world had ever heard of Rome. You will find old trackways trodden out by tin-streamers, and bridges of one huge stone. One trackway not far from here is called the Abbot's Way."

"One moment," said Anger. "A memory strikes me. Does this road lead to Abbotsford?"

"I cannot tell you; I do not know of any ford so named."

"Do you know of a stream of water called Nympha?"

"I have not heard the name before."

"It exists and I am to find it," said Anger. "What other wonders may I hope to see?"

"Stone coffins."

"They will not interest me. I desire the things suggesting life and energy."

"You cannot look for them in stone remains. There are circles of upright stones and avenues approaching them. These are supposed to have possessed a sacred meaning."

"Primitive temples and approaches to them?"

"That is the idea, but it is a matter of theory entirely."

"It is wrong," said Anger. "Regard me as a savage. Suppose that I desire to offer worship to my God. Should I surround myself with a circle of upright stones and pray in them? Decidedly not, for my God must be the sun, and to sacrifice I shall ascend to the highest point and make my altar there."

"You speak as if you meant it," said the nurse.

"I ask you to regard me as a primitive man, a savage who could know nothing except what had been revealed to him out of Nature. Such a man, being at the mercy of the elements, suffering all winter from numbing winds and ice-cold rain, must have regarded the sun as the superior deity of his life. He would perceive how the sun made the growth of spring and brought what must have been to him the heaven of summer. Even now we associate the joy of life with sunshine, and shrink from rainy winter as a time of sorrow."

More he would have said, but checked himself, conscious that Nature and his mind were pulling different ways. There had been little sunshine upon the streets of poverty, but he had not noticed the lack of it because the lamp of religion had given light enough. His life had there been full; now it was empty. The joy of sacrificing himself for others had made sunshine.

During the month of August fever left him, and the door of the prison was thrown open. Anger received permission to leave the house and walk a short distance along the road.

"But, doctor, he cannot go," the nurse protested. "He has no clothes."

"They are there," said Anger, indicating a wardrobe the door of which had closed four months ago.

"They are useless to you now."

"Of course," said the doctor, laughing. "You are by sixty pounds a different being from the man who wore them."

"The hill, which has changed me utterly, now tells me to discard religion," Anger muttered. "It will not permit me to wear the clothes of my old life. And if I could wear them—" he went on, thinking of the tale of the emperor's new clothes which did not exist in fact, but were to be seen in all their brilliance by those of his courtiers who were wise and fit for office—"some voice might whisper, 'he has nothing on.' Well then," he said to the others, "we must send for a tailor."

"I am going into Ashburton this afternoon. I will send a man out to measure you," the doctor promised.

The tailor came next day with tape and patterns. Anger forgot to mention his profession, and not feeling in the mood to resume black, which the man assured him was unsuitable for the moor, he selected such stuffs as a country gentleman might wear. These were made up in due course and sent to "John Anger, Esquire," who assumed strange garments without any sense of shame, persuading himself that while he remained on Dartmoor it would be advisable to dress for the place. Clerical clothes were not adapted for moorland ramblings. When the time came for his return to London the garments of the church might be resumed.

"A priest in any sort of coat is still a priest; but I am to regard myself for the present as a holiday-maker," Anger murmured when he found himself at last alone among the granite.

He was fully awake, remembering Billacott and the Wiggatons, writing to them sometimes—but never to Mary—telling them of the wonderful change that had taken place, while reserving details to himself unpleasant. Each day he was set a longer pilgrimage; with the return of strength he went out morning and afternoon into the severe and solemn wilderness, beside the soft rivers, through the deep valleys carved through moorland rock. There being no further need for the nurse, she departed, and he was left alone with the housekeeper in his little house which faced upon the hill.

His former terror had departed, for that had been induced by natural weakness, yet still he walked in wonder. Even to a man accustomed to travelling, a change from the banks of the Thames to those of the Dart is apt to provoke amazement; and Anger had been in every sense a man of town life till recently. He had been born, schooled, and had always worked in London; his few holidays had been spent in some other crowded centre; the agricultural country of England was unknown to him; and now he had been transported into scenery which even to travellers appears alien. Anger found himself in a district wholly unlike the England he had known, inhabited by a people proud and independent, no more related to the men and women of his streets than were the Breton onion-sellers who tramped the trackways with strings of bulbs upon long poles. The free man was a revelation to one who had mingled with a folk inclined to whine for charity. This self-reliance was, he supposed, a matter of temperament; no man could feel weak while striding through the mist of the upland on the roof of the west with a roaring gale behind; but it was also, so he soon learnt, born from a conviction that the Celt, and not the Saxon, was the genius of the country. These moormen might not know history, but it spoke in them, whispering with tradition's stubborn voice of the past when the English invader struggled to subdue the Cymrians of the impregnable tors, and of a period far later, when Devonshire had been incorporated into the Saxon realm, while Dartmoor remained still part of the West Welsh kingdom, speaking its own language down to Shakespeare's day. The descendants of men who had never been conquered might well acknowledge no master except their own wild weather; knowing that the great storm-beaten granite stump called Dartmoor could only be habited by people of fierce strength and fiery passion, and that the historian who should relate the time when, and the act by which, the proud district was incorporated into the Saxon realm was likely to remain unborn.

It was not until the end of summer that Anger received permission to extend his wanderings into the unknown land. Then, released altogether from medical supervision and pronounced "free from trouble," he began those expeditions which unconsciously brought on the fatal sleep. The routine of walking would, he imagined, quicken his mind, but it was not so. A gardener may apply manure to a plant to force it into flower, but the plant may fail to bloom and run to wood instead; and these rambles through rich air did not awaken Anger's mind, but closed it up, while adding fibre, blood, and muscle to his body. His friends seemed parted from that present life by a kind of death; he grew careless, cared for nothing beyond the enjoyment of a holiday which only waking up need put an end to, as his tradesman-father had left him ample means, and he had gone to the Church, not out of necessity, but with a clear vocation; and now with perfect health there came a vision of the apples of the tree of life he had not tasted.

Yet he was not altogether happy. The new body was somewhat brutal, a bit of a bully; a mischievous rogue, inclined to smile with affection not quite spiritual at maidens; with no definite religion, no fixed principles; easily tempted to enter wayside taverns and take a nip as a counter-stimulant to the strong air of the hills. The new body was a thorough son of Dartmoor, although the old mind belonged to a priest who had carried the lamp of charity in slums and vaguely longed to do that work again. Anger was restless; all the day walking, and in the evening struggling against a growing sense of loneliness, for he had no comradeship of men or books, having no knowledge where to find the one and no great inclination to procure the other. Had the good merchant Billacott come to the house, declaring he would not return alone, his presence and speech might have dispelled that increasing indolence, and Anger would have been restored to his old life, not the same man, but capable of resisting the new master which the wind off the mountain had transfused into his blood.

Early one afternoon Anger passed into what had been once the hall of a mansion and was now a drinking-place. It happened to be Saturday, therefore a number of men were seated around the walls passing the time with songs and liquor. The weather was rough and prematurely wintry. Anger took a chair among these men, who regarded him at first with unfriendly faces, supposing he had come to spy upon them, but unbending one and all when he invited them to drink at his expense, and began to ask them questions about the house they sat in.

"'Twur a mansion once. Rich volk lived here," said a man whose shaggy beard brushed, as he spoke, the sloppy table.

"There wur coloured glass in that window," said another, pointing at the commonplace panes. "I never saw it, but my vaither did, or might ha' been his vaither. A chap chucked a pot through the glass one night, and that wur the end of the picture."

"The arms of the family," suggested Anger. "Do you know the name?"

"Vigar," cried several voices.

"I seem to have heard that name," Anger murmured.

"The house be called the Vigar Arms. The old board outside wants painting," said the man with the shaggy beard.

"Have any of you heard the name of Brimelford? I have looked for it upon the map, but cannot find it."

There was a doubtful muttering, during which the bearded man sat deep in thought. Presently he put up his head and spoke.

"Why, sir, the place of the stepping-stones over the water down under, about fifty paces from this inn, ha' been known time out o' mind as the Brimmletake. A sight o' brimmles grows there now."

"Brimelford is the ancient name of a manor-house," explained Anger.

"Be it though?" said the bearded man with interest. "Then I tell ye, sir, this house must be the one, though I ha' never heard 'en called that name avore."

"Nor me," said one and all.

"Jonas Hard will tell ye," continued the chief speaker. "Jonas ha' got the wonderfullest memory in the world, and wi' a few pints in mun, and a parcel of gude listeners, he'll sing a hundred songs without once stopping. You go and see Jonas, sir. He'm ninety now, and too weak to go abroad, but he can sing. He'll die a-singing, and start again when he gets up to heaven."

"What is the name of the stream which is crossed by the stepping-stones?" Anger went on.

"Some call 'en Wallabrook, and some Wallbrook," came the answer.

"Wester Wallbrook?"

"Wester and Easter be west and east hereabouts. There be a proper lot of Wallabrooks, and this one might as well be west as any other."

Excitedly Anger stared round the dark old room, from the great fire-place, heaped with glowing peat, to the smoked and grimy timbers of the roof, trying to imagine Mary and her parents there; for this had been no doubt the home of their ancestors before it had passed into the possession of the Vigar family. Here, in grim, high-backed chair, some old Squire Wiggaton had sat beside a dreary rushlight, listening to the storm of wind and the howls of savage people, hearing perhaps the tramp of tinners passing by. It was a long day away, but the house remained, patched up, remodelled, and turned into an inn; its glory departed, and the memory of its mediæval holders gone. Even the Wiggatons knew nothing of the place—what a world distant was the brick warehouse where Mary worked at knitting for his poor! He alone held the secret. There was romance in that.

Some of the drinking songmen put their heads together, glancing sideways at the stranger, indignant to think they might after all be entertaining some "paper chap" sent to spy out their ways. Perceiving their attitude Anger made haste to reinstate himself by mentioning that a descendant of that manor's former owners was his personal friend; he added the name, but all heads were shaken, until the man with the trailing beard said wisely, "Churchyard be the likeliest place to look vor they."

"No Wiggaton has lived here since the seventeenth century," said Anger.

"Then they ha' gone vor gude," said another. "All gravestones more than two hundred years old ha' been took vor building. Parsons and volk were the like a time back. All careless lads I'm thinking."

"They tore down one place to make another, and they broke back more than they built up," added the chief speaker. "You won't find the name you'm after on church wall, and I'll tell ye why. They Wiggatons could never ha' been the first family in the parish, and the man who wur squire in them days wouldn't let the name of the man who wanted to be squire be shown wi' his name on the wall of church. Understand what I be telling ye," he went on, speaking in free fashion. "They ses all volk be equal in the church; but the man wi' a hundred acres never would let the man wi' no more than a yard of ground sit in the seat avore 'en. A man what be big in the parish ain't going to fancy himself any smaller when he gets inside church door."

"What is the name upon the memorials in the church?" asked Anger.

"I ha' forgot; but it b'ain't Wiggaton vor certain," came from the bearded mouth.

"Do any of you know?"

Some said one thing, some thought another; but nobody knew with any certainty. Every man explained that he was chapel. It was their way of covering up a want of observation.

"Willum will know. Where's Willum to?" cried the giant, who sat at the table like Barbarossa, with beard sweeping the slops.

The majority might have answered, since the name William belongs to every third male on Dartmoor. Yet any of these men, by some mystic intonation of the name, could make known which particular William he was calling.

"Who is Willum?" asked Anger pleasantly.

"He looks after parson and digs the graves. He likes his pint," came the matter-of-fact answer.

"Here he be!" cried voices from a corner near the fireplace. "Wake up, Willum. Open your eyes, will ye? Gentleman be telling to ye."

Comatose Willum was prodded as if he had been a bale of wool, while the matter of Anger's question was poured into him. The operation took time, as the sexton's intellect bobbed about in beer like a cork in troubled waters. At last the query reached its mark, and Willum answered with a bubbling and babbling of betas, "It be Billacott."

Anger was speechless for a few moments, during which the life before the change came very near him. Modernity rasped ancient history and made him smart. Regarding the Wiggatons not the least tatter of a memory survived, but the Billacotts lived on triumphant. Even here, in the tavern which was Brimelford, the Billacotts, or at least their relatives, conquered; for Anger remembered how the merchant had quoted from his household book the name of Vigar. Time had been pitiless to the gentle Wiggatons; while the bouncing Billacotts had been parasites on time.

"Are there any Billacotts about here now?" he asked.

"None that I knows of, master," came the answer, out of the mouth of Barbarossa. "A name don't last for ever. He dies like the volk what used 'en."

"Are there any Vigars?"

"None in our parish, but plenty out in the country. I knows nought about they. They'm foreigners."

"Plenty in Youlstone parish," a voice muttered.

"Where is Youlstone?" continued Anger.

"It lies beyond, t'other side of Dartmoor, and nigh to Riversmeet. A wisht place, Youlstone," said the bearded man.

"Aw, 'tis so surely," agreed murmuring voices; and Anger did not like to ask another question, but addressing the assembly, which had increased since his entry, he invited all to have their mugs refilled, and then called for a song of olden time.

"What sort will ye have, master?" asked a ballad singer.

"The oldest that you know."

"A song of women?" the man suggested.

"I leave it to you," said Anger, hardly remembering he had changed his clothes.

Thereupon the man arose and sang a bawdy song; while the others listened with fierce faces, never smiling.

"I would rather hear an old ballad," said Anger, willing to rebuke but afraid to speak, when the rough voice ceased.

"None older than that, master," said the singer.

"A different one, then."

"I'll sing ye one as old as yonder hills," cried another man; and without rising from his seat, he chanted solemnly, beating time with his mug and gazing steadfastly towards the roof, the north-country ballad of the old grey cloak, which had reached the west and entered the repertoire of the ballad singers before the Wiggatons had left that house, having been made popular by no less a songster than Will. Shakespeare, gent., of Stratford town. Hugh Billacott, who had left that parish to settle at the Sign of the Unicorn in Cheapside, might well have shouted those verses while the fair cousin scraped the melody upon her fiddle. So past and present clashed again. Anger listening, moving restlessly, felt a longing to silence the singer who insisted on disquieting his mind; for the parable of the cloak fitted his case too neatly.

> "My cloak, it was a very good cloak,
>   It hath been always true to the wear,
>   But now it is not worth a groat;
>   I have had it for forty year:
>   It will neither hold out wind nor rain;
>   And I'll have a new cloak about me."

Other ballads followed, of little interest, but Anger sat on, until a younger man, who had been "abroad," awoke the echoes of the crumbling house with the nonsense of a music-hall song. He went, and as it was still early, in spite of low rain-clouds and the darkness cast by them, he asked the way to the cottage of Jonas Hard, and being directed with that vagueness which belongs to a spacious atmosphere, he took to the moor, where there was neither road to guide nor a bush to shelter. Less than an hour of crooked rambling brought him among hut-circles, and beyond, where the side of the moor was heaped with clatters, he saw a small patch which had been taken in, to his sight like a piece of green cloth sewn upon an old grey garment, and in the middle of it the cottage he was seeking. "You cannot mistake it," he had been told. "Vor 'tis the only dry cottage hereabouts."

Dry seemed an adjective misapplied, because the modest house stood among bogs, and the pathway to its door was first cousin to a stream; but the masonry was dry, that is to say the blocks of granite—known as hand stones to distinguish them from larger masses which a man could not lift unaided—composing its walls were not secured by mortar; and yet neither wind nor rain went through the chinks, although within many a modern house, well built by skilful craftsmen, sweat would break out and moisture roll; for width of wall, not mortar, is the only trick which baffles Dartmoor weather; and the walls of this humble home were four feet thick.

The illiterate historian, who had never read a word nor penned one, but was himself the book of a million words which others had dictated, sat alone beside a chimney-piece of unhewn rock. The daughter of threescore years, who minded for him, had gone out to collect some reek. Jonas welcomed the visitor gladly, for he was near his end, and the only pleasure left was talking; begged him to be seated opposite, and not too far away; invited him to stir the turves and make a blaze; and began conversation with the usual preface, "You'm a stranger."

"I come to you for information," Anger said.

"Them who comes to me vor that carries plenty away wi' them," said Jonas. "I would sooner sing than tell to ye. I be ninety

past, master, and I ha' a bird in my throat yet. I touches the high
notes, but I can't bide on 'em. I'll sing to ye avore you goes," he
said determinedly.

"I shall be glad to hear you. Some of the men have been singing
for me already in the Vigar Arms," said Anger.

"None of they can sing," cried Jonas. "They'm like old jack-
frogs in a bog. Volks blow and whistle now, and think they'm
songmen. They sings Methody hymns and such like trade. Proper
old windy stuff, I calls it. Wait till you hears me sing, master. I'll
sing ye ballads of love what will make ye crave vor maidens. And
I'll sing ye ballads of war what will make ye wonder you warn't
a hero. And I'll sing ye ballads of monks what used to live in
Buckfast. You'm pretty near one o' they yourself, master."

"How do you know?" cried Anger.

"I knows the attitudes. Your varmer sits all nohow, as if he
didn't care whether he sits or stands. Your labourer sits all together
like. Your squire sits wi' his legs abroad. Your tradesman sits wi' his
hat under the chair. But your parson sits up like a woman, wi' one
hand held by t'other, and his butes be always touching. I'll sing ye
ballads of shepherds. And I'll sing ye ballads of blind beggars——"

"Will you answer my questions first?" Anger broke in.

"I'll sing ye ballads of Dartmoor, and I'll sing 'em when the
wind be rough. And I'll sing ye ballads of winter what will make
ye draw the chair up near the fire."

"I want you to speak first," shouted Anger.

"But I won't sing ye Methody hymns, and I'll sing gentle so as
not to frighten ye," Jonas added.

"Can you tell me if the name of Wiggaton survives in this
part?" asked Anger despairingly.

"There b'ain't no such name, master, and there never have been
from the beginning of the world till now, and if there had been I
would ha' told ye all about it," replied Jonas; and in his annoy-
ing way went on to recite a list of all the names he had heard of,
which used up nearly a quarter of an hour, for his memory was
extraordinary.

"Thank you," murmured Anger ungratefully, when the list had

been completed from Alpha to Omega, resolving to be more wary in his questions and to put as few as possible. "Now will you tell me where I can find the water of Nympha?"

Jonas was cornered. That was obvious, but he could not spoil his credit by confessing it. He shifted uneasily, feigned to be obtuse, and finally implored the stranger not to proceed in that direction. "'Tis a wisht old watter. There be plenty of better trade than he," came the disdainful utterance.

"This water is supposed to possess salutary qualities—if a man is ill it will do him good to drink it," Anger explained.

"Why, master!" exclaimed the old man, trembling, partly with excitement, and partly with indignation, because the visitor had presumed to simplify a phrase which he had not understood, "You mean the sleeping watter. I ain't heard tell of he, not vor sixty year, I ain't. Who told ye about the sleeping watter? Be you a wise man?"

"I am afraid not very," answered Anger, failing to understand the question, which had a supernatural meaning.

"There b'ain't a man living, except me and you, what ha' heard of the sleeping watter," went on Jonas. "Volks ha' forgot, vor there warn't nothing to make 'em to remember; nought but a story, millions of years old I reckon, about volk what wur crossed in love, or had done a murder, what used to come to the watter and drink mun, vor when they had drunk they forgot what they had done. You can't tell a tale like that to volk nowadays, master, without setting 'em to laugh at ye. Proper smart volk ha' got nowadays. Laugh at pretty nigh everything, 'em do. I'll sing ye a ballad about the watter avore you goes. Can you swear you b'ain't a wise man?" he repeated suspiciously.

"I can," replied Anger, still not understanding the question, but plainly perceiving a negative was wanted.

"I fancy you b'ain't," said Jonas more easily. "If you wur a wise man you wouldn't want to come here, 'cept to tease me. I'll sing ye a ballad of wise men presently. Now I'll tell ye where to find the watter. You be wrong about the name, master, vor the watter ain't never had that name from the beginning of the world till now, and if it had——"

"It is called Nympha in a deed from the Abbot of Buckfast," said Anger.

"Them monks wur fearful liars. I'll sing ye a ballad of their lies avore you goes."

"'From La Haven to Gnatesburg, and so by the waters of Nympha,'" quoted Anger.

"Bide a bit, master. You'm all wrong. There b'ain't no such places anywhere. There be Heaven, and that be away to Youlstone parish, and there be Knattlebarrow, and if you walk out t'other side of Knattlebarrow, which be a hill covered wi' white stones, you'll come to the sleeping watter. 'Tis nought but a bit of a stream vull o' trouts."

"Is it far?"

"It b'ain't what us would call far, but 'tis a fairish bit of a way. 'Twill take ye all the day to get to the watter and back home again."

"I shall go to-morrow," declared Anger.

"Don't ye drink the watter," cried Jonas.

"Why not? I would not laugh at the story, but as sensible men we know it is nothing better than a myth."

"It b'ain't never safe to meddle wi' that trade," said Jonas uneasily. "Volk ha' forgot the story, but mebbe the watter ain't forgot. I ha' known of volk what ha' lost their memories. How be I to know they didn't drink the sleeping watter?"

"I intend to drink it, and, I promise you, shall forget nothing."

"You'm young and you ha' got a modern understanding," said Jonas peevishly. "I won't sing ye a modern ballad, vor I don't know none. I be agoing to begin now," he threatened, clearing his throat noisily. "Move the chair back a piece, master. I ha' a dreadful voice; I wouldn't like to scare ye. I'll take the first song gentle. Will ye ha' love first or last?"

"First and last," said Anger; then started and wondered what had made him say so.

"Well, master, 'twill make a gude beginning, and I don't know how 'twill make a worser ending. I'll sing ye first a ballad of the shepherd boy and the butiful lady. He ha' been sung from the beginning of the world till now, but he won't be sung no more when I be took. Take the poker and shovel, will ye, master, and beat 'em together when I puts my hand up. I likes a bit of music whiles I sing."

CHAPTER III

MISTY HOURS

THE morning brought letters to Anger: one from Billacott, full of questions and exclamations, making it not unlike a piece of music; and another from Mary Wiggaton upon business. She desired to know what was to be done with an old woman and her broken-down husband, who were about to be evicted from their precarious tenancy of one room, and were even then calling upon St. Joseph and Father Jack to rescue them from the State, the landlord, and the workhouse. She also enclosed a document which looked insanitary, but was human: a sheet of paper, dirty and much folded, from both sides of which signatures, with crosses scrawled for such, had been propagated without forcing beneath a neatly written invocation, praying for the return of the young shepherd to his flock. No doubt the appeal was selfish; the field of clover was more in the mind of the sheep than he who had guided them with the crook; they missed the hand which found rent more than the tongue which recited well-worn phrases; but they also felt the need of the sympathetic presence which had given itself with words of consolation.

The appeal, however, did not reach "Father Jack"; it fell into the hands of one Anger, a countryman, and was by him received with feelings of annoyance. These people wanted him back merely to dip their fingers into his pockets; he had spoilt them, and they in return had tried to spoil him. While he grew weaker not a single voice had begged him to make better provision for his own body; all had whined on and begged for more. Anger's new nature thought contemptuously of these shameless mendicants, these tattered and too often idle Teutons, as he compared them to the

independent Celts around him; men such as Jonas Hard, who lived
with pride of majesty in a hovel, and could live, and would have
scorned the hand of charity.

"I like the spirit of equality," he said, while thrusting the sad
document in his pocket. "The people here all live on the same level.
They do not ask themselves whether they grovel at the bottom, or
kneel in the middle, or tiptoe on the top; and if they regard me as
somewhat lower than themselves, it is because I break no rocks
and have no land to till. These creatures at home admit they are at
the bottom, and no strong wind arouses them into a desire to rise.
They regard every man who is in a position to give as somebody
much higher than themselves."

With that he made a start to find the stream of water called
by some Abbot of Buckfast Nympha, not being in the mood for
letter-writing, or for any other business of sitting-down—since his
recovery he had been moving as if bitten by a tarantula—and while
he walked the argument he had started continued to work with
his strides. This young man, like many a slum-worker, had been
tempted to take the shilling of King Socialism, without knowing
what was meant by the service, and quite unable to find a captain
worth respect; not knowing that an improved social condition could
not be forced but had to be evolved gradually out of natural causes.
Socialism could only exist so long as the people who practised it
did not know they were socialists. Now that Anger walked upon
Dartmoor, which once he had feared, a region little troubled until
recently by modern ideas, the problem was cracked and a kernel of
truth emerged. The folk of the moor had been socialists for centuries, content and fairly prosperous; but they would have been greatly
annoyed had they been called by that name. It was true the parochial
spirit was overwhelmingly strong, and the inhabitants of different
villages were divided as Jew from Gentile, but within each parish
communism flourished. There was no competition, and property
was distributed equally. Each man had an acre or two; when a building was required there were stone quarries held in common; for fuel
the peat-bogs, for gravel and sand the rivers; horses, cattle, and sheep
fed upon the commons, which provided their masters with sticks

for the fire, reed for thatching, fern for bedding, materials for hedge making. And yet, when these people left their homes, and became swallowed up by the towns, they very quickly departed from the traditions of their ancestors, allowed themselves to become dependent upon others, and would cry aloud that Socialism was the only remedy of the evils which they suffered from; when it was in fact that very state from which they had wilfully divorced themselves because life was lonely and had no evenings.

"I grow wiser," declared Anger, as he found himself in a solitude which might have been unexplored territory, so entirely was it lacking in every sign of human occupation, and looked upon a region of furze and heather, shining bogs, and stony upland. "We Londoners call country-folk provincial, but we are more narrow-minded than these commoners. They look at the horizon; we stare at a wall. Only a primitive race can live happily under Socialism, only under primitive conditions is the state possible; when civilisation is forced in that direction it reaches anarchy."

He went on, perplexed by numerous waterways descending upon every side, all eager to make rivers, hoping he still walked beside the Wallabrook, but growing doubtful when he crossed by a clapper where four streams met. Water was everywhere too abundant, and he could not fail to note how varied were the colours. He had hitherto regarded water as a dull-coloured liquid, but here, in its home and birth-place, all the young element was touched with the complexion of flowers and fruit; one stream red, another green, another blue or saffron-yellow. He determined that the water he searched for would be red and impregnated with iron. If pilgrims and sick folk had flocked to it, there might be a cross erected, or lying prone beneath the heather, to mark the pool their trusting heads had dipped into. The hill rising yonder was no doubt Knattlebarrow, and, according to Jonas the singer, the waters of Nympha were to be found at its foot, creeping quietly northward with their secret.

The hill looked near, but was not. Anger walked an hour before he reached it, crossing many a bog by means of tussocks, avoiding those patches of grass and watery green where liquid mud was fathoms deep; brushing through heather, nearly three feet high, which hid crevasses in the peat, all wet, some dangerous; and so to a slope of turf which trembled beneath his weight, consisting of spongy matter bright with the seed-pods of asphodel and the fleshy plates of sundews, and dripping heavily at its broken edges, more like a rain-cloud than a bank of soil. Beyond, firm ground was reached, and here climbing began, for Anger had reached the hill and could see the white stones gleaming.

Being an imaginative man, he could not wander there alone and keep romance away. The tales he had listened to in child-hood became retold; falsehood and truth were mingled together; history and myth kissed each other. The folklore, which Jonas the singer stubbornly believed in, the rites and mysteries of his own Church, the deed from the Abbot of Buckfast, the mystic powers of consecrated water, became to his mind the chapters of a story which his own life was to continue, a dream-like story to which he must add realities.

"I should find here," he murmured, "squatting in a hole among the rocks, some old hermit, who would tell me all the secrets of the hills and provide me with a clue to find the water. No story can exist without the human element, and here there is nothing but space. The hermit of the moor might tell me perhaps these white stones sleeping on the hill for ever were once the bodies of pilgrims who sought for the water in vain, and for their failure were so punished; and if I fail, I too may be condemned to remain on the moor, like stone, for ever."

He went on, crossed the spur of the hill, then started round and flung his arms out. Distinctly he had heard a human voice, not speaking coherently, nor appealing to him, but calling in a freak to frighten him. Space behind and around was empty; there was no place where any man could hide, and the voice had been as close as voice could be. The sun had disappeared; the moorland became quickly haunted by all manner of strange creatures, many of them with human voices, and from every bush of heather came a mut-tering, while solemn murmurs rose from slabs of rock. This meant nothing but a change of weather, and the wind was getting up.

"I could have sworn some woman was calling me," Anger muttered, hurrying on, never pausing to look beyond at the distant
rock-masses already wet with mist. A moorman would have taken
his bearings and set his face in the direction of home, advancing
without a swerve from his course; but the townsman, who could
not read the alphabet of the weather, and discovered nothing
ominous in the spasmodic shrieks and sullen muttering, forged
straight ahead away from Wyld, merely admiring those clouds
which were soon to roll around him. A man who had spent the
years which made his life about a couple of acres of close streets
was not to be smitten with any idea of being lost.

Upon the other side of the hill a pleasant resting-place was
waiting. Another brook came racketing down a cleft between
round boulders; some way beneath jutted out comfortable shelves
and tiny terraces planted with hanging ferns. Anger descended,
reached the water, found a snug spot beneath a rowan-bush; and
in a bower of whortleberries he reclined, quite out of sight of the
plateau, enjoyed his sandwiches, then rested for an hour, remaining so still that a jay hopped near and helped itself to crumbs. The
air was close, not cold, but presently it grew so dark in the little
gorge that the stickles lost their sparkle, and Anger parted the
fronds above his head to admit more light.

"Somebody has fired the heather!" he exclaimed, for a dense
smoke was drifting across the gorge.

He climbed out quickly, and stood in the open wrapped with
shrouds of mist; all the prospect was hidden; eyes could not see
more than a few yards, while the wind began to find itself at
freedom. There was no rain; merely earth-rolling clouds filled
with those human voices of glad mutterings.

"I shall not find the water to-day. I have rested too long," said
Anger. "Now I must make for home."

He set out with full confidence, and walked on briskly, exhil-
arated by the blanket touch of gentle clouds, certain he was
returning by the way he had come, recognising as he thought a
certain stone-circle, later a clapper bridge upon which he had lingered to watch the black trout darting under; but actually taking

the opposite direction, describing the inevitable curve, and never aware of the mistake until another hour had passed, and he came out upon the very gorge where he had rested.

"The mist will not clear before evening," he reasoned, wiser than he had been. "I may be condemned to spend a night upon the moor."

Beginning to feel afraid because the air was darkening, he made a fresh start, remembering what his nurse had told him: "When lost upon the moor, descend until you find a river, and follow it down stream." To reach a river it would be necessary to find a cleave, and being upon the upland Anger could not decide in which direction to face, or which brook to take as a guide, for the little tributaries were numerous, some going north, some south, while all, robbed now of sunlight and half-hidden, were simply ways of water without a difference. He followed the largest, wondering at its rapid rush since the ground seemed level, and keeping closely to its bank, went with water, wind, and wool-like clouds, hurrying until the ground descended, and he came to a pool which might have borne the name of silence, for it lay in a hollow so that the wind passed over it, and the water was sluggish, and the spear-like reeds which lifted from its mud were hardly shaken. A bird soared upward, and was gone.

There was a faint whispering near Anger's feet, less human than those other voices, and parting the heather he saw deep down a runnel which entered the pool with a slight murmur and a thrill which kept the surface shuddering day and night.

"I am lost," he cried. "There is no place like this within five miles of home."

The brook which had brought him there curved back in its fickle way as if bidding him retreat; pool and brook had no connection, for a dozen yards of peat divided them, while the whispering runnel led a life apart. Anger went on, perceiving an eyot no larger than a fair-sized table covered with cotton-sedge; and upon approaching the other side of the pool, which was barely ten steps in length, he heard a singing sound, for the ground was broken where the overflow splashed down into a perfect basin worn out of rock by the ceaseless drip of centuries. So wonderful was this piece of nature that he stopped to gaze; so clean was the basin, so pure the water, that he stooped to drink, for he was thirsty; but he could not reach the brimming basin until he had stretched his body on the turf; and, clutching with both hands the tussocks, had lowered his head, smelling the soaked peat, hearing more clearly the siren-song of falling water, feeling bubbles burst against his face, and at last cold lips on his; and he gasped and drank those kisses.

Clambering to his feet, a voice from his inner consciousness spoke clearly, "You have drunk the holy water of the Nymph."

"Why, I had forgotten," he cried, answering himself. "Old Jonas told me I must walk a long way out, past the hill covered with white stones, then downward. And so by the waters of Nympha," he muttered, gazing into the drifting clouds, then hurrying onwards with a shiver towards the old guide which made a maze-like pattern with its coils. "Well, I have drunk the sleeping water," he cried out loudly. "Now I must find a place where I may sleep."

He began to run, laughing away fear, talking aloud as an imaginative man will when much alone: "The kisses of the Nymph were cold, and work slowly. The mind which connected sleep with that bubbling basinful of water had little sense of what was fitting. Old monks of Buckfast would not have been above a joke which brought them patronage. They invented a rumour that the water possessed medicinal qualities—possibly the Abbot came each Easter to bless that basin—and when one legend failed another was invented. All crossed with love, or suffering from sorrow, were called to drink, forget, and pay their fees. Forget the past! My memory is wide-awake. I am here until winter freezes; two more months I wander on the moor, then away to the old life and work. I would like to know whose lips were dipped into that basin before mine."

So he laughed and talked to supply himself with company, his mind being far from easy as the clouds grew darker, and there came each moment a cold spot of rain. The descent continued, the brook became more rapid, but there was no break in the moorland, no wall nor enclosed field, and nothing that had ever been a home except hut-circles. Anger's courage failed, until he hardly dared to look ahead in search of lighted windows, too fearful of seeing the dreadful pale blue candle hovering in mist. He could have welcomed beast or bird or creeping beetle; anything which suggested an existence allied to his; but nothing seemed near except rushing water, living rock, and juicy plants; life in full strength but unrelated.

Pausing to regain breath, for those last few moments had been spent in running—and he was no longer thin priest but burly countryman—there came from far below a different sound, a roar of water falling swiftly; and Anger felt more easy when, at the end of a few more steps, he came out upon a shelf of rock, looking down into cloudland, knowing that he stood at last upon the summit of a cleave, and below was the river which had worn it out. The slope was steep and heaped with rocks, making slow progress necessary. The guiding brook turned aside towards a cleft of its own creation, and Anger left it, requiring its aid no longer, and clambered down until he reached the friendly river making its march of triumph towards the place of men.

"The dangerous part of my journey is over," cried the wanderer.

Hardly more than an hour of daylight was remaining. Encouraged by passing beside a wall, which suggested civilisation but might have been built before the first mud hut of Londinium, Anger scrambled on and soon reached walls of a different type, rectangular, mere foundations of what had been the dwelling-place of tinners. The lost man in his ignorance called them modern. He was now struggling among boulders, some as great as houses, some logging, some like tapering spurs projecting from the bank; he jumped from one to another, not always wisely, sometimes slipping back into a crevice, or plunging forward into heather which flourished strongly, finding a roothold somewhere. Faster than his progress went the light; heavier came the rain with a sting of sleet in it; and still there was no prospect of shelter for the night.

The descent ceased and Anger found himself walking upon level ground. A roar from the right suggested the fall of some invisible tributary down the hill opposite. He had left the rocky ground, but not his difficulties, for the peat became more spongy as he entered a region where reeds grew waist-high, holding his feet which thereupon sank swiftly into mud. No longer came the cheerful noise of the river to urge him on, for the stream had ceased descending a rock-strewn bed, and was now flowing smoothly in a deep channel between banks of bog.

Anger stopped at the edge of a deep slough, which at least was modern, for peat-cutters had made it. Many a saturated vag[1] lay around; and in fury at being beaten by the mist he raised a piece and cast it in the water, shouting as loudly as he could, "Help! Help!"

Heavy masses of cloud lifted slightly, as if disturbed and frightened by the splash, and Anger saw, two steps ahead, a bright green bed of bloated mosses. He jumped aside, landed upon a tussock, and seemed to be in the midst of an earthquake, for all the ground shook from side to side, tossing like waves, with a stink of rottenness. He stood upon peat-bogs well soaked by recent rains, supported upon those fathoms deep of quag by nothing more solid than moss and grass-roots.

"During the last few moments I have walked in peril of a loathsome death," he cried in a sweat, while the surrounding bogland sympathetically shuddered.

He consoled himself with the thought that peat-cutters had been there; but they would have passed in summer, and would also have known where it was safe to tread, while he was in the dark. It had become impossible to remain by the river which penetrated the heart of the morass, although in leaving it he lost his only friend. Now it was difficult to see a yard ahead, while the rain beat down in fierce autumnal fashion. This Dartmoor, a foster-mother to him in time of sickness, now scourged and tormented the body she had strengthened; placing him like a Spartan mother on her roof, telling him to hang on or perish.

Stepping delicately from one ridge to another, Anger came out upon firm ground, where the turf was like that of an old lawn and

---

1 Provincial English: dried peat or turf for fuel. [Editor's note.]

walking was easy. He seemed now to have reached a garden, sheltered from wind, planted at more or less regular intervals with neat
furze-bushes. So he continued with more spirit, until his progress
became barred by the steep side of a hill. Turning by good fortune
to the right, he kept beneath the slope for the best part of a mile,
finding a pony-track to follow, and coming out once more among
stone masses. It seemed as if the pony-track went upwards, and
snatching eagerly at the merest suggestion of a path Anger clung
closely to it, feeling at last exhausted as the wind reached his body
again, but pressing on to yet another hill-top knowing it might be
death to fail.

When the false pathway came to an end, he still ascended,
reached a tor, descended upon the other side with the wind
behind, and walked until the darkness caught him upon a slippery
trackway where it was certain carts had lately passed. He seemed
to have descended several thousand feet. The continued motion,
with jarring against rocks, had brought on dizziness, and his mind
was torpid, so that when the trackway divided, within fifty yards
of a perfectly invisible farmhouse, he selected without hesitation
the lower track, going downwards out of custom, hearing again
the brawling noise which told him he was upon a cleave through
which another river plunged its way.

He went to disappointment, but not at once, for it seemed
to him he had *stopped* a few minutes to regain his strength; the
track disappeared, and he had no mind to struggle back, for this
was the steepest descent he had made. Groping and plunging he
continued, and at last came out beside a very white and broken
watercourse, which divided the steep moorland from a dense and
sheltering wood. He could hear the flutter of leaves, the motion of
branches, and from time to time was able to catch glimpses of the
black and rugged boles of ancient oaks.

"This means safety," he murmured. "I must have reached the
edge of the moor. I could not have endured that wind and rain
much longer."

He saw no bridge, and the great stepping-stones were submerged by water as well as mist, for this stream, which Anger felt

sure was no nameless brook but a titled river, was bearing towards
the lowlands the rainfall of a week. As it was not possible to enter
the wood, he advanced along the opposite bank, dimly conscious
of having reached the bottom of some lonely glen which very
possibly made the last barrier between the heather and cultivated
fields, and trusting to the same descent to bring him out. Again he
clambered among rocks, some fifty feet above the river, feeling the
ground before him with his stick, fearful of stepping too near the
edge. Here, he fancied, was a place more romantic than any he had
wandered through. Caves gaped in the side of the cliff, and above
were bushes of wild-rose, with scattered oaks and rowans, and
many a holly tree; while on the other side whispered the hanging
garden of the wood, flinging a roof of branches across the river
to get the leaves baptized at birth with spray. As a blind man will
pass his hand across a face judging its beauty by the sense of touch,
so Anger, guessing the outlines of that scenery by the contact of
stems and branches, was ready to declare he had reached a goodly
place.

There was also a sense of mystery suggested by the thick and
murmuring wood, where a benighted traveller might have met a
crooked witch with nose and chin which touched, or a young girl,
just awakened from enchantment, walking plaintively in search of
the lover who had been enchanted with her; and with the mystery
a horror, for between two black and polished walls of rock the
river flung its white and ghastly volume from a slate-flat bed to a
cauldron of rough granite far below, where the water seemed to
boil with heat of motion and to steam with spray. Anger drew back
from that chasm, where mist and water met; and still clambering
downwards discovered a sort of foot-track just wide enough for
him to pass beside the cliff by clinging to the ferns and roots. Thus
he passed a cavern half-full of water, then lowered himself into a
gully which brought him near the level of the river, and here was
a shaft cut deep into the rock, now filled with slime and chanting
frogs. There seemed no way out, but after much groping among
thick ivy, he discovered a stone ledge jutting over the river, and
venturing upon this he passed safely round, regaining the footway

which led into a deeper gully. To the right another gloomy tunnel went far into the hill; in front appeared a stone wall, and above, branches were hanging down to help him climb. He dragged himself up, stood among alders and great furze-bushes, but made no advance, for he smelt smoke caused by the burning of peat and wood, and he saw two bright red sparks gleam and go out above his head.

"A cottage cannot be here," he muttered. "There is no place where it could stand, and no road to it. Nor would any moorman be camping out on such a night."

Not a sound came except the roaring of the river close beneath. It was very dark on the side of the cliff, for in addition to the moonless night and misty rain, trees spread overhead. Anger had been praying for fire and shelter, but now that both seemed near, hanging as it were in cloudy space between the rocks and river, he began to shiver. Again he felt thirsty, and remembered what water had last touched his lips.

A few steps onward and his groping fingers met a wall. Extending both arms they touched large well-shaped stones piled one upon the other without benefit of mortar. Out of a chink darted, lizard-like, a gleam of light, which led him towards a corner near the river; and when he had rounded this the light spread softly, and Anger perceived an entrance covered not by door but with a piece of sacking. The building showed no window; the roof was low, and by the touch he judged it was thatched with heather; the hut was no more than ten feet square.

Still not a voice, nor any sound of motion. Fighting down nervousness, Anger gently called, "May I come in? I am a traveller lost upon the moor."

His cry aroused no sleeper. Putting out his hand he ventured to draw aside the sacking; a moment later he had passed inside out of the mist and rain; then stood in wonder.

No living creature was there, yet one had been prepared for. Upon the roughest kind of hearth burnt a good fire of turves and furze-roots. He saw a lighted lantern, its wick turned low; in one corner a quantity of fuel; and along one side a bed such as an animal might have slept on, made of dry fern heaped upon the ground, with an old stuffed sack for a pillow and three well-worn blankets. A steaming kettle stood near the fire; in a rough box were some provisions, and a few articles such as teapot, frying-pan, and tinware. Shivering with excitement, Anger knelt by the fire, warming his wet hands, hearing the water from his cap hissing as it dripped, made by the welcome heat, fully conscious that the building and the fire were real; but who was the owner, and why was the place unoccupied? It seemed to Anger in his exhaustion that the rough shelter had been prepared for him, and when he had departed from that fireside all would vanish. It was part of the enchantment of the glen and hanging wood.

Rain soaking into the thatch of heather, mist drifting against the loose walls, and darkness pressing down, were forces without noise; rough wind could not reach that corner. There was no sound except the plunging of the river which suited the calmness of the place. Anger felt dull in his wits; his mind would not work, being held in the knot of a problem which reason would not cut. This dwelling was entirely primitive, yet no rough owner was suggested. Time had been set back a thousand years, but modernity was not absent; for the interior was clean, tidy in a sense, and from a fold in the topmost blanket protruded two knitting-needles and a scrap of shy woolwork.

The sacking which made a door was snatched aside. A horrible face, white, wild, and mad flashed across Anger's eyes, followed by a scream which touched the lowest note of human terror; while Anger was alone again, and the silence was full of shuddering, and the man who had been so daring as to shelter his body in the witch's kitchen covered his eyes and could not look again.

"Down Whippety! Lie down, will you?" a voice muttered.

Anger turned, fearfully dazed, but winning courage from the voice, expecting to see a woman and her dog standing in the light of the lantern; afraid of seeing more and worse.

It was dim light, and at first he thought the hut was full of spirits. He brushed the moisture from his eyelids, and saw more clearly—no dog, but the same white face which had flashed before him, ghastly indeed but human, belonging to a wild creature of the wood whose body quivering with passion was controlled by a queenly mistress.

"Who are you?" she asked, not less frightened than the visitor, but much more sane.

"It is the Princess Eglantine," muttered Anger. "And this is her bower."

"What are you doing here?"

Anger had been seated upon a long flat stone, which represented in that strange abode a fireside chair. He rose and stared somewhat wildly at the girl, supporting himself by placing a hand against the wall. She was young, of course, because this was the valley of romance, and she was natural and wonderfully healthy; brown beauty at its best. Her face was almost the colour of peat so deeply was it tanned, and upon her cheeks and lips glowed strong red life like fire-light. She would be under the spell of some enchantment, condemned by the witch of the wood across the river to live in that hovel until some man, strong in the wisdom of the world, and pure of spirit, should find his way there in the mist and break the spell.

"Down, Whippety, I tell you!" she cried more sternly; and the wild boy flopped at her feet, curled up like a dog, and lay there growling.

"Are you human?" murmured Anger. Had he not wandered half the day, lost and perplexed, terrified by solitude; and was it not night in a place of wonder? His mind and body had been thrown quite off their balance.

"Of course I am," she said seriously.

"I might ask why you live here, but I am confused. I must explain my presence. I have been lost on the moor—I am lost still."

"Now I understand," she said, greatly relieved, her manner changing as she came lightly forward. The boy uncurled himself and followed. She pointed to a heap of fern beside the fire, and the poor creature slunk there and lay down, showing his teeth at Anger.

"I was frightened when I saw you," she went on. "I thought you might have come from the village."

"What village?" he asked.

"Oh, you are quite lost," she said, still without smiling. "Youlstone lies upon the top of the cleave, about a mile away."

"I have heard of Youlstone. The Billacotts and Vigars live there."

"Then you are not quite a stranger. I am Petronel Vigar."

Again that dizziness. After all, he had not gone back a thousand years but merely a couple of centuries; and somewhere in the mist above Hugh Billacott would be writing his household book, while here in the primitive hut below was the comely wench his cousin, who had been engaged as a help to the mistress, and was now driven out because the master would make love to her. "I won't let him have her," Anger muttered to himself.

"You must be very tired and hungry. Let me offer you some hospitality," said the re-incarnated girl. "The kettle is boiling. I can give you nothing but tea, and a pasty which I made myself. It will be better than nothing."

"It is most kind of you," he answered with difficulty. "I had no right to come in, but I could not resist the light and warmth."

"Your clothes are soaked. Will you not take off your coat and hang it upon this stone?"

"Thank you," he said sleepily.

"Take off your boots as well."

"I shall be glad to," he said; but did not move.

She glanced at him quickly, then moistened her splendid lips; his face, well-filled now, looked a fine one in the firelight. She bustled about, spread a white cloth across a slab of rock, brought forth tin plates and cups, a neat dish of pasties, another of small cakes; splashed boiling water into the teapot, murmuring to herself. Pouring out the great beverage of the world, she asked the guest whether he took sugar, just as if they had been living in the twentieth century, then invited him to eat and drink, with apologies for the fare she had to offer.

It was all pure romance to Anger, and the feeling of enchantment remained until he had drained the cup three times and made a strong attack upon the store of sweetmeat pasties. Afterwards his body recovered and began to discover some modernity.

"I have robbed you," he exclaimed, with an idea she must be very poor. "I force myself into your cottage, I drink your tea, I eat your food; and it seems now very late to thank you for having saved my life."

"But I have not done that," she said more brightly. "You would soon have been off the moor and down among the farmers. I wonder you did not find Youlstone instead of wandering into this cleave. There is more food than I shall want. To-morrow morning, if it is clear, I must go back home."

"I shall look upon you as my saviour," said Anger boldly. "At first I thought you lived here. I was dazed when you entered."

"This has been my hiding-place for a good many years," she answered. "Once it was a refuge for miners. My brother and I cleared it out. We removed nettles, brambles and tons of loose stones; then built up the walls, made a roof and thatched it. He has been gone a long time. When I saw you leaning over the fire, I wondered if you could be the dear lad."

"I am sorry to disappoint you. I have no sister," said Anger, somewhat too gently.

She looked at him again with a certain eagerness. Their eyes met and for some moments both were troubled; yet they looked on, he admiring, she welcoming; the guest ready to put out his hand, the hostess asking him to stay for a little, give some human friendship, and help to break the spell of enchantment which condemned her to pass long nights in that hidden hovel. Each had a story ready, and both were willing to listen; but they were strangers meeting in the mist, introduced to each other by elemental forces. Even there, in the midst of all things free and natural, they could not be man and woman; custom, and the clothes upon them, were too strong. Had Anger been a primitive man, rubbing the sleep of chaos from his eyes, he might have said, "You are very beautiful. You are the very spirit of the moorland. My desire is to watch your movements and to hear you speak." It would have been no sin to have spoken thus; yet it would have broken a commandment, not known during the youth of granite, nor ever written, but stronger than the ten. And she might have answered, had she been natural,

"It is a pleasure to give you shelter, to offer you food, and to see you sitting by the fire. I am lonely. My only companion is the wild boy of the wood."

"Whippety lies here," was what she did say. "He keeps the place dry and has a fire ready for me when I come. Nobody wants poor Whippety."

The boy looked up with eyes that lacked reason but not love, and dragging himself across the floor began to lick her shoes. He at least was natural. She pushed him away gently, saying, "Lie down, Whippety. Good Whippety," while she stroked his hair, making the wild tongue whine for joy.

"He does his best," she said to Anger, "but I cannot cure him of the habit of licking my shoes. I call him Whippety because unkind people beat him. I am afraid he does steal, but he knows no better."

"In any other place he would be removed to an asylum," said Anger pityingly.

Hardly had he spoken when the boy sprang at him, and had the mistress not seized her slave, Anger would have been bitten in the leg. She caught up a stick, intended for the fire, and lashed the boy, who cringed and grovelled, yet was happy because it was the mistress beating him.

"Go back to your bed, and do not dare to move again," she cried; while Anger was thrilled to know she was furious because it was himself the lad had turned against.

"He understands the word asylum. It expresses to him just what the grave does to us. Probably he will be taken some day, but he won't live long in captivity. I am so sorry he showed his teeth at you."

"I am sorry you beat him. He will hate me now."

"He would have hated you in any case—for speaking to me," she added.

The boy had taken his rod to the bed, and was licking the part of it which her hand had gripped.

"It is past eight," said Anger. "I should be going."

"You are a prisoner," the girl murmured, turning from him. "There is full mist, and the rain is heavier. It's none too easy to get out of the cleave when the night is clear. Whippety could guide you to Youlstone, but he wouldn't, and I could not trust you with him now. He is fierce and strong."

"I am here for the night!"

She murmured, "Yes."

"I am thinking of you. In every place are people who speak unkindly," he said painfully.

"Nobody will know," she said, speaking coolly. "We will keep the fire up. There is enough oil in the lantern to last. When I am here I lie down just as I am. Will you sleep there?"

"It is your bed," he said hoarsely.

"You are very tired, while I am fresh. You require sleep."

"I insist upon you lying down."

"I could not sleep. I will sit by the fire and go on with my knitting."

"What is that?"

"Only an owl. The wood is full of them. Please lie down and rest."

"I cannot. I should like to watch over you," he said.

"Whippety will do that. He sleeps like a dog. This is my home," she went on, smiling. "You are my guest. It is a very poor resting-place, but there is no other."

"For that reason I will not accept it. Miss Vigar, you will drive me out into the mist and rain, to be lost again."

"If you will not sleep, neither will I," she said firmly. "Please, stranger!"

"I am no stranger. I know you, I know of your family," cried Anger. "I will be, if I may, your friend. Let me tell you part of the history of your family."

"This is wonderful. Tell me all you can," she cried. "Then may I tell you my story, the history of myself?"

"I will hear that first," he said too eagerly.

"I have never been free," she murmured.

"But now—now that some power has guided a friend here?"

"I may be."

So they talked through the night; and perhaps before morning were seated hand in hand. Only Whippety would know, and he was natural. And outside the mist went on drifting, and the rain beat down upon the thatch of heather, and the river roared, and the witch's owl was hooting, and the spell of enchantment remained; and if there were voices in the wood, where the child's eyes and brain of the man are one, and a whisper was intelligible, it was that of the immortal mystic Princess Springwort, muttering:

"I salute thee, Nymph! When the moonbeams enter the hovel, and touch the hearthstone, let the sleeper go free."

CHAPTER IV

FREE FOLK

YOULSTONE parish presented a patchwork of physical geography; much of it moorland, comprising acres of peat-bogs, granitic hills, uplands bristling with furze and black with heather, deep cleaves and white rivers; the central portion a network of fields where little flourished except universal grass and root-crops; oats were sown sometimes, but the harvest was claimed as a sacrifice by Æolus. Westerly the ground sloped so sharply that legs descending were forced into rapid motion, while to ascend kept the mouth of man or beast wide open; but when land more level was reached, after the hurried drop of seven hundred feet, Youlstone lost severity and laughed.

Here squatted farms which accounted for the greater part of the population. One hundred and seventy human beings gave the place justification for calling itself an occupied district, but how these people used their material forms passed understanding. The majority appeared to glide about invisibly; there was never a crowding at the centre, which was called the church-town of Youlstone, made up of church with stunted tower, parsonage with thatched roof, inn, and a number of cottages, all huddled together so that a great sheet let down from heaven would have hidden the lot, in imitation of a cluster of great rocks such as were to be found

hard by on common land, or ponies driven by wild weather to the
side of a bramble-patch. Ponies outnumbered people in Youlstone
parish; without adding cattle, sheep, pigs, geese, and fowls; while
every man owned a dog; nor was there any woman catless; so that
had war been declared between man and beast, human beings
would certainly have been repulsed with great slaughter. The little
street seemed always empty, the same people passed every day; the
stranger would have learnt to recognise about twenty faces, while
the twenty-first might have made him stare. Youlstone in short
appeared to be inhabited by beasts and a score of human bodies,
together with one hundred and fifty imperceptible phantoms.

Decidedly the most obvious of the bodies was owned by
Bobby Billacott, who also owned Quoditch which seemed to be
the name attached to one of the geological glimpses Youlstone
was lavish of. From the centre of the church-town proceeded a
nervous little road, swerving first to one side then to the other,
when it could so easily have run straight and boldly, and presently
giving a violent shudder which carried it beside a hedge topped
with lop-sided beeches, and fifty yards beyond losing its nerve outright and breaking off with some display of hysteria, adding by its
lack of confidence much beauty to the landscape. The geological glimpse was startling in its suddenness. The little road gave up
because it could not continue; the ground yawned where the rock
was rotten, and the soil, composed chiefly of gravel, shifted easily
so that the mischievous little stream, always to be heard but often
not seen, ringing its bell-like note below, had done nothing very
remarkable thus to have scooped out Quoditch, rain being plentiful and time no object. Upon the other side hard rock abounded;
therefore that region, called after a strange fashion Stiniel, was
lifted high above the gravel and mud, looking down contemptuously upon moist Quoditch. One problem before the early inhabitants had been the making of a cart-track from Stiniel, where
the upland leading towards the peat-bogs was reached, across
Quoditch, and so into Youlstone by way of the nervous road. This
had been solved by using commonsense, a virtue never wanting
among savages. Being practical engineers, they adopted the zigzag

method, which is nearly as old as time, starting their road from the end of the trackway above Stiniel, cutting a terrace out of the crumbling cliff to the right, another to the left, and so descending unto the bottom of the cliff; and here they built a bridge, bringing huge blocks of granite by horse-power, rolling them down with man-power, and shifting them into place with iron-power. The opposite side of the cliff was ascended by means of similar terraces. The work was good, but horses had to sweat to get a load up. The highest and sharpest turning on the moor side was called the Stiniel Pinch; that on the Youlstone side the Quoditch Pinch. At these points came the pull which decided all things; and if the cart-wheel sank at either Pinch a day was wasted.

If the house Stiniel stood at the beginning of the zig, then the cottage Quoditch wobbled at the end of the zag; or had one of those rounded masses of granite become detached from the height, it would, after the rebound from Stiniel, have crashed into the roof of Quoditch, which would have been a lamentable disaster, for, even if the cottage was not worth preserving, its owner was necessary. All healthy laughter heard that side of Youlstone proceeded from his throat.

"This must be a place of great beauty during the green months," Anger exclaimed, when he had the glimpse from the shudder of the road; a certain amount of time having passed since that day of mist. "It must always be solemn," he added.

Apparently it was always muddy; the bridge, which served also as a viaduct, presented to his boots a sticky surface, composed of water, shredded peat, cow manure, with sufficient clay to make the mixture binding. On the right rose a cliff perpetually dripping; on the left, where the bridge ended, a gate appeared leading towards the wonderful farm of Quoditch; remarkable because it was unlike any other; consisting of three fields, shaped like the fantastic figures which appal the schoolboy who glances for the first time into Euclid, with a little house which defied every principle of geometry, architecture, and building by-laws. A farm of swamp, rushing water, precipitous banks, which had neglect stamped all over it, ruin imminent, bankruptcy sure and certain. Hedges were tottering in one place, bulging in another; here and there a shower of stones had fallen, and lay upon the turf half-covered with brambles, testifying that the hedge had not given way lately and the owner was indolent. The gate marking the entry to this farm of hopelessness was the greatest wonder. Very long ago it had been constructed with the usual five bars and cross-pieces, but now only three bars partially remained, and these lichened pieces of wood were eked out with furze-bushes, and held together by scraps of iron torn from some old bedstead, while one gap was draped with a sack and another was filled with a sheet of tin, and the entire barrier was kept from toppling by blocks of granite fixed upon either side.

Out of this, or over it, or through it, appeared with bird-like motions a small man, black and covered with dirt as if he loved it; a little round-headed, laughing man, who jumped across the road and cried excitedly, "Seen any bullocks going yonder?"

"There are none between here and the village," Anger answered.

"The beasts go abroad. Hedges be broken, gates be lying in pieces. You fancied I wouldn't see you go by," said the little man mirthfully. "I watched ye come creeping down the cleave."

Anger had no love for this creature, who seemed offensive and was certainly impertinent. He did not understand this was good-fellowship expressed in a primitive fashion, with nothing but a good heart and ignorance behind; and so he would have passed on towards Stiniel had not the little man stopped the way and kept him back, demanding with the same rough rudeness, "What ha' you brought to me?"

"Why, nothing, of course," said Anger sharply.

"You'm a foreigner. When a stranger crosses Quoditch, he brings weather. One brings rain and another fetches down snow. Don't ye bring along wind, vor I don't want none."

"I hope to bring you sunshine," said Anger, beginning to smile and to perceive the little man was willing to be friendly.

"That's a proper thing to say. I ha' spoke to plenty of foreigners, but none of 'em hoped to bring me sunshine. Us can put up wi' that. Plenty o' sunshine makes plenty o' pleasure. I'll shake hands with ye, I will sure enough. I don't shake hands wi' every man, and you'm only a foreigner, mind ye."

"I may improve while I am here," said Anger gravely, trying not to flinch from that hand which had benefited in no way from the surrounding streams.

"You'll learn, if you ha' a mind to," the new friend declared. "You tell to me when you be passing. I ha' plenty o' knowledge, and I uses it vor the benefit of others. You'm glad to be here, I reckon."

"Youlstone is well worth seeing," said Anger.

"This b'ain't Youlstone. 'Tis a *far better* place."

"It must be very healthy," Anger went on.

"'Tis a hundred times healthier in Quoditch."

"And the air is very fine."

"You catches it in Quoditch. Youlstone be mucky wi' smoke."

"May I ask your name?"

"I be wonderful well-known."

"But then I am a stranger."

"I knows you warn't here yesterday. I be Bobby Billacott."

"It is a good name," said Anger, wondering what connection could be possible between this dirty little farmer, who was exceedingly lazy and did not know his business, and the brisk merchant; both were from the same stock, but the man before him was a Billacott who had not advanced, and supposed he was a man of importance in the world because he was well-known in unknown Youlstone.

"You ha' heard tell of me," said Bobby with contentment. "Fame be the like to me as water be to trouts—I swims in it. Every foreigner who comes to Quoditch ha' heard of me."

"How long have you lived here?"

"From the beginning of the world, I reckon."

"I am speaking about yourself."

"Ever since I wur born and a bit avore."

"I believe your family came originally from Wyld."

"Wyld be a wonderful way off. I ha' never been as far, and I don't crave to go. A man who leaves his parish be out of the world. There may ha' been volk to Wyld who took my name. 'Tis a famous one."

"What has made it famous?" Anger ventured.

The little man looked at him uneasily. He was not accustomed to be pressed with pointed questions.

"It be famous," he said emphatically. "You can't alter a thing what be. The sun shines—that's my argument, master—he shines. The Billacotts be famous. 'Tis a fact. You don't know why it be."

"The sun is necessary," began Anger; but Bobby would not let him continue, for his method of debate was to refuse the other side an opening.

"No Billacott ha' worked 'cept vor himself," he rattled on. "Us be free. Us ha' never been without a bit of land."

"Is that a sign of freedom?"

"You ha' plenty to learn," said the farmer scornfully. "A man wi' land be free, and a man without ain't got his freedom."

"I have no land," said Anger. "But I am free."

"You ha' got money," replied Bobby. "That be the like to land where you come from. When you can buy a bit of land, you'm in the like position of a man who bides on his land."

Perceiving sense in the argument, Anger did not continue it. He knew sufficient history to be aware that the countryman without his plat was compelled to be a hired labourer, the lineal descendant of that human clod of earth—the serf; but he was astonished to find how tenacious was the idea of freedom in thought and action being dependent upon the ownership of land. Property made the man, gave him power to vote, to speak as he liked, to call himself master. Now he understood why every man in all the parishes of the moor possessed at least his one small field, which he clung to and regarded as the best thing he had, even though he might neglect it altogether, and would not clear it, and left it to be covered with furze and bracken. It was his own land, the holding which gave him the right to call himself a freeman. Merely as a farm, Quoditch, with its ruined gate and tumbling hedges, was a hopeless spectacle; and yet without it that little dirty man would not have held his bullet head so proudly, would certainly have lost his trick of easy talking, and no longer would have styled himself as famous.

"I'll take you round my property," said Bobby, beginning to unravel the problem of a gate. "The trouble be like the pleasure, and that be nothing."

"Do you suggest I may not be interested?" asked Anger.

"I ses what be a trouble to you b'ain't no pleasure to me," explained Bobby, and added to himself, "He'm fearful ignorant."

"I have business yonder," said Anger, shrinking from the path of liquid mud. "Another day I will give myself the pleasure. Are you married?"

"I ha' a proper woman. Her volks wur always wonderful vor pigs, and Thirza favours 'em."

"Have you any family?"

"A proper lot of little pigs. Mother will show 'em to ye. I calls her mother, though she'm my wife really."

"I mean children."

"Us ain't got any of they. Vunny little things they be, but useful to come after ye. Mother would fancy a few, but I ha' no opinion what you would call decided. The bridge be narrow, you see, and if us had children they would be running in and out of the gate, and a cart might come by and knock down a dozen of 'em. What do you think of the house?"

"It might be bigger," said Anger, looking at the toppling mass of iron, stones, turves, and wood, very little better than Petronel's hiding-place beside the river.

"I'll have a proper house some day. I don't know when 'twill be, but I ha' set my mind on having a house as big as Stiniel, and 'twill come I tell ye. When I craves vor anything I waits vor't."

"Are those two horses yours?"

"They'm mine, and if you want to beat 'em you must travel. I calls the horse Scribe, and the mare Pharisee."

Anger was going on, seeing an opening, but Bobby had not done with him. Putting out an arm he caught hold of the visitor, whom he supposed had come that way to call upon him, and said querulously, "Bide a bit, will ye? You foreigners be always in a hurry. You knows my name, but I don't know yours. I calls to volk when they goes by, but I can't call to you unless I knows your name."

Anger told him, somewhat sharply, for the little man's tenacity annoyed him.

"I see you b'ain't satisfied wi't," said Bobby, whose faculty for misunderstanding was well developed. "Us can't all be Billacotts, master. A bit of room must be left vor the volk down under. What be your profession; be you one o' they chaps what works from eight to five, and puts out his hand on Saturday to take as many shillings as his master likes to give?"

"I have been accustomed to work longer hours than those," said Anger. "It was a labour of love; I was not forced to it," he added, more to himself than to this wormer out of secrets.

"You b'ain't a varmer," said Bobby with derision.

"That is true."

"You don't come from a town."

"How do you know that?"

"You'm lusty. You favours the commoner."

"Perhaps I am a teacher," said Anger lightly.

"A schulemaster! I would never ha' thought of that. Be you vull o' buke learning?"

"All that I know would not amount to much. I am learning now," said Anger.

"You mean I be teaching you," said the hopeless egoist. "I likes a talk wi' schulemasters, but when I asks 'em how much gude their bukes ha' done 'em they'm mostly deaf. You teaches children to read and write; you don't teach 'em nought else, vor that be all you knows yourself—don't ye get peevish, master; 'tis learning you be getting—and when you ha' done with 'em they'm only fit to teach others how to read and write. They'm gude vor nought till they come on the land and forget what you ha' taught 'em."

"You can learn without reading, and you can live without writing," replied Anger. "The state of ignorance may be a happy one; but when you die you leave a world which you have never really discovered, you depart from a life which you have never shared in, and you abandon for ever a wealth of beauty which has never been revealed to you. The reward of ignorance is a dull kind of self-conceit. If you were to read a dozen of the best books, you would talk less, my friend, and think more; you might not be satisfied with your present conditions; you would rebuild those hedges and repair this gate."

Bobby Billacott was staggered. Muttering, "No man ha' ever spoke like that to me avore," he fell back, giving his dangerous opponent the right of way. The greater part of Anger's meaning was lost upon the little bullet-head, which meant to do well and wisely, but was stuffed with independence and stupid pride in place of brains. He had been called ignorant, told to read books, advised by a loafing stranger to learn his own business. No wonder he was silenced for the moment, during which the schoolmaster escaped and went his way. The man of Quoditch was not crushed, but stunned by the intellectual hammer which had fallen on his folly. The shrewdness of the Billacotts was stirred into some kind of activity by the calm rebuke. Villagers called the farmer wise and openly admired his trick of ready speaking; strangers made a point of calling upon the local celebrity and flattering him with irony he could not see through. No man had ever suggested the plain truth.

Thirza was in the living-dining-cooking-room sorting potatoes, placing the sound ones in a sack, hurling the discarded ones broadcast; if a window was broken it could not matter much where anything that was whole seemed out of place. Thirza worked in a hurry, thus adding to her labours. Her figure was enormous, and to it strength was added sufficient to have lifted Bobby and carried him up hill if necessary, never failing at either of the Pinches. She was a man for work, her feet and hands were large and tough, yet her face was unmistakably feminine, very wide and marvellously red, but soft in places, almost child-like, and her good clear eyes were somehow innocent. How much she weighed was not known with certainty, but the little room shook while she bustled to and fro; and if ever Bobby, during some hour of energy, determined to shift a rock, he found it an easier task to call for Thirza and invite her to cast her weight upon the end of the bar of leverage, while he stood by and watched the boulder lifting. Ease, necessary to all women, was unknown to her; so were womanly clothes. She toiled in a shameful skirt, boots made for a ploughman, a ragged cloth cap, a sack around her shoulders.

"Scat you, woman!" cried Bobby, as a rotten potato struck him in the stomach.

"Stand out of the door, will ye?" called back Thirza, not ceasing from her labours for a moment.

The farmer entered, seated himself, scratching his nailed boots upon the cement floor. Industry gave no heed to idleness until the word went forth that energy should cease. Then Thirza looked round, and perceived that all was not well.

"I seed you telling with a gentleman," she said.

"Schulemaster," muttered Bobby. "I can stand parsons, I can stand lawyers, but as vor them there schulemasters—I hates they."

"How did he tell to ye?" asked Thirza.

"He drew me on. He wur confident wi' me. He wur artful, he wur deceitful; and then he turned on me. He told me I wur ignorant."

"Did you ever hear the like!" gasped Thirza.

"Told me to go under and read bukes."

"My dear soul!" cried Thirza.

"He had the last word, then left me, so as I shouldn't answer 'en."

"Us won't let 'en pass over Quoditch if he insults we," declared Thirza.

"Quoditch be mine. If I ses he can pass over, you won't stop 'en. A cruel, artful, cunning toad of a schulemaster he be. I ain't done with 'en yet. I'll learn a thing or two and answer 'en."

"Let 'en bide, Bobby. If he beat you once, mebbe he'll beat you again."

"Told me I wur ignorant," groaned Bobby.

"You'm the cleverest man in Youlstone parish," cried Thirza, returning to the potato-picking. "Where do he come from?"

"Wyld," replied the unhappy voice.

"Tell ye how 'tis, Bobby. Volks got telling him how wise you be. He ha' come to wrastle with ye," said Thirza earnestly.

The powerful influence of tradition told her how frequently it happened in the old days for the sage of one parish to travel into another to engage in a trial of wit with some noted rival. A ballad-singer would hear of another living in a distant parish, and at the first opportunity would travel in that direction and issue his challenge; the two would then sing against each other in some public place, ballad against ballad, and he who continued the longest was declared the winner.

"He ha' spoke now. He ha' told all he knows," she said hopefully. "Now 'tis your turn, Bobby."

"I ha' got the learning," declared Bobby, "but he ha' got the words. He ha' got a fearful lot of words."

"He couldn't ha' got 'em unless he made 'em up. You can do the like," said Thirza.

"I ha' never put my mind to it. Learning can't talk against words. Learning gets all smothered up and choked wi' words. 'Tis like snow on a vuzzy-bush, falling and falling till you can't see no bush but only snow."

"I saw schulemaster going beyond. He went up over," said Thirza, extending her mighty arm.

"Did he go to Stiniel? I wur too mazed to watch 'en."

"He went through the gate. I saw 'en. Stopped a bit, walked on, then stopped again."

"He never come here to tell wi' me, then," muttered Bobby. "He gets over from Wyld this morning. He goes first thing to Stiniel. He'm a friend of Nicholas Vigar."

"He b'ain't Bert come home," said Thirza, lowering her voice.

"He warn't a Vigar," agreed her husband.

"Wur there a posy in his coat?"

"I b'ain't certain."

"Wur he wearing gloves?"

"I knows he warn't, vor I looked at his hands to be sure he worked without 'em."

"He b'ain't going courting then," said Thirza.

"The maid wouldn't fancy a schulemaster."

"Her would fancy any man what took she away from that old devil. Her wur screaming again last night."

"Shut your noise, mother. Us don't talk about it," said Bobby angrily.

"Us be near to it. I be afraid of something what will make us wish Stiniel wur miles away."

The little man jumped up and went to the door, wishing to hear no more of his wife's forebodings. Being in the way, he was directed to move, so he made a couple of steps forward as if intending to leave the house, but changed his mind quickly, hurried back, and shut the door.

"Curgenven!" he whispered.

Thirza left the potatoes, wiping her hands, looking innocent no longer. She turned her head to spit on the floor, then muttered, "Which way?"

"Down from Stiniel."

"He'm up there plenty," was her comment.

"Hoped he would bring me sunshine," went on Bobby. "Foreigners bring nought but foul weather. The schulemaster ha' brought Curgenven along. Proper old gleam o' sunshine he be!"

"What wur his name, Bobby?"

"Anger, he ses."

"Like enough," she whispered.

"They'm together, think ye?" said the farmer, actually appealing to his wife. "This Anger ha' gone on to Stiniel, and he only come to Youlstone town this morning. Anger goes up to Stiniel, and the devil comes down out on't."

"When volk meet they talk," said Thirza, coming to the window and standing beside her husband.

Free they might be, but there was no boast of it then; independent they called themselves, while in the grip of a master, like serfs subject to the tyranny of their lord. That man coming round the Stiniel Pinch was prince of Youlstone in the mist; a man at a distance insignificant, being hardly more than five feet high, more of a court jester than a king; a dwarf to the eye, barely a man, but a rough model of human parts; a creature without a neck, whose chin seemed to dig into his breast, whose shoulders were fearfully square, whose backbone and skull were close together. Strongly he walked, each footfall sounding like a judgment, while the two Billacotts looked on, trusting to see him cross the bridge and disappear.

"He passes by," said Bobby.

"He turns back. He'm coming! How much do us owe?"

"Two pounds, two shillings, no pence," muttered the little man.

The dwarf was beside the gate. Now it was easy to see how massive were his arms and what great heaps his shoulders were. Those arms fought with the gate, which gave in every part yet would not give admittance. He stepped back, lifted his foot, crashed it against what was already wreckage, smashing rotten wood, sweeping aside iron-work, breaking furze bushes, crumpling the sheet of tin.

"He'm scattering my poor old gate abroad," cried Bobby, with passion, foolish if pathetic; for this was merely disarrangement of his rubbish. "Will you please to step outside and talk to 'en, Thirza?" he went on humbly.

"I b'ain't master," she said sharply.

"What be I? He'm calling me!"

"Go out, Bobby. Face mun, and say you ain't got the money, but please God you'll sell a beast and pay next week"; and Thirza pulled the door open and pushed her husband out.

"Ah, friend Bobby, my little friend Bobby!" said Curgenven. "Busy as usual! Always hard at work, without time to visit your friends or to think of little bits of business. How is the woman? Call her out. Tell her an old friend wants to see her."

He spoke pleasantly, but without a smile, his sunken eyes fixed upon the wriggling farmer, and his face as hard as the granite against which he placed his squat body, prodding the turf with an iron-pointed stick as if inactivity was to him impossible.

"Her's fine, master. So be I. Thirza! Mother! Come out and tell to master."

The strong woman appeared, "with a knife in one hand and her fist in the other," according to her own description, to signify her readiness to attack the enemy should he set his foot by some malicious accident upon one of her young chickens. Curgenven welcomed her with an idle compliment, then added, "A pretty little place, Quoditch. I was thinking as I came down from Stiniel what might be made of it. A house at that end, the fields turned into garden, the side of the gorge planted with shrubs. A nice bit of property, Bobby."

"Aw, master! you b'ain't going to be hard on us," cried Thirza.

"Hard on my neighbours," exclaimed Curgenven. "I, who help you, give you good advice, set you straight when you get into difficulties. I was suggesting what might be done with Quoditch. Half a moment, Thirza, my dear. You are the farmer. Master Bobby runs in and out, buzzing. See that old gate I had to trample down before I could get in. See those hedges tumbling. It won't do, my dear. The place must be kept in proper repair."

"I ha' got plenty of potatoes—fine ones, master," said Thirza irrelatively. "I'll sell a load next week and get some money."

"Money!" said Curgenven. "Ah, yes, I seem to remember. How much is it?"

"Two guineas, master."

"Overdue? Not much. I can't keep these little things in my head. A month or so? Bad business, neighbours, makes bad friends. Keep straight in your accounts, my dear, or you will soon run crooked with your creditors. I'm easy with you—always have been. Quoditch is what some people would call a romantic spot. Wouldn't it sell, neighbours?"

The farmer and his wife said nothing. Silence for a moment was disturbed only by the water rushing down the gorge, roaring gently, never even in the flood-time of winter lacking music, like the strong dwarf's voice.

"Shake this man of yours," he went on, less pleasantly. "Turn him out early and make him work. I can afford to work with my tongue, Bobby; you can't, I can stick my hands in my pockets; you can't. I can pay my debts; and you must."

He moved away, looked back, and said, "Mind the hedges and gate, Thirza. They are mine, my dear, and I must have them seen to."

"I'll do my best," muttered Thirza. "But I be mazed wi' work."

"Come along with me, Bobby," called Curgenven amiably; and the little man tramped like a dog at the dwarf's heels until they reached the ruin of the gate.

"You can't go along like this, my friend. The place is growing rotten for want of money. It's your duty to keep everything in good repair, and if you won't do it yourself, you must pay others to do it for you. Quoditch is yours, even if I do call it mine, for a bit of a joke, and I want you to keep it. You can't do that without money. This is Tuesday; to-morrow, busy; next day, busy. I'll be round on Friday with a bit of paper; fifty pounds will be enough. That will make a hundred. One's as easy to you as t'other. I'll make it easy, neighbour. I give you another fifty; you scratch another cross on a bit of paper. Pretty way of getting money, ain't it? But you must work, my man, and do me credit. Keep the roof tight, or the rain will leak in. I'll look after mother and you, keep you straight, see you don't get into the hands of money-lenders, steer you clear of difficulties. Remember the gates and hedges. Build 'em up and you'll soon grow rich. When the stones roll out the house begins to tumble. Good-day, my lad. I'll come on Friday with the paper."

Curgenven went across the bridge, his feet splashing like a horse's hoofs, his chin on his breast, head and shoulders like lumps of granite deep in heather; and so departed towards his little principality of Youlstone church-town.

CHAPTER V

AT THE STINIEL PINCH

STINIEL was a square house, hugged by moorland on two sides, opening upon the terrace road westerly, and fronted northerly by its steep and sunless garden, thrusting an arrow-shaped end into the marsh of Quoditch. The farm consisted of a group of fields along the river some way behind the house, with, above the zigzags, two large plats where stood the necessary buildings, barn, cow-byre, and stables, all in good repair. The house was modern; people of old had been tempted perhaps by that level strip of land; but they had not taken it to build upon because the sun could not strike there more than once during the longest day. The father of Nicholas Vigar, who built, had somehow overlooked the sun; he was an earnest Christian, and possibly the light of his religion, shed from the Wesleyan chapel, had atoned to his body for the lack of lesser warmth; it was otherwise with his home, which remained dark and grew gradually damp, while the garden gave no produce. The good soil, ready to bring forth, gasped for the love of the sun, and for the need of it stayed barren; soured by moisture which produced mildew, and those crops of darkness, moss, spongy fungi, and all manner of cryptograms, things of a secret marriage which love dark places. One week of the sun upon that slope would have killed these children of shadow, and forced into existence the fragrant plants which revel in the joy of the day and are not ashamed to wed in openness.

The strip of land being sheltered, trees and bushes grew well, but nothing of bright green; only dark firs, fleshy laurels, and rhododendrons which rejoice in sodden peat. Nothing of sweet savour grew in Stiniel; no rose-lit garden could be there, no lily held its cupful of pollen to the bees. The bushes held possession, spreading their black leaves to the unwarmed atmosphere, leaves like the flesh of animals, fat and pulpy, unpleasant to the touch. Small wonder if Petronel ran often from a home so shadowed to hide in her cot at the bottom of the glen of sunshine. Even butterflies did not play in Stiniel, and birds only tarried for what they could pick up and went elsewhere to sing.

Not the place a sleeper would choose to dream in, yet Anger approached with a kind of elation. The life before his illness grew marvellously dim, and his old friends were shadows. He had come to Youlstone—to complete his cure; and by so doing had cut himself entirely from the past. Anger was in danger as he climbed the Stiniel Pinch. Fond of his friends he was hiding from them, loyal to his faith he neglected it, still a churchman he was passing as a layman; nor did he place these matters before his mind because heaviness had settled upon it, stupor caused by the weight of flesh he carried mastered him, while the new blood in his veins made him a man like others. This period was a break, a holiday, a time of refreshment, of rebuilding; it was not sleep. Before the first gale of winter roared and shook those roofs, he would be Father Jack, tending the sacred lamp, claiming the life of Mary, spurning her love as falsely as before.

The cause of his elation was clear. He had discovered Youlstone, although that by itself was not sufficient; he had come upon Vigars and Billacotts, although that was not enough; his meeting with Petronel had been romantic, the touch of her hand had thrilled him, her story had touched him deeply. All these were not reasons, but rather side-lights upon the truth, which was reached by a simple argument: he was a priest, although brown beauty had not been told, and he was bound to continue his work as if no break had occurred; listen to confessions, stroking the suppliant's hand tenderly, and speaking sympathetically with brotherly love in his eyes; aid the sufferer to the best of his ability; devote himself to free her from sorrow. That was the duty; he was proposing to himself no new thing. Where was the difference between fighting for Petronel, and rescuing a poor girl of the town from the clutches of some dealer in low traffic?

He hesitated between black rhododendrons beside a white

gate bearing the name Stiniel in pitchy letters. All was as different as possible from Quoditch. No sign of neglect, no tumbling
hedges; even the gravel walk was neatly weeded. Yet it was dark
and damp, and pitiless somehow. Restored Quoditch would have
been a better place by far.

Slowly Anger advanced, longing to hear a disturbance caused
by human energy. Stiniel became now like the spell-bound castle
where Thorn-Rose slept for a hundred years, and with her all things
that had life inside the hedge: servants over their work, pigeons on
the roof, flies upon the wall, and even the fire in the hearth. Yet
that feeling of elation would not go. Fearfully as Anger walked
his spirit exulted. His was to be the helping hand, his the guiding
mind, and his the soul to release brown beauty from the beast. The
voice of duty, the voice of religion, the voice of self-love, called
him to the tryst appointed by the new man's heart within him.

A porch, and beside it a window near the ground—the path
curved suddenly—and close to the glass two chairs supporting a
body with rigid limbs and a face too white. Anger shivered at the
shape so silent, suggestive of a sad ceremony rather than healthy
sleep, as he came nearer the window and looked boldly in. The
body seemed forgotten. It was alone with a large bee, which
thumped itself against the glass, seeking some outlet into space, as
if it had been the soul of that body eager to start and travel.

"This must be the master, Nicholas Vigar," Anger muttered;
and he rattled his knuckles against the glass.

More knowledge might have made him much less daring. To
visit houses had been a part of Anger's daily life, therefore it was
with confidence he woke the sleeper, ignorant that in Youlstone
a visitor was not welcomed unless sent for or invited, while the
unwanted stranger was on a level with the tramp. The rigid
figure went crooked very suddenly, rolled off the chairs and again
straightened, now standing, gazing at the figure in the garden,
and presently making signs towards the gate. Stupid with sleep,
thought Anger, and did not go, but waited for Nicholas to throw
up the window, which action he declined since fresh air in a living-
room was little to his taste; but disappeared and quickly came out

upon the path, ordering half fiercely, yet in a voice subdued, "Get out, will ye? Go out, sir. You must have seen the gate. 'Tis large and white enough. The trackway goes beyond, not through my garden."

"I have come to call on you," said Anger.

"I don't want to buy, and I have nothing to sell. Left your pack outside, have ye? Well, take it and be off."

"I am no pedlar."

"I have told you once—I've nothing for you. If you want to buy, go to them that sell. I do no business."

"Mr. Vigar! I come to you in friendship."

"Waking me from sleep; I get little of that. I know you, I can see through those fancy clothes. Your sort comes to the village sometimes, but not to me, never to me before to-day. You have come all the way from God knows where to preach the gospel to me."

"I have come to see your daughter," said Anger quietly.

"Who are you, sir?" cried Vigar in a different key, looking about him in a frightened manner.

"My name is Anger."

"Are you a friend of that cursed Curgenven? Do you come from him? No, no! he is about himself, I heard his voice—he would not use another," said Vigar quickly. "My God, sir, take care what you do—take care or there may be a hump upon your shoulders."

"I do not know the man you speak of. I came upon your daughter a week ago by chance. I was lost in the mist all day, and towards evening reached the hut where she goes to hide, as you know, Mr. Vigar, to hide from her mother."

"You are a brave man, sir, very brave to speak so carelessly," said Nicholas bitterly.

"Did she not mention me?"

"I have heard nothing of you. Yes, she goes to that hut," he muttered. "She must go, it helps her to live. But she is proud, and very strong. She would not speak such secrets to a stranger."

"She told me everything," said Anger earnestly. "I was compelled to stay in the hut all night. We spent it sitting beside the fire and talking. She put off her restraint and told me all, she gave way, she cried; and I promised to be her friend, to stand by her, and not to leave her until she could tell me she was happy. I am here to keep my word."

Vigar was obviously moved. His face softened, but there was terror in it. Again he glanced round, then approaching Anger seized his hand furtively and murmured, "I am sorry I mistook you. Nobody comes here but enemies and pedlars. A little word to you, sir, a word of advice, as small a word as I can think of: go!"

"I keep my promise," said Anger firmly.

"Turn round, sir. Pass through the gate, return to your lodging, leave Youlstone, go back to your own home, and forget there is a house called Stiniel."

"You must give me reasons."

"You admire my daughter."

"As a friend."

"You will love her."

"As a brother."

"No, no! A young man is no brother to the maid he pities. I should have a poor opinion of you if, after being Petronel's companion for a month or two, you did not love her. I presume you are natural. Now then, sir," he went on sternly, "go, and never let me see your face again."

"If you order me to leave your garden, I must do so. But I shall remain in Youlstone, and I will see your daughter."

"She will tell you to go."

"I should not leave her."

"She may have told you much. There is more," said Vigar, wavering in speech and manner. "You wish the maid well; you have a feeling of kindness for me because of her. Would you hurt her?"

"God forbid," said Anger with a start.

"You have thought of seeing her as a wife. Don't tell me of friendship, for you are young, and while you talk I can see you change from friend to lover. Would you see her in white, like a bride, white all over, sir, but deaf, blind, and dumb, as you found me stretched on those chairs, and as stiff, but not able to move when you come to knock upon the window? Will you go now, Mr. Anger, or will you stay?"

"You are excited, Mr. Vigar; you say too much," said Anger hoarsely. "There may be danger from passion and madness, but there is no fear of death. I will see to that," he said more strongly. "Are we not in a civilised country, are there not laws, is violence to go unchecked? This has gone on too long already."

"You are a stranger. What right have you——"

"I claim the right of protecting Miss Vigar," broke in Anger. "Call it love if you must. Give it any name, only know that I will keep my promise, and will take it upon myself if necessary to invoke the arm of the law, and put an end to this mediæval system of torture."

"Curgenven," groaned Vigar. "You will never get past him."

"Now, Mr. Vigar," cried Anger, not hearing what he said, "let me see your daughter."

"She is not here."

"Where shall I find her?"

"She is out upon Dartmoor."

"Then I will wait near the gate until she returns."

"You are brave, sir, and, I might add, foolish."

"Will you invite me into the house?"

"I will," said Nicholas, after a moment's thought. "But I shall not be the one to tell you to leave. Please to step inside."

The air was beginning to darken, so that it was gloomy in the house, which was poorly furnished and seemed to contain no luxuries. The floors were of cement; some of the walls were unplastered, and here drops of moisture could be seen standing like dewdrops. Vigar introduced the guest into the room where he had slept, then turning to him asked in a sullen fashion, "Now that you have forced your way inside, what do you want to talk about?"

"This," said Anger at once, putting out his hand towards a picture. It was not so dark that he was unable to see the red and brown face of little Petronel, a child of about twelve with glossy hair upon each side of her face, the whole well painted.

"An artist did that miniature, and gave it to the child. A pretty thing to the father. Perhaps a pretty thing to the friend?"

"It is very beautiful, and very true," said Anger simply.

"Her face has grown hard since then. She is painted with a smile, you see, and that is not true."

"She has become a woman. Life may harden a face without spoiling it," replied Anger.

"It is a small picture, and there is not much light in here. Yet you found it at once. There is always a light about those things we want to see," Vigar went on in a more friendly fashion.

"That is true."

"And we create our own darkness around those things we do not want to see."

"That is natural."

"Hang the picture on its nail. Turn its face towards the wall; then say good-bye, Mr. Anger. The door is open. It is not too late to go."

"You do not wish me to go," said Anger clearly. "Now that you know me better you are glad I am here. Your face has changed; your voice asks me to stay. I declare myself your friend, Mr. Vigar."

The man who owned Stiniel, but was not master, trembled a little, then put a hand to his head, and stood like a philosopher in thought. Anger went near and touched him, but Nicholas did not move. He was struggling with pride, finding it hard to break down family tradition which could not brook the interference of a stranger. It was evening time and they were both seeking for the light, which could not return until the night of dreams and darkness had been crossed.

"You have just arrived in Youlstone," Nicholas said at last. "A lonely parish; to you perhaps a savage little place. Our lives are public; neighbours know what happens, they talk about it, but do not act; they have no right to do so, because when the door is shut upon moor or street all that takes place behind is secret in a sense; guessed at, known, or discussed behind other closed doors, but sacred to the family concerned. There is no action. No commoner of Youlstone would walk into my house as you have done.

It would be an offence against the custom of centuries, but to you it is nothing. Travellers do not respect the customs of the folk they stay among. Is it worth while, sir, do you think, to leave your home and its secrets, that you may force yourself into mine; to leave a well-lighted place in order that you may explore the corners of a dark one?"

So low was the voice of Nicholas that Anger could scarcely hear him. The use of his ears was claimed by a sound more ominous.

"What lies beneath this room?" he whispered.

"A cellar."

"I heard a voice calling."

"Your ears are very keen, sir; but they are, like your mind, mistaken. I hear no sound."

"Do you make use of the cellar?" demanded Anger, not then prepared to shrink from any question.

"We keep peat in it, sacks of potatoes, many things."

"It would be cold," said Anger somewhat wildly.

"Very cold."

"And dark?"

"There is no window; and it is damp," Vigar went on. "I have seen toads and long-legged spiders."

"Mr. Vigar," almost shouted Anger, "will you swear to me your daughter is not locked up inside that cellar?"

"I told you she has gone out. She is rambling upon Dartmoor," muttered Nicholas. "Perhaps she has gone down to the hut; the wild boy keeps it warm for her. She is not in the house; she would be with me else. Nobody knows, Mr. Anger; they can only guess. Why don't you go? There is the gate, with the sunshine beyond. Go now, do ye," he said coaxingly.

"Take me below," cried Anger, forgetting himself entirely, claiming his right to search the house. "Open the door of this cellar and let me see for myself. If you will not lead me, I will find the way alone. It was her voice, calling her friend; and I am in Youlstone for no other purpose than to save her."

He spoke loudly, incautiously, and more boldly than he had ever shouted at some drunken bully of a wife-beater in the slums.

Young and strong, and thrilled with tender pity for the brown maid, who had received him so kindly in the hut, and had spread her store of food before him, and wounded him so sweetly with her eyes and story, he cared nothing for the devil in fleshly form as man with a hump or woman without soul. He was ready with his own hands to light a lamp, then rage through the house, forcing doors open, exposing dark corners, tumbling the skeletons out of their cupboards. No question of right arose, for he was a stranger, and local custom was nothing to him; only the great facts and passion of humanity troubled him then. He had been a priest; disease had made him a man; mighty winds of Dartmoor had breathed fierceness into him; its gods had divided his mind among themselves, and the greater part had been claimed by the god of the glen whose temple was the hut beside the watercourse within the shadow of the wood. Anger was far from home, lost in other mists, and it was not now possible for him to retrace his steps.

Vigar went to the window and did not move. The room was darker, but not silent. It seemed to Anger that a beast had come upon the doormat, and was lying there, weary after hunting, breathing heavily. He crossed the room, stared out, and felt, no loss of fierceness, but that shrinking and spiritual collapse which attend the shocking vision of a thing unnatural. A figure he saw, somewhat tall, its tumbling hair plentiful and colourless; a different face beneath it would have made it pure. Here was the living witch of the wood able to change the life of the young and happy by her enchantments. Faintly the warning had reached him, when it was getting dark as he came out upon the end of the trackway to discover the river and the wood: "Take care not to go too near the castle." But it had been misty then, so that he could not see which way to go; and it was necessary that he should hurry on towards the hut which was all on the way to the fatal castle, and become entangled in a spell which should not have concerned him as a priest. Now the light had disappeared; he felt very sad, and looked about him, wondering which way to turn; and he seemed to see the grey walls of the fearful castle showing through the tangle of brambles and nettles; for they too were under the spell and could not become fragrant plants until the witch was conquered. He was within the magic circle; dark night had come; all nightingales were owls; and here was the witch with her terrible red eyes, and upon her lips the words which could transform the man who had put off the protection of the priestly mantle. Already he could not move, but remained fixed like the white stones upon Knattlebarrow, unable to stir hand or foot until she gave permission.

The seaman about to be engulfed, as the wave of his destruction topples, may read in one moment the forgotten history of himself; the soul entering the world may in the pangs of birth behold for the last time till death the spiritual realm it is then cut off from. So Anger, past the turning-point, and about to make a choice of paths, and to take that one marked desire, had the glimpse, not now geological, but vital, seeing the past in one clear flash of light, the present in a mist, the future darkly outlined. The charm cast by the woman at the door could not be wholly evil if it gave the vision of a life more natural. Surely the past had been wrongly spent; and because he would not see the path marked out for him, disease had been sent, expelling him from the town, driving him into lonely places, that he might be changed and given shape to fit this work.

"It is Mrs. Vigar," said a hollow voice.

As the woman moved Anger stepped back. She came on, glaring at him, until he had pity for her too. Seeing her face more clearly, courage returned, for his religion was still strong enough to wrestle with the powers of darkness. Before him was a vice, a sin, a fury. He had only to invoke the aid of perfect womanhood, and she would shiver.

"Who are you?" she said in a hoarse voice.

"A visitor. A friend of mine," said Vigar loudly.

"Hold your noise. The man can talk. If you have any business, speak to me," said Judith Vigar to the guest. "I'm master here."

"My business is with you," said Anger firmly.

"Who has sent you?"

"I come on behalf of your daughter."

She went into a rage at once; screamed out, and ran at him, while Anger stepped aside, and as he did so heard again the voice from below. Nicholas came forward, shaking pitifully, but Judith threw him back as if he had been an infant. She did not speak, but howled and appeared to be a beast devoid of reason, until seeing the little picture left upon the table she snatched at it, broke up the frame, but dropped the miniature in her rage, and before she could stoop Anger had it held behind him.

"Go out!" cried Vigar, trying to be strong. "You have done too much."

"I will not go," said Anger.

"I'll welcome him," howled Judith.

She ran at Anger, forced him back into a corner, then jumped like a cat and tried to claw his neck, making senseless noises and breathing furiously. He forced her back and held her at arm's length in the pride of his new strength, while Nicholas groaned, and kept on striking matches which went out.

"The gentleman is a stranger, Mrs. Vigar. The stranger is a gentleman," he kept on muttering. "He will go. He will leave us if you stand aside."

"Give me that picture," she screamed.

"It is mine till you are sane," said Anger.

She spat at him, and when he shrank from the filthy missile she pressed forward with a blow which missed its mark. Her strength was borrowed from passion. It was easy to hold her back, even with one arm. Not a strong body, but an evil spirit, was fighting with the guest. Vigar was helpless and hopeless. When he reached the lamp there was no oil in it. Natural terror of his wife hindered him from going too near. So he kept on scraping matches and letting them burn out.

"The brute is all fat," she screamed. "I can't get hold of him. Fetch me an iron bar, old Nick, and then I'll shift him."

"I have no fear of you," said Anger quietly. "I shall beat you. A girl must be protected against an unnatural parent; and if her father cannot do it, a friend must." She let him go. Fury was in her eyes, yet she restrained it, and he perceived she was cunning, and a coward when opposed by a stronger mind. Anger stepped forward from the corner, shivering a little, resolved to force his victory to its conclusion.

He pushed Judith Vigar aside contemptuously, and said to her husband, "That is the way to use her. Show her she has a devil. Frighten that, and you frighten her."

"No, no!" murmured Nicholas. "How fearfully he can talk!"

"Shut your noise, you blasphemous old fool," she snarled.

"I understand her," Anger went on, somewhat too loftily. "She is no woman. She ceased to be a woman years ago; after she gave birth to a daughter who is a woman and a perfect one. Evil entered into her in place of the virtue she then lost. You have given birth to a daughter, Mrs. Vigar," he went on, thrilling with youth and strength, "who is good enough to be among the angels; and you have made yourself a devil with strong drink. I smell it in your breath."

"Go on," she snarled, but weakly. "I like to hear you."

"You have driven out your son. You torture your daughter."

"She defies me. She curses me. I hate the creature."

"Because an evil nature loathes a pure one. I am your daughter's friend, her brother. I come to release her. You have locked her in the cellar beneath this room."

"She shall stay there."

"I am going to set her free."

"He breaks all laws and customs. He is fearful. How good it is to be a stranger!" muttered Nicholas.

"Who are you?" gasped the woman.

"I claim the right of entry here in the name of love—God's love, which I have spent my life in seeking."

Judith Vigar stared at the enemy mockingly, then laughed. "A preacher!" she cried. "Afraid to wear a black coat. A preacher in disguise, running after the bodies of young women to save their souls. If you were a man, and not a shivering idiot," she shouted at Vigar, "you would take this lying rascal by the neck and throw him out."

"Strangers are full of guile. He has deceived me. He said he had not come to preach the gospel," Nicholas muttered; then added more cheerfully, as Anger made towards the door, "He is going. Good-evening to you, sir. Please do not call again."

"If he does, I'll set Curgenven after him," said Judith.

Anger did not make for the porch, but in the direction of a narrow flight of steps made of rough granite which was cheaper there than wood. He tramped down quickly, each step making a hollow noise which sounded in the room he had abandoned, and brought Judith out. She followed, but could not pass him, because the way was narrow, and though she caught at his arms the trespasser kept on, and reached a dark door lighted by the last gleam of day struggling through a small window sufficient to show him a key protruding from the lock. This he turned, wondering at the woman's silence, but guessing she was stunned at this outrageous act. The door fell open, and it seemed quite natural to find Petronel standing before him, not as she had done in the hut, a fine picture of red and brown softened by mist and raindrops, but cold in every sense and looking smaller; with defiance also on her frowning face.

"So I have found you," he cried triumphantly.

"What are you doing here?" she asked coldly.

"I have come to take you out of this horrible place," he answered, moving aside when a movement behind suggested Judith was about to push him into the cellar and imprison him as well. "I heard you calling," he added.

"I did not call you. I did not know you were here," she said sullenly.

"You are free now," he said weakly.

"Hear him!" the woman mocked. "You are free. The preacher wants you. . . . He has bought Stiniel. He owns us all. You had best go with him while you have the chance."

"You have no business here at all," said Petronel. "It is no affair of yours what goes on in this house. You forced yourself on me once before, and I suppose you could not help it then; but I won't have you coming into my home and interfering between me and my relations."

"Forcing myself upon you!" exclaimed Anger, then checked himself, hearing a joyful whisper close behind.

"I suppose I may clean out this cellar if I want to," she continued, speaking almost as violently as her mother.

"I cannot go until you leave this awful place," he answered faintly.

"I may please myself. Who are you except a stranger?"

"A friend," he answered.

"I don't want your friendship."

"Throw your love where you throw your rubbish," cried Judith. "How do you feel now, preacher?"

"You mean what you say?" said Anger stupidly. "I may not help you?"

"Now the dog whines," cried Judith.

"You are nothing to me. I had forgotten having met you," the girl answered.

"I will go then," said Anger quietly. "I will not apologise for having done my best, for I believe any other man, even your enemy, would have done the same. Have your key, Mrs. Vigar. The miniature I left upon the table upstairs. Yes, the face has changed. I ask your pardon for my violence. You at least had not seen me before, and had not asked me—but that is no matter. If Miss Vigar is satisfied," he went on bitterly, "if she does not complain of being imprisoned in this cellar, if she declares herself in no need of friendship and declines assistance, then I admit my conduct is inexcusable. I will say good-bye, Mrs. Vigar. I will not trouble you again."

"Thank heaven," murmured Petronel.

"You reject my help?" he cried once more.

"Of course I do."

"I will leave Youlstone. I perceive I am mistaken."

"A preacher right enough. He has all the tricks," said the satisfied woman. "First, second, and last, he's a wrong 'un. There goes the dog, slinking over the stairs. Next time you run after a woman," she howled, "make sure she's got a dirty mind like yours."

Anger reached the head of the stairs, feeling cold and at last frightened. He passed out of the door, the master following. It was almost dark; owls were gliding over Stiniel. A smell of decayed leaves and sour moisture filled the air. The old life had been a success after all; the new one was a failure.

Nicholas still followed, and Anger, when near the gate, turned to him and asked, "Are you my enemy?"

Vigar muttered some incoherent words, while Anger paused, longing for friendly sounds. "A word will call me back," he whispered. "You are afraid of your wife. I am not. She too needs protection."

"Please to leave Youlstone. Better to-night than tomorrow," said Nicholas slowly. "No more talking, sir," he added sternly.

"Are you friendly to me?"

"I hate everybody. I hate this place, and the world, and if I didn't hate death the most I'd kill myself."

Nicholas turned and ran like a hunted man towards the house. It was very silent there. Anger closed the gate and walked easily down the Stiniel Pinch, feeling the free air, not yet recognising that he was bound, and murmuring, "How beautiful with that scorn upon her face!" But he had to pause on the Quoditch Pinch for lack of breath.

CHAPTER VI

A DREAM

RETURNING to his hotel, which was the Youlstone beer-house, as ugly a place as could be found, but possessing some very decent bedrooms, Anger asked for the landlord, discovered he was dismembering a pig and would not be presentable until late in the evening, at which time his presence would be required within the bar. The visitor suggested that somebody with local knowledge should be invited to wait upon him. The landlady believed the bar-room was empty at that moment, which seemed untrue as Anger distinctly heard the sound of voices. Had the landlady ventured to speak plainly, she would have confessed her inability to discover a commoner who would consent to be shut up in a private room with the foreigner, a creature strange in every way, who would talk in a manner hardly intelligible, expect answers to be delivered in his own language, and might ask for information which it was not right that he should have. It was the duty of strangers in Youlstone to ascertain facts by their own shrewdness. Plainly they were not wanted; if they insisted upon coming they were tolerated according to their spending powers; but they were not to take it upon themselves to catechise the lords of the land.

There was, however, one man quite different from his fellows; and it so happened he was engaged in a certain pastime, which added to the ruin of his hedges, when the landlady returned to the bar and mentioned what the gentleman had said. His presence there was hardly a coincidence; it was more like habit.

Anger ascended to his room, noticing how much more light there was at the top of the village than in Stiniel. Sitting at the end of the bed, he looked out upon the saddest prospect. That side of the building made one of the boundaries of the churchyard; apparently a few feet had been stolen by the innkeeper, so that the portion of room occupied by the bed was actually above consecrated ground, and when the guest slept it would be with the dead. The place was in that condition of neglect common in moorland parishes, and not unknown in bustling cities. Headstones had fallen and were left, cracked and moss-grown, names and dates gone out of sight and mind; brambles and nettles grew unchecked; even the furze and fern of the moor were creeping in, and pieces of glass in the windows of the church were broken—and who cared?

"A dying church surrounded by the dead," said Anger, not cynically but sadly, for the thing seemed true. "How can they argue Protestantism is no failure?"

"If you please, schulemaster. Here I be to tell to ye," answered a cheerful voice; and good master Bobby, who had lost his fit of depression as readily as a bird parts with a feather, entered without knocking, seated himself without invitation, and chatted on without encouragement. "You had the better of me this afternoon, but then you took me unawares and you beat me when I warn't prepared. I played fair wi' you, but you took advantage of me. I told you I wur learned, but you didn't tell me soon enough you wur a schulemaster. If I had known I would ha' been more artful.

You told me I wur ignorant. That's a strong argyment, master, and now I'll answer ye. You be ignorant. I don't know as I ha' ever seen a man so ignorant. Now us be quits, but mind out what you ses, vor now I knows ye I'll be ready."

"That is the simplest form of answer. We call it the *tu quoque* argument," said Anger lightly, glad in his heart to see the little man again, and hoping to secure him as a friend.

"I knew how 'twould be," complained Bobby. "You fetches up words of your own and throws 'em at me. It ain't fair dealing. Stick to the dictionary if you please, master. How be I to answer words what ha' no meaning? Might as well listen to the blab-blabbery of a brook."

"You have a word there which has too many b's for me," said Anger. "You have beaten me this time. I cannot answer you, Billacott."

"I come prepared, you see," said the little man of very great conceit. "A sprung trap catches nought. I come here open, so I catched you easy."

"Will you tell me something about Youlstone?" Anger went on.

"Church-town or parish? There's a mighty difference."

"To begin with: who lives in the low thatched house, surrounded by a wall, opposite this inn?"

"Parson lives there. A very worthy gentleman he be, but he ain't got a woman," replied Bobby. "He be a scholar, same as me and you, and he'm a pious Christian holy gentleman. He don't tell to me now. I ha' beat him every time."

"He must find Youlstone a most sequestered place," Anger murmured.

"Now you'm fangling up words again," said Bobby sulkily.

"I am sorry. I should have said Youlstone is very much out of the way."

"It be quiet when the winds don't wrastle," admitted Bobby. "It b'ain't what you calls a racketing place. Volks do get time to breathe in between jobs. There be plenty o' strangers coming though, and they ses Youlstone be getting more like London every year. There wur nigh upon a dozen here last month, and 'em all telled to me and said Youlstone wur a proper place, and they wur sorry they had never come last summer, and they would be sure to come next, God willing, and bring more volks along with 'em; and I had the last word wi' the whole lot."

"These people come and go," said Anger in a low voice. "They stay for a few days and admire the purity of the moorland, but what do they hear and see? They pass the actors in a tragedy and call them simple countryfolk."

"Just what I tells them, schulemaster. 'You volks,' I ses, 'you come up along, and you walks all day, and you casts your eyes abroad, and off you goes wi' the idea you ha' seen everything; and you fancies I be a simple country gentleman till you tells wi' me and finds I ha' got an answer ready to beat the wisest of ye.' I ha' noticed strangers be cruel fond o' laughing, vor when I ha' done with 'em, they goes away wi' faces blown to busting. Tell ye what 'tis, schulemaster, us scholars do get laughed at by the vulish."

Anger agreed, to preserve his friend's good humour, and went on, "There will be other learned men beside ourselves. This Curgenven for instance—who is he?"

"Bide a bit. You'm going along too fast," protested Bobby. "Turn and turn about, master. You had last question. Next be mine. You ha' been to Stiniel?"

"Quite true," said Anger. "Now will you answer my question?"

"Not till you gives me a proper answer. A tedious schulemaster, you be. A question be to get learning, and you ain't given me none."

"I gave all the information you asked for. I have been to Stiniel. Now I suggest that you know about Curgenven?"

"Quite true," said Bobby.

"Now you are tedious, to reply with your own epithet," said Anger, when his answer had been turned against him.

"He b'ain't an epithet. That be words wrote on a tombstone. I ha' beat you again, schulemaster. 'Tis my turn to ask a question. You know the Vigars?"

"I do. And you know Curgenven?"

"I do. Be you related to the Vigars?"

"I am not. Is Curgenven a friend of yours?"

"He be."

"We are not getting on," said Anger, smiling. "You must ask a wider question."

"I ha' got one ready," said the parrot. "Be the Vigars friends of yours?"

"I cannot honestly say yes or no to that. A week ago I was lost in mist and wandered out from Wyld until I came near Youlstone. I happened to meet Miss Vigar. To-day I went to Stiniel to thank her for the kindness she showed me then."

"You'm courting she?" inquired Bobby.

"I had only seen her once before."

"A man don't crave to see a maid unless he'm courting she."

"Now will you tell me what you know about Curgenven?"

"Well, 'tis your turn to ask. Mr. Curgenven be a little gentleman, what you would call a hunchy gentleman. A very kind and gude gentleman, I tell ye. He'm fond of all the volk in Youlstone, and there bain't a man nor woman he ain't helped. Now 'tis my question," said Bobby, who would have blown his head off rather than speak an adverse word against the dwarf. "Who let ye into Stiniel? Did ye see the maiden? Wur she gentle? Did her mazed old mother sing to ye? Us calls it singing."

"A very good euphemism," Anger murmured.

"What wur that word?" said Bobby sharply. "Talk fair, schulemaster, or I'll have to crush ye."

"Mr. Vigar let me in," Anger said quietly. "I saw his daughter. Mrs. Vigar appears to have no control over her temper."

"Night and day she'm singing. Her's a vunny woman, sure enough," said Bobby with less cheerfulness. "Like old Dartmoor wind in December time her be. Volks keep away from Stiniel. They let 'en bide."

"Is she supposed to be insane?"

"Us don't quite know what she be. Some ses mazed; some ses rotten. But if her wur mazed Curgenven would ha' she put away."

"Is he a relation?"

"He'm the friend of Youlstone," said Bobby simply.

"How long has she suffered from these fits of temper?" asked Anger, stating the case mildly.

"Years and years. Between you and me, schulemaster, wi' nought but walls vor company, her won't never be quiet till her be put down under wi' a gurt big lump o' granite laid atop o' she."

"Is it supposed she is cruel?" asked Anger carefully.

"Her drove out the boy; young Bert, a gude lad, but a bit of a coward, I fancy. Her terrifies the old man proper, and her uses the maiden shameful. Me and Thirza, down to Quoditch, hears plenty, but it ain't our business to interfere. Mrs. Vigar would sing a new song if us went up to Stiniel; and Mr. Curgenven wouldn't like it neither. He knows what be right and what be wrong. Us be sorry vor the old man; but the maid can give as gude as she gets. Her be lusty, and they ses her b'ain't much better than her mother."

Anger winced at that, knowing it to be untrue; and yet how fiercely she had glared at him.

"Her goes vor days and nights to a bit of a shed down the cleave. I fancies her ain't always there alone. Mebbe she took you there?"

"I was driven into it by the mist and rain."

"Bided there all night?"

"I was forced to. We sat by the fire——"

"If her would take you in, her would take others. You'm an artful schulemaster, I reckon."

"She is a good girl, wonderfully good, considering what her home is," cried Anger.

"I wouldn't ha' she vor wife," said the little dirty man.

"Do you know the history of Mrs. Vigar's family?" Anger went on, to give his comrade other stuff to think of.

"Her vaither wur a bit of a roaring lad. The like o' she, I fancy. They ses his wife died natural, but us misdoubts it. He wur mazed on liquor, and when he wur drunk he would kick his own shadow; he kicked she sure enough, and beat she cruel; and when her wur dead he gave she a fine funeral, and put up a proper big tomb-stone—if it warn't dark, I'd point it out to ye from this window: 'Wi' Christ, which be far better'; that's what he put on the stone. So it wur, I reckon."

"I have one more thing to ask, Billacott," said Anger, wondering why the use of that name did not bring his friends of London near his mind, "Is there a lawyer near? To-morrow I should like to go to Riversmeet and consult one."

"Why, of course there be one, and he'm the best lawyer in the world," cried Bobby in great astonishment.

"What is his name?"

"Ain't us been telling about him! 'Tis Curgenven. There b'ain't no other. My dear life! Mr. Curgenven wouldn't let no other bide there."

"I will call upon him," said Anger, beginning to understand certain matters more clearly. This solicitor would naturally be interested in all the affairs of Youlstone, and would also be keeper of every conscience. Each family history would be known to him, and if he had a kind soul as well as the heart of a man of the world, he would be anxious to see happiness restored to Stiniel. No doubt he desired to take some action, but could not find the way.

Now that Anger had obtained the information he required, Bobby was given hints to retire, which were useless, and when speech more definite met with the reply that the morrow was a long way off, Anger turned to action, backed out, and left the farmer in possession.

Night had settled upon the insignificant church-town; life seemed present only in the form of bustling wind. Even the occasional blur of lamplight, shivering from some cottage, looked distant, and might have been a nebula in space. The satisfaction of walking there in the mud, surrounded by the loneliness of black hills, was undefinable, yet strong enough to spoil the mind for other places. Anger could not rid himself of the small idea that in Youlstone he was no humble servant of the people, bustling through a crowd unnoticed, but a man of consequence, a schoolmaster indeed.

A labourer and his wife cutting fodder from a rick of hay by lantern-light began to shout. It was nothing but an outbreak of ordinary conversation—high wind being taken for granted—noise without words to the stranger, who drew towards the lane where he could see the light beaming, and heard the knife slashing; himself making no sound, and being well separated from the workers by a high hedge and three yards of smooth darkness.

Definite words escaped, like dim characters breaking through the text of a palimpsest, from the shouting, and Anger guessed this new life of his was under discussion. What motive could he have in meddling with the mysteries of Youlstone? The woman was feminine enough to know that desire for a maiden—and such a one, she shouted, thanking the god of the mountain for providing her with better—provoked the stranger's interference.

It was maddening to stand and listen to English in disorder, catching the subject word, while guessing at verb and adjective; but the male worker became a trifle coherent as he wiped his knife, speaking slowly with a bull-roar, saying, "The man who goes after she will be pixy-led vor certain."

Anger went on, careless of direction, hearing the woman worker's shout against her sex, but unable to translate it. Every tongue in its own way warned him to depart, and to shrink from assisting a life which must spoil his. "She is neither evil nor harmful," he cried, as the descent began; seeing again that fine figure in the hut, queen of the boy without a mind, feeling the warmth of her welcoming presence. How kindly had she made herself hostess, giving her fire and food, more ready than a sister to make him comfortable; and as night went on, how gently she had rested her hand in his, a hand which throbbed and fluttered like a heart. If that day she had looked upon him coldly, and spoken like an enemy, preferring the cellar to the hut, her mother to himself, memory would not receive the record. The first picture prevailed; false colour would not lie upon it.

"What am I doing?" Anger asked himself, when the land seemed cut away before him, and Youlstone was a mile behind. "Running away! Well, let me see where the spirit is driving me."

Steep and stony fields sloped to the valley; to enter the first a stile made for giants had to be climbed; and over this rolled a careless pigmy, his nailed boots slipping on the stones, preceded upon the descent by some object, turnip-like, which fell and bounded as if full of life. Sufficient light came through a rift in the clouds, where a half-moon struggled, to make the brown thing gleam and laugh.

"Stop 'en, master," called the happy boy; then fell and pounced upon his toy.

"What are you doing with a skull?" asked Anger sharply.

"I found 'en," said the boy, hugging his treasure. "They lifted a rock what had been blasted, and I saw a bone, so I loosed the earth and fetched mun out. Vunny old chap, b'ain't he?"

"You must bury it," said Anger.

"Not me. He ha' been buried long enough."

"What will you do with it?"

"I'll knock in his eyeholes," said the imp, spitting upon the skull for luck, then rubbing the spot dry with the flat of his hand. "I'll put a bit o' lighted candle inside, and stick him up on chapel wall. Feel his old grinders, will ye, master?"

"It is useless to preach to a boy," Anger murmured as a dark cloud came up and put the light out.

He might have turned back had not that merry, ghoul-like urchin appeared to stir up his soul and restore religious thoughts. Scenes of the old life swept back, dim pictures without a background, making the solitude hateful for the moment. Anger climbed the stile and ran as if pursued, his face towards the valley lights, and in his ears the whistling of the boy, who ascended towards Youlstone with his toy.

"My church—of the Resurrection," Anger cried. "There goes the acolyte."

The gloom, the great expanse, the overmastering wind of the mountain were made unbearable. Reason called upon Anger to leave what was too strong for the old mind, if only for a night, and to pursue a gentler Nature through the lowlands. The vision of the streets presented itself, with the life which swelled at full tide when the country began to sleep, reaching at midnight a carnival of carelessness as if the Erlking was chanting through the town, shaking the feet of one and all. Return was not impossible, although obstacles were presented: the pathway was lost, great boulders had to be surmounted, hedges climbed, until a trackway of running water was attained, then a brawling river, and upon the other side swamps, thickets of willow and spiteful brambles. Yet it was easy to press on, for it seemed a duty; and that red star hanging upon the side of the moor was a lamp of the former life, marking the railway; a train thundered in the distance. Some shillings' worth of travel might break the spell.

"Mountain, let me go," cried Anger; but only brambles held him, and human force could deal with them.

Quiet moorland spread, and far below the lamps of Riversmeet blinked sleepily. The station high above the town was near; it was open and busy, for although night seemed old upon the moor, it was still evening in the centres. Already people in Youlstone would be ending the day; here townsfolk were beginning to enjoy leisure. As if by some arrangement a train came in from the east, and learning that it was a fast one, Anger entered it with a ticket for Plymouth, and found himself again a normal being, travelling with commonplace people, who were reading papers, or glancing at his disreputable appearance with superior eyes. This journey of impulse, in search of the missing spirit, had some romance in it; for Anger had been taken from the old world early in the spring; it was now strong-smelling autumn; and during the interval every part of him had been altered, so that he seemed born again. The motion of the train was familiar, the sight of a great town could not be new, yet these things, together with his services to religion and the vows he had made, belonged to a previous existence upon the other side of a death which his personality had survived.

To pass from a primitive state of existence, where old custom stood for knowledge and a charm would be muttered to cure toothache, into the heart of modern civilisation required half an hour's motion, and one small piece of money; the two extremes were only separated by a few acres of hills. The three towns facing Cornwall and the sea, famous for docks, but much more remarkable as presenting a dream-like contrast to their tempestuous background, spread from the railway in the form of a gigantic stage of players. In truth, nothing that night seemed real, not even night, for Youlstone had long been dark and slumbering; and here, with thousands of lamps for sunshine, children played in every street as though it had been midday. To Anger it was his London, but not the same, because of the change in himself and his long sojourn among fierce realities, which made all this bustle false. The streets were crowded, although work was over for the day, therefore the crowd must be at play. The broad illumination conquering night, the almost barbaric places of pleasure, the sham of colour, paint, costume, could no longer deceive the man whom wild Nature had so thoroughly restored. These people should have worn masks; they were not living, but trifling with hours meant for sleep. The towns were revelling to a fête, as if the inhabitants had been summoned from their beds to rejoice over a victory; yet the same drama was played every night, the only victory rejoiced over was the conquest of daily work, and the Te Deum of thanks was somewhat blasphemous.

"I lived with this," said Anger, as he tramped the streets, "I thought it was chiefly good, or at least natural. I mistook the canvas for solid timber and the pasteboard for masonry. Here human nature after dark is tinsel."

Judgment in haste earns quashing. Human nature was everywhere triumphant. Deeper into streets of endless struggles went Anger; a drizzling turned dust to mud upon the roads; a closer atmosphere made him gasp. A woman stood bareheaded, calm, but in an agony. A gaslight, placed behind a bottle of green liquid in a chemist's shop, made her face terrible. She stood and swayed; and following the direction of her gaze towards a newsvendor's across the way, Anger saw in that needless horror of green light the latest evening paper rumour; and a ship had been wrecked; and she was a widow who stood there staring. No idle pleasure there, no mask was wanted on that countenance; but surely a fine nature to remain so calm.

Again, a small lad came tottering by laden with a bag of coal too heavy, and, slipping in the mud, he fell, bruising himself, while the sixpenn'orth of costly stuff was scattered. Loafers and other children laughed, but one man, rough-looking and uncouth, hurried to lift the boy, and wiped his clothes with a handkerchief taken from his own neck, and collected the scattered coal for him. Was this done to please an audience the rough fellow never glanced at?

Once more, when Anger reached a turning, two old men were settling themselves, one with harp, the other with violin. They were wandering musicians, and they appeared indifferent to the drizzle as they played a good sound piece of music, disdaining rubbish; and while at work, which was also pleasure, they could be seen smiling at each other, nodding encouragingly, and murmuring, "Take it quicker, Jack" or, "This is the bit we like"; so enthralled by their music as almost to forget the coppers. They were artists, even if they shared one small room and a little food; they were old and very white, yet they would not give up. They did all they could, and remained gentlemen; and the nature in them was worth a young man's study.

The district ahead was more thronged, ill-lighted, and soiled with poverty. Streets of houses, each room hiding a family, spread upon either side of the highway where Anger walked, between public-houses and small shops where business was done in coppers, searching the faces of those who were not ashamed to eat their suppers in the street. It was night at last, but the people of this region did not seem able to rest; they too were players, and at the same time spectators of each other's drama; unable to spend money on places of amusement, they hung about the always open street, finding it in the damp more cheerful than their homes. They drifted to and fro in the half-light like so many ghosts condemned to wander till the cock-crow.

The atmosphere was blood-warm. Walking on, conscious of weariness, Anger found himself beside a church, and he hesitated, perceiving an open door where young men passed in with heads uncovered. The place was dark, almost forbidding, yet an atmosphere of gentleness surrounded it.

"I will go in and rest," he said.

Back in the gloom of the porch the Vicar was standing, his face hardly visible. He put out his hand, saying, "I am so glad to see you," as if he and Anger had been old friends, and gave the stranger a heart-grip of the fingers, drawing him in towards the church as a fisherman might drag his net to land.

Anger moved forward, saying to himself, "He is no clergyman, but a priest"; then started, and smiled dreamily when he saw the red lamp again, the altar of sacrifice, the stations of the Cross, the Crucifix and sacred pictures; and distinguished the religious odour of that morning's incense.

He knelt in his mud-spotted layman's clothes, and tried to look at the altar, but could not see it clearly, for his eyes were misty, and Stiniel was in his mind. He longed for Petronel to be kneeling there, as a sister, by his side, and to see her fine face uplifted towards the eternal picture of Mother and Child, with a tender thought for himself as a brother who had ministered beneath that picture and had preached its miracle.

"When these heretics imitate, they beat us," he murmured, perceiving a book of Common Prayer before him. "They are free to take what is best; we must take all. I have dreamed of a church like this."

It was a late service for men only. A shortened form of Evensong was used, with chants and hymns, followed by a sermon from the Vicar. Anger discovered his thoughts wandering away into that land of dreams he had referred to—thoughts not without religion—and he was again a boy, standing in the chapel of his school. This service was so like that one; this chant was the same; he had heard it often during the days of carelessness, for Anger had been educated as a Protestant although the Church teaching of his school had been advanced. He had not seen that church before, neither had he actually dreamed of it, but he had stood day after day for years within the chapel which that interior recalled.

The music became a spirit of enchantment. It seemed to Anger as if the Vicar had turned towards him, and was watching the sleeper with pitying eyes. He saw the kind face, where strength and tenderness were finely blended. His heart went out towards this stranger who had greeted him like a friend. He longed to feel that grip of the hand again.

Not eloquent, thought Anger. He has a better gift; he speaks with his soul.

Indeed, the Vicar was not preaching to his congregation of young men. Leaning from the pulpit, with clasped hands extended, he spoke like a father simply asking the children to be good.

"Many of you have a sister whom you love. Remember, in all your dealings with young women, they too may be loved sisters of good men."

Still Anger could not restrain those wandering thoughts. As he heard the pleading voice it was an autumn day, years ago, and he was a boy, very small and white and shivering, standing in a long, gloomy corridor, almost dazed by what seemed to him the brutalities of schoolmates.

"Love of a kind is unhappily the cheapest of all things; it should be a thing money cannot buy; it can be bought with the meanest coin. If you degrade love to the level of commerce, you will be paid as you deserve, with degradation. I ask you to aim at the highest, to give and ask for gold, to regard love as a sacrament and great part of your religion. Let your heart be as the lamp always before the altar. Let your desires be as incense offered up to God. You will be tempted by beauty; remember it is base when lacking virtue. You may be fascinated by cleverness; see that the heart is there. You may be led into a woman's life through pity; be very careful the snare of the hair of Lilith is not set. Pay the full price for virtue, give yourself; goodness is cheap if you give all you have; immorality is ruinous at any price. Bear in mind, when you love that you are being dealt with by a passion which is at the same time sublime and horrible, a passion which has made history and broken empires, which has destroyed princes and has ennobled peasants, a passion which has caused destruction with the sword, and has bestowed freedom with the pen, a passion which brought God Himself through death to save us. You will not escape, you would not wish to; but build up your strength that you may escape the horrible and attain to the sublime."

Another boy was approaching the child Anger as he cringed against the wall; a senior, wearing the cap of the football fifteen, a tall, athletic youth, old enough in the eyes of the new boy to be a master. Dispersing the rabble of persecutors, he came to

Anger, and placed a hand upon his shoulder, saying kindly, "Don't be afraid. I went through it when I was your age. You will have your innings later on. I am going into the chapel to play the organ. Would you like to come and blow for me?"

"Oh yes, sir," said Anger eagerly.

"I am not a master. I am captain of football."

They went into the chapel which was so like that church; another big boy joined them with a violin; and the two seniors played sacred music, while the little new boy listened so zealously that he sometimes let the wind out of the organ.

"A splendid fellow," murmured the man in the chair, his mind struggling between past and present. "The strongest boy in the school, and he used his strength to protect the weakest. He would let me prepare my lessons in his study. I cleaned it out. Once I broke some china that he valued. He only smiled and said he knew it was not my fault."

The last hymn was over. The congregation of young men went out with grave faces, but a few stayed behind to speak in private with their spiritual father. Pausing at the door, Anger perceived an old man carrying a bunch of keys, and going to his side he whispered, "What is the Vicar's name?"

"Mr. Lyson, sir."

"And once he asked my name," muttered Anger, as he stood against the dark wall of the church, the rain beating upon his head which was still uncovered, the crowd beyond still passing by; and the doors of the low public-houses were swinging, and steam poured from windows of shops where fish was being fried for midnight suppers.

"We were strangers then, and boys. To-night I asked myself the name of that priest who advised me from the pulpit, and I could not answer, though I recognised his face dimly—and we are strangers still."

He hesitated, then turned away from the district which that church lighted to find a lodging for the night; but the spirit of enchantment was over him, very different from the spirit of Youlstone, much more gentle and religious; and if Petronel was a sister then she wore the monastic working dress. The Vicar had stood in the porch and given him the hand of welcome; and the recreant priest had once broken the china belonging to the faithful priest; and if he broke his own life, he knew strong old Lyson would smile and say, "I know it was not your fault."

CHAPTER VII

A DEN

RIVERSMEET town, lying in a hollow upon the edge of the moor, was among the sleeping places. It woke up on market-day, and rubbed its eyes for the rest of the week. Except upon the Friday so little business was done that the shopkeepers might as well have been playing bowls. Some sat in their offices, wasting stamps on sending out accounts to those who would not pay; money was always scarce in that district, but a summons for debt was not to be thought of, since any legal action would have made merchants unpopular and might have deprived them of what trade they possessed. Others yawned behind their counters, or mused upon the policy of the government in power; too many of them were argumentative politicians, and this also was bad for trade. Wealthy folk of the neighbourhood could not patiently give an order to the tradesman who spent much of his time declaiming upon their vices in the market-place. Besides, they were weary of receiving the answer, "We have not the article you require, but can get it for you"; especially when the getting might require a lunar month or even a luni-solar year. These shopkeepers were really agents who accepted orders for manufacturers; their stock lay in dust to become soiled and out of date. Commercially eager, and sometimes enterprising, they lacked intelligence; the housewife who ordered marmalade was not to be astonished if she received plum jam, as being equally suitable if a trifle more expensive; and was it not upon record that Alderman Toprail, who it was believed aspired to Parliamentary honours, had, upon receiving an order for garden lights, packed up and sent off a parcel of Chinese lanterns?

The exception was there, of course, between the rivers; however one might enter the town, a torrent had to be crossed, bearing down old pots, boots, and frying-pans towards the sea. Little James Woodland was a man of substance, a twenty-thousand pound man if it was possible for report to come near the truth; one who boasted neither of his religion nor of his politics, who had nothing to do with any council chamber, and was not seen at public meetings. This man with broad forehead and conspicuous stomach was unlike his fellow-tradesmen; he talked little and read much; he had studied business and regarded it as a science; and thus it came to pass that he owned, not a shop, but the Stores of Riversmeet.

When a stranger came for some trifle Woodland often declined payment, saying, "I make you a present of that, if you will be kind enough to accept it." The stranger remembered that. When a housewife from the country sent an order for groceries, he would enclose a shillingsworth of stamps, with a remark that all letters received his personal attention. The housewife remembered that. All market-day the stores were crowded. Every farmer, dissatisfied with the dilatory methods of the other tradesmen, which were perhaps too much like his own, came at last to the one house of business where he was sure to receive satisfaction and good value.

It was afternoon upon one of the sleep days, and the store-keeper rambled in a region upstairs, overhauling a quantity of china with the idea of selling the lot at a sacrifice which would yet yield a fair profit; when one of his sons mounted the ladder, calling, "Young man from Curgenven."

"I know all about it," said Woodland. "He is sent to remind me. Say I will be round at the office in quarter of an hour."

He went to a small window, dusted the cobwebs from it, looked at his watch, being the only man in Riversmeet to whom quarter of an hour meant fifteen minutes, then rubbed his forehead as if to dust the cobwebs from that, and began to address the stacks of china in a deliberate fashion:

"I am a man of scruples, and I am going to meet a man who has none. I believe in honesty; I don't say it pays in every profession, but it does in mine. In my business the secret of success is to be well spoken of. Cheat one man, and the whole country speaks badly of you; down go the receipts. Let your customer think he has cheated you, and back he comes to do it again; up go the receipts. This idea of Curgenven's sounds well enough, but there is dishonesty in it because it comes from him. Poor old Doctor Palk don't see that; he's a good simple fellow; he reckons Curgenven would split on the rocks rather than deceive him. It is a case of rabbit and weasel there."

He drew out a very dirty tin box, which had once contained tobacco, tapped and opened it, took out a quantity of snuff, which he piled in a pyramid upon the back of his hand, then supped it up greedily, cleaned his face, and went on, "This is the position: Curgenven is the landowner, and he intends to contribute brains. I don't think much of 'em. He is cunning with his tongue, but he gives his own reading to the law, and he comes of a low stock; still, he is popular, and at present it looks as if he might die respected by everybody—except one. Palk is the medical man who is to prepare the advertisements. I am to be financier. I know little about law, and nothing about medical science, but I do know how to spend money; and Curgenven knows something about getting it. May it not be something like this?" he whispered, addressing a group of dust-filled champagne-glasses. "May this plan be nothing but a trick to screw an odd thousand out of me? I will carry that thought along with me," he went on, moving briskly towards the head of the ladder. "My boys and I play chess of an evening, and 'tis a mighty good game for a man of business. Curgenven will tell me I'm king of the game, but he won't add the king is only there to be checkmated. I know a move worth more than all his gambits." He passed down to the ironmongery department, and went out at a side door, saying, as he passed, to his eldest son, "If I'm not back in an hour, come for me at Curgenven's and say I'm wanted."

He crossed the road, hurried along a crooked lane, called, somewhat in the grand style, River Street, plunged through an ancient gateway which strangers loved to sketch, crossed a court of foot-racking cobbles, and entered a long building which might have been a prison, for coldness was stamped upon it and fierce iron bars protected every window. It was built upon an outcrop of shining rock jutting over one of the rivers; safe short of an earthquake, if rather terrifying to behold from the opposite bank. Within, the idea of a prison departed and was replaced by the suggestion of wine-vaults; the walls were of whitewashed stone festooned high up with cobwebs, while offices of clerks were veritable shades. No shred of carpet lay upon the floors of stone. A door of green baize supplied one touch of comfort, mouldy though it was. This was drawn back to admit the tradesman, with the sullen grating of a rusty spring; a heavy door one yard behind was also opened; both were closed behind him, one with a clang, the other with a snap; and Woodland heard the rushing of the river beneath and saw the tame face of Dr. Jonathan Palk heavy with its long black beard.

"Good day to you, gentlemen," said the tradesman pleasantly, seeing only one man but knowing the other was there.

Directly he spoke laughter proceeded from the opposite side of a table piled with documents and dockets. It increased in depth and volume, like wind from the moor or a sudden flood of waters. Palk nodded in a simple fashion, while Woodland braced himself; that laughter had something to do with business and he misliked it.

Very gloomy seemed the office to a man who worked in the light. The day benefited that interior with a few dusty gleams which, after struggling through the dirty window, had scarcely strength to reach the opposite wall, stained with green patches of moisture and crumbling fast. The noise went on. A giant might have caused it, yet when Woodland stepped round the table, his feet rustling through dry parchment deeds carelessly thrown there, he saw no great figure, but only a head very little higher than the blotting-pad, rolling in mirth upon two shoulders which looked like mounds of earth. An extraordinary face, though. Every feature hard and sharp; almost a handsome head, but grown in sport from an elfin body.

"Sit ye down, Woodland man," gasped Curgenven at length, pushing at the tradesman with a hairy hand. " 'Tisn't the bottle;

that stays in the cupboard till the shutters are drawn. A pretty bit of business always tickles me. Right in the middle of old Riversmeet, we three assemble, good fellows, dear old sportsmen, three of the best, pledged to work out a scheme which will alter the neighbour-hood, wake up the town, and make us fat. Anybody would laugh at that except bedside Jonathan. Capitalist, doctor, lawyer; a beau-tiful combination, as pretty a group as ever was photographed, a threefold cord which all the folk of Youlstone will never break when it comes to the tug of war. We shall pull the lot over if we hang together. Sportsman Woodland can advertise his business; Palk and self ain't allowed to hang out the sign, 'Law and Physic cheap to-day.' But we are poor souls if we can't do a little climbing on the back-stairs."

"This is our first meeting, and, as far as I am concerned, it cannot be a long one. I should like you to put the scheme clearly before the doctor and myself," said Woodland briskly.

"Youlstone Limited. Dear little Youlstone, may it prosper!" cried Curgenven, glancing at the two solemn faces, and digging a letter-opener into the soft wood of the table. "You know the village pretty well, my dear," he said to Woodland.

"It is a favourite Sunday afternoon walk of mine."

"What think ye of it? I seek the opinion of an artistic mind."

"It is without much doubt the most beautiful place upon Dartmoor."

"The country shall think so. Now, Palk, my Jo, let's hear the medical verdict."

The man with the heavy beard looked up and answered, "I believe I put the idea into your head."

"You did; it was capitally well put. You mentioned that it was rather an extraordinary fact that a village standing over a thousand feet should be so well sheltered from fierce storms."

"I also mentioned another fact, which is of far more impor-tance," said the doctor. "It is a place where sufferers from asthma, or any nervous complaint, do most remarkably well. I have made experiments in a very small way by sending a few cases at my own expense into lodgings there, and the results have been astonishing. They were stubborn cases, and in each instance a cure was effected."

"Gorgeous!" murmured Curgenven, glancing at Woodland.

"I do not know what causes it," Palk went on. "In other places, not far distant, results have been quite different. Apparently the piece of moor occupied by Youlstone village is exceptionally healthy."

"That fact is sufficient," said Woodland.

"A poor place," added Curgenven. "I will quote you Shakespeare: 'Barren, barren, barren; beggars all, beggars all; marry, good air.' Youlstone is a place of great natural beauty; it is unique in its ability to cure sufferers from certain types of disease which Palk may more fully specify. Now for my point, and I know Youlstone better than any man. It has not yet been discovered."

"It would be more correct to say it has not become popular. People do go there every summer," said the doctor.

"A mere dozen, who paddle in the streams and look for white heather. It is unknown as a health resort."

"Its secret is sure to be discovered by others."

"You are the only doctor who has set foot in the village during the last twenty years. We can afford to move by jogs. My point is Youlstone remains in the dark. How many Riversmeet folk ever climb to that hollow among the mountains? The place is cut off from the world. Even the political agent has not found his way there."

"Briefly, Mr. Curgenven, your plan is to convert the village of Youlstone into the town of Youlstone?" suggested James Woodland.

"A garden city; that idea seems popular. The garden is there. We have only to pull down the cottages, cut up the fields into sites, build a couple of hundred villas, make a few roads; the rest is advertising."

"Your 'only' will require some thousands," said the tradesman. "It is a highly speculative venture. I don't like bricks and mortar, gentlemen; I never did."

"I think it is safe. If we build the houses we shall get the people," was the doctor's comment.

"And the right sort," Curgenven added. "None of your bag-carrying thirty-shillings end-of-the-weekers, but elderly folk, solid folk; old ladies of fortune, retired military men, wheezing bishops, and broken-winded merchants; folk who have lived too fast for their nerves. A cure or two will bring a hundred applications for houses, and our town will grow and prosper automatically."

"We have heard the points in favour of the scheme," said Woodland. "Now let us have the other side. In the first place; we are setting up a rival to Riversmeet."

"This ancient borough must work out its own salvation. We shall benefit personally," said the lawyer, beginning to fidget.

"So will the town," declared the optimistic Palk. "Its chief industry at present is the letting of lodgings to summer visitors. These would increase. Youlstone is sure to become an expensive place owing to its position and the class of people who will be attracted to it. Those who could not afford Youlstone prices would go on farther than Riversmeet——"

"Well done, doctor!" cried Curgenven.

"Owing to its position," repeated Woodland. "That is my second point. I believe it is impossible for a place to flourish when it is difficult to get at, and it is very certain no railway can ever touch Youlstone. The roads to the village are mere trackways, full of loose stones, and running with water half the year. We propose to cater for people who will be more or less invalids. What will they say when we tell them the worst part of their journey begins when they leave the train?"

"Roads can be made," said the lawyer.

"With money; and every autumn they will be torn into gutters by the rains."

"The remedy rhymes with your difficulty—drains."

"More expense."

"I am for leaving the roads as they are," said Palk. "Invalids will put up with an uncomfortable journey when they feel sure of benefiting at the end of it."

"Very well," said the tradesman. "Let us suppose we are sure of patronage. The next question is how are we to acquire the land?"

"Leave that to me," said Curgenven, brightening up. "If you will furnish the capital for building, I will provide the land. The people would never sell to strangers, but they will to me; and they will sell cheap. Give me six months and I will show you deeds for every acre of Youlstone village, including the property of the church; that pretty piece of moorland which slopes towards the edge of the cleaves west of Stiniel. The Vicar is anxious to sell; it brings in nothing but a pound or two; and permission could easily be obtained."

"Should we not be depriving the commoners of their homes and fields?" said Woodland deliberately, turning to face the wriggling little figure; while simple Palk shifted in his chair and murmured he had never thought of that.

"We should leave a certain number of cottages—I have kept this matter before my mind, doctor. We must see that the present inhabitants of Youlstone benefit as well as ourselves. They will lose their land certainly, but it is of very little use to them. They will be far better off as servants of their betters. I could give you the names of several moorland villages, not one of them comparable to Youlstone, which have become during recent years popular resorts of holiday-makers. Twenty years ago the inhabitants of these places were beggarly; now they are in flourishing circumstances. The man who works to-day in Youlstone for himself snatches a bare living. Twenty years hence, if our scheme prospers, he will have made his fortune. We are not here to harm our fellow-creatures and to break up homes. It is our hope that the entire neighbourhood will benefit by our enterprise."

"But we come first?" suggested Woodland.

"We reap. The gleaners follow," laughed Curgenven.

"Youlstone people are a strange lot. I cannot force myself to like them; neither could I injure them," remarked the doctor.

"Woodland fancies I am in too great a hurry," Curgenven went on. "Because I have set the whole picture before him, frame and all, he thinks the venture is beyond us. As a matter of fact I propose to move very cautiously. There is only one thing which must be done thoroughly and at once—make sure of the land. We are not indeed compelled to do anything more, except advertise the place. With its reputation made we could easily dispose of the land in parcels at a profit of several hundred per cent. Still, it would be a good thing if we could lay out an acre or two—that pretty little corner of Quoditch would do nicely—and put up half a dozen villas; nothing leads to building like building. Perhaps an artistic hotel with thatched roof would be better. There is no really satisfactory accommodation at present. Stable our patients well, and immediately they find themselves recovering they will want to buy an acre and build for themselves. Their medical attendant would be able to advise them. Building is very cheap, as the only expenses worth mentioning are labour and timber. Stone is to be had for the taking, sand for mortar is everywhere. With a capital of five thousand we could make a big show. Shall we go into it boldly, my dears, and make the capital ten thousand? What do you say, old sportsmen? 'Youlstone Limited. Capital ten thousand. Only shareholders Woodland, Palk, and Curgenven.'"

"I am good for one thousand. If I had more I would give it," said Palk, his simple face aglow. The doctor's practice was extensive in regard to ground covered, but if calls were frequent pounds were few, so that the sum he offered represented the savings of twenty years; but then this bachelor had hobbies as expensive as wife and children. Palk was fond of his profession; he desired to obtain a competence, ease, nights to himself, and days in a laboratory playing wizard tricks with rays and drugs. His vision was narrow, his mind a poor thing outside its own groove. A pedlar would not have deceived him into paying the price of gold for a brass ring, because he was skilled in chemistry; but a dealer could very easily have sold him a wretched picture as a costly work of art.

"By an effort—and some curtailment of my charities—I could manage two thousand," said the lawyer, seizing the edge of the table and dragging his mountainous shoulders clear of it. "Now for the rich man. What is his contribution? Which of the figures will he throw? A seven, Jimmy Woodland, man. Make a seven."

The tradesman's eyes were fixed upon the table littered and heaped with deeds and papers. For some minutes a sheet, torn roughly from some schoolchild's copy-book, had been troubling him; for he could not refrain from reading what was written there by the same schoolchild's hand:

"Mr. Curgenven. Dear sir. Grandfather did not know about the interest. When you gave him money you said it was to help him and when he signed the paper he thought it was a reseat. Please sir, Grandfather knows you are very kind and he's getting money for some ponies and his roomatism isn't better yet and he will come with the money after the fair. The Ponies are good ones sir and Grandfather wouldnt cheat you. Please sir if there are mistakes in this please excuse them for Grandfather cant write himself."

Letters of this sort get dropped about by some elemental good-fellow as a warning to others. Possibly a puff of wind had carried it Woodland's side of the table and turned it upward; a shabby blot of an appeal, stained with the domestic life of a poor man's dwelling; evidently a nailed boot had trodden on the paper. Upon it was scrawled in pencil, "Half an acre, stream through, decent site, cottage would make stable."

The tradesman remembered how hard he had worked, how impossible it seemed to get a living out of the little china shop his father had bequeathed to him; what a struggle it had been to give his lads education, food, and clothing; and now he was a wealthy man, while others were selling ponies to pay an unjust debt; and the tempter looked towards him, offering to double his capital, while plain Jonathan Palk, entirely selfish, stared with the same expectancy; and that scrap of paper made the answer simple.

"Nothing, gentlemen," said the little man firmly, folding his hands upon his prosperous stomach. "Not a penny. 'What I have I hold' is the motto of men about here. I am ready to enter into any scheme which is practical and cannot cause injury to others."

"I have demonstrated to you——" began Curgenven; but the tradesman smiled at him deferentially and went on:

"This idea of turning Youlstone into a popular health resort is too much in its own good air. I do not gamble, gentlemen. I have found in my business a small profit upon a large number of articles pays very much better than a big profit upon a few. In the same way a safe two per cent upon capital pays in the long run better than an uncertain five. I sleep well, Mr. Curgenven. It is not every business man who can say that."

"This is no gamble," muttered the lawyer; while Palk added, "I am ready to stake all I have upon it."

"Your professions bring you into touch with a great deal of poverty and misery, none of which is ever brought before me. I don't speak offensively, gentlemen, but perhaps your feelings get sometimes a trifle dull," Woodland went on. "I am not satisfied that we could carry through this affair without inflicting a grave injury upon the people of Youlstone. Everybody knows how attached Dartmoor folk are to their cottages and fields. Even if they live in a ruin and cultivate a plat which is chiefly rocks and furze-roots. The cottage is home, and the plat has belonged to their ancestors. I am sorry, gentlemen, but I'm not in it. Good afternoon;" and he took up his hat and hurried out.

Under the prison-like archway, evidently waiting for the lawyer to be disengaged, stood Anger, smelling no longer of incense, but of earth. Hearing the approach of Woodland, he started round and asked, "Are you Mr. Curgenven?"

"He is in his office," replied the tradesman, smiling a little, and adding, "I am not much like him."

"Pardon me," said Anger, attracted by the good forehead and open face of the man before him; "you live in the town?"

"I am the proprietor of the Riversmeet Stores."

"I am a stranger. Will you permit me to ask you a question?"

Woodland bowed, anxious to hide his face which looked astounded. The stranger gave him the impression of a man in perfect health, but very weary, and in some mental trouble; possibly he was temporarily embarrassed. If so, he could not do worse than go near Curgenven.

"Will you please to come to my house?" he said.

"That is not necessary. I do not wish to trouble you. We can talk very well in this court."

"I will ask you to step into the street," insisted Woodland, not wishing to be seen by Curgenven. "You will find it as private there as here. Riversmeet is very quiet to-day," he added apologetically.

"I wish to ask your advice upon a matter of importance to myself," said Anger, prevaricating without much skill. "I do not wish you to praise, and I cannot expect you to abuse, a fellow-townsman, but I should be obliged if you would tell me plainly whether my business is likely to be safe in the hands of Mr. Curgenven?"

"May I ask if you are staying any time in the town?" asked Woodland.

"I am lodging at Youlstone."

"Not for your health, sir?"

"For no other purpose," declared Anger.

"Were you recommended to the village, may I ask?"

"I came to it by chance."

"I should think, sir, the place has done you good. You look very well and strong," said Woodland, beginning to wonder whether it would be possible to outwit Curgenven. If the stranger beside him had come to Youlstone a sick man, Palk was unquestionably right; he had not spoken words which the lawyer had dictated; there must be healing air in Youlstone, and somebody was sure to reap the benefit of its discovery. Towns and villages upon the fringe of Dartmoor were already playgrounds for holiday-makers, the great upland was becoming well-known, and inaccessible Youlstone could not remain hidden in its rock-basin for ever. If the primitive village was to be exploited, an honest man would harm its inhabitants less than a careless knave.

"I have been very ill. I am staying in this neighbourhood to make my cure complete," said Anger.

"You are not thinking of settling, sir; up over, I mean?" asked Woodland, glancing towards the tors in their cap of cloud.

"I have made no plans. Please answer my question," said Anger impatiently.

Then Woodland was convinced his first impression was no wrong one. This stranger, who had become a moorman by some process of transfusion, was troubled in mind, and the secret of Youlstone was the cause of it. "Mr. Curgenven will do his best for any client," he said deliberately.

"He is honest?"

"Nobody would say he is not."

"He would not take advantage of a man in difficulties?"

"Well, sir, this is a poor place, and his office expenses must be heavy."

"You mean—in any question of money——"

"A country solicitor has many temptations," Woodland went on when Anger hesitated. "If you study the newspapers, you must have noticed some do fail in their trust. Some cannot resist when a poor man's acres lie in their power. But Mr. Curgenven is popular, he has an excellent reputation, he subscribes impartially to charities. He is especially clever, I understand, in settling difficulties out of court."

"Thank you," said Anger shortly, and he went back, while Woodland walked towards his place of business thinking.

"What an office! There is actually moss upon that wall," Anger muttered when he had been ushered through the doors and left alone, as he supposed, seeing no sign of any living creature.

"This is too bad, my dear sir, much too bad," cried a deep and croaking voice, which made the visitor shiver with surprise and nervousness. "Come round the table, will ye? I am a little fellow and big books hide me. Still, I am not the only man whose personality has been hidden by his books. How are you? Very well, I hope. I am so very glad to see you. Excuse me if I don't rise. Once in this chair I revolve and remain. My feet do not reach the floor."

"I apologise," faltered Anger, his mind drawn towards the dark wood, when his eyes fell upon that human lump with its marvellously vital head and hairy hands, thinking of the witch who might have given birth to such deformities. "I saw nobody, so I spoke my thoughts."

"These walls are perfectly harmless; I admire the green stains— that one, you may observe, is a streak of copper—and the moss, I hope, will increase and make a wall-paper. We have a river below, and a river at the side, and most days of the year a river of rain above; but the moisture of Dartmoor does no harm to any man. Have you walked in from Youlstone?"

"You know me then?"

"Our visitors arrive with the strawberries, and go with the plums; when they come with the blackberries we take notice of them. You are Mr. Anger. I am glad you have entered my den, for I was intending this very day to visit you. I am interested in Youlstone; so is my friend, Doctor Palk. There is a rumour that Youlstone air works miracles. The doctor and I collect evidence on that point; he will be anxious to hear of your experience. You are not seated. There is no moss upon that chair."

"I have only spent a few hours in Youlstone; yet you know my name."

"This office is a hive, you see, where the little bees of rumour bring their honey."

"Now I am just from Plymouth, where I spent the night," Anger went on.

"Without much sleep, I fear."

"Its atmosphere seemed to stifle after the moorland."

"Too much like London, where your home is."

"What more do you know?" asked Anger, shrinking from this monstrous child's body and giant's head.

"A suspicion of cockney dialect clings to you telling me you have listened for years to the speech of the poorer classes. There is a vast difference between your churchtown and Youlstone. You discovered it in a mist."

"Next you will be reminding me how I drank the waters of the Nymph," said Anger heedlessly.

"Eh!" cried the lawyer sharply. "Now you are teaching me—a son of the moor."

"A tradition, a myth," Anger murmured. "There is no reason why I should not tell you"; and he went on to mention the story of the Abbot's Pool, and how he had come to it, and, having drunk, had passed on to the cleave of the wet wood and the brown girl's shelter.

"This is of great interest, Mr. Anger; possibly of some value," said Curgenven. "The one thing wanting," he murmured deeply. "Our health resort becomes a Spa. We must tell this to Doctor Palk; he will analyse the water. There is no sleep in all the rivers of Dartmoor; they are full of life and motion. A cloud of superstition surrounds folklore. Some call it the poetry of rural life; we call it humbug. This water is full of iron no doubt. Palk will find out. And after drinking the water you groped through the mist until you came to the very cave of the Nymph herself."

Here the laughter began to rise and fall, while the cold eyes glittered.

"There you received a hearty welcome. Pardon me, Mr. Anger, pardon me. Water may leak through the walls, but words never leak out. We lawyers, we clergymen, we are all men of the world at night time."

"Do you make suggestions against Miss Vigar?" said Anger smartly; and Curgenven, changing at once, shrivelling into his chair, put out a hand and said gently, "I speak from knowledge. Will you come a little nearer? Some words are better whispered. Now, Mr. Anger, you come to visit me after a few hours spent in Youlstone, and you are going to ask me questions about the Vigar family. Are they quite respectable? Are Mr. and Mrs. Vigar the sort of people I should not be ashamed to own as my wife's parents? We are all human where women are concerned. I am glad you have come to me, but you will understand that to a certain extent my lips are sealed."

Anger tried not to forget how everybody spoke well of this man. He appeared earnest, even sympathetic, yet his finger-nails were scratching at the table, and his feet were straining at the chair-supports. Deep in his eyes glowed passion, hunger, and perhaps some pain to know himself as others saw him; it was illusion perhaps, but those fingers went on scratching.

"You are mistaken," said Anger, wondering what made his own voice sound so passionate. "It is true I desired to speak to you about Miss Vigar. That night in her hut she made me unhappy by telling me the story of her life. Yesterday I went to Stiniel. I will not relate what happened there, but when I came away I resolved to seek a lawyer and to ask him whether the law permits a mother to abuse her daughter. I was recommended to you."

"You will have been told I am frequently at Stiniel, keeping the peace?" the lawyer suggested, speaking as softly as any woman.

"I had only time to make a few inquiries."

"You wish to interfere?"

"In the name of ordinary humanity."

"To free the daughter? To get the mother sent to an asylum?"

"That is my idea."

"Remember, Mr. Anger, you are a stranger still, and you know little. Knowing everything, I have not interfered. You will argue either I am a brute, or I am in the right. . . . I must also tell you that the Vigars are my clients."

"Can you see the girl tortured day by day?" said Anger bitterly.

"She is not tortured."

"I had the story from her lips. I saw her imprisoned in the coal-cellar. I experienced her mother's violence."

"You are the victim of a false impression. It is true Mrs. Vigar has a temper; but it has been made—devilish if you like—by her daughter's conduct. The girl's a liar, Mr. Anger. If she were nothing worse I would leave you one illusion. Recall to your memory any form of vice you may have shuddered at during your life in the lowest streets, add that to Petronel, and you will still be using her with charity. You think the mother is behaving cruelly to the daughter. The mother is protecting herself against the daughter. I must say no more," Curgenven muttered, wiping some perspiration from his forehead. "I cannot divulge family secrets. You come to me for advice and I give it. Have nothing to do with this young woman."

"If I have been deceived, I was blind and deaf that night," said Anger hoarsely.

"No more of this," cried Curgenven.

"I promised to save her."

"From herself?"

"No, from her mother. I have looked into Petronel's eyes, I have held her hand."

The lawyer turned aside, feeling the heat of the young man's soul. A movement convulsed his great shoulders as if some creature had been burrowing through them; and presently Anger heard a strong, deep voice:

"Keep your faith. I will say one thing more. There was a son called Bertram whom this girl hated. He is supposed to have run away, but the summer after his disappearance a will-o'-the-wisp was seen night after night playing over a bog which lies at the top of the wood opposite the hut you know of. Do you smell anything?"

"No," cried Anger.

"Then I will say one thing more. When next you visit the hut, search among the brambles which grow between the wall and the face of the cliff. Force them aside, cut them down if you like; and if Petronel should be with you, draw her attention to anything you may discover; ask her to explain, then look into her eyes again. There is time to make the search before dark if you feel in the mind for it. I see you are in a hurry to go. I will visit you soon—if you stay on at Youlstone. Mind the spring of the baize door. It catches one's fingers sometimes, and it pinches like the devil."

CHAPTER VIII

BROTHER AND SISTER

DAYS of weltering hours followed, when books became necessary, and of these Anger had too few. The muddy season was near, and an autumnal pageant of the weather ushered it in: a Sunday of clouds rolling along the ground, a Monday of wind too strong to be faced, a Tuesday of ceaseless rain, a Wednesday of snow-showers, a Thursday of flesh-flaying sleet, a Friday which was a blend of all the seasons, followed by a Saturday which was April out of date.

While the atmosphere played its drama, Anger hid behind the scenes, penned in his room overlooking the churchyard, studying old thoughts with a new mind. Sometimes he ventured out, soon to be driven back soaked to the skin; and then he would change his clothes and look down the village street from the room where his meals were served, glad to use his eyes whenever a cart appeared or a living creature passed. Very little work was done that week. A few loads of granite came sliding down the trackway, accompanied by men in oilskins, like slippery seals. The only voices came from the bar-room after dark.

Night indeed was the pleasantest time. The days were charged with sluggish thought for company, while in the drama of the outer atmosphere three figures stood out clearly, those old figures which have always made romance since they were evolved from allegories of earth, night, and magic, and made to suit three human types: the witch, her son, and the princess. One character was lacking until Saturday; the sun which thawed the bonds of the earth princess, finally delivering her from the black witch, night, and her cruel son, magic; and the usual type of the sun was a young David, a shepherd who was king's son in disguise; and his victory was won, not by strength, but through superior cunning, just as the sun drove out the night by casting faint beams of light, increasing them cunningly when the enemy began to move away in fear, then stretching the bow and taking the golden arrows from his quiver.

Having cast himself to play the part of sun, Anger could not feel more than a godlike loneliness. He would not believe Petronel was anything but good and virtuous, although no man had a kindly word to throw at her. He felt sure the crookedness of Curgenven reached to his soul, although every man spoke well of him. The idea that Judith Vigar was possessed by an evil spirit remained. What he would not recognise was the spirit of new life which possessed himself. How was it he desired to lose his old friends and become attached to new ones? Why was he doing his best to hide and forget the part which had been assigned to him? Why had he no longer the active wish to resume the priestly office? Such questions were ignored, for they were called in a voice too small to reach his consciousness. During the earlier part of his illness he had prayed for health in order that he might return to be a servant of the poor, and secretly he had renewed his vows. But the restoration had seemed a birth into another world; his spirit had passed through space, not so much from London to Dartmoor as from earth to another planet, and the old body had been left behind. The past was dead because it was the past of another existence, and he was free to make a new start, reincarnated. He had wandered through mist, like a spirit lost in space, had baptized his new body in the waters of the Nymph, had come out upon Youlstone where the new state awaited him—so much was clear; and all of the former life yet clinging to him suggested he had been brought there to perform a duty, still to exercise the priestly functions of a former life and to save from sin and suffering a mother and her daughter. He made no vow, but stood resolved to remain in Youlstone until that duty was accomplished.

With the fine day he hurried down the cleave towards Hut Dangerous. The river was roaring in a flood, while the wood was red and dying. It was perfectly true that the space between wall and cliff was rough with brambles which grew, supported by a thorn-bush, ten feet high, but only hands in gauntlets could have parted them. Anger trampled the outskirts of the defences but could make no entry; he knelt and tried to look behind, but failed. He hacked with a knife, but soon retired with bleeding hands, and muttering, "It was a trick to frighten me. He would not tell me what is hidden here because he could not. Still, I will borrow a hook and some gloves and clear these brambles to confound him."

A quaint, bird-like sound disturbed him; and turning, he saw, beside the entrance to the hut, close to a furze-bush which looked black, the ghastly white face of the imbecile. When their eyes met the poor creature trembled, and pushing a finger into his mouth, sucked at it, shifting from one foot to the other with a kind of rocking motion.

"Whippety!" called Anger gently.

The boy went on sucking his finger, deaf and dumb.

"Do not be afraid. I will not hurt you. Have you seen Miss Vigar?"

"Pretty!" murmured the boy.

"Yes, the pretty lady; your good and beautiful lady," said Anger, finding it pleasant to utter the words of admiration. "Has she told you when she will come to the hut again?"

"Pretty house!" murmured Whippety, removing his finger, and pointing at the mossy walls.

"The pretty lady!" repeated Anger. "Tell me if you have seen her. You love her, Whippety, because she is good to you. I am her friend; I love her too. I am going to look after her, and take care of her."

He stopped abruptly, almost frightened at his voice, no longer chivalrous, but lover-like, which mingled his confession with the river's roar below; but the imbecile, who took no part in the common life of his species, yet could love, gazed about as if Anger had not been there, listening for the only voice which reached his soul.

Anger approached and Whippety retreated, always looking away from the visible man and keeping his eyes fixed upon vacancy where he appeared to see another being whom he feared, and muttering words which sounded like, "Stick! Gurt stick!"

"Who beat you?" said Anger, then added to himself, "It is hopeless. He seems to be afraid of some creature at my side."

The sun in its course cast upon the ground the shadow of a point of rock projecting some twenty feet above. The rock itself seemed shapeless; so was the shadow, yet while Anger looked, and understood this was the portent Whippety found frightful, the blot of black suggested a limbless trunk, a mighty pair of shoulders with a strong head midway. The artist sun behind the rock played with human fancy, as in cloudland, painting studies in chiaroscuro, blending the art of caricature with a knowledge of life and form upon a planet controlled by its influence, if not visible from its fires.

"That shadow is very like Curgenven," exclaimed Anger.

As he spoke the boy howled, plunged through the alders, dashed into the river, and went from rock to rock across, to vanish in the autumn of the wood. Anger heard the breaking of dry sticks with other trampling noises, then turned and trod upon that shadow, following the boy's flight mentally with simple reasoning: Curgenven was an enemy of his species, of the moorland which he would have civilised, of the sun which mocked him by a caricature, and of the wild boy. Whippety, more of an animal than human being, had by his actions proclaimed a truth which the owner of Quoditch had not sense, nor the proprietor of Riversmeet Stores the courage, to admit.

"I am advised by the sun and warned by shadow; but it is the imbecile who has answered my question," said Anger; and after a pause added, "I seem to be asleep, and the whole of this moorland and all the figures which inhabit it are visions round me."

He made a few steps and came before a well-shaped furze-bush which was in bloom, not only with its own gold but with roses, while pieces of bread and meat were secured to many a prickle, and here and there a scrap of ribbon fluttered. Here was more enchantment of the nook-shotten garden, although Anger soon perceived the roses were made of paper, while he could guess the food was placed there for the birds. Impatient tits were fluttering on each side. No wild boy of the wood had twisted those paper roses on the thorns of furze. Petronel was the lover of the birds; these were her false flowers and foolish ribbons. Here before him was a proof of kindness, the sign of a good heart. Here was the truth. All evidence on the other side was perjured.

He passed into the hut, seeing it for the first time in sunshine. A fire of wood smouldered, well covered with ashes, as if the flames would be needed later on. The floor of beaten earth had been swept with a broom of heather, simply made by tying a few handfuls of tough stems around a stick. The crockery was spotless, and upon flat rocks here and there stood gallipots, gathered by Whippety from refuse heaps, and these were filled with the last flowers of the year, and sprigs of foliage. That shed was cleaner by far than many a cottage home above in Youlstone.

"I thought she might be here, hiding from me," said Anger. "A day so fine would tempt her. Storms have passed across the moor since last I saw her—an enemy. Here she was a gentle sister. What storms have raged in Stiniel?"

Stirred by a breath of wind, the piece of sacking fell across the opening which served as doorway, darkening the windowless hut. Anger listened, confident he would hear a footstep despite the roaring of the river, but only a certain footstep and a light one.

"I could stay here," he murmured. "Though I have been accustomed to comfort, a room to sleep in, a room to dine in, and a room to think in; I could abandon them all, and serve my time here, sleeping on the earth, enduring any sort of hardship through the rain and frost of winter, if I might minister. I could draw water from the river, I could go into the wood for fuel, I could eat husks, if my work might be blessed, and my food seasoned with the happiness of that misty night. I have been surrounded by the faces of women all my life; I have admired beauty, I have been inspired by beauty, I have pitied beauty; but never have I known the desire for beauty, the longing to make it my own, and to lavish myself upon it. What is there in Petronel which the thousands who have passed me lacked? It has a name, and yet I cannot find it. While she stood there looking at me, I knew I had come to Youlstone either to live or to die. One part is dead," he said, going out slowly. "It must be dead, for I cannot make it move; it will not speak nor open its eyes, and I can find no motion of its heart. I am not the murderer of that part; it died upon the bed where my body lay six months; and if there is anything new in me, if I am more a man, learning how to live, understanding at last the call of Nature, it is my destiny, it is the spirit of creation sent upon me. No man is master of his birth-mark."

Outside, the character of the shadow had changed already; now it was the wood, no longer the cliff, which became assertive. Anger remembered the territory upon the other side of the river remained unexplored; he had not wandered through the rusted bracken, beneath the wealth of oak grown from acorns scattered by the wind and buried beneath leaves in the autumn of old time. So he crossed lower down upon pinnacles of rock, black although beaten by white spray for ever, and passed into a solitary glade.

The wood was ancient, a relic of the age of forests yet always young, because at that season every foot of ground was a nursery for young princes and princesses, golden children of royal oaks, still nestling in the cradles of their cups. Wandering in that romantic territory, Anger could almost have believed he had been sent upon a mission to win certain things by outwitting those who kept the treasures guarded. On him was set an elementary task, which might prove to be an enterprise of peril; a task pleasant to the senses, and one which almost every man would undertake with readiness, and pursue in a holiday-making spirit, enduring a thousand trials if he could gain possession of the golden apples, and by delivering them to the king, might claim, as a reward, his daughter. Love, after all, was the same in kind as the spell imposed by magic; the winning of the woman released the lover from his enchantment as the fulfilment of the conditions of the spell dissolved the charm. No man could refuse the spell; it was useless to take precautions against it; he might be warned, but he could not be saved. Ordained to kill his brother, he might travel to a far country to evade his fate, but neither accident nor enemy could harm him until the day arrived when he quarrelled with a stranger, fought with him and left him dead, and so became his brother's murderer. On the other hand, the man who was born to good fortune might drink poison or leap into a furnace with impunity; death could not come near him until the good things had been won. Even the lords of life and death were bound by a law which prevented them from expurgating a single sentence from the book of fate.

This was rhapsody, not philosophy; the argument of a savage who desired to kill and devour a saint in order that he might acquire the good man's virtues. It was true that every young woman who smiled at a youth incurred a responsibility to heaven; but strength of mind would conquer any spell whose name is woman. Anger had only to force himself free from those surroundings, and if fatality pursued him like a huge lumbering Cyclops, he had merely to avoid the mountains hurled at him, then tilt at the giant's one eye. He would not own to himself the simple truth which rode like a jockey on his heart, how, during illness the priest had been sloughed off, while the man remaining had since been shaken and divided by that singer.

For it was Petronel singing somewhere in the wood. Anger stood leaning against an oak, remembering the priest Felix who, doubting God's word, went into the wood alone to confess to Nature; and, while musing, his heart kindled at the singing of a bird; and he listened, feeling his doubts departing, then returned to the monastery, where all things were changed and faces were new; for a thousand years had passed while the bird reproved the doubter in the wood.

This song was not sweet; the voice was harsh, and its theme was melancholy:—

> " 'Tis a piteous sight to see around,
>   The leaves lie rotting on the ground."

The singer missed the message of autumn, mistaking re-birth for death; but why did she chant at all?

Another song swept through the wood, one far better and more musical—rune-staves of the wind. Merrily the dry leaves rained upon Anger's head. That myth of the piper accompanied by the organ of the river should have lured him rather than the lamentations. Yet the immortal music was sound only; the discordance had more sweetness. The listener could not remain in that shower of leaves. Through bracken, heavy as fossils with moisture, and black-fruited alders and wild apple, he went downhill. The wild boy had been a messenger—and Petronel sang. He was not far away—and she sang. That garden of ferns in a hollow had its charms, but it was empty.

He came out into sunshine, divided by the river, which there swept through a narrow gorge, from the cliff of the moorland and the overhanging rocks heavy with ivy. The voice had ceased, making the loneliness intolerable. Anger, gazing and wondering, observed a burr upon his coat-sleeve, removed it, but another was soon clinging, while a third fell upon a mossy stone. High grasses past their prime, and stems of foxglove bare of flowers or fruit, fluttered in the breeze without a whisper; but that thing of active life, returning like a brown bird to its nest, did not belong to the order *digitaria*, although it had fingers. Anger felt a burr in his throat as he climbed the last rock and looked below.

"There is no room," said Petronel, sitting upon the narrow shelf above the river as if she had flown there, her heels tapping the black granite, her face detrimental to all philosophy. "If you advance, you fall, and then the splash."

"I felt sure you would be out to-day. I searched in the hut. Then I heard you singing," said Anger, leaning over with a feeling of contentment, seeing just then only a nut-brown neck and a dress of flaming red.

"Singing!" said she. "I had to use my voice because the sun shines, but you cannot call a frog's croak music. What were you doing in the wood?"

"Looking for you."

"Finding every nook and corner that I hide in. I shall tell Whippety to dig me out a cave at the top of the wood and make it the centre of a maze where I may sit in peace."

"Do you want to be alone?"

"Yes, if you please. I was dreaming of golden birds and apple trees until you came along."

"You were singing very sadly about the leaves rotting on the ground."

"Dreams are not happy things," she said, in the most careless fashion, picking a sodden blackberry and playing at catch with it.

"The first time I met you," said Anger, without any idea of going, "you were yourself. The second time I believe you were playing a part. Now you are incomprehensible. I like you best when you are serious."

"Preaching and using polysyllables," she cried, snatching at the berry she had thrown out too far, and almost following it into rushing water; so indifferent was she then to life and feeling. "Speaking as if I was his daughter!"

"I am very little older than yourself."

"I am to do as he bids me. I shall be told what dress I am to wear, how I am to arrange my hair."

"Miss Vigar! Did you not ask me——"

"When I am serious he approves of me. When upon my dignity I'm an actress; and when I laugh and chatter, then I'm Heaven knows what—incomprehensible! I'm an elf without a soul sitting on a pixy-stool. And the man's a stranger!"

"Did you not promise to be a sister?"

"One promises anything during a fit of the horrors. No more brothers who run away. What are you doing in Youlstone? Go home, and do some work, and support your wife and children."

"You will force me to leave you," he said sadly.

"What do I know about you? A man dropped out of the mist, out of the moon for all I know; not out of the sun, for you're too solemn—and you like me best when I'm in misery. Don't cast yourself about upon that rock, because it logs. I don't want to be crushed beneath stones and strangers."

"Whippety told you I had come. Why did you sing?"

"Because I was in the mood to make a noise; and I wanted to frighten away the bird."

"What bird? You are fond of them. I found the furze-bush which you had covered with food and paper flowers and ribbons."

"I have bird-friends, and that bush is dedicated to them, O stranger-man, who must know everything. First come the tits, who devour meat like little boys, darling wee fellows with golden waistcoats and black ties. Then come the robins, who prefer fresh worms but cannot always find them and will then eat bread. The paper flowers are decorations for their table, and are to make my friends forget summer is over and gone. The ribbons frighten away the bad birds, the strangers, who come out of the mist and steal food which was never meant for them."

She turned round to be sure he was there. Her face prevented him from going. She was too splendid a wild bird to be bound by the laws which govern sparrows.

"Now you will demand an explanation of the bird I was trying to frighten by my singing. Look above. You see a rowan-tree hangs over me, and there are left just three bunches of small berries. These are the apples; we give them that name in this part of the world. Every night a bird comes and feeds upon them. It is the golden bird which lives by day in a wooden cage hanging to the wall of a cottage somewhere in the wood. He is released at midnight and comes here to drink from the river and to feed upon the berries. Catch him, and you would make your fortune; but he cannot be caught. If you sat up and watched all night under the tree you would be bound to fall asleep. If the stranger likes me when I'm serious, how he must hate me now!"

"You are growing serious."

"While I talk nonsense."

"There is a healthy grain of truth in every fairy-tale."

"You think that," she exclaimed, then laughed again and went on: "He is a bad bird because when he has eaten the last apple winter begins, and then he stays in his cage. Catch him while the apples are still red upon the tree and the summer would remain for ever. Sometimes he is supposed to drop a golden feather, and then the winter is always very mild."

"Who finds the feather?"

"Some child, of course. Children always get the best of everything."

"We cannot complain."

"Do we all have a childhood? You are wrong. Some of us are not allowed to have one."

"Now you are yourself," he said more tenderly.

"Then I am only myself when I forget myself."

"You have explained the singing; but what about the seed-heads of that burdock?"

"When burrs are blown about some are bound to stick," she answered, not in the least ashamed.

"You threw them at me."

"I am tired of sitting here; this rock is clammy now that the sun has left it. Fine weather is in such a hurry this time of the year. Would you like to reach out your hand and help me to climb?"

He did so quickly enough, and after a jump on her part and a pull on his they stood upon the same level, seeing each other clearly, and he noticed she had freckles slightly showing, while she observed his face was good but somewhat sleepy. As they turned to gain the pathway a bramble caught at her flimsy sleeve, tore it to the elbow, and he saw upon the rich brown arm, pricked permanently in blue, a hand clutching a cross which was interwoven by a scroll inscribed, "To the memory of my dear brother."

"Was that your work?" asked Anger, longing to confront Curgenven with that arm. "What a pity to stain your skin," he added heedlessly.

Vexed that he should have seen the cross and scroll, Petronel hurried forward, but tripped, for she went blind suddenly.

"It must have hurt you," said Anger gently.

"To make those pricks," she muttered almost scornfully.

"And to lose him."

"I would have driven the needle into my heart if that could have done him good. I would have pushed it into my eyes and through my tongue—that pain is nothing. Now like me, for I'm serious."

She threw her arms around a tree, held on to it like the hand which clutched the cross upon her arm, and sobbed aloud. The wind which swayed the tree moved her as well; and her cry, "Oh, Bertram! Bertram!" moved with more force than wind the soul of Anger.

He reached her side, himself blind and moaning. This was the girl whose vileness had wrecked the peace of home and her mother's mind, whose hands had made away with the brother whom she sobbed for. If she was false, creation had outdone the devil. Those marks upon her arm, those tears, her attitude of ivy on the oak, proclaimed her sinless.

"My sister! Be my sister! Let me take his place."

So he whispered; but these were not the words the rider on his heart had meant to utter.

"Nobody has seen that, except you. I would never have shown it to anyone—and you are a stranger."

She walked away with her words, holding her head proudly.

"I cannot remain a stranger. I have seen you now three times. Nobody on earth is better known to me; nobody can ever seem more near," he cried, and followed her.

So they came to a kind of pathway crossed by branches, and stood still.

"You cannot be my brother," she said bitterly. "I was glad to see you that night because I felt more lonely than usual, and had reached a breaking-point. I welcomed your offer of assistance as some poor creature might pick up a purse of gold without stopping to consider whom it belonged to. Who are you? A man here to-day for your own pleasure, and gone to-morrow. We met in that place yonder, and talked sentimentally, and agreed to be brother and sister. It was pretty, it was romantic; but two lives cannot run into one so easily. No stranger can play the part of brother. Bertram was good and strong——"

"He left you. He played the coward."

"I advised him to go. Had he remained he would have killed our mother."

"He does not write to you?"

"He did at the first. Now he is dead—drowned. I saw him in my sleep, rising and falling on a sandbank held by seaweed. But this is no affair of yours."

"There are rights I may claim."

"You shall not follow me about," she cried fiercely. "That evening, when you were lost in the mist, you could not help forcing yourself upon me. You had no excuse for coming to Stiniel, and—and—oh, what a brute you are to make things harder for me."

"Petronel," he cried, "all the leaves in the wood shall be witnesses that I call your name beloved. You have confessed more than you meant to. Forgive me for the impulse which made me hurry to your home immediately I set foot in Youlstone. Forgive me, beautiful sister, proud sister, sweet sister. With the knowledge I had caused you pain I was driven and tormented all the night."

"Are you not a clergyman?"

"I was before my illness."

"Then you are one now. What are you doing here; and in those clothes?"

"I hardly know," he said in dazed fashion.

"You are hiding from your friends."

"I have done many things of which I have repented afterwards. I have never done anything of which I am ashamed."

"Do you include your religion?"

"Write to my Rector—I will give you his address—and ask if Father Jack ever failed in his duty until now."

"You are a Catholic priest!" she exclaimed.

"I was. I became ill; I seemed to die—I lost something. What it was I do not know. Now, at least I have a man's courage, a man's strength. I shall not go back."

"I know now why he claims me as a sister," she murmured; and then aloud, "I came out in a red dress to enjoy the sunshine. You meet me and bring up storms. Don't you think it was unfortunate that you were lost in the mist?"

"I am still. I shall never get clear of it until I see you happy."

"Then you must wait in darkness," she said bitterly.

"Can you believe in me? Will you trust me?" he cried earnestly.

"What is the use? Strangers we are, and strangers we must remain."

"When you call me stranger, you are avenged for what I made you suffer," he said quietly, although his heart was at war and the longing on it was riding to its fall.

"If I say I do believe in you, will you leave this place and never return?"

"I cannot."

"Shall you continue to follow me?"

"I must."

"I have no good reputation. You will make it worse."

"Let it fall upon me."

"My friend may be compelled to help me."

"I am here for no other purpose."

"My brother will place himself in a position of great danger."

"Danger for your sake is my happiness."

"If I tell you to go, if I command you, if I entreat you?"

"I remain."

"I have heard nothing like this before," she murmured, and went on a little, being afraid lest he should see her eyes.

"Still you must leave me, and you will do so. You are very honest with me. I will be plain with you. We are at the beginning of a friendship; we both look forward, but the future I can see is very different from the one you picture. What is the end, Mr. Anger? Do not come near me, please. Call me Petronel, if that gives you pleasure, but never touch my hand, and do not dare to pity me again. When you came into my hut you brought the mist. It is clearing from you, but it increases around me. I saw your eyes then." She looked round. "I see them now. The next word lies with you."

"I love you."

Again she stopped, melted by his voice, and fell to crying, but had the strength to tell him to keep his ground.

"What will you do for me?" she whispered.

"Any deed that may be lawful."

"No more?"

"Any deed."

"Who knows?" she called to the trees of the wood, holding her hands a moment before her eyes. "We are young. Is it a great happiness to love me?"

He was trembling all over.

"It is the only thing on earth."

It was also fearful.

"Yet you cannot marry me, for you are a priest. Say nothing yet. When I finish speaking and turn away from you do not answer, leave me at once, let me stay here alone. Be at the hut every day, early in the afternoon, until I come. Now listen, and keep away and be strong. I am mortgaged, I am claimed. I am in the power of a humpbacked dwarf."

CHAPTER IX

COLD FOLK

HISTORY of work was made that day of glad weather. Living-rooms were deserted, and doors left open to clear out six days' smoke; men and women, insect-like in their nature, hurried into sunshine to prepare the plats for winter's sleep or to lift the last potatoes from their patches. Getting-up-time, according to the proverb, was five for those who would thrive, and seven for those who had thriven; morality in proverbs being much under the rule of rhyme. There was little prosperity in Youlstone, yet its inhabitants acted as if they had thriven, rising for the most part long after dawn, and they were right; for when went the order forth that men should dig by lantern-light? Every day gives light enough for labour, and they who toil eight hours have done enough.

Good workers lived in Youlstone—half of them women— quiet folk, cold in their manner, a trifle deaf, without time to come out of their own lives and stir about others; but Vigar and Billacott were not of that company. The farmer of Quoditch watched his wife sweating, and placed the credit of work accomplished to himself. The farmer of Stiniel felt he had done his duty when the beasts were fed and his round of the fields was over. The one basked in the ignorance of idleness, while the other had lost interest in energy. Both were abroad that morning; with a brave show of muscle Billacott heaped a quantity of manure precisely in the middle of the road, and in response to Thirza's grumble told her to move it elsewhere. Vigar repaired a gap in one of his hedges with furze and stones. The solid house of Stiniel looked down contemptuously upon the wobbling cottage of Quoditch, tough-ness of granite sneering at such rottenness; but Quoditch was the stronger of the two.

Presently Nicholas descended the steep garden, entered

the boggy strip of pasture, which separated his property from Quoditch, and wandered about this useless strip of ground, covered with sand and rushes, until he heard voices. Going to the hedge he looked down, and saw his neighbour chatting with the doctor of Riversmeet.

Hearing him they looked up, and mutual salutations followed.

"Come along down, neighbour," called Bobby. "You aren't been on my side once this year, I fancy."

The party hedge was in a ruinous condition, so that it was easy for a two-legged being to ascend or descend; but because of its steepness bullocks could not break through. Nicholas climbed down, shook hands with Palk, who was spying out the land where it had been agreed development might commence, and expressed a hope that nobody was sick in Youlstone.

"There is always somebody ill; even here," Palk answered.

"There be them who smoke too much, and drink too much, and don't do no work," explained Bobby, diagnosing his own state accurately.

"The most dangerous disease is old age, and that seems infectious here," said Palk lazily.

"Doctor ha' been admiring my bit o' property. Calls it the prettiest piece o' Youlstone parish. Ses two o' Stiniel ain't worth one Quoditch," rattled Bobby at the ear of his old neighbour.

"I made no comparison between the houses," said Palk.

"I ain't afraid of none. Houses get burnt, but the land bides."

"It is all a matter of sunshine," the doctor went on. "You get it here from morning till night. Look over there," pointing up the slope. "You can trace the line beyond which the sunshine never passes. On this side the bushes have grown strongly because the soil is sweet; on the other the ground is covered with plants which love the shade."

"Yes, the garden is very sour. Nothing does well except onions. If the side of that hill could be blasted off, I would have done it long ago," said Vigar.

"If the old hill wur busted, where would Quoditch be?" asked Bobby.

"Underground, I reckon," replied Vigar.

"It will crumble in time," said Palk. "The sun may get to Stiniel a few thousand years hence."

"Mr. Vigar had best go and get buried and bide till then," said Bobby. "Doctor ses Quoditch be the properest little farm on Dartmoor——"

"Steady, Billacott," interrupted Palk. "I said it could be made worth more than Stiniel. Mr. Vigar has to put up with the damp; you could get rid of it. The whole place wants draining."

"Dartmoor watter b'ain't serious," declared Bobby, getting stubborn.

"I know it is not detrimental to health; but continued leakage sours the ground. It would not take you six months to drain your fields, and the work would pay for itself the first year."

"How wur it my vaither never put in drains?" demanded Bobby.

"Perhaps he lacked the energy."

"How wur it his vaither never put in drains?"

"Very likely it never occurred to him."

"They wur gude men. You don't see their like now when I b'ain't visible. They could carry queer old chaps of stones up over the Quoditch Pinch, which be harder by hundreds than the Stiniel Pinch, and never drop 'em. If the land had wanted draining they'd ha' done it."

"Doctor's right, neighbour," said Nicholas. "A drain across a sour field does work wonders."

"A drain across Quoditch would sour my vaither's grave," said Bobby. "'Twould be like teaching mun his business now he'm gone."

Palk had expected some such answer to his criticism. He liked ignorant Bobby Billacott somewhat as he might have liked a harmless beetle, while regarding him as a savage settled upon the land his ancestors had squatted on for two or three centuries; and savages, whether white or black, had to move ditchwards before the men of progress. Civilisation, which was all wise, could not bear with fools. Palk was a humane man but too simple; he could only face a fact, and not a fancy. Procuring a piece of land at a bargain was the fact; the grief of the former owner was the fancy.

As he went towards his horse, Nicholas detached himself from Bobby and followed, saying as he reached the ruin of the gate, "May I have a word with you, doctor?"

"Certainly," said Palk, settling his face professionally.

"Mrs. Vigar is getting dangerous."

Palk unfastened his horse, stroked his beard, hesitated, then asked, "In what way?"

"Crazy bad," the farmer muttered.

"Has she shown you any violence?"

"She assaults me with her tongue. This morning I found her standing behind me; she moves about so quietly I do not know when she is near. She pushed me, but that was nothing. She swore at me, but that also was nothing. She told me that Curgenven hates me, he wishes to take Stiniel from me, and to occupy the house himself. There may be nothing in that, but who gave her these ideas?"

"Not Curgenven. He is very fond of you Youlstone people," said Palk sharply.

"He would not leave Riversmeet to live up here. He could not do it, even if he wanted to," said Nicholas, who knew nothing about "Youlstone Limited."

"She is not insane, Vigar. You know where the trouble lies. It is the man of Law you want, not the man of Medicine. Have you told Curgenven?"

"No, doctor. I am afraid of him."

"Why, you are foolish. Tell him. He will advise you. If she assaults you and Miss Vigar, she must be restrained. As a doctor, I can only tell you to keep her from the liquor. If it becomes impossible to live with her on that account, you must consult Curgenven concerning a separation. Do you want me to visit her?"

"Not yet. I should have to suffer for it when you went. I will take your advice and consult Curgenven. At least, I say I will," the farmer murmured.

"He is the man. I am very sorry to hear this, Vigar," said Palk, dragging himself into the saddle. "A bad business, but Curgenven will settle it for you. It is drink, you know—nothing but drink. Common enough. Good-bye."

"There is nothing you could give her?" suggested Nicholas, stepping up as the horse began to move.

"A bottle of medicine won't cure temper. Keep the other bottle under lock and key. You are too dark up there. Diseases of all kinds breed in gloomy places. You want sunshine in Stiniel."

"Right enough," muttered Nicholas, as he went up towards his barn. "But we shan't get that without an earthquake."

Taking mattock and spade he worked, cutting a trench between a piece of bog at the top of his highest field and the gully below. Thus situated he could see almost every roof in Youlstone, as well as the strip of common and the winding roadway which led merely to his home and then to the moor. While he laboured the sun fell behind the tors and the air grew cold, stiffening the muscles of the man who was prematurely aged and unable to move with the rapidity that warms a body. The mud and sluggish water depressed him; clay numbed his hands. Straightening himself, and answering the scream of a lapwing with a curse, he looked out for the last time. Light was still wonderfully clear upon the road, as if some ray of sunlight lingered there. A wagon loaded with granite was heaving and swaying as it made the bend for home; and when it vanished a figure started out, as if it had fallen from the tail of the cart, and began to run towards Quoditch Pinch.

"No man goes towards Dartmoor this time of day," said Nicholas, leaning upon the handle of his spade. "He would hardly be in a hurry to get to neighbour Billacott."

Shouldering his tools, Nicholas went down the field which ended in a bank above the zigzags along which the runner would have to pass if he continued beyond the bridge. So still was the air that the farmer could hear already the beat of footsteps.

"I wish it was my old Bert running back home," he murmured simply.

Reaching the hedge he waited, tingling somehow and feeling frightened; for an idea had come to him that the figure, which he seemed to recognise, had no intention of stopping at what passed for Quoditch gate.

"He is slow in running. He carries a lot of flesh," Nicholas went on, rubbing the cold clay from his hands. "'Tis a good thing I saw him. He means to make trouble, but he means well. I might do worse than make a friend"; for he knew that the running man, and the visitor who had almost forced himself into Stiniel, were one person.

"Go no farther, sir. Here is the man you want," he called in a guarded voice, afraid of some echo reaching his home, as the runner came hot and panting up the track.

Anger stopped and looked up, while his face, distressed by this unwonted speed, tried to express its gladness. He had dreaded the approach to Stiniel; had feared to face its mistress; had felt sure he would never reach the master. When a man loves he acts upon the impulse; and when he does that he has nothing but good luck to hope for.

"Thank God, Mr. Vigar," he gasped. "I must speak to you upon a matter of life or death."

"I guessed it would come—a matter of life or death. It seemed to me like that when I was twenty. I warned him," Nicholas murmured; and then aloud, "Climb up here, sir. Somebody may come along the road. We will go into my barn for privacy."

"Which way?" cried Anger.

"Any way you choose," was the reckless answer.

"This is the nearest," said Anger; and he dragged himself up the bank by means of docks and nettles—feeling no stings—plunged through the hedge, breaking rotten wood, heedless of thorns; while Nicholas smiled grimly and remarked, "That's the way to get through difficulties."

The barn was near, yet Anger snatched the tools from Nicholas that he might hurry; and immediately they passed in he flung his burden down and seizing the farmer's clammy hand held it in a grip given him since last winter, and gasped out the whole of his new world in a single breath:

"Mr. Vigar, I have come for your permission to marry Petronel."

"Why did you run, sir?"

"Heaven knows there is no time to waste; for her sake and my own."

"I thought it might come. I did not expect it so soon. Are you not a bit of a stranger to us, Mr. Anger?"

"No, a friend, a son. Give your consent, and let me act as a relation."

"You want to be my son. I was looking out just now, and when I saw you running I wished you were my son, escaping from death to find his father," said Nicholas heavily.

"I will take his place," cried Anger, acting, thinking, speaking, by force of impulse.

"My name is as good as yours, I think; but our clothes are cut differently," Nicholas went on. "You take me, sir? We Vigars are Dartmoor folk; we are a bit rough, and we eat our meals in the kitchen. In the matter of education we have always been a little higher than our neighbours. I don't go home to change; I sit in these old boots all the evening. Your own parents might look the other way——"

"My father and mother are dead. I have no near relation; nobody to offend or please. Give me your daughter, Mr. Vigar."

"Don't speak so loudly. Stiniel is below," said the farmer, looking out upon the blue and perfect evening. "I cannot find an answer," he went on. "It is not the custom here for a young man to ask for permission to marry a maid. If she consents that ends the matter. Has Petronel promised herself to you already?" he asked wonderingly.

"She knows I love her. We met by chance in the wood, and I was forced to speak."

"What was her answer?"

"You can guess."

"Something about Curgenven?"

"Yes, that devil, who tried to make me believe she was as black as his own soul and shoulders. Let him dare to touch her and I'll maul him."

"Steady, sir. You must not shout like that; sounds carry in this silence," said Vigar, drawing the young man back, then closing the door of the barn so that they could hardly see each other. "So Petronel told you. I think she must like you. Yes, I do think so. What more did she say? She did not make you any promise."

"She would not let me speak to her again, but she promised to meet me. I came as fast as I could to find you," said Anger, beginning to raise his voice again. "I felt if I could obtain your consent I might at least show Curgenven he is beaten. He may tyrannise over the ignorant folk of Youlstone, but he can't frighten me. Give me your answer, Mr. Vigar."

"Gain her consent, sir, and you will find me your friend," said Nicholas. "I know what is in my mind, but I do not know what is in my daughter's. She may love, she may not. One moment she submits; the next she fights. Life owes her a good deal, but I might say the same about myself. I suppose we get what we deserve," he murmured drearily.

"I cannot give her what she deserves, but I will give her all I can," cried Anger joyously. "If I save her from Curgenven, that surely will be something."

"What do you think of it?" asked Vigar sharply. "Do you suppose she would have him?"

"Left to herself she would; I am sure of it. She may hate him, but she would never find the strength to resist, because he terrifies her; and more, he is able to cast a spell upon her, he can bewitch her. When I stood in his office I felt that power. I knew if I should weaken he would crush me."

"So you have visited him. A powerful little man, sir, and nobody has ever beaten him yet. You believe in the evil eye," Nicholas chuckled. "We Dartmoor folk are not so much more superstitious than you Londoners. Well, sir, if there is any truth in it, you and I and Petronel can cast the evil eye as well as Curgenven. The person who gets the glance in first will win. Let me tell you this: Curgenven before my wife and Curgenven before my daughter are two very different men."

"What does that mean?" cried Anger.

"He does not frighten Petronel. She has somewhere in that fine body twice his strength. She is not the woman to knuckle before any man, whether she loves or hates him."

"You would not say that had you seen her in the wood. I have met your daughter three times only, but I believe I understand her best," replied Anger, with the tremendous self-confidence which a lover must needs sport openly.

"I will only say this," Nicholas went on, "I have never for a moment believed she would marry Curgenven, nor do I suppose he wants her much. In his life there are many secrets, and he would not be able to keep one of them from Petronel. Now I must leave you."

"Have you nothing to say; no sort of feeling to express, no good wish?" asked Anger, beginning to cool.

"Well, sir, I know little of you, but I think you are a worthy man. I believe if you marry my daughter she will have no cause to complain. When are you meeting her?"

Anger repeated what the girl had said.

"Would you like me to be present? You must not come to Stiniel. Mrs. Vigar sometimes sleeps in the afternoon—very heavily," said Nicholas in a meaning voice. "Until that happens it would not be wise for Petronel and myself to leave the house; but a sleep will soon be due."

"Come by all means, and if Petronel will have me we can make all arrangements," replied Anger. "I am not wealthy, but I have enough."

"I am poor," said Vigar. "Still, I have made some provision for my girl. I saved for the boy; now it will make her dowry. Petronel has returned home," he went on, as a light broke out in Stiniel. "Do not cross the field with me. Your shortest way lies down the gully. Good night, Mr. Anger."

"We shall be father and son soon."

"Well, I will hope so," the farmer answered, adding in a low voice, as he crossed the plat towards the gate, "I have many doubts. Petronel does not take to love like most girls."

Somehow Anger was none too elated as he walked to Youlstone. Vigar's manner had repressed him. The father had not expressed a proper amount of enthusiasm for his daughter or sympathy for her lover. He seemed to distrust them both; Anger as a foreigner, Petronel as a near relation, knowing nothing of the one and too much about the other. What looked like suspicion might be prudence, since it was not in the common way of things for a visitor, whose life happened to intersect and not run parallel with that of Youlstone, to hurl his body at a resident, demanding his daughter after three times seeing her.

Going towards the village, still at a high rate of speed although the impelling force was quieter, he heard an asthmatic wheezing, then perceived a yard or so ahead the rounded form of a meat-fed pug. Dogs were plentiful but, with the exception of this highly-civilised type, they were all fierce collies kept for business. A few more steps, and Anger distinguished in the increasing darkness the big black figure of the fat beast's master. A handkerchief fluttered, scenting the keen air with violets; a voice highly refined called tenderly, "Come along, Dora!" and the pug responded with machine-like noises. The queer couple passed ahead, while Anger followed with a distinct idea that the elegant gentleman had become aware of his proximity and was very much afraid of being spoken to. Again he quickened his steps, drew near the mysterious being, who halted abruptly opposite the inn, and a moment afterwards the noise of a door slammed back into the wall preceded the leisurely tramp of footsteps towards the low thatched house.

Making inquiries, Anger knew, was hopeless work, yet he asked questions of the landlord, and received the usual answers:

"A very kind gentleman, Mr. Hanson. He is respected by every one who knows him; one of your real gentlemen and a scholar. Don't interfere with folk neither. Two services regular on Sundays, and always punctual for weddings and funerals. He ain't seen abroad much; he'm too busy. Yes, sir, the folk do go to chapel, but everybody likes Mr. Hanson. He ain't got an enemy in the parish."

Anger was not looking forward to the hours of solitude till bedtime, and had half decided to make a call at Quoditch; but then he made the bold resolve to visit the Vicar, who was unlikely to pay that compliment to him. The passage to Billacott's rude home was dangerous after dark, with its manure-heaped road and sundry pitfalls, while the subsequent entertainment promised insufficient compensation for these perils. Besides, Anger felt an increasing appetite for the company of a social equal. So he ventured forth presently, tried the gate in the wall and was not surprised to find it fastened; then, noticing a bell-pull nestling amid ivy he tugged it hard, and the iron beyond began to clang as if all Youlstone was on fire.

"Paying a call here is something like a real adventure," Anger murmured.

Footsteps came hurrying up the hidden pathway; a key was turned, numerous bolts were shot back; at last the door yielded, and the custodian's voice asked sharply, "What do ye want this time o' night? It's gone eight. Couldn't you bide till morning?"

"I am a visitor," said Anger.

"Oh, I ask your pardon, sir, I'm sure. 'Tis the gentleman to the inn, I fancy. I'm sorry, but I couldn't see ye in the dark."

"If Mr. Hanson is not engaged I should like to see him."

"Well, sir, master be always busy, but I'll tell him. Please to walk inside, sir. Be careful of the step, sir. 'Tis a bit sudden-like in the dimsy."

Anger was ushered through a garden, which gave him the impression of being a pleasant, as well as a secluded, place; he could see tall firs, thick shrubs, and beds of white chrysanthemums by the light from the kitchen window. The rest of the house was heavily shuttered. Showing him into the hall hung with thick curtains pleasantly scented and dimly illumined by a lamp of many colours, the housekeeper departed, and did not return. The Vicar himself, tall, pale, and intellectual, in clerical evening dress, walked out, extended his hand, and remarked in a voice which lacked sincerity entirely, "I am delighted to see you. A visitor is a rarity, and so more welcome. Will you come into my study?"

Very conscious of his muddy boots and rural knickerbockers, Anger followed the Vicar into a large low room, and immediately felt muddled, hardly believing it possible that he stood within a stone's throw of rough Dartmoor, that upon the other side of the high wall surrounding the garden were the wretched cottages, the comfortless inn of a dark and muddy village a hundred years slow by the clock of civilisation; and beyond, the rock masses, tearing rivers, mossy bogs, ravines, and chasms. This luxurious room suggested the better part of London, with its sumptuous furniture, artistic decorations, rich screens and carpet, hot-house flowers, and violet-scented atmosphere; the exquisite owner dressed as if expecting lords and ladies; the newspapers, journals, and reviews; the slips of "proof" draping the central table. As an embassy is held to be part of the territory of the country it represents, so was this study of Youlstone Vicarage a part of the capital in which the spirit of the Vicar lived, and where his life was spent, although his body had been exiled to the moorland.

"I must apologise," gasped Anger. "First for intruding upon your privacy; but I intend to make a long stay here. Secondly for coming in these clothes."

For his life he dared not add the nature of his own profession.

"It is a weakness of mine to dress in the evening," came the slow and stately answer, spoken in the voice of perfect breeding. "I was unwilling to break myself of the custom when I came here, nor did it appear to me expedient to do so. A good deal of negligence is often shown in the country regarding clothes, and this seems to me bad from a moral point of view. A gentleman ought never to forget he is one. He should impress the fact upon the common people, in my opinion, as frequently as possible. They will respect him all the more for his insistence."

"You have held this living a good many years, I believe?" said the visitor, feeling himself forced to act the part of interviewer.

"Yes, a long time. I was compelled to leave London on account of very indifferent health, and by a chain of circumstances, all curious, was led by divine grace to purchase the advowson of Youlstone. It was a wild place then. Have you seen this month's reviews?" the Vicar hurried on, with a change of voice, exchanging a disagreeable for a congenial subject. "Here is an article of mine upon 'Vedic Mythology'; and here another upon 'Some Theories of the Ice Age.' I do not know if it would interest you to read them."

Anger returned the only possible answer, and went on, "Science is little more than a name to me. Your time must be pleasantly occupied with these studies."

"That is very true. The air of this region is highly conducive to excursions in the mental field. It is also good for the general morale. My days are well filled, while the months pass with amazing rapidity. I am at the present engaged upon a study of Neo-paganism in its application to the present generation. You will have noticed the advent of this spirit."

"I have given the matter little thought," said Anger uncomfortably. "I fear my presence interrupts you," he added.

"Not at all," said Hanson, rising quickly, and proffering a silver box containing cigarettes. "It is delightful to receive a visitor."

"Thank you; I do not smoke," said Anger, shrinking from the silken coat and scented cuff when they were brought almost into contact with his coarse tweed and flannel. "May I ask if you have applied your researches to this particular parish?"

"Only from a geological point of view. The parish covers a considerable area, and I have not yet found the opportunity to explore it thoroughly."

"I have not seen the interior of your church," Anger went on.

"It is scarcely worth a visit. A very mean structure, terribly out of repair. It does not contain one single point of interest. The village is striking. I like the peaceful conservatism of its inhabitants. This opposition to progress, as it is called, must react favourably upon the morale."

"You would describe Youlstone as a well-conducted place?" suggested the visitor.

"Most decidedly," replied the visionary, whose spirit was not, and never had been, resident in the parish. "The zeal displayed by the people in their work and recreation amazes me. They cast their energies with such thoroughness into the smallest detail of the daily round."

"It is a happy place?"

"Marvellously so."

"There is no immorality?"

"None; certainly none whatever."

"Nor any drunkenness?"

"I believe none. The morale of the place is the joy of my existence."

Anger reflected it was indeed true that the Vicar lived in his study. It was impossible for him to see the bar-room of the inn, or any portion of the village, because of the great wall surrounding his garden; and what he could not see with his eyes had no existence.

"There is a chapel, I notice, at the far end of the village," he continued. "Do you find it draws the people from the church?"

"To a certain extent," came the calm answer. "It is indisputable that the people, whose minds are innocent and child-like, do prefer a simpler type of service than those which are provided for them by the established church. The archaic language of our prayer-book, tender and beautiful as it must always be to you and me, remains a source of perplexity to them. It would be astonishing if they did not on the whole prefer the extempore prayers of a minister who is their equal in point of birth. I never lack a congregation, however. 'When two or three are gathered together'—you know the rest. A few good old folk, with a sprinkling of religious-minded young people, attend the church—I will not say regularly—as a sign of their respect for me. I am much touched by their devotion."

While speaking, his mind was evidently far away, and his eyes were resting upon yesterday's London newspapers. This intellectual man, who was spiritual master of Youlstone in mistland and had bought the Vicarage that he might use it as a workshop, actually lived between Fleet Street and Kensington. All that he knew concerning the parish was the fruit of his own fancy.

"Although I have been here only a short time, I have already found acquaintances, even friends," continued Anger.

"The people are most friendly," murmured Hanson.

"Upon my arrival I happened to meet Miss Vigar of Stiniel."

"Let me consider. I have at present no recollection of her."

The visitor drew a picture, somewhat thoroughly, while reflecting he would hardly be tolerated in that house when his intentions became known.

"A very striking and handsome girl; a perfect type of moorland beauty," declared Hanson blankly.

"What is better, a good and pure-minded girl," added the visitor.

"Entirely so."

"I have become acquainted with her parents. You may know them."

"Mr. Vigar—yes. One of those gentle, hard-working farmers who are the salt of the land. Mrs. Vigar—poor woman—suffers, I understand, from some incurable disease which makes her irritable. They do not attend a place of worship. I do not judge them. I have not been in Stiniel within my recollection, but then I do not visit. The men are always out by day, while the women are busy, and the coming of a stranger embarrasses them."

"I have also made the acquaintance of the Billacotts," resumed Anger.

Hanson repeated the name with a suspicion of annoyance. If the guest had only discussed aspects of mediæval art, or origins of primitive religions, he would have made himself more welcome.

"They live below, in Quoditch," explained Anger.

"I remember them distinctly. The wife a most excellent woman. The man industrious, sober, painstaking, but not without grave faults. Much too self-confident, and fond of displaying a spirit of irreverence, to me distressing."

"I know him merely as a well-intentioned man blown out by ignorance which he mistakes for knowledge," said Anger, surprised to find Bobby selected from all others as the one bad character.

"His attitude within a sacred building approaches blasphemy. He is addicted to somewhat gross forms of frivolity, and has been known to make an audible joke during the most solemn moments of a neighbour's obsequies. I will cite you an instance. When asked at his own wedding the awful question, 'Wilt thou have this woman for thy lawful wedded wife?' he answered loudly and distinctly, 'No!' making the congregation and the unfortunate woman at his side suppose he had suddenly changed his mind. He explained that it was merely a joke caused by an excess of high spirits; but he remained unable to appreciate the fearful blasphemy of his conduct."

Anger smiled at the shocked voice and pained expression of his exquisite host, who was unmistakably chafing at being detained so long in barren Youlstone, and was fretting to return to a more congenial spiritual condition. Clearly the visitor's presence was a nuisance, and his act of calling was regarded as impertinent. One more remark he felt compelled to make; curious to know if that would strike the same dull spark of unreality:

"I have also made the acquaintance of Curgenven."

"Ah, you know him," said Hanson, with a voice on the edge of animation. "But you could hardly fail to do so since he finds his way to the heart of every one. A wonderful, an amazing, almost an unique, individual. Never ill, perennially active; about the moorland by day, working by night. It is often said by unthinking persons that when a man is little more than a dwarf and suffers from the infirmity of crooked shoulders his mind must be warped like his body and his soul will be deformed like his spine. Curgenven's life furnishes us with a complete refutation of that theory."

"You would call him a worthy man," exclaimed Anger, trusting his note of irony would be missed; as indeed it was, if heard, for the Vicar went on clearly:

"He is in truth the father of this people. He controls their lives, manages their affairs; not even a christening can take place without Curgenven. He is a man, I do assure you, who, unlike so many lawyers, would harm himself rather than offend a fellow-creature."

Anger sat spellbound, watching the fire, hearing the pug snoring on its cushions; nor could he find another question.

"Unwilling as I am to deprive myself of your company, and let me say at once I trust this will not be your last visit," Hanson went on, fingering a sheaf of papers delicately, "I am compelled to mention, against my inclination, that two hours' work await me before the day's work is over. An editor is pressing me for matter which must be posted off to-morrow. Otherwise I should decline to close my ears to your interesting conversation this side of midnight. Good night," he said, taking Anger's hand, and leading him absent-mindedly towards the door in his eagerness to be alone again. "If in your walks you should make any geological discovery,

I trust you will inform me. I am myself too busy to get about much. The latch draws back—allow me! The outer gate opens in precisely the same manner. It was so good of you to cheer my solitude."

And then the door was closed somewhat vehemently; Anger went out into Youlstone church-town; while the Vicar hurried back into his study and sent his spirit out to Fleet Street.

CHAPTER X

KNITTING PEOPLE

THE proprietor of the Riversmeet Stores had suffered all his life from that nervous affliction known as a sense of duty. As a child in the china shop his highly-developed conscience had been troubled by the small labels attached to various articles advertising the price to purchasers. It was not right, he thought, that half-a-crown should be charged for a candlestick which had cost his father sixpence; such a profit was not only obtained through dishonesty, but was dictated by bad principles of business. So the boy would seek sometimes to redress the balance by going to defrauded customers and handing them small articles taken out of stock with the remark, "We make you a present of this"; until the father discovered these pilferings and sought to flog a proper commercial spirit into him, without success because conscience made the boy a thief.

"It's no use leaving the shop to Jimmy," the china-merchant said often. "Two years after I die he'll be bankrupt, and the name of Woodland will be wiped off the street. He robs his own parents, he gives things away, he would ruin me if I didn't watch him. The boy has no more instinct for business than a tramp has for digging."

Later on, the orthodox tradesman introduced a sympathetic neighbour into Jimmy's bedroom, and complained with increasing bitterness, "Only seventeen years old and a freethinker already. He might have waited till he was twenty-one. Look at his books!

Political economy, elements of logic, philosophy of the mental and moral powers of man—good Lord! He reads books of science by the hundred. Goes out looking for birds' nests; that's natural, but he keeps the eggs, sticks 'em on cardboard, and writes Latin underneath. He brings home plants too, squashes 'em in the letter-press, and kicks me if I touch 'em. Look at that! 'Tis what he call his cabinet of science! What's a man to do with such a son?"

Old Woodland had died worth about twenty pounds of ready money; and now his fool of a son was the richest man in the town, having accumulated his wealth by those methods which the old man had flogged him for. He could not help being honest, but the virtue had paid well. If a customer remarked that the price of some article was too high, Woodland would reply, "It is too dear," and would immediately knock off his profit—and yet it paid. Those books and the cabinet of science, which had horri-fied his poor father, made the son a scholar in the worthiest sense; even the astronomy and the smattering of Latin had been a help; nor had the love for birds and botany been proved a hindrance. Natural studies had shown Woodland that it was not necessarily the orthodox types which survived. Those which accommodated themselves to ever-altering circumstances flourished, while stron-ger neighbours, who could not face variety, were squeezed out.

This nervous sense of duty, which was in some respects a disease not less a trial than actual neurasthenia, drove the honest man towards Youlstone to find the stranger who unaccountably played bogey with his mind. It was an unusual act to call upon a visitor, even one who came out of season; but the apparition of Anger, his absent remarks, and the mystery about him were impel-ling factors. There was also the great land question of Youlstone. By all the laws of business and propriety Woodland was con-demned to be silent in Riversmeet; even had his wife been living he would not have entrusted her with the lawyer's secret. He had already babbled it to the moor, but that was no relief. So he went in search of the visitor.

"He will take his luncheon at one o'clock. If I reach the inn by half-past I shall find him at leisure," said the practical man.

Anger was leaving the inn when Woodland turned the corner of the lane. They met beneath the high wall of the Vicarage, where Hanson would be wallowing in cold science, and Woodland stepped up in his brisk manner, respectfully pleasant, and asked for an audience, adding, "I had the pleasure of speaking to you once before."

"I remember you perfectly," said Anger. "I fear I was short with you that morning, but I had something on my mind. You have not walked up here on the chance of seeing me?"

"Once a month I allow myself a day upon the moor. It does me good, sir. It enlarges my mind, which is in danger of getting small in Riversmeet. But I should not have come to-day had you left Youlstone."

"I am glad to hear that," said Anger in a low voice. "Half my time has been spent in a hopeless struggle to get information. The people will talk about weather and potatoes, but not a word of truth on matters of importance."

"Because you are a stranger, sir. I should not be so ready to speak if you were not one. We are both foreigners so far as this village is concerned. You know as much of the secret life of Youlstone as I do. I know who can pay debts and won't, who would but cannot, and who can and do."

"Will you walk with me?" said Anger. "I am going down the west cleave." He added hurriedly, "I have an appointment later on."

"I shall be very pleased to accompany you, sir. That has been a favourite walk of mine since I was a lad, and I am still almost the only inhabitant of Youlstone who goes there. The wood has been untouched during my lifetime. There is some question, I believe, as to whom it belongs."

"Curgenven?" suggested Anger.

"I do not think so. But he is there almost every day. He tells me he has trodden out a footpath."

"A crooked one."

Woodland gave a bird-like start, then laughed and said, "You have given me an opening and I will take it directly we get clear of the village."

A few steps up the lane, along which Anger had fled after the visit to Stiniel, across a piece of common covered with flat stones, not unlike a long disused burying-place, then beside the wall of a barren plat, and so to solitude and the springy peat. Woodland drew a deep breath, coughed, slapped his chest; then opened his mouth again and appeared to drink the air.

"Strong here, sir," he called. "This wind is like a woman, changing in a moment. We may live with it, but we never get to understand it. It blows life into us for eighty years; then it blows death."

"Eighty years—is that the limit? I had bargained for longer," Anger murmured.

"Not many get past fourscore. This is the healthiest upland in the world, but few reach ninety, and no commoner has ever celebrated his hundredth birthday."

"Yet there are centenarians in the slums and workhouses of London."

"None here, sir. There is no disease in pure air, but there's death. The wind which cured you killed others. Anybody would be the better for ten years of Dartmoor, but the worse for twenty years. Fighting the wind wears a body out. You have seen plenty of men drunk with liquor. Have you ever seen one the worse for wind?"

"You are the very man I have been looking for," cried Anger.

"A small one, sir," said the tradesman, not without a slight inflation of the chest. "Taught by the atmosphere we walk through, and fed by what spoonfuls of knowledge I could swallow in my youth. But now I am well past fifty, and another twenty years will fill my time up. Twenty more bluebell mists—nothing at all, sir. Nothing but twenty dreams."

"You would like more?"

"Yes, sir. I should like a second innings. I should not tire of the game. It's a grand one if you keep the rules. Give me one more June at the age of twenty, and I would suffer any number of Decembers. We may live for only a portion of our time—you know that time, when we go out tingling all over—but, by heaven, sir, we do live then; that time makes up for everything. When I am asked, 'Is life worth living?' I merely answer, 'Are you worth life?'"

"The best men go to trade," declared Anger. "Your place is in the study helping misery to bear its burden. The man who has it in him to preach a happy doctrine, which is also true, comes far before the doctor and the priest. I say the priest, because he may only use set phrases, he is forced to walk in the rut, he remains a machine and must never be a son of Nature. You are free, happy Mr. Woodland."

"Are you not free, sir?"

"Not yet; I have all these dreams about me. But when I do awake I may find the chains have fallen off."

The little man started, but continued to gaze ahead, and immediately continued, "You place me too high. I am in public life a bustling tradesman. It is only when I take these walks I can allow myself to think of poetry. This is my study, sir. Cut up these blocks of granite and build them around me as walls, and you will find a very dull companion."

"Your question is still in my mind. I have not seen a man drunk with the wind, but I know it is possible," cried Anger. "I have been drunk myself; I have reeled about the rocks shouting; I have answered invisible companions, and spoken to beings who have no existence; but this intoxication is not harmful."

"Did you not find it made you inclined to speak rashly, and to act upon the impulse?" asked Woodland gently.

"To make mistakes," mused Anger. "Why, there's some truth in that. I have these ideas as well as you, but they remain latent somehow. Your suggestion brings them out."

"You told me, sir, you were here for your health," Woodland went on. "You have been ill. My own eyes tell me you are cured. We are still discussing Youlstone air," he added.

"Never since boyhood have I known such health," cried Anger. "I feel strong enough to break chains. And only a few months ago I was tottering at the very edge of the grave, a thin, shivering creature without a spark of courage in me."

"Youlstone air!" exclaimed Woodland. "It can work miracles."

"I was not cured here," said Anger. "I have been beyond, in the parish of Wyld. There is a big rounded hill beside the village, and that healed me. It hung over my bed, breathing new life into me."

"I fancied you had been the whole time in this parish," said Woodland.

"I might have recovered here more quickly. Wyld air was like its name. It is softer here, more like food and drink. There is Wyld blood in me," declared Anger. "Now I am adding Youlstone air to make it gentler."

"You will think me curious," said the tradesman, "but may I ask you which place you would recommend for any sick person?"

"Youlstone, because it is more sheltered, and much more beautiful, than Wyld. Had I known of this place I would have come to it at once."

"You understand that the village is not yet well known."

"It is very much in the dark," said Anger in a startled voice, adding, with the same surprise: "You have a message for me."

They had reached the shadow of the wood. Appointing himself guide, Anger turned beside the river, away from the region to him enchanted, and they walked along a slope of turf towards a hill composed of titanic pebbles which had been cast there in confusion before the human mind had received its freedom.

"I have no message for you," the tradesman whispered, as if fearing lest wind and water might carry the echo of his voice to Riversmeet. "When we met upon a day which is memorable to me, I had just left Curgenven, and you were about to visit him. You asked me questions."

"And you shuffled," said Anger bluntly.

"I answered as well as I could, not having the opportunity to prepare myself. I suspended truth, but I told you no lies. As we left the village you made a remark——"

"That a certain pathway trodden through the wood must be a crooked one."

"Is it possible that Curgenven spoke too plainly?" Woodland murmured.

"I cannot hear you," complained Anger.

"You spoke of freedom just now; we tradesmen who live in a small town enjoy little of that; we wear a curb till we have made our fortune. You know how it was in the old days; a word spoken against the king was treason. Many a country town has its king; and a word against him means death to the speaker's reputation. Nobody fears the lord of the manor, the squire, or the parson; their day is over. The local king is the blackmailer."

"Let us give black its proper colour," said Anger. "You have come to put me on my guard; you wish to tell me Curgenven is a scoundrel. I know it."

"How you came to make the discovery is your own affair. Do not give too much credit to me, sir," said Woodland warmly. "I have not come to warn you so much as to relieve my mind. I am not one of those men who can carry a secret which implies a conspiracy against the lives of others. My motive is a selfish one; I have been guided by selfishness throughout my career, and now that I have done very well for myself, I should like to help the neighbourhood a little. Selfishness again very likely. We may give a hundred pounds to the building fund of some church, or a shilling to some beggar, caring nothing at all about the particular church or beggar, but conscious we are paying a premium towards good luck. Still, the church gets its bricks, and the beggar his beer. And by making you my confidant—confessing to you as if you were a priest—I may be helping Youlstone."

By force of habit Anger inclined his head and murmured gently, "Do not be afraid to speak."

"Climb with me to the top of those rocks. I want you to look out over."

They ascended, and from the summit, looking over the brow of the cleave, Woodland pointed out three large plats sloping westerly, entirely free of stone. In the lowest appeared traces of a long-abandoned garden, and here were also two bare walls and remains of others.

"You mark those fields, sir?"

"I have walked across them, making a short cut," Anger answered. "They have been well cultivated, for the grass is long and rich."

"Now let us go down," said the nervous tradesman.

They returned to the former level, and when standing opposite an eyot covered with golden and fading fronds of osmunda, symbol of dreams, Woodland continued, "A pretty little property, if far from a road. One hundred years of labour have been given to those fields. They belong to Curgenven."

"Preach upon that text," muttered Anger.

"He lets those fields to a farmer upon a yearly tenancy. I am about to tell you why he will not sell them."

"I would like to know how much he gave for them."

"The former owner was a rough, illiterate commoner, rather too much in the bar-room, but with no other fault worth mentioning. He dealt with me and I found him honest. But he could not resist Curgenven's offer of a loan, understanding nothing whatever about the law of mortgages, or the necessity of paying interest, or indeed of raising a new loan to pay off a former one. When the blow fell, and he came to mention he could not pay a few shillings which he owed me, the truth slipped out. Those four acres cost Curgenven fifteen pounds. I could only assure the man that as his ancestors had paid no money for the land, which they broke back from the moor, fifteen pounds were quite a fair price for the hundred years of labour."

"Did he not warn the other commoners? Could he feel no resentment against Curgenven?" cried Anger.

"These men are close to each other when it comes to any dealing with a lawyer," answered Woodland. "The poorer the commoner, the deeper his independence. How can they have any feeling against Curgenven when he is always blessing and helping them, when he is in and out of their homes, present at every marriage and funeral, godfather at every baptism, and sometimes stuffing little presents in their hands? When they lose their fields they believe Curgenven at least has not benefited. The land they regard as useless to him, as he is not a farmer, and at present there is no demand for fields in Youlstone. They only perceive he has lost his money. He would sympathise and say something like this, 'Well, my dear, 'tis a cruel bad business. You ha' lost, and I ha' lost. We'm partners in misfortune, but here's a shilling or two to comfort ye.

I'll share wi' the neighbours while I have a few pounds left.' Now, sir, you begin to comprehend Curgenven."

"I know all this. I seem to have overheard him talking in his office," muttered Anger; then added strongly, "I will report him to the Law Society."

"You must do nothing of the kind, sir; not unless you are prepared to leave the place, change your name, and hide for the rest of your life. Besides, what would be the use? Neither you nor the Law Society could collect a scrap of evidence against Curgenven. Who would whisper suggestions against his honesty either here or in Riversmeet? The very men he has defrauded call him righteous. Curgenven is the idol of the people, and the man who throws stones at him must know how to run. If a farmer likes to part with his property for fifteen pounds, and does not even think he has been cheated, the more fool he. The solicitor has done nothing illegal. The victim would declare he understood the terms of the mortgage perfectly; touch a commoner in the matter of ignorance and you tread on his tenderest corn. It's the old story, sir, of the cunning man among the simpletons. Youlstone will become enlightened one of these days, but so far those who have profited by education emigrate, while the old and the dull stay on; and tradition dies hard with them. Now, sir, for the matter which brings me here." And he went on to tell all he knew of "Youlstone Limited."

"A good scheme," said Anger, when the little man had finished. "A town for the old village, and weak bodies in the place of strong ones. Again I declare I had these ideas, but they remained latent, and your suggestion has brought them out."

"The idea is good," said Woodland. "I fully believe that by investing in this undertaking, without scruples, I should come out richer than I went in. However, my scruples remain, and it is there Curgenven has the advantage."

"There is nothing illegal in his action either."

"Why, no, sir. On the surface it is all straightforward bargaining, and Curgenven is going to make sure nobody will ever find out what happens below."

"Is not this Palk a dark bearded man, a doctor? I have seen him somewhere."

"An average doctor, a clever surgeon although nervous, but simple as a man. He will follow Curgenven's lead."

"You have thought over the matter," Anger went on. "What decision have you come to?"

"I am prepared to move against the lawyer, but it will be necessary to work in the dark," Woodland answered. "I should have no objection to Curgenven getting a fortune out of Youlstone if he could work honestly, leave the village untouched, and pay a fair price for the land. He will do none of these things. He means to get hold of every field and building, with the exception of the church and vicarage which cannot be bought or stolen."

"Stealing a village is burglary on a big scale," muttered Anger.

"Magnificent, and unfortunately possible," said Woodland excitedly, bringing out his tin of snuff, enjoying two pinches, then offering the stimulant to Anger, who declined decidedly. "Nothing like snuff to rouse the brain," he went on. "It is useless to think of warning the commoners. They would not listen and Curgenven would hear of it. I can only act indirectly. I have the money, sir, I am the warmest man in the two parishes, and I am prepared to spend a large amount, some thousands I tell you, to preserve the homes of Youlstone. I shall lose nothing, for when the sense of duty drives it is always in the right direction. A little sharp practice pays, I have been told, and so it may be, a beggarly one and a half per cent; but honesty, sir, brings a certain five in the long run, and good nights besides."

"You are looking for the man," said Anger. "I am on the spot and will do as you advise."

"We are moving," said Woodland. "I will supply the money, sir, if you will give yourself. Will you stand forward as a speculator, interested in the development of this part of the country, and make the attempt to buy up Youlstone?"

"Proclaim open war against Curgenven!" exclaimed Anger.

"That's what it will come to. I cannot do it because I have my boys to think of."

"Have you not already made yourself his enemy?"

"He hopes I shall change my mind. He would not fight me unless he knew I was opposing him."

"If Curgenven supposes I am a wealthy man?"

"He will try to win you over by explaining you would do far better in partnership with him. Failing that he will use his shoulders."

"What can he do?"

"I should advise you not to walk too much in lonely places."

"I am on your side, Mr. Woodland," said Anger.

"Thank you, sir. To-morrow I will go to Exeter and have an interview with the head of a firm of solicitors who conduct their business as I have always tried to conduct mine. The name of the firm is Lyson and Wiggaton; I tell you, as you may soon expect to hear from them."

"Names of my friends," cried Anger.

"I shall explain everything to Mr. Lyson, and will mention it is my desire to buy all Youlstone, but he is to deal with you as principal," Woodland went on. "I don't say that we shall succeed, as Curgenven is sure to warn the commoners that you have evil designs against them, but he won't dare to go too far when he has Lyson to deal with; and the commoners, like most men, will listen to the voice which promises them the most. In any case we can force Curgenven to submit to stalemate; for if he calls in his mortgages we step in."

"You are sure he has mortgages?"

"Certain of it. I have a strong idea that all Youlstone, with the exception of church property, is in bond to him."

Stiniel as well, thought Anger. That is my own affair. "I will work with you gladly," he said. "If we succeed, what will you do with the property?"

"Play at hazard with it," said the tradesman. "I shall leave the village as it is and gamble with the fields surrounding. Youlstone's long sleep is nearly over. We would awaken it to fame; our rival to ruin. When Curgenven developes his side of the lane, we will develop ours. Competition will not hurt us, but it must harm him, for when he puts down five hundred pounds I will put down one thousand. We will keep him busy, I promise you. 'Youlstone Limited,' with its capital of three thousand, shall find itself confronted by the 'Youlstone Development Company, capital twenty thousand.'"

"One question, if I may ask it," said Anger. "Have you any personal feeling against Curgenven?"

"I hate his methods, sir. You can keep within the law, and yet be a villain. Human nature is so diversified that it would require an eternity of law-making to control it against wrong-doing. The men who live by their wits, to use the common expression, are far more clever than the legislators. There was never a law which some rascal could not frustrate, except the *lex talionis*; simplicity made that perfect. You can struggle through a complicated hedge, but you can't climb a plain brick wall. Curgenven breaks all the rules of decent living, which I have done my best to keep, and I mean to show him my way is the best. You may leave me, sir, with the idea that I am a man of great conceit. I admit it; I am proud of myself. I was given a shabby education, and I inherited what was little better than a bankrupt business. My father used to tell me political economy wouldn't help to sell china, and he may have been right, but it taught me there are other things in the world besides china. Now, sir, my sense of duty, which is not a possession I am proud of since I had nothing to do with the making of it, calls me back to Riversmeet. You shall hear from me soon."

"No, I am not a mason," said Anger, when Woodland made a sign.

"It is a good warrant of assistance anywhere. Well, sir, good day and thank you. I return to my business more easy in my mind than when I left it."

Woodland bowed and was soon lost to sight among the furze-bushes, while Anger followed presently towards the hut, understanding why everybody spoke so highly of Curgenven, comprehending also the position of Petronel. She was mortgaged along with Stiniel to the lawyer; and that was the peril Anger could now avert. He had the money, and when Curgenven had been paid his power would leave him. "I am now the master of Youlstone," he mused. "I, the despised stranger, have the commoners in my hands. I am to bring the light of civilisation here, and when it comes, why then, we shall all wake up."

The hut was indeed well occupied. Nicholas sat upon a stone with his boots against the glowing logs; while Petronel was knitting in a matter-of-fact way, looking for her a trifle pale, and showing no warmth as she glanced up, nodded at her lover, and merely remarked, "I thought you were never coming."

"I have waited a long time for you," Anger reminded her. "I am late to-day because I made a longer round."

Nicholas looked up and put out his hand. He seemed disposed to be merry as he called, "Good day to you, Mr. Anger. You see I can keep a promise, though you do not want me here; but then a father must look after his daughter if he can."

"How is Mrs. Vigar?" asked Anger.

He could see Petronel was smiling. Presently she broke into a laugh, cheerful like the noise of the river, yet harsher.

"Mrs. Vigar is fast asleep," said Nicholas drily. "We saw it coming on early this morning."

"She was yawning," murmured Petronel.

"By noon her drowsiness became pronounced," Nicholas went on. "Soon afterwards she fell into a peaceful slumber which is likely to last for some time."

"Tell him at once the old brute is drunk," cried Petronel in a sudden passion.

"Do not speak like that," Anger pleaded.

"It is quite true," said Nicholas, in the same merry fashion. "My wife is a brute, and she is drunk. Could I put it more plainly?"

"It seems to me we are going to be natural," said Anger. "I am with you, Mr. Vigar; I will speak as plainly. Nobody can hear us."

"Whippety is beside the river with a jay he has tamed," said Petronel. "If anybody should come near, the bird will scream to the boy, and the boy will howl to us. It is all very natural," she added, looking at him gravely.

"I wonder sometimes whether I should have met you had I not drunk the sleeping water," he murmured.

"Oh, why?" she cried, while Nicholas kept on chuckling.

"Because you remind me of the moorland through which I walked that day."

"Very good, sir. Very well put, but not very kind," said Nicholas. "Dartmoor does its best to kill us three days out of five."

"It was meant to be kind."

"I like it," declared Petronel. "No man could have paid me a better compliment. Serious, serious," she whispered, narrowing her eyes at Anger.

"So is my love," he whispered back, while Nicholas slapped a flat hand on his knee.

She was more nymph-like, softer, and had a flush of beauty almost delicate, as if she had worn out her strength. A pallor beneath the peat-brown of the skin restored to her face the romance which had not been present since that night in mistland. She was tender then as at Stiniel defiant; in the wood careless first, afterwards melting; and now she seemed anxious. What was the constant epithet he could apply to her?

"I have not changed, Mr. Vigar," said Anger, looking away from the man who was just then grotesque. "Now that you have come at last with Petronel, I shall ask her in your presence if I may join her life with mine," glancing at her fingers busy with woolwork as he spoke. "Her head is down. That is a good sign," he mused.

"I cannot look at you. I am counting stitches," she said.

He went up to her and cried heedlessly, "Tell me now that you hate Curgenven."

"No; why should I?"

"At least you would not marry him?"

"Now you are teasing me."

"Remember what you told me."

"I do. I won't be bought. I shall not marry him."

"She always keeps her word," piped Nicholas—somewhat sadly, Anger thought.

"I will make it impossible," he cried. "The day after I came to Stiniel I visited Curgenven, knowing nothing about him except that he is the patron saint of Youlstone. I went to ask him whether it is possible by law to restrain Mrs. Vigar——"

"You dared!" cried Petronel.

"Strangers dare anything, my dear," said Nicholas.

"Curgenven assured me that what I mistook for cruelty was, in fact, self-protection," Anger went on. "He piled lie upon lie to make me believe that the daughter—pardon me, Petronel—was no better than a murderess."

"Nobody except myself understands him," said Petronel quietly. "He makes towards his own end in a peculiar way. Listening to him, you must remember he may not hate the person he abuses, but by a show of hatred he is trying to mislead his listener."

"He declared you had murdered your brother Bertram."

"Ah, did he?" She gave a moan, and brushed a hand across her eyes. "He went too far. He must have lost his temper."

"I am afraid you will remember that, my dear," sang Nicholas.

"It is down against him," she said simply.

"What I am about to add will sound ridiculous," continued Anger. "He told me to clear away the brambles behind that wall——"

"So it was you," she murmured.

"Then to confront Petronel with what I discovered, ask her the meaning, gaze into her eyes."

"Well," she said, looking up. "What do you see?"

"My own life and happiness," he said loyally. "I only mention this to give you a full-length portrait of the villain. I found bones in the sand, and portion of a dress."

"What possessed the man to talk so wildly?" cried Nicholas, dropping the merry mood. "Bones of sheep and ponies are to be found anywhere on the moor, and as for rags they get blown into secret corners."

"Temper," she said. "I have seen him like that."

"Curgenven hid those bones himself," declared Anger. "I have a feeling they are human, and to make sure I have taken one and will submit it to an expert when I have the chance."

"They had better be cleared out, my dear. Such bones are nasty things to lie about," said Nicholas nervously.

"They do not trouble me," said Petronel. "Don't you understand

Curgenven now?" she went on, looking half impatiently at Anger, her fine face as open as a printed page. "He regards you as an enemy, a rival if you like, and his abuse of me is meant to beat you. But he said too much. He does not believe that I—— Ah, he has bitten me at last. He said he would. You may smile now, for you have beaten him."

"I have not done," said Anger. "Now, Mr. Vigar, what is this idea of selling your daughter? Why do you fear Petronel may remember Curgenven's vilest lie? You are her father, not his agent. Do you defend the man who would be glad to bring you into misery?"

"Never mind me, sir. Do not listen to me. My talk is nonsense," muttered Nicholas.

"If you will not speak sense I'll dictate it to you."

"Family secrets, sir. Respect them, if you please."

"I will root them out of their cupboards," threatened Anger.

"Nothing, sir; nothing to you, even as a son-in-law," declared Nicholas. "I am a commoner, and I'll keep my independence."

"You have lost it long ago," said Anger scornfully. "You, and all Youlstone, have permitted yourselves to be governed and oppressed by a creature with half a body and no soul. I'll dictate your answers to my questions. You have played into the hands of Curgenven. I cannot tell how much you owe him, but I do know that your property is mortgaged from the grass you tread on to the slates that keep the rain off your head, that Curgenven is threatening to deprive you of Stiniel, and the price of the redemption of those mortgages is the life and happiness of your daughter."

"It's no use talking. Strangers know everything," said Nicholas feebly.

"Guesswork is easy after a hint. The hold your wife has upon you is equal to the hold she has upon Curgenven."

"What makes you say that?" asked Petronel.

"Reason."

"As near the truth as water is to ice," moaned Nicholas.

"Your wife arranged these mortgages. She forced you to sign," Anger went on. "Talk no more about liberty, Mr. Vigar, for you are a prisoner in your own house. Give me the figures."

"I am a poor man, but money won't buy me," cried Nicholas, trying to show spirit.

"Yet you would sell your daughter," said Anger bitterly.

"I must save Stiniel," said Petronel, beckoning Anger to her side, then laying a soft persuasion on him with her hand. "I am fond of the dark old place; I was a child there, and it's home. If I had married Curgenven, all would have been square, but he would have lost—I don't say what. Believe me now, I hate him."

"Come here, sir! Here, Mr. Anger!" cried Nicholas. "Who talks of property? Didn't I tell you I had money put away, a sum saved for the boy, and now it's for Petronel. I have two hundred pounds. Don't laugh at it; a little bit of money, but a fortune in Youlstone. I have known a man lose his head over ten pounds."

"Why did you borrow, having this money?"

"It was my mother's work. You told him so," cried Petronel.

"Mrs. Vigar did have something to do with it," confessed Nicholas. "She knows nothing about the nest-egg. That's safe in the post office. I will draw the money out and give it to Petronel on her wedding-day."

"Tell me the amount of your debts."

"Speak the truth, father. There is more than one."

"Yes, a little family of mortgages, growing up fast, getting mature. There was one, then another, and so they ran on; five in all, sir, and each for one hundred pounds."

"How were you going to raise five hundred pounds? You can hardly scrape a living out of Stiniel."

"'Tis a mystery how one does live," said Nicholas pleasantly. "I can't tell how neighbour Billacott manages to go on. I fancy he does it on potatoes."

"Think of yourself. How could you ever pay your debts?" said Anger.

"That is Mrs. Vigar's business. Leave these things to the women, sir. They will not settle, but you can forget."

"I thought myself a poor man of business, still I can teach you," went on Anger. "It seems to me the commoners of Youlstone are children, taking pocket-money from their master, and never dreaming of a day of settlement."

"They put off pay-day until to-morrow," said the girl plainly. "And so it goes on until they die."

"To borrow money, or to accept a loan, knowing it means the sacrifice of home, is the act of a madman," said Anger. Then he approached Nicholas, and laying a hand on the farmer's shoulder, shuddering when he felt much bone and little flesh, went on clearly, "Whether Petronel consents to marry me or not, the offer I am about to make holds good. I will pay off your debts, or if you prefer it I will purchase Stiniel upon the understanding that you remain as my tenant. The transfer must be made at once. Which shall I take over, Mr. Vigar; the mortgages or Stiniel?"

A quiver passed through Nicholas. Turning, Anger saw Petronel looking towards him with admiration, her hands and her knitting upon her lap. Never had he seen her in so fine an attitude; serious and longing to be free, leaning forward conscious of approaching liberty, straining towards him from the bonds which held her. She reminded him then of the upland being released from winter by the warmth of the first spring day.

"You know what this means, father," was her cry.

"I am scarcely a religious man," Nicholas muttered. "But I do believe God meddles with us sometimes."

"You and I are free," cried Petronel.

"You must sell," said Anger, beginning to tremble with excitement. "Then you cannot sign another mortgage."

"Not leave old Stiniel. Take the mortgages, sir, and let me have my home."

"Sell, father. I will see to the rest," said Petronel, going to him. "It is settled," she cried to Anger. "He sells. Stiniel is yours."

"The price, Mr. Vigar."

"Eight hundred pounds," said Petronel. "Say nothing, dad. Do you know what you are doing, man of all men? I'll not call you stranger any more. You are paying my debts as well as his."

"And you, Petronel? If I buy Stiniel and give it to you? Mr. Vigar, do you consent?"

"Let the maid answer," said Nicholas, leaning over the fire and in a sudden fury of excitement scattering the logs with his half-baked boot.

"Will you, Petronel, let me give you your own home?"

"Catch!" she cried, throwing him the ball of wool. "Stand over against the wall while I knit and think. Hold the wool tightly."

Anger did as he was told, delighting to humour her fancy. Seating herself again she went on knitting, her face aglow, her lips moving with her fingers, murmuring in sheer delight; and soon the strand of wool between them tightened, and Anger was drawn one step towards her; while Nicholas with his back towards them warmed his flesh in silence.

"What are you knitting?" Anger asked.

"Something for you," she answered.

"There was another question," he reminded her.

"You shall have the answer as fast as my needles will knit it."

So she went on drawing him towards her by the thread of wool. The sacking being well drawn back, the hut was filled with a cold clear light, while moisture stood upon the walls. All the surroundings were charged with the solemn roughness of the winter season. This game required a warmer time, a different setting. It might have been played in the drawing-room of the Wiggatons, when the curtains had been drawn, and the lights were burning brightly. In this miserable place, with harsh furze-prickles scraping the stones, and the old man huddled over the fire, apparently lifeless, it was somehow tragic, for it suggested the playing of a tender comedy before dark hangings.

"Keep your hand down," she whispered.

Only a yard divided them. Petronel drew in her feet, then knitting her fastest brought the lover to her knees, and raising her hands to the level of his eyes worked on until he could come no nearer; and then the wool fell noiselessly, she passed her arms about his neck, and closing her eyes whispered, "Yes" and kissed him; while Nicholas knew little of these things; and the wool settled at Anger's feet as a tangled skein.

CHAPTER XI

SATURNALIA

IT appeared that a ceremony known as "Tasting the Cider" was observed each year upon the second Saturday in December; a form of revel not found elsewhere, and having its origin possibly in some pagan sacrifice to the god of agriculture. Why such a custom confined itself to Youlstone, a village well above the fruit-line, was not clear. During early morning the barrels were brought up in a decorated cart, driver and horses decked with ribbons; and any parishioner who called at the inn could taste without charge until the supply became exhausted; while the church bells kept on swinging to supply the sanctifying touch. Bells, which were silent upon many a Festival of the Church, rang their loudest in praise of that little pot-bellied old deity Silenus and his troop of satyrs.

Not that any drunkenness worth preaching at was seen while the light remained; after midnight came the rolling home, when the barrels were empty, and the next year's tenant of Lomyns' Furze had been elected. All the day people in their best black loafed about the street, tasting at intervals, talking about nothing and laughing at the same. Even the children tasted, because that was the custom, then walked in a procession singing hymns: a curious mess of religion, holiday, and apple-juice. The vicar, passing through with a geological hammer in his pocket, remembered the feast, forgot to ask himself the name of the saint, but merely murmured, "I like these old country festivals. They are so good for the morale."

The inn became noisy soon after midday, and Anger determined to go into solitude until dark. Passing the principal room, which was given over to the ceremonial, he perceived a small figure standing in the midst of the laughing men, and at once recognised the father of the people, now their jester, his gigantic head fantastically crowned with a wreath of evergreen, and further adorned with a false nose and comic spectacles. Curgenven was playing the fool for his purpose, telling funny stories to amuse the grown-up children and to make the chains of his parental authority lie upon them lightly. It was fitting, thought Anger, as he passed out, conscious that the pasteboard nose had been pointed at him, that the lawyer should play at carnival with his head, for this festival was a test of the head, and he who had the strongest took the prize, while Curgenven's was the head that ruled. There was some meaning beneath the madness.

For Anger there was only one road; it went by Stiniel and ended in desolation among lichened boulders and frosted heather. It was a pleasure to see the peat smoke from the last house that way. Nobody was to know of his engagement to Petronel, least of all her mother. Yet it was hard to believe that any action could provoke an avalanche, so peaceful were those surroundings in cold light: the simplest life, idyllic on the outside, the primitive little buildings, and, beyond, the silent moor mortgaged to winter.

"Stay at home, Bobby," called Anger, as there ascended from Quoditch the little dirty man, in trousers too large, coat too small, and a hard hat dented. Thirza was working in her usual rags, while the master went out to drink and play, announcing his intention without shame:

"Bide home! Why, schulemaster, you'm dafty. 'Tis revel day, and I be agoing to tell to the volks and make 'em laugh."

"They have one fool already. Curgenven is amusing them," said Anger heedlessly.

Bobby exchanged his grin for an expression almost fearful. Plunging his hands into pockets, which appeared to reach to his knees, he whispered, "Be you calling Curgenven a vule?"

"At this moment he is."

"My dear soul! A proper vule?"

"Who knows very well what he is doing."

"When I comes along you means to say there will be two vules!"

"A dangerous and a simple one."

"If that b'ain't the like o' calling me a vule, what be it?"

"You have reasoned it out," said Anger.

"Bide a bit," cried Bobby. "Schulemaster, you ha' insulted me. It b'ain't the first time neither. You comes to Youlstone to tell agin me, and you reckons I be vulish first time us met, and then I came along and beat you, and 'stead of lying quiet when you'm crushed you comes along on revel day and tells me agin, vor the second time, I be vulish, and you ses Curgenven be vulish, and you reckons, I fancy, 'tis mighty fine to be the only scholar in the world."

"You are going to the village," replied Anger. "You will taste cider until you are muddled; that is the act of a fool. You leave your wife to do the work; that is the act of a knave."

"I ha' done it vor twenty years."

"Then you are twenty times fool and knave. Turn back, Bobby Billacott. Go and do some work, or walk with me upon the moor."

"It b'ain't a work-day," said the farmer sullenly.

"That day is always to-morrow," said Anger.

"What's the gude of walking up on Dartmoor?"

"If you had a mind you would know."

"My mind be a proper one," said Bobby, somewhat staggered at the swiftness of the answers. "I'll crush ye with it to-morrow."

"I should like to open your eyes, Bobby," said Anger, in his preaching manner. "For the sake of your name I would help you; but so long as you remain in idleness, and keep your face set against education, you must remain a fool. Your ignorance places you at the mercy of any unscrupulous man. If I liked to rob you I could do so."

"How would ye do it?" asked Bobby, looking ugly.

"By employing Curgenven's methods." Bobby drew a hand from his pocket and wiped his grimy face, thinking of his hatred for Curgenven, which was inspired by terror, and the suggestions which Thirza had whispered; for the strong woman could see far deeper than the man.

"Look at the state of Quoditch, which may not be yours much longer," Anger went on. "You spend your days in idleness; you are in danger of becoming a drunkard; you may end a pauper. Unless you change your way of living I will have nothing more to say to you. Now go up to the village and get drunk."

These words cut, but could not conquer, Bobby; for he was a free man, settled upon his own soil in what was to him the centre of the universe, while his opponent was merely a barbarian. Besides, his pockets were full of money which he had not worked for and could never repay, but the feel of it made him a lusty fellow. "Aw, go your ways," he cried, looking from the retreating figure of his adversary to his mortgaged fields and the spectacle of Thirza toiling among the pigs. "You'm a vule and so I tells ye. I be a commoner, and I be agoing to drink, and I be agoing to make a bid vor Lomyns' Furze, which be a thing you can't do, vor you b'ain't a parishioner. Talking b'ain't all, schulemaster. Learning ain't no gude when you can't back it up wi' land. You'm a vule, schulemaster." He shouted again and again at the figure descending Quoditch Pinch, "You vule! You vule!"

Fanatical Protestants had been Anger's only enemies during the old life. The new state found him at war with a village and a town; the spirit of ignorance yelled behind, while the mind of oppression awaited him within that shape which was leaning against a menhir engraved with some rude characters of the Age of Stone.

"I left the creature far behind; now he is in front of me," murmured Anger when the voice of friendship called him. "A low comedian one moment, flying through the air the next, and now a country gentleman; but this new mask is like that pasteboard nose."

"A good nesting-place for an eagle," cried Curgenven. "I can sweep the village and see the dear people without glasses. There was a little drama just now between wisdom and ignorance, ending with the cry of fool upon both sides. Don't spoil that little saphead. His type is worth preserving."

"I am wondering how you came here. Did I not see you in the inn as I passed out?" asked Anger.

"Making the lads laugh," said the lawyer, pulling the false nose from his pocket. "I could have done a turn upon the stage. 'Tis a glorious thing folly; not your sharp and witty comedy, but sheer inanity. That catches everybody, except the philosopher with his everlasting toothache. Make a neat epigram and two people in a hundred laugh; clap a false nose on your face, and bray like an ass, and the ninety-eight split their sides. Popularity is the father of confidence, and popularity can always be won by playing the fool. The lawyer who can shout a comic song will get more clients than his rival who frowns with common law. How did I get here? While you walked round I cut across. And now we meet," cried the dwarf, waving his cap to the inscription on the column, "beside some relic of the worship of Baal-Dartmoor."

"Then you meant to meet me," said Anger.

"To return your call, which was not a business one unless you insist."

"I came on business, otherwise I should not, as a stranger, have entered your office."

"But I approach you as one man of the world seeking the companionship of another," said Curgenven. "'Tis a dull place, Riversmeet. Palk, my good friend, is one of the best sportsmen, but when I open my mouth in wisdom, such as 'tis, he will open his in sleep. There is no other except Woodland, good man, dear man, honest man, but dangerous, dangerous, ah yes, dangerous. Come! let us move for a mile or two, and set our blood in motion. This is my own ground. No mist baffles me. Blindfold and turn me about, but I will still make for home. Had I been with you that day you were lost——"

"I should never have reached Youlstone," finished Anger.

"I did not say that. Youlstone or Wyld—I would have brought you on a bee-line. We are glad you found us out. The folk like you. They appreciate a quiet man who does not interfere with them. 'Tis the meddler they rise against. Turn this way, and you smell the Atlantic clear from the coast to the banks of Newfoundland. Turn again, and you get upon your face the wind off twenty miles of the sweetest upland in God's world. 'Tis pity human beings should quarrel in this atmosphere. One good smell is lacking," and Curgenven, producing cigars, held out one.

"I am no smoker," said Anger, shrinking from this pasteboard friendship.

"Then you lose. The man who can rise to the level of a good cigar, and is never sick upon the sea, has no need to pray for blessings. Money—yes! But any fool can get money. We have all got heads and hands. Getting money is like learning to swim: a splash, a bit of a struggle, then all is easy, and we have nothing to fear except cramp, cold currents, jellyfish, and sharks."

"We are going uphill. You are walking too fast for me," protested Anger.

"I like to go up. It gives me the right feeling. The wind gets stronger near the clouds. Then comes the dash downhill which makes you tingle."

"I am surprised to hear you call Mr. Woodland a dangerous man. I had formed a very good opinion of him," said Anger warily.

"The best fellow in Riversmeet, but too keen a sportsman. Hunts the game too close. Gives nobody else a chance. So he has found you out," Curgenven chuckled. "Little Jimmy Woodland has a rare nose for the scent."

"I approached him," said Anger. "I needed information which he gave."

"And he happened to cross your path. That's his way, a very good one, and his own. He marked you down. Quite right. Good business, tell him so from me, but mighty dangerous when he starts to shoot—never misses though the bird may be nearly out of sight."

"But why dangerous?" asked Anger.

"A rich man, Jimmy Woodland—an honest, a red-hot, man, and, mind you, one of the best. But I have found that when a man is fortunate himself he brings bad luck to others. Suppose Jimmy asks a friend to stand in with him, what happens? He comes out richer, while the friend may find himself in a fix. Jimmy has too much money, he is always trying to find a good investment, and for that purpose he is fond of tackling people and asking their advice. If he has a fault it is this; he is a little shy of being principal. I tell you there is no more honest man alive, but he has a trick of making corners. Quite right, but it makes him dangerous. Jimmy knows I regard him as dangerous. So is a twenty-thousand pound hammer to the apprentice who meddles with it."

Anger stole a glance at the diminutive figure which was advancing with quick strides and elf-like hops, bending beneath the natural pack upon its shoulders. The face, which was very similar in colour and texture to the red rock common to the cliffs upon the moor, was bright with good-fellowship, and stubbornly strong, but not clever. Those eyes did not flash with intellect. Therefore Anger came to the conclusion he had nothing but a narrow-minded rascal to wear down.

"Point out to me the direction of the magic pool which still contains the enchantments of the Middle Ages," Curgenven rattled on, satisfied by Anger's reserve that the tradesman had nibbled at him. "We must ride out one day with dear old Palk— not with Jimmy Woodland; he would bottle the water, offer it for sale at the Stores, and his luck would do the rest; if the water was ordinary stuff from the clouds he would make a fortune out of it. You see how dangerous he is. He anticipates everybody with that keen commercial mind. He has ruined half the tradesmen in Riversmeet. Quite right. 'Tis business. I should do the same."

"I don't know how we stand," said Anger.

"Going south-east. Yonder is the way to Wyld."

"Then the pool lies midway. I shall not visit it again. It is best to clear our minds of legends," said Anger.

"Why should we regard it as a legend?" cried Curgenven. "Even humbug must have a root to grow from. Deception is one of the secrets of success. Call a pill a pill, and nobody would buy it. Swear that it contains the elixir of life, and the public will buy because they want to be deceived. We live by deception, and we die deceiving ourselves."

"Not all of us," murmured Anger.

"Every man and woman," declared the lawyer. "The priest deceives his people with romances; the tradesman sells rubbish as first-class goods; the doctor tells the dying patient he will be about in a week or two; the lawyer is the worst of the lot, he is the prince of deceivers, he makes his living by swearing sinners are saints. The biggest rascal can hear himself described as an angel of light if he possesses a few guineas. I am a rogue, my dear; you have guessed as much already. Suppose I see a man committing a murder, and suppose later on I am engaged as the solicitor for that man's defence. It is my duty to save him from the gallows, and I am going to lie to the last to do it. This sort of thing is called straight-forward dealing. It is understood that we are all deceivers, and so the biggest trickster wins the world's best honours. To return to the mud-hole. There are such things as medicinal springs, and why should we not find one upon Dartmoor?"

"The pool of the Nymph is water and romance," said Anger. "Romance in a bottle can have no value. Let the doctor analyse the stuff if he wants to." Then he went on to describe the pool and its surroundings.

"A pleasant journey on a fine day. A nice jaunt for lazy people," said Curgenven. "Make a pilgrimage to the mystic pool, drink and live—or go to sleep. It is my hope that the village below will prosper some day," he went on lightly. "Woodland may have told you."

"I believe you suggested it yourself," said Anger.

"Very likely. It is much in my mind. Observe the wonderful colour of these mosses. Youlstone is far healthier than any of the popular watering-places. Do you think of settling?"

"For a time certainly. The place attracts me," replied Anger, keeping his wits about him.

"And the people?"

"Interest me."

"You must stay," cried Curgenven. "When we catch a good man we do not let him go. I have one or two fields down there— see them sloping towards the edge of the cleave two hundred feet above the wood. Why not have one—cheap to a friend—and run up a neat house?"

"I shall think about it," said Anger quietly.

"Time is on your side. Under forty a man should build; over forty he should buy. My fear is this," said Curgenven earnestly.

"While longing to improve the place, I have not the means, for my type of rascality has not made me fat—not in the sense of Jimmy Woodland's good round stomach—and it is possible I may be forestalled by some wealthy man who might treat the villagers harshly, get them out of their homes, deprive them of necessary fields. Dear old Jimmy believes I am capable of doing this. I love the place and its people. I regard the village as my home and its inhabitants as my relations. If a woman has the toothache she must come to me about it. When a man loses a distant connection he must have my sympathy. These pleasant relations must never be disturbed. If any outsider tries to hurt my people I will fight him to the last. Our little Jimmy Woodland has a remarkably glib tongue."

"He has," agreed Anger.

"I thought as much," Curgenven murmured to himself. "You are getting tired of my company," he said aloud. "I do not interest you. To be plain, you do not like me. My shape does not appeal to you."

Anger shook himself together. He was about to fight this man, but some weeks must pass before the challenge could be issued. All he could say was, "I remember our first meeting."

"When you found me in an ill-humour. I gave you advice, not as a client, but as a friend. I guessed something feminine detained you in Youlstone, but was I not right? Why, are you ashamed, my dear?" he asked in a tender voice. "You accept the romance of the sleeping water. Why shrink from the romance of life?"

"You told me a shameful story about Petronel," said Anger strongly.

"Christian name already! You are past advice," said the dwarf, beginning his big laugh. "Where would you expect to hear shameful stories if not in a lawyer's office? Could you look into the documents wrapped up in cobwebs inside my strong-room, you would find secret histories which might make you blush for your fellow-creatures. My business is to keep such matters secret, and to warn others from getting mixed up in similar affairs. One associates tragedy with this open moorland," he went on carelessly. "It is hard upon the upland, and yet amidst lonely surroundings it is not difficult to commit a crime and escape the consequences."

"I am as firmly persuaded as ever I was that Miss Vigar is as good as she is beautiful," said Anger firmly.

They were now striding down-hill towards the village, and the shouts of revellers made themselves heard.

"You shall marry her," cried Curgenven, laughing furiously. "Decidedly you shall marry her. Buy one of my fields, build your house, take your bride, and let the future be all roses, apple-blossom, and forget-me-nots."

"Why the last?" muttered Anger, who was drawing a little way ahead.

"Did you not discover in that old shaft bones wrapped in a woman's skirt?"

"Bones of a sheep," cried Anger.

"Do ewes wear petticoats? Dry bones do not go with orange-blossom, but let that pass. Good-luck to you, my dear, Woodman's luck!"

"I have heard a report that once you proposed to marry her yourself," said Anger, stung by the other's manner.

"It was Mrs. Vigar's idea, not mine," replied Curgenven, laughing still louder. "You won't believe she abuses the white-haired lady. Quite right. You love her. You are for the defence. Go your way, my dear," he said, repeating Bobby's phrase. "I tried to warn you, I would have held you back, but if love leads you must go. Cupid has two shafts to his bow and one of 'em is a poisoned arrow, but they both strike in the same way. Buy the land—you shall have it cheap as a wedding-present from an old friend—and marry the murderess——"

"Mr. Curgenven, I'll hear no more of that. It is a vile charge, a vile lie, from the lips of a vile man."

Anger had stopped and was standing in a blind passion, shaking both hands towards the laughing dwarf, who hopped forward pleading, "No, no, my dear. No bad words between good sportsmen. Deception must be practised. A lover may say anything. Others may regard him as a madman. Quite right to curse me. I'm a rogue, but I wish you well. Take my hand. It's hairy but I can't help that."

"I will not touch you," shouted Anger. "Let there be no false feeling between you and me. I hate you, and that's the truth of it. You meant to have Petronel, get her somehow, treat her like a brute, and you speak these vile lies to frighten me away from her. I'll beat you—I have beaten you. She has promised to be my wife."

"Come, come!" said the lawyer, always laughing. "Let us walk on a bit without words. So this is love. I have seen the real thing, and it's fine. I'll bring no more charges against Miss Vigar. We will go down into the village, taste some cider, drink her health. Walk along, Anger, walk straight. Hate me," he muttered, ceasing his laughter. "Why, everybody loves old Curgenven."

"I cannot speak to you now. If I have said too much I will try to apologise; I do not remember what I said," Anger whispered with difficulty. "But I must be alone now."

He went off at full speed down the side of the moor, his head in a heat and his heart beating wildly; while Curgenven stayed and looked after him, cold and rigid like the red rock of the quarry, and muttering Bobby Billacott's last words, "You fool! You fool!"

There was no sign then of the revel, apart from men shouting against each other beneath Anger's room, and all that remained to round off the day was done in secret. Excluded from the common life, the visitor, after partaking of a meal badly cooked and smelling of apple-juice, was driven again by disturbances into the street which was full of clouds. His mood was still tempestuous. An idea came to make for the hut and spend a night away from those voices; but he mistrusted the wild boy. So he kept to the usual track, and had gone some fifty paces across the common when a loud voice reached him out of cloudland, "Hi! Stop my cow!"

Anger became conscious of a rough pony cantering upon the turf, snorting and wild-eyed; after it a figure reeling from side to side, waving a stick, using language never printed, one who had obviously tasted and gone again. Only Bobby had a head so round as if a lathe had fashioned it. Anger felt his wrath increasing, as the little farmer looped his boot in a bramble and became a lump upon the ground, still yelling, "Stop my cow!"

"No cow is here. You have been chasing a pony," he said fiercely.

Bobby had risen; he staggered to and fro stammering, "Where be the cart I fell out of? Didn't us go over something? 'Twas a fearful bump vor certain."

"You came here on your fool's feet," said Anger.

"I wur driving the old cow home. Where's her to, master?"

"Gone with the cart and your senses."

"That's a vunny old thing to say. My dear life, if it b'ain't the vule," stuttered Bobby. "Give me you hand, vule. Let's be telling to each other free and easy. Us had words, but us b'ain't enemies. Us be brave two of a trade chaps. I ha' tasted the cider, vulemaster. I ha' done my duty and I b'ain't mazed yet. Where's my old cow to?"

"Keep away," said Anger roughly.

"Don't ye be peevish," implored Bobby. "One word leads to another when scholars get to telling. If one ses, 'You'm a vule,' t'other answers, 'The like to you.' 'Tis the proper law of argument. If you ses to me, 'You'm vull o' learning,' I ses the like to you, and if I don't you spit at me. That's how 'tis between scholars. I ha' lost the old cow vor certain. Her broke through the hedge and be gone abroad, and Thirza be waiting wi' pail to milk she. Shall us ever get home to-night? I ha' tasted, and I ha' no fault to find except 'twur gritty to bottom o' barrel. Oh, dear, schulemaster, I be got so windy wi' the trade, and I ha' sour apples in my nose, but I ain't done yet. Where be my old cow to? When I fell out o' cart I missed she. I could hear she snoring in the mists beyond, when the tail o' cart slipped, and old Jack wur saying, 'Mind out, Bobby. Us be going over the humpy bit.' Where did he go wi' the cart, master? I reckon he never missed me, vor I wur on behind. 'Twas after I left you my brother come along. He'm my uncle really, but I calls 'en brother. He ses, 'Jump in behind, Bobby, and us'll drive to Riversmeet and back avore Court time.' So I jumps in, and us drives off, but us never got no further than the inn, and I reckon us must ha' gone in and out, aw, and up and down, till us got a bit mixed like, and then I sees the old bullock going abroad, and I starts to drive she home. Come along wi' me, schulemaster, and let's ha' a taste avore I goes down to Court, but, aw my dear life, I won't never get Lomyns' Furze next year, vor I started a bit too quick like. Pity you b'ain't a parishioner. You'd get the plat easy. You could stand the tastes, I tell ye, vor here 'tis dimsy and you b'ain't mazed yet."

The little man might have babbled on an hour, but Anger could listen no longer. Passion, aroused by Curgenven, became reheated by this useless creature, glorying in ignorance, stammering nonsense, slobbering over him. Snatching his stick, he gripped the swaying farmer by the coat-collar, swung him round, and thrashed him well, exclaiming hoarsely, "This may make a man of you. I don't care who you are, whether you are a commoner or a hired labourer, but I'll cure you—that's for the fool in you."

It was a first-class hiding. Bobby scarcely cried out, but flung himself from side to side, gasping with pain, moaning with horror, cursing with shame, getting sober rapidly, striking out wildly, threatening terribly. The full significance of his act did not at the moment occur to Anger. A despised stranger and a townsman flogging a free and independent Dartmoor commoner! Such a thing had never been done before, nor even contemplated. Had there been witnesses to the dark deed on the misty common, the beater might have been expelled that hour from Youlstone with sticks and stones.

A gust of cold wind passed, staying Anger's arm. He dropped the rod, released his victim, and stepped back feeling frightened. Such violence was new, like the blood in him; never before had he been overwhelmed by passion; never had he dared to strike any man, nor even a mischievous boy. Yet he was unrepentant, and could still stare fiercely at the round-headed farmer, who had staggered into a furze-bush, and was beating his hands together, and moaning like the whipped child he was: "He ha' beat me wi' my own spear. Schulemaster ha' bruised my bones. Where be I? Master, find my old bullock, and let me go home. I be a commoner, I be a free man, I be owner of Quoditch, and he ha' beat me, he ha' bruised my buttocks, he ha' torn me all abroad."

"Go home," said Anger coldly. "If you turn towards the inn I will beat you again. You may be old enough to be my father, but I will treat you as a child, and teach you as one. Go home to bed. Get up and rebuild your hedges, and pay Curgenven what you owe him. I am your master, Bobby."

"I be cut to the heart, and that be broke," wailed Bobby. "Don't ye touch me, master. I can't bear it. Where be old Jack and the cart? I be bleeding to death, I be injured internally, and my hands be tored."

"Get away from the furze," said Anger more gently, taking hold of the farmer, who shivered and moaned afresh. "Nobody saw me beat you, and nobody will ever know. That is the way to Quoditch. Now go!"

He turned Bobby round and pushed him forward so sharply that the farmer fell forward upon hands and knees. Without another glance Anger returned to the village, while Bobby picked himself up and staggered home still crying, his little cowardly spirit crushed by the schoolmaster's rod. To speak of his shame was impossible; even Thirza, who could well have avenged that whipping, was not to be told.

Night had fallen. A few laughing women hung about the cloudy street, where some gaily dressed children were playing at carnival with lighted lanterns. Suddenly depressed by these attempts at merry-making, Anger entered the inn with the idea of going at once to bed, and immediately found himself among a group of men passing from the room where cider had been tasted, and making with uncertain movements towards a flight of steps which led below. Anger went with them unnoticed, for there was scarcely any light, and the men were heavy with liquor. Those behind forced him down the steps, along a passage, and into a cellar, damp and chilly, barely lighted by a smoky lamp hanging from a meat-hook in the roof. Anger blinked his eyes, then stared again as he lowered himself upon a common bench. If that night visit to Plymouth had been a dream, this was a nightmare. A trestle-table stood along the centre, half covered with glasses and huge crocks; and in the centre he saw a scrap of candle, unlighted, upon a piece of slate;

while near the table, along the floor of cement, appeared an ordinary lath which rattled as his feet touched it. The stranger recalled whisperings he had overheard that day concerning the Court of Lomyns' Furze. Now it was about to be held, in this cellar, and at the head of the table sat the president, the smallest man there, looking at Anger with calm and steady eyes.

"Curgenven again! He must be in everything," Anger muttered.

"What be you doing in here? You b'ain't a parishioner," inquired a voice beside him.

"I came with the crowd," said Anger moodily, and rose to go; but that moment the door was shut, and Curgenven rapped smartly upon the trestle.

"Time is up," he called. "Shoot the bolt, and let's get to business."

"There's a stranger here," cried several voices.

"Quite right. He is a witness," said Curgenven. "He is my friend, well known to many of you, and he is here by my especial invitation. He will soon be a parishioner, as he intends to build a house and settle in Youlstone. I appoint him my referee. Pass the candle."

The lawyer took a rule from the man nearest him, and after a moment stated, "One inch exactly. According to custom," he went on, "and for the benefit upon this occasion of our friend, I declare the meaning of this Court. It was established some two centuries ago by the will of one Lomyns, who bequeathed a field to the parishioners, to be held by one of them annually as a pasture, no commoner to enjoy the tenancy two years in succession. Lomyns, I presume, was a merry soul who loved his bottle, and the conditions he imposed were these. The Court was to be held in the strictest privacy; no minister of religion was to be present; at the word of the president one inch of wax candle was to be lighted; competitors were then to be called upon one by one to drink a glass of cider without staying to take breath; when the candle burnt out, the president was to test the condition of the competitors, and the most sober was to be declared tenant for the forthcoming year of Lomyns' Furze."

He lighted the candle, passed it to a man who placed it upon the piece of slate. A glass of cider was poured out, and Curgenven, bringing a list of names near his eyes, called, "James Griffey."

A competitor stepped forward grimly, took the glass, drained it, and returned to his seat, wiping his mouth.

"Peter Dummit."

Another stepped forward and drank.

"William Southcott."

This one lurched as he came forward and swallowed the draught with difficulty.

So it went on, while the flame of the lamp flared up the smoky glass, and on the table beneath the little ghastly candle shook its spear of light. Anger, leaning now against the wall, powerless as the sleeper to escape from the vision round him, watched Curgenven, then like a mountain gnome, and knew the lawyer was also watching him, smiling in a friendly way, yet taunting and mocking the guest, proclaiming his own mastership in Youlstone and his power over its inhabitants, putting Anger's courage to the test, daring him to challenge himself before these men to say by what moral or legal right he presided at that Court.

"See how easily I defeat you," those eyes seemed to say. "Even now, when I am in a sense playing into your hands, since no Court of Law would justify my present action, or uphold the will of Lomyns, you have not the courage to oppose me on my own ground, in the presence of my own people."

"How long will the candle burn?" Anger muttered, hardly conscious he had spoken aloud, until an unsteady voice replied to him, "Half an hour. Likely a bit more."

"James Griffey," called the merry Curgenven, beginning the second round.

Most of the men were smoking. The cellar was filled with blue clouds in addition to the reek of the lamp and the stench of cider; and yet it was cold. The floor was damp, the stone walls were dripping; the light of day never entered there. Anger began to gasp, then fell into coughing. Curgenven's face was swimming in mist. The flame of the candle looked blue.

This might have been a joke two hundred years ago, he thought, when men were rough and customs ruder, and drunkenness was accounted a thing to laugh at. If civilisation could do nothing more than introduce a better fashion, it was well worth bringing. Anger secretly renewed his vow to fight; he remembered how Bobby would be moaning in Quoditch over his bruises; the white strip of wood caught his eye. Presently the candle would gutter, the wick would fall, its light be extinguished; and then the terrible dwarf, playing with these drunken men as a potter plays with clay, would marshal them, and order them one by one to walk the lath, giving the field to the man who walked the straightest. It was a good old custom, but it could not last.

"James Griffey," came the call; and for the third time the competitors came forward.

Anger was on his feet, breaking free from these visions, believing himself at last awakened. He pushed men aside, stepped forward, threw out his arms trying to wave aside the smoke and see clearly the face of that grim president, calling as loudly as he could, "I cannot stay here."

"Go on!" cried Curgenven. "Stop for a moment, and you are all disqualified. Never mind my friend. He has drunk too much. This is new to him. He has lived among the ladies. Peter Dummit. Drink up, my sportsman!"

"I have no right to be here," cried Anger. "I am a minister of religion."

There was a movement and a muttering. The president called in vain, for all eyes were fixed upon Anger, and William Southcott forgot to answer to his name.

"Lomyns may be dead to you," the visitor cried on. "But what of his soul in purgatory? Will that ever be released while this Court is carried on?"

Curgenven rose from his chair, beginning his big laugh, then hopped forward, and brought a crock down on the candle.

"The Court is adjourned. It will not sit again," he cried. "My friend is right. It was getting out of date. We will find some other way of administering the will. My dear friend reminds us of souls in purgatory. We may not accept that doctrine, but then we are not members of the holy Roman Church, we are not priests, we are not Jesuits in disguise—splendid fellows all of them, and our friend the very best. The disguise is lawful. Our friend will tell you that, and I shall uphold him. We might even sing a hymn before we go."

The last sound heard was Curgenven's tremendous laughter. Some man, unseen, and no doubt drunk, struck Anger upon the back of the neck as he went out.

CHAPTER XII

LACRIMA SAXIFRAGA

THERE are dark hours in the year, but four o'clock of a morning in mid-December cannot be blackened. At that time Anger was aroused by a tapping upon the window, which he kept uncurtained and the upper sash let down for his health's sake. Half out of sleep he murmured, "owls," having heard the birds earlier screaming around the sycamores; but soon drew himself up and choked a cry; then fully awake leapt out; and as he did so there came a crash, and glass fell upon the bed. Wan light covered the window which was twelve feet above the level of consecrated ground where the dead seemed restless in their sleep.

It is an attack, he thought. Curgenven has turned the village out against me. But, while groping, his eyes discovered a pole, forked at the end, protruding through a hole in the glass; and his ears distinguished the comic lamentations, "Aw, my dear life, b'ain't this a queer old business! I ha' been and took schulemaster's window all abroad."

Drawing on slippers Anger went to the window muttering, "It's the fool," threw up the lower sash, and beheld among the tombstones the man he had lately thrashed, clothed and sober, clutching a ten-foot clothes-prop, with a stable lantern upon an altar-tomb beside him.

"Bobby Billacott," called Anger solemnly.

"Me sure enough," replied the vision.

"What is the meaning of this prank?"

"First of all I be got sober; second I ha' put my mind to thinking; third I be sorry about the window, but the old pole slipped. I ha' plenty o' money, and I'll pay damages."

"What do you want? And why do you come in the middle of the night?"

"B'ain't the middle neither. 'Tis nigh cockcrow. 'Twas a likely time to find you indoors I reckoned. I ain't been to bed. I ha' sot rubbing grease on my buttocks, and thinking till I got fair mazed. Schulemaster, I craves to tell to ye."

"Wait a moment," said Anger, then went back into the room to put on his dressing-gown and a scarf worked by Mary Wiggaton; while Bobby withdrew the pole and extinguished the lantern, exchanging crepuscule for chaos.

"Where are you?" called Anger.

"Same place. Between the grave of parson Bulliver and granfer Blackaway and atop of someone who be anonymous. Us can tell in the dark, and it be safer. Schulemaster, you ha' beat me."

"I lost my temper, Bobby."

"You beat me wi' words. Then you beat me wi' a stick. You'm the better man, schulemaster. That's what I come to tell ye. I couldn't say it in the light, but us can't see one another now. When I got home Thirza ses to me, 'Bobby, you'm a vule,' and I hadn't the heart to call she liar. And the old cow was standing nigh the gate, and hadn't never been abroad, and her went on chewing and seemed to call me vule as well. I wur cut, schulemaster; I wur fair cut."

"Cheer up, Bobby. You are on the right tack now."

"Schulemaster," whispered the eager voice from the graves, "if 'tis certain I be ignorant, and I don't say I'm vulish mind, but if so be I b'ain't wise, will ye learn me?"

"Certainly I will. You shall become a real scholar, Bobby, wiser than Curgenven. You have the right stuff in you. I felt sure of that when I heard your name. We will build up Quoditch, we will grow wise together, and you shall teach me something. You offered me your hand some hours ago. I am sorry I cannot reach it now."

"Thank ye, schulemaster. Between me and you in the dark, you'm just a bit of a vule yourself now, b'ain't ye?"

"I am," replied Anger. "We all have a bit of that breed in us. Are you still there?" he called when silence fell for a few moments.

"I wur working," the voice answered. "It do seem I runs up agin something hard and prickly when I gets to think. You ha' heard my name avore ever you come to Youlstone?"

"A Billacott was my greatest friend. He is a merchant in London."

"He'm my cousin," said Bobby. "Leastways I'll call him that. When I learns to write I'll send him a line asking how he be."

"I must do that—some time," the other murmured. "Bobby," he called, "I shall want you to stick to me. You may hear hard things said of me to-morrow. I broke up the Court; there will be no more burning of the candle for Lomyns' Furze. And I have made Curgenven my mortal enemy."

There came gaspings and stumblings from below, before a voice muttered, "Scat your old tombstone, parson," and then pleaded, "Bide a bit, will ye? I can't think fast enough. Broke up the Court, did ye? My dear life! Set Curgenven agin ye? My dear soul! Schulemaster, you be a scholar."

"What will the people think of it?"

"They won't think. Us gets back to work in the morning. Time enough to think when revel-day comes round again."

"What will Curgenven do?"

"Take ye by the hand and say he loves ye."

"Bobby," called Anger. "Answer this question truly, or I will have nothing to do with you. Don't hesitate. Answer without thinking, straight from your heart. If you speak falsely now, you stand to lose your home. Do you like Curgenven, or do you hate him?"

"He'm a kind gentleman," muttered the voice which suggested a sinking ship.

"Answer the question. Nobody will know of it except myself. Answer it, or I shall find it in me to beat you again."

There was a pause, followed by more gaspings and stumblings

against sharp-pointed altar-tombs; more struggles to break down custom and become natural.

"Now, Bobby!" cried Anger encouragingly.

"I hates 'en," came the whisper.

"Tell me why."

"I used to like 'en," said the trembling Bobby. "I fancied he wur a mighty pleasant gentleman. 'Twas mother who set me agin Curgenven. 'What do he want walking about the place as if he owned it?' her said. 'He b'ain't kind to we vor nought,' her said. 'I don't like the face o' mun,' her said."

"Why does every man sing his praises?"

"Because he'm neighbourly. He ha' helped many chaps out o' difficulties, and they don't ask the reason why."

"How much money do you owe him?"

"Who told ye I owes 'en money?" came the excited whisper from the graves.

"I guessed it."

"You'm the wonderfullest man what ever lived, I reckon. I said you was a better man than me, though I warn't certain of it, but now I knows you be."

"What do you owe him?"

"A hundred pounds."

"I am glad it is no more. What made you take the money?"

"He comes and gives it me. 'Here, Bobby my man,' he ses, 'us must help one another.'"

"He helps himself first."

"He'm mazed on Youlstone volk."

"For his own ends. Why should he be so anxious to help you? He is a man of business, and not wealthy; neither does he give. You have to pay interest. The poor man who buys money is on the edge of ruin. He might as well be buying health with his own life-blood."

"Listen to mun!" exclaimed the admiring Bobby. "A wonderful learned gentleman, I ses."

"The day will come when he will call upon you to return the money, knowing perfectly well you cannot pay," Anger went on. "And then he will take your farm and make you homeless."

As he spoke the cock crew, and night began to shiver on the hills.

"Don't ye try to be too clever," said Bobby confidently. "Curgenven don't want my land; he b'ain't a varmer. Pen and ink be his trade. You talks too loud, you'm getting vulish, I tell ye. If Curgenven took my land all the volk would be agin him. I'll be going along home now," he added, beginning to croak. "'Tis mighty cold near dawn. When be ye coming to Quoditch?"

"Very soon."

"You'll be bringing the bukes along?"

"Which ones?"

"Them you stole your words from."

"Not yet," said Anger. "The ground must be dug and cleared of weeds before the seed is sown."

Shouldering his pole Bobby groped out of the churchyard, while Anger returned to bed and slept heavily until awakened by a knocking and the announcement that Mr. Vigar was waiting below desiring to see him at once. Dressing in haste, he went down, and there being no privacy in the building they walked to the common, and soon found themselves alone among coughing sheep.

"Yesterday we had a visit from Curgenven," began the farmer in his long-suffering way. "He congratulated us, and gave it as his opinion that you were one of the best fellows he had ever set eyes on. I know what that means."

"I lost my temper with the man. He forced me to speak," said Anger.

"You made two mistakes; Petronel and I have suffered for them. Mrs. Vigar turned the key upon me last evening. Luckily I had a lantern in the barn, so Petronel and I were able to go down to the hut."

"You were turned out of Stiniel by your wife! Why can't you show her you are master?"

"Because her tongue is stronger than my body. She was wild enough to have burnt the house if I had stayed."

"What did Curgenven say?"

"Very little. Laughed the whole time, and declared we were all dear people, while Mrs. Vigar was making him a present of my property and swearing she would poison you."

"I can understand her hatred of me; I am a stranger; I came to Stiniel and crossed her," said Anger. "But why is she so anxious to marry Petronel to Curgenven?"

"We won't talk about that. You must leave me a few secrets," replied Nicholas.

"Does he want her?"

"I don't pretend to read his mind; but I am quite sure he is afraid of her."

"I had an idea Petronel had promised to marry him," Anger went on.

"He has never asked her. You must understand that Curgenven is an old family friend," said Nicholas bitterly.

"So is the devil," muttered Anger.

"There was a sort of agreement between him and Mrs. Vigar that if the marriage took place he would return my deeds; but that was only part of the agreement. The rest is my secret. As you had to come along, Mr. Anger, you could not have chosen a better time."

"If he is afraid of Petronel, I wish she could have dealt more firmly with him," Anger murmured. "Will you tell me if Mrs. Vigar has any hold upon Curgenven?"

"She has," replied Nicholas. "But that is another of my secrets."

"I do not get much out of you," complained Anger.

"But I must get something out of you, sir," said Vigar, rubbing his cold hands together. "You have let out our secret. What do you propose doing now?"

Anger thought for a few moments, then asked, "Where is Petronel?"

"In her hut."

"Where are you going?"

"Back to Stiniel. I have the bullocks to feed."

"I will go down to the hut at once, and take some breakfast. My poor girl will be hungry," said Anger. "We will make our plans, and Petronel shall tell you of them later."

Leaving Nicholas on the very spot where Bobby had been thrashed, Anger returned to the inn, and there found a letter from the firm of Lyson and Wiggaton, requesting him to call at their office at his own convenience. Quickly deciding to make the journey that same day, he gave an order to the landlady to put up breakfast in a basket. She replied with a stare of amazement, followed by the announcement that the temperature was not far from freezing point.

"I cannot alter that," said Anger. "I have a fancy to spend the day upon the moor, and I will take breakfast with me."

"Be you going abroad wi' teapot and sausages?" he was asked.

"Give me the sausages, with some bread and butter," said Anger impatiently.

"Will you take them cooked, sir?"

"As they are."

"Will ye please to take the frying-pan with ye?"

"I only take what I ask for."

"There be a window, sir, broke in your bedroom," she went on stolidly.

"It was an accident; I will pay for the damage. Do not expect me back until this evening."

The landlady departed with another unfriendly glance. She had been told of the fiasco in connection with the bidding for Lomyns' Furze; she knew that the lodger was a priest in disguise; and there was a rumour connecting him with the Vigars, who were known to be strange people. Curgenven had also hinted to her husband that his friend, although a splendid fellow morally, was not sound mentally. Guests who ruined business and their windows were not worth having.

Ignorant that a plan to get rid of him was simmering, Anger hurried on a well-known route to make his own. First he saw Whippety swaying about like a mystic dancer, and hovering near him, equally clumsy but unnaturally friendly, was the jay, that shyest of moorland birds, which yet had some affection for the wild boy who seemed able to talk to it in its own language. Whippety was cold; his thin, yet babyish face looked patient as he danced outside the hut imitating the sounds of bees and birds.

Then he saw Petronel, also cold, and leaning over a fire which would not break into flames. A lamp had been added to the furniture of the hut, and this was lighted. It seemed like night, when the sacking which made a door fell back.

Their eyes met, and carried out of his own cold life, Anger held her, and cried, like a determined man at last, "Petronel, my sweetheart! My own wife!"

She kissed him without passion, murmuring, "I am glad you are come. I was getting out of patience with the fire which will not burn, and my father who is like it. Whippety irritated me, and I had to turn him out. You at least bring some warmth."

"And some breakfast!" cried Anger. "Darling, you are shivering. Lie down, and I will cover you. Come, child! I am your master as well as servant; you shall obey. Lie down, and let me warm you. You see I am the strongest."

"Could you lift me?" she said with a half smile.

"Easily."

"Try."

He made the attempt, while she closed her eyes, and made herself wilfully heavy so that he was beaten; and then she ceased opposing him, and he was able with ease to lift and place her upon what passed for a bed. Afterwards he took off his coat and wrapped her in it, kissing her hair and eyes.

"You could not have moved me had I not helped you," she said.

"But you gave way; you uplifted your spirit towards mine. Tell me you love me, darling," he cried fondly. "I know now it was love which came to me when first I set eyes upon you. I had seen nothing like your beauty in my life before the change. I became hungry even then for your life and soul. Say they are mine. Let us begin our great romance in perfect unity. One glance will answer me."

"I will love you," she promised, still shivering. "But I shall have moods when you will think me fierce. You have not shaved this morning."

"I had no time," he said, somewhat chilled.

"Don't think me unkind. I had a fearful night, and it seems night still. I am too tired even to look at you. If I am cold, remember the time of year, and wait for me till spring."

"That I cannot do. My Petronel, we have enemies in Youlstone and Riversmeet. Your father warns me there is danger in delay. He is afraid Stiniel may be burnt, or you may be spirited away."

"My father is cowardly, and you are full of fancies," she said wearily. "This is a place where much is said and nothing ever done. Mrs. Vigar will wear herself out in time."

"Before then anything may happen. Sweetheart, we must be married at once, before the winter is over."

"Where are we to live?"

"Anywhere except Stiniel. We might go into lodgings."

"In Curgenven's town of Riversmeet!" she exclaimed.

"He could not harm us."

"How little you know him! Curgenven does not break the law, but he manages to break his enemies. I will not leave Youlstone. That is settled. If you are going to be master of Stiniel, why shouldn't I be mistress?"

"Is that really your wish, Petronel?" he asked wonderingly.

"Yes, I am bound to my old home. It is no worse than other places in winter, while it is cool and dark in summer. Give me Stiniel, and I'll marry you when the snow comes."

"That might be to-morrow, or not at all. You grow mischievous, darling."

"It is my fancy. When you look out and see the moor all white, you shall find me in a white dress too."

"Stiniel shall be yours, and you are mine, sweet girl," said Anger, bending again over her. "I would rather take you far away from Youlstone, to some place more sheltered and free from memories, but not less beautiful, where in some peaceful home we might find the happiest life. You are still cold, my darling."

"Let me see to the fire; I shall never get warm lying here," she cried, pushing him away gently, and going to the hearthstone where the peat merely smouldered. "The kettle is bewitched," she went on, raking out dead embers; then placing two sticks cross-wise against the stones to work a charm. "Now it will burn. Sit there, while I get breakfast ready, and talk as much as you like. People when they want to cheer you up talk of the big funerals they have attended. You will want to talk about wild January which is likely to bring the snow. Did you ever dream a year ago you might be sitting in a hut watching a wild girl preparing your breakfast? What were you doing then?"

"At this hour I might have been in church," said Anger dreamily, glad of the change in her, but still loving her best when serious.

"Now you have left it altogether. What have you done to release yourself? I make my fire burn by means of a cross of sticks. Do you get rid of your profession like this?"

She kicked the two sticks and sent them flying.

"We both have memories to escape from," said Anger, shrinking a little. "Any man is at liberty to change his coat. Once I did all I could for the Church; now it stands in my way because it denies love to its ministers. It has two very different definitions for one word. I am not bound. I merely step aside."

"If you had not met me?" she suggested.

"I should not have gone back."

"You may love me, but still I know I am standing in your way," she declared, with a feeling she had not shown before.

"You cannot be in my way when you are at my side. We are together, we shall soon be one," he said loudly, coming to her again. "I have served the dead. From henceforth I devote myself to the living you."

"The dangerous me," she said more meaningly.

"According to Curgenven," he added; and went on tenderly, "Come, darling, we must hurry, for I propose walking from here to the station. I have business in Exeter which concerns us all."

But Petronel would not hurry, although the fire glowed and the kettle was singing like a bird. She put her arms round Anger's neck, clung to him closely, and in that position said, "I will release you from your promise if you feel any doubts remaining. If the old life still calls, go back and leave me. If you feel I am not fit to be your wife, tell me so and go. I am not fit—I warn you—I am as wild sometimes as the weather, far wilder than Mrs. Vigar. I am Dartmoor born, and its storms are in me."

"Sweetheart," said Anger in a gentle whisper, "the only punishment which could make me suffer now would be my liberty. Until my illness I had been slave to a system. With my recovery came the knowledge of a freedom which I did not know how to use. I learnt when I saw you. Whatever happens, you and I are bound till death. Without you I should become again a lonely wanderer, looking for another star to lead me on. I loved my duty, that is true, but it only kept me at a certain level of spirituality, and not high enough; it merely awakened a part, it made enthusiasm mechanical, and sympathy a matter of the calendar. You have awakened all, and given me the enthusiasm of devotion as a whole, with perfect sympathy of mind and body. A man who has never loved a woman can only half love his God."

She hesitated, still holding on, her hair upon his cheek, her lips quivering at his neck. It still seemed very much like night. To Anger this was religion; it was doing good and helping another; and he came to the ceremony fasting, as he had gone to the daily Mass; but now it was no difficulty to dismiss base thought, and to uplift his mind, because the elements of adoration were alive and with him. So this was to him the perfect sacrifice.

"I love you; I do love you," she cried, as if upon her trial and pleading. "A man who can speak so well must know his heart. When I am wild with you, as I must be sometimes, remind me of this hour, and I'll be calm again. I am hungry for your soul; I am yours. In this dear little hut I have found all the happy hours of my life, from the time when I piled up the stones to the coming of the wet stranger in the mist. We will not leave it altogether when the snow falls."

"The misty stranger and the lovely brown girl will make a little shrine of it all their lives," he whispered.

"Now we will get breakfast," she said. "Then I will walk with you through the wood and wave you on the way to the station."

A few moments later Anger was sitting upon a flat stone cooking sausages in a frying-pan. The descent from deepest feeling to this trivial act seemed easy and natural, because food was, after all, as much a part of love as sighs and kisses. Petronel made ready the rock which served for table, then stood beside it, looking down and saying nothing, warming her face near the lamp-glass, wandering away into side-scenes of thought. Anger, with his back towards her, talked on, not referring to his conversation with Nicholas, but speaking about Lyson and Wiggaton, and the forthcoming visit which might result in Stiniel passing to himself, and so to her. But Petronel was not attending; she heard his voice, but not his words, for she was passing through a land of her own. The time of her freedom drew near, but she could not see the present for memories.

"After Stiniel, what then?" Anger was saying, like a cheerful boy, while he shook the crackling sausages which made his own thoughts simple. "We must have some rudder to our lives, and a harbour to steer for. We shall never be content to rust in idleness. I began in London, and would like to end there, doing a little good. You are silent, sweetheart. What do you say to the streets—crusade against vice, a mission to aid your sex and mine?"

A cracking sound, not from the pan, started the eager speaker. He turned to see a wire-like thread of cleavage running round the lamp-glass, and when the circle was complete, the topmost part fell, the flame turned to smoke; while Petronel looked up with big sad eyes.

"A tear ran down my cheek. It must have fallen upon the lamp-glass," she said quietly.

Anger was at her side, to kiss her eyes, to murmur, "What was the tear doing upon your cheek, my darling?"

"Scorching out a furrow; it felt like that. I had only one lamp-glass, and now I have broken it. What a destructive thing a tear can be!"

"If there is another let it fall upon my heart, and be like a sweet strong plant thrusting its roots into the rock," he whispered, loving her the more for that gentle attitude. "But what brought it? Did I say anything to hurt you, sweetheart?"

"It was not the first tear you have made me shed, though it is the first to be destructive," she confessed. "The stranger who came to Stiniel made me cry. So did the brother in the wood. You have brought me nothing but tears. It is the lover now. Soon it may be the husband. A life of tears! Some of them like this, which has put out the light, happy ones. All your words and actions bring them into my eyes because I know you waste yourself when you love me."

Darkness was in the hut save for the light of the fire which had then burnt low; so that the sense of night was real. She broke from his arms, went to the piece of sacking, and held it to one side, admitting the poor daylight of December; and more, a wandering flake or two of snow. Hurrying forward, Anger caught sight of crystals vanishing in the warmth of her hair; while Whippety beyond was dancing with the bird, knowing nothing at all of good and evil.

"It is the announcement of our wedding," Anger cried. "My winter's bride!"

The air was gentle, the earth asleep; only the waters roared. Wild boy and bird, brown girl and lover, were alone among the elements, surrounded by rocks and cold things, drawing inspiration from each other. Had Whippety been struck down, the jay would have gone back to its own kind. Had Petronel been swept away by the next storm, Anger would have departed from that place for ever. He and the bird would never have been drawn together, nor could he have formed companionship with the spirits of empty space; for he was a stranger among those mists, and he was not able to interpret the immortal mutterings which the wild boy and the jay could answer to. They would pass through the haze of twilight, knowing no hindrance; while he would be lost.

"This is only the announcement of winter," said Petronel. "The clouds are breaking over the cleave. The ground will not be white till January."

CHAPTER XIII

MATTERS OF LAW

EXETER CLOSE looked modern, with the exception of one fine corner where swashbucklers should have been lounging; but, hidden from the road, were scenes to feel bygone in. Opposite East Peter's, Anger was directed to a door, heavily studded with iron and half as old as Methusaleh. Within he came upon a tiny court where Richard Humpback might have stood in terror of the name of Rougemont, then a castle, now rubbish. A Latin text ran round the walls, which were further decorated in summer by wreaths of greenstuff. It was a place where a scholar might have hidden himself to compose iambics, or a monk might possibly have been discovered mixing his gold and silver colours afresh before painting in his missal the initial of his Lord.

A typewriter's click destroyed illusion, and going to a door whereon the names Lyson and Wiggaton were painted in dull letters without any illumination, Anger passed into the clerk's office and gave his name. Almost immediately he was shown into a low room, and there advanced to meet him a man of massive figure, tall and broad; his face lined, sallow and serious; his eyes piercing. He would have been hard on eighty, yet he moved well, and carried off his years with clothes and manner. He was indeed the best-dressed man Anger had ever seen.

"I come as a stranger," he began, when seated beside a desk which was a marvel of order, even pens and pencils being placed exactly one inch apart. "But the name of Lyson is very well known to me because I was at school with your son."

"Then you are no stranger, but a friend," said the old lawyer with absolute sincerity. "Which of my boys?"

"Edward, now the priest."

"The eldest; I do not say the best, for each of my boys is to

197

me first among equals. I am a happy man, Mr. Anger, for I have
no failures in my family. Yet, strange to say, I have no grandchil-
dren; so I am not without my disappointment. Edward is the most
earnest. He will not be a success, in the eyes of the world, because
he is an advanced churchman; yet I think he has chosen well. He
went to a slum occupied by people who were very little better than
heathen; and now he has changed all that. To my mind he deserves
some honour. We give a medal to the man who rescues a would-be
suicide from the river. We try to suppress a priest who saves many
a soul, because his ways may not be our ways. Now let us get to
business. You will pardon me, but I grow talkative when my boys
are mentioned. A few days ago I had a visit from Mr. Woodland
of Riversmeet, and he told me a most extraordinary story which I
need not repeat."

"About Youlstone, which you know, of course?" suggested
Anger.

"I do not."

"It is a village hidden away among hills above Riversmeet,"
Anger went on. "Its inhabitants are ruled by a lawyer, whose name
you must have heard. He enters into the common life, and calls
the people his relations in order that he may bleed them. He lends
them money, actually forcing it upon them, and in exchange takes
mortgages upon their property. It is now his intention to convert
Youlstone into a health resort, or, in other words, to deprive the
people of every bit of their property. It is my hope, Mr. Lyson, that
you will report this Curgenven to the Law Society——"

"Gently, Mr. Anger," broke in Lyson, putting out a hand. "We
must not pass sentence so hastily. Gossip as a rule is not the truth.
I do know of Curgenven."

"A mere dwarf, a conventional goblin," cried Anger.

"He is not your friend, it seems. Have you been preaching in his
pulpit?"

"I have promised to assist Woodland in saving Youlstone from
him, and I intend to marry the girl he has set his mind on."

"Ah, then, you must not expect him to be friendly. Regarding
this duplicity of his, I can set your mind at ease. If Curgenven is

acting illegally, as you maintain, by inducing ignorant people to sign mortgages under the pretext of taking receipts from them, we can very easily pull him up. But do not think too badly of him, and remember what temptations may assail the small country solicitor. He often finds it hard to get a living. He is brought into daily contact with people, more or less of an ignorant type, who insist upon regarding him as infallible, and will cheerfully hand over sums of money for investment. The temptation to divert a portion towards his own expenses will sometimes prove over-whelming. We city men are closely watched by suspicious rivals, but the country solicitor stands alone and practically unmarked."

"The man is a blackguard," insisted Anger.

"If so we can spoil his game," said Lyson, smiling at his client's violence. "Supposing your story to be true, it is probable that a clause is inserted in these mortgages naming a certain day for the repayment of the principal. According to the Court of Law, if the money is not paid upon that day, full enjoyment of the various properties passes at once to Curgenven. But, as he knows well enough, the Court of Equity waits behind. I will not weary you with professional details. Let it suffice to say the mortgagors have always the right to reclaim their property, and if the mortgagee should enter into possession, he must keep accounts, and when he has received so much as will suffice to repay the money lent, with fair costs and interests, he is bound to re-convey the estates to their former holders."

"None of the people will be able to exercise their right of redemption," declared Anger.

"Then we step in," said Lyson. "The lands will be put up for sale. Curgenven may propose to buy them for himself, but we oppose him, and win by virtue of the longer purse. We bring no suggestion of fraud—Mr. Woodland's instructions are explicit upon that point—unless Curgenven should be foolish enough to compel some action, which is most unlikely. He will retire from the contest, seeing that he is beaten; and then Mr. Woodland may carry out his plan of re-conveying the cottages and fields to their former owners. Now you will perceive, I think, that your mediæval village is not controlled by mediæval law."

"I cannot believe Curgenven will be beaten so easily," Anger doubted.

"A solicitor may give his own reading to the letter of the law, but he cannot fight against the spirit of it," answered Lyson.

"Shall you put yourself into communication with Curgenven?"

"Certainly not," said the old man sharply. "He must go his own way, and if we meet it will not be in this office, nor in his."

"So far you have been dealing with me as agent for Mr. Woodland. I have now some business of a private nature," Anger went on. "I wish to buy the house and land called Stiniel from Mr. Nicholas Vigar, the owner and occupant. He is prepared to sell, although he would prefer to grant me a lease."

"Is this property also mortgaged?" asked the old man, taking a pen and making a note of the instruction. Having listened to the client's reply, he added, "Then Mr. Vigar cannot make a lease without permission, which might not be granted if the mortgagee is Curgenven."

"It is just as well," said Anger. "Now I know he will sell, but I shall have to bring him here to sign the deed. His wife would destroy any document sent to Stiniel. That is another, and a stranger, Youlstone story."

He went on to tell it, using a single colour—and that one black— while the old gentleman leaned back with eyes half-closed, now and again making a slight movement with the hand that held the pen, until his client concluded with the declaration of war against Curgenven. Then he smiled and murmured, "We city men are sluggish, it appears, if primitive warfare such as this is going on around us. Women of Mrs. Vigar's type are not so rare as you suppose, but they are generally widows or spinsters. Disappointment in love in one case, a life without motive the other; nips from the bottle do the rest. It is a kind of insanity, but we do not interfere with the unhappy creatures. We let them go on until they hang themselves. Has it ever occurred to you that the woman may have a passion for Curgenven?"

"Never," cried Anger. "It is impossible, for the main object of her life is to marry him to Petronel."

"We are considering a woman whose mind is decayed, and whose moral sense is lost," said Lyson. "Her husband she hates because he has long been indifferent to her; implacable hatred towards their child has followed. She has been scheming how to get the man she loves under the same roof with her. It matters nothing to her if the man is married to her daughter. She knows his character perhaps; she may long to be avenged upon her daughter, or at least to see her married to a man who may not treat her well. Decidedly you are wise to purchase Stiniel."

"I wish the house and land settled upon my wife," said Anger eagerly.

"Ah yes, I congratulate you," said Lyson, giving him a sudden glance. "We will see to that when the time comes. Pardon me for thinking of anything which must jar your feelings; remember I am an old man, *in loco parentis* for the moment, and the father of your old school-fellow, but permit me to ask whether you are confident happiness will be brought to you by Miss Vigar?"

"I have no doubt whatever. Nothing that any man could say against her would shake my confidence. I could not listen, even if you were her accuser, Mr. Lyson."

"That is quite right. I do not attack Miss Vigar. I am doing my best for you," said Lyson, his voice growing sonorous. "This suggestion of cruelty disturbs my mind. I want to know more about it. You believe this woman persecutes her daughter in every possible way, tortures her, locks her in a cellar. Have you ever seen any marks of this violent conduct?"

"I have not," said Anger.

"No scratches, nor bruises? No sign of ill-health?"

"None whatever."

"Has the father ever described to you any specific act of cruelty?"

"He told me about the cellar, and I found her there myself."

"Has he ever, to your knowledge, witnessed the mother forcing the daughter into this cellar, or ill-using her in any way?"

"I do not know that he has."

"My dear Mr. Anger, I make no charge, I bring no accusation; I merely beg of you to proceed with caution," said Lyson. "Being in love you do not reason with an open mind. Let an old man argue the matter for you. This girl, who is perhaps not the equal of those you have mixed with elsewhere, comes like a flash into your life. You know little about her, you hear nothing that is good. Her beauty has bewildered you. No, you must please listen. I cannot forget that as a child my Edward watched over you and saved you from the bullies. I do not say Miss Vigar is unworthy, but few women, perhaps none, can attain the height to which the lover's fancy flies. The mother tortures her, yet she shows no sign of it; she actually wishes to live on at Stiniel, when married, with that mother——"

"She knows I will protect her," Anger interrupted. "Mr. Lyson, I cannot listen to this, I cannot bear it. I stand by Petronel."

"You shall hear no more," said Lyson, bending over the desk. "This matter of the purchase of Stiniel shall be put through directly. Get all details from Mr. Vigar, post them to me, then I will write to Curgenven for his account against the property."

"The deed must be signed first," cried Anger.

"I have to see you are getting a good title. The estate may be encumbered in all kinds of ways," protested Lyson.

"I will risk anything. Nicholas shall sign before Curgenven hears a word. He would rage about Youlstone, and stir up Mrs. Vigar. She might burn the place, murder Petronel——"

"Gently, gently!" cried the lawyer impatiently. "If you like to take the risk, that is your own affair. One more thing before you go, a little word of advice, Mr. Anger," he went on, rising and beginning to pace the room, flicking invisible dust from his coat-sleeve. "I imagine you will not take it, still my duty is to give it. I ask you to keep your eyes open and to watch the Vigar family carefully. Prowl about the place by night and listen; do not be deterred by any foolish fancy that you are suspicious of your lady; remember you have a future to make or mar. I also beg of you to be guarded in your speech and actions. Receive the advances of Curgenven in a friendly fashion, and if you must hate him do so privately. Above all keep to yourself as much as possible. If any stranger, whether man or woman, accosts you, have nothing whatever to do with that stranger."

"You bewilder me," said Anger.

"I hope my words will impress themselves upon your memory. If anything out of the common should happen, let me know at once, however trivial the incident may appear to you. In regard to the larger business of Youlstone, Mr. Woodland will keep me posted. Good-bye, Mr. Anger—and beware of strangers."

The client went out, and lingered for a few moments beside an ancient pump, trying to translate the Latin of the text. It seemed to him the man of business was less clear-sighted than himself, but that was because Lyson had dared to cast a stone against the brown girl. He stayed because his mind was waking up. The noise of a city, the old buildings, even the quiet Latin painted on the walls, disturbed his slumber and recalled him to one act of duty. Returning to the clerk's office, he asked permission to write a letter.

Some minutes later he came out with a feeling of greater ease, and going from the old-world atmosphere, he dropped into a pillar-box his letter addressed to the earnest Frenchman, his late rector. It served the purpose of a weighty document although in number of words it was a note. Anger had nothing to say concerning his body, nor the sixty odd pounds of flesh made in mistland added to it. His mind, he explained, had changed, giving him a new set of definitions for such words as duty, love, religion, and sacrifice. The church was his, but he could be its slave no longer; he was going to forget altars, brass candlesticks, and artificial flowers; he was for the hills, the only sun, and the fresh blooms of the earth. Like a new Joseph, he had put on a coat of many colours, his uniform of freedom, and had discarded the black of imprisonment for ever.

It seemed proper to write that letter, and natural to post it; for the free man knew his mind was astir, even if he could not hear it protesting beneath those sixty pounds of flesh, knocking against its walls, and trying to signal such messages to the brain as, "What pain will this give the rector? What thoughts will it raise in the heart of Mary? Why couldn't you tell them you are leaving the

Church just because you love a woman?" Then it went on passionately, "Take me back to the slums and the little dim church. I want
the red lamp, and the ceremonies, and those poor pinched faces.
I was happy there and I was at rest. Remove some of this stifling
flesh, Father Jack, and lift me out, and take me home." But Anger's
brain could not receive these messages.

Long before the train reached Riversmeet, darkness had fallen.
There was no longer any promise of snow, for every cloud had been
swept off the sky, which was then the colour of a calm Atlantic, and
brilliant with stars, planets burning on the hill-tops, and meteors
flashing through a frosty atmosphere. Anger descended into the
town, preferring the roadway to open moorland. At a turning
Palk went by, muffled to the nose, seeing nothing but the stones
he walked on. In the street of business Woodland could be seen
behind the only windows which were well lighted, supervising the
arrangement of some winter goods. A carriage drawn by a pair of
horses rolled by, and Anger remembered that people of some dis-
tinction had their homes in the wooded valleys to the north, enjoying a view of Dartmoor which was to them unknown land. Then
he heard a voice which made him shudder, and looking along River
Street perceived a small figure stamping along between the lamps,
shouting tremendously to every man and woman, "Good night,
my dear. Get ye home to the fireside. 'Tis brave frosty weather, my
dear."

"Get home yourself, Curgenven," called a woman's voice from
some hidden doorway.

"Presently, my dear. I'm looking for a few sticks and a bit of
coal to steal," cried the lawyer; and the last sound Anger heard was
River Street noisy from end to end with laughter.

The little town possessed one church and five large chapels,
which seemed enough. One of them was situated at the bottom
of River Street, where the town ended at the edge of precipitous
fields. "Zion" was painted coldly above its doorway. Lights were
in the windows, and the place was filled with the sound of voices
singing a popular hymn. An anniversary service was taking place,
and a special preacher had just finished his oration.

"Noisy in Jerusalem," muttered Curgenven, glancing at his watch. "Well, it will please them if I show myself."

He mounted the steps, and as he put out a hand to the door it was opened for him. The most respectable and the most popular man in Riversmeet faced and shook hands.

"Ah, Mr. Curgenven! It does me good to see you," whispered the doorkeeper.

"I wanted to take my part in the rejoicings," said the lawyer warmly. "I am a bit late, but I come in, as usual, for the Benediction. I'll slip into a back seat, Wadge. Look out for me afterwards."

"Does that mean some business, sir?"

"Some more of your pretty handwriting," said Curgenven.

"I am always happy to be your agent, sir," replied the doorkeeper.

When the service was over Curgenven shook hands with men, women, and children, bestowing his blessing upon all, making a joke with one, expressing sympathy to another, arranging a business appointment with a third. Everybody was anxious to have a word with the popular little man who was able to remove financial difficulties and could set a mind at ease with his advice. Even the preacher was proud to receive congratulations and a devout, "God speed ye" from the ruler of a thousand households; and afterwards Curgenven was left alone with Wadge, who moved reverentially about the dismal chapel, collecting hymnbooks and extinguishing the lights until only one was left. He was a middle-aged man, grey-bearded, and almost handsome, although his face was flabby and his eyes were puffed up with flesh. He was the model to young Riversmeet, pointed out as an example of a devout man who, if ready to denounce the faults of others, was in his own life a credit to the place. Curgenven had been attracted to him by the discovery that Wadge was skilled in a style of handwriting likely to be useful in a certain line of business.

"A beautiful service, Mr. Curgenven. So full of heartiness. The young man who preached was filled with the Holy Spirit. He is sure to make his mark, and he should make money," said the respectable man as he approached the popular one.

"How is Zion going? As strong as last year?" asked the lawyer.

"Better, sir. Our 'city set upon a hill' goes from strength to strength. We have never been more prosperous; subscriptions and offerings increase monthly; and, what is far more important, fresh souls are added to the Lord."

"Not every chapel has a zealous whipper-in like you," said Curgenven.

"Well, sir, I have done my share, though I am only a doorkeeper in the house of my God," said Wadge earnestly. "I am much indebted to your kindness and the work which you have given me. It has enabled me to increase my subscriptions largely."

"I have a ten-pound job waiting for you. It is a bit more risky than usual, but it's necessary. You will have to keep yourself very close, my friend."

"I know, sir, secrecy in all legal business is the first essential," replied Wadge. "You may trust me. I do not forget my Master's injunction, let not the left hand know what the right hand doeth. All work, sir, however unworthy it may appear to others, can be performed to the honour and glory of God. It is the spirit behind the pen and not the pen which will be judged."

"That is sound reasoning," said Curgenven. "There is nobody hanging about the chapel, I suppose?"

Wadge walked in his stately fashion to the swing-doors which opened upon the end of the street. He looked out and returned saying, "We are alone, sir."

"Listen, then," said Curgenven amiably. "A young man called Anger is staying in Youlstone. He pretends to be a layman; he is actually a Roman Catholic priest."

"That's enough description, sir. He cannot be up to any good."

"As a matter of fact he is playing the devil with the people, he is trying to undo my work, he goes about slandering me, and although he cannot marry he is actually making love to Miss Vigar of Stiniel and has asked her to be his wife."

"To punish him would only be doing God's work," said Wadge in a voice which seemed to suggest that the Almighty without himself was impotent. "You wish me to expose him, sir?"

"Clear him out," said Curgenven, with a sweep of his long arms. "Go straight for him. Hit hard. Make the country too hot for him to walk in."

"The ordinary methods may not be strong enough. I must bring direct pressure," said Wadge deliberately. "But it will be a noble work."

"Act at once. I will look after you. Here is a sovereign for out-of-pocket expenses. There is another matter, Wadge. Come a bit nearer; this holy place echoes damnably. Frighten Woodland."

"Mr. Curgenven, you surprise me!" exclaimed the doorkeeper, a flush of colour rising in his flabby cheeks.

"Attack his business. Spread a report that he keeps a woman secretly."

"Mr. Woodland guilty of adultery, sir! Mr. Woodland! I knows he is careless in his life; he attends no place of worship, I doubt if he has opened a Bible this twelvemonth. But I did think, sir, I did think he was moral."

"I have been making discoveries about him lately. It is a bad business, Wadge—an old friend, a good sportsman, like Jimmy Woodland. We may be a help to him."

"I shall work with that hope, and with the earnest prayer that my humble efforts may open his eyes to his awful wickedness," said Wadge in a trembling voice. "There are many men in Riversmeet I have my doubts of, but I felt sure Mr. Woodland was moral. I feared he had not found his God, but I never suspected that he kept a woman."

"Our friend is wealthy. He must do something with his money."

"He could present Zion with a new organ," said Wadge with fervour. "Had I one half of Mr. Woodland's wealth, I would build a chapel in every street. There cannot be too many. You have no quarrel with Mr. Woodland, sir?"

"Have you ever known me to quarrel with any man?" replied Curgenven, pulling at the arm of the doorkeeper who towered over him like a giant. "I love every good sportsman in Riversmeet, and Jimmy Woodland above all. He sits with me sometimes of an evening and gives me good advice, for he's got the soundest headpiece in the country, mind ye, and he'll pull out the heart of an argument while I am nibbling at the skin. Woodland and Palk are dear to me as brothers; but look ye, Wadge, I can't take Jimmy by the hand, and stare into his eyes, and tell him I know he is sliding down the road of good intentions. He might take it badly, or call me a liar. He might lose his temper and take a stick to me. We should be enemies ever after, and that would never pay in Riversmeet."

"How shall I begin, sir? With letters appealing to his conscience, or post-cards appealing to the public?"

"I leave it to your own judgment, which is as cunning as your right hand. The polished style to Anger; the illiterate to Woodland. Yours is a gift to be proud of, Wadge. Had you ever been criminally inclined, you must have turned forger long ago."

"I have been tempted, Mr. Curgenven," said the other, with the same straining after earnestness. "When short of money, or in difficulties about making up the pastor's stipend, I have found it hard not to devote my ability to imitate any kind of handwriting to some practical purpose. Can it be wrong, I have argued, to deprive a wealthy man of money which I should apply to the needs of Zion? Conscience has always answered that it would be wrong. I am thankful for the gift which enables me to unmask a priest and to bring our leading tradesman into the way of virtue. You said ten pounds, I think, sir. Cannot you make it twenty?"

"That's a round figure in this hard-up place," muttered Curgenven. "We will not quarrel over a pound or two. By the way, Wadge, conscience is all very well, but you mustn't get too sensitive. Say twelve, and all expenses."

"Mr. Woodland is big game," said Wadge, fingering the gas-jet. "He might retaliate. Our action is capable of being misunderstood. Say fifteen pounds, sir, and I put the light out. This gas is costing money, and Zion is poor. A subscription list for a new organ will soon be opened, and it would bring joy to my soul if I could put my name down for five guineas. Nobody would beat that sum, I fancy."

"You shall have it," the lawyer promised; and the next moment the chapel was in darkness.

A dinner was held that night in the principal hotel of Rivers-meet, an annual affair in connection with a sale of fat stock held at the Christmas market; and this was practically the only social function which Woodland felt bound to attend, partly as the leading man of business, partly as a prize-giver, chiefly because his absence would have given offence to many of the farmers who dealt with him. A titled landowner presided over a motley assembly of gentlemen-farmers in evening-dress, middle-class farmers in Sunday black, and very small-holders in gaiters and raw collars.

During the tedious speeches, which never varied in subject or congratulatory matter year by year, Curgenven started and stared suddenly along the table. Many a face passed within range of his vision, as many a thought flashed across his mind—a fear lest Wadge should go too far, a vision of Youlstone as his town, the idea of Petronel, but not as she was then, a determination to get rid of Anger—but he saw one face only. Woodland was sitting low down in his chair, an elbow upon its arm, his chin resting upon his hand; and he too was thinking deeply, and his eyes were fixed in a steady stare upon the lawyer whose body until then had been turned away. For a moment neither man could change his attitude; Woodland could not remove his gaze; Curgenven could not smile. It was the stare of a man who had forgotten prudence, and it told Curgenven that the tradesman was his enemy; money was about to be brought against brains, Youlstone was to be taken from him, its people were to be set free.

Woodland made a motion of his hand, but it was then too late.

Early the next morning Curgenven sent for Wadge, and said with a burst of hilarity, "A bit of good news has reached me. That story about Woodland is all humbug. We must leave him alone. I am thankful to know the truth in time."

"Hardly in time, sir," said the professional letter-writer in his confidential whisper. "I posted off a batch of post-cards late last night. You will find one among your correspondence."

"I wash my hands of it. 'Tis a beastly low-down game," Curgenven muttered.

CHAPTER XIV

AT THE QUODITCH PINCH

THAT night Anger awoke suddenly to discover a lamp burning dimly on a table beside his bed. He became also conscious of unusual weakness; there was little vitality in him, while his head was light and his limbs felt numb. After repeated efforts he dragged his body upright, reached out a hand to the lamp, which memory assured him had been left extinguished upon the other side of the room, turned up the wick; and immediately a great terror fell upon him.

"Am I out of my senses?" he whispered. "I came to bed in perfect health; I am now weaker than I was in London. This is my room, but it has been altered; even its shape has changed, and the window is no longer broken. Am I ill again? Have I lost consciousness and missed a day? Have they put me into another room? Is this Youlstone?"

He sank back out of weakness, hearing the wind rushing by the walls and the creaking of sycamores around the church. He was indeed in Youlstone and as certainly awake and ill; but who had placed that table and lamp beside his bed and left a book lying there, with a pad of writing-paper and pencil?

"I swear I am conscious," he went on. "Yesterday I was in Exeter with old Mr. Lyson. When I came back I saw Woodland, Palk, and Curgenven in the town of Riversmeet. I know all these men; they are not names to me. And I am to marry Petronel when the snow comes. And I am about to buy Stiniel. I remember it was very cold in the train, unnaturally cold."

Another effort and he had reached out a hand to the writing-pad, and discerning a faint line or two pencilled he read what had been written by some woman's hand. The sight of the address gave him another thrill. "The Tors Hotel, Youlstone." He had never heard it called that name before.

A start, almost convulsive, followed as he read:

"DEAR MISS WIGGATON—I received your letter this morning and must apologise for not having written yesterday. Curgenven is getting more of an enemy. Dr. Palk thinks the best thing Father Anger could do is to murder him and bury the body somewhere on the moor! If he does marry Miss Vigar, that will not help him much, I fear, as he has quite decided to purchase Stiniel, and unless he can get rid of Mrs. Vigar there is bound to be awful trouble. Father Anger is such a fatalist. He believes he has been brought here to save Miss Vigar. To-day he is in Exeter—"

Here the writing broke off. Anger lay motionless, hardly conscious, wrestling with the shadows round his mind. What was the name of this woman who composed letters and placed them unfinished at his bedside, who knew of his secret affairs, and had the impudence to write to Mary concerning them? What had she been doing in his room at all? Was she near then, and would she come if he called out? How was it possible that anybody in that place could know of his past life, or even guess at the existence of the Wiggatons?

"Now I am getting at it," he whispered at last. "That man Curgenven is capable of anything, and I verily believe he possesses supernatural powers. He must have seen me passing through Riversmeet; he followed, and when I was asleep crept into this room and drugged me. That accounts for the altered appearance of everything, for this half-dead feeling; I am still under the influence of the drug. This scrap of a letter he dictated to some woman in his employ, hoping I may take the suggestion, which he pretends was given by Palk, and try to murder him. The creature is half-elf, half-devil. Therefore he knows of Mary. I am half-fainting—I must make a note of this."

It was marvellously difficult to control the pencil; but he managed to scrawl upon the sheet of paper, which he was certain would never reach the hands of Mary: "I am fully awake and in my right mind. Curgenven has tried to murder me. If I am found dead let my body be searched for poison."

Folding the sheet he placed it beneath his pillow, trusting it might be discovered by some honest person. Afterwards his brain began to wander, weakness increased, and he longed to sleep again. Everything disappeared from his sight except the fat red volume upon the table. It seemed to him he had not read for weeks and months. Somehow he managed to get hold of the book without discovering that it was a copy of the poetical works of Shelley. It opened at the tragedy of the Cenci, and half unconsciously he read.

This must have been a dream, for he appeared to be floating through the air with the book hung round his neck and the terrible story rending his mind. Count Francesco had become a woman whose name was Judith Vigar, Petronel played the tragic part of Beatrice, while Curgenven was the Pope behind the scenes. Here was Petronel plotting with himself to destroy her mother. There was Stiniel, a gloomy castle among moorland crags, up the walls of which he climbed as an assassin. Then the horror of struggling at death-grips, the fall of a strangled body, a hellish battering at the door, while all Nature was upheaved by thunderous winds and each window was a flame of lightning; and now the flight, the capture, and the trial before Curgenven in flaming red robes, the torture and grinding of racks, the confession, the trampling outside of those who were setting up the scaffold. . . .

Anger cried out. No knocking came upon the door, but it seemed as if a woman had entered; not the figure of tragedy, but a kind and natural being; another creation of fancy, as Anger went to sleep and saw no more.

Rising at the usual time in a state of perfect health, Anger went down to breakfast, which was never ready; and while he waited the postman came along and he heard a muffled conversation at the doorway, accompanied by those chuckling noises by which some women express the words, "I thought as much." Presently the landlady came to Anger and held out to him a post-card, saying, "I suppose that's right, sir."

"Evidently it is intended for me," said Anger, trying to smile when he read the address: "Father Anger, Jesuit in Disguise, The Hotel, Youlstone"; while upon the other side was set forth a certain version of his character.

The landlady withdrew with a typical Dartmoor stare, and after a long interval returned with breakfast. She set it down, retreated a few paces from the table as if in mortal terror of the teapot, hesitated, and said at last, "My husband has been having a bit of a talk with me, sir. He says it b'ain't hardly worth while keeping the rooms open all winter. Us would be sorry to lose ye, sir, but that's what my husband says. It don't pay to keep the house open vor one gentleman, not unless he pays a lot more than what you'm doing now, sir."

"You would like me to leave," said Anger. "Very good. I will go to-day."

Having breakfasted, he put his things together, settled his account, including the broken window, the glass of which had evidently been valuable, then went off to Quoditch, and discovering Thirza knee-deep in pigs told her at once, "I am coming to lodge with you, Mrs. Billacott."

"Bless my life!" cried the startled woman. "Us ha' no place to put ye, sir."

"Then Bobby must build on another room before tonight."

"Well, sir, ask 'en. He'm coming wi' a load of slats."

Half a dozen light turves made up the load which Bobby panted under. Anger advanced, explained he had been evicted and knew of no place to hide in except Quoditch, and having come it was his intention to remain.

"Us will manage to make ye welcome, schulemaster," said Bobby. "Me and mother can shift into the shay, and you can bide in our room. He'm as gude as the one you'm leaving, but you'll please to stoop a bit when you goes under."

"And now we will commence our studies," said Anger. "By day we work on the farm, side by side, Bobby. You shall teach me to build hedges and cut ditches. After dark the books come out."

"I ain't got no itch vor they," was Thirza's comment.

"You'm a woman, mother. You don't need learning. Us scholars can't do without it. Will ye work wi' me on the land, schulemaster?" inquired Bobby eagerly.

"Every morning. It will do me good."

"There be strange tellings about you in Youlstone," said Bobby with a wagging of his head. "They ses you'm a priest, and you'm here to buy land vor to build a gurt monastery vull o' golden idols."

"How much do you believe of that?"

"I believes what you tells me. First time you came down through Quoditch you beat me wi' words. T'other night you beat me wi' a stick. I wouldn't tell she o' that," he whispered, pointing to Thirza who had gone back to the pigs. "When a chap beats me I believes in mun. You promised to bring me sunshine, and I fancies you will."

"I have been a priest," said Anger. "Now I will be a farmer for a week or two; and before we have done with each other we shall both be better men. Now let us get to work."

"What be us to do?" asked Bobby helplessly.

"We will start with that hedge. I am going to have it built up before dinner. Then we will go for my luggage, and this evening you shall have a reading lesson."

"That makes a mighty long day," grumbled Bobby. "Yonder old hedge ha' been broke these five years."

"We are starting in business, and I am going to be senior partner."

"Who taught you to build hedges?"

"Get the tools," cried Anger. "Take off your coat, and I'll show you the way to put a farm in order."

At that Bobby hurried off for sledge and mattock, indignant at the idea of being taught his business by an amateur. Soon they were tackling the first pile of stones, while the gap above filled quickly—for hedge-building is simple work when the principle of overlapping has been mastered—and when they moved on to the second gap Anger suggested quietly, "Now we are building a wall against Curgenven."

"Not we," said Bobby. "He can hop over a bigger hedge than you can build."

"I mean you are at work, and that brings in money, and money will keep out Curgenven."

"I don't get money vor building my own hedges," said Bobby.

"This is the first step. When the hedges are finished we will build a new gate. Then we will drain the fields. We shall get a good crop of hay in the summer, and that will bring in money. Leave the pigs and potatoes to Thirza. We will attend to the pasture land. The hundred pounds must be wiped off, Bobby."

"He won't ask vor it; not vor a long time anyhow."

"He may be down upon you any time," said Anger, ceasing from his labour. "You signed a paper without knowing what it meant. It was a mortgage, Bobby, and by it you handed over your house and farm to Curgenven and agreed to let him be the owner until you repaid all the money he has lent you. If you do not pay the money upon a date which is mentioned in the paper he can step into Quoditch and take it as his own."

Bobby dropped his mattock, wiped his face, and muttered, "That b'ain't true."

"You promised to believe me," Anger reminded him. "Curgenven lent you that money because he knew you could not repay it, and he does not want you to do so."

"What do he want then?" asked Bobby sullenly. "He don't want me, he can't want mother, he wouldn't want the old house."

"He wants your land."

"That's what I don't believe. What's a bit of old marsh to him?"

"He wants your land," said Anger impressively, "because he knows how to sell it at a big profit."

Bobby stared stupidly, then sent his hammer clattering among the stones and turned away.

"Where are you going?" called Anger.

"If it be right what you ses, I'll do no more work. I won't build hedges vor Curgenven. Why didn't you tell me o' this avore?"

"You would not listen. Come back, Bobby."

"I ha' done wi' work. If I ha' sold Quoditch without knowing of it, I'll just smoke my pipe and spit on his ground. This bit o' land ha' belonged to we Billacotts vor hundreds o' years—aw, vor thousands I reckon. Us owned the whole lot once, from the river to them old high stones up the hill. Stiniel wur ours, and all they vuzzy fields along the cleave wur owned by my volk, but it got

and slipped away from 'em somehow. There be nought left but
Quoditch plats, and now they'm going too."

"I will show you how to keep them," said Anger. "Pay Curgenven the money he has lent you, take no more from him, and
then he cannot lay a finger on your property. Sell the place to me."

"Schulemaster," said Bobby sorrowfully, "you'm teasing me
again. How can I sell land what don't belong to me? I ses Quoditch
be mine; you ses it b'ain't. Be that as 'twill, the man who takes it
from me will ha' to get past my gun. I won't give the place up, and
I won't sell it neither."

"I did not say Quoditch was lost to you; but if you mean to
keep it I must help you," replied Anger. "You made your mark on a
piece of paper, and by doing so Curgenven became owner of your
property until you pay back the money. Where will you get that
money from if you don't take it from me? And how can I lend it
you without security? If I take over the mortgage, Curgenven will
force more money on you. If I buy Quoditch, you are safe from
him for ever."

"I won't be safe from you," said the little man cunningly. "If a
cat be druv up a tree by a dog, her don't worry about the name of
the dog."

"You will sell Quoditch to me for three hundred pounds, and if
you refuse again I'll beat you," said Anger fiercely, groping into the
hedge for a suitable ash plant.

"Thirza wouldn't let ye," said Bobby manfully.

"Then I shall go to Curgenven and offer to buy Quoditch from
him."

Bobby wavered at that, and his little dirty face began to quiver.

"I will be a good landlord," Anger promised. "While you will
have a nice sum of money to start with, and at some future time
you can buy back the place."

"If I wur to sell Quoditch," whimpered Bobby, "all the Billacotts
what ever lived would get out of the ground and walk abroad."

"Did they walk when Stiniel went?" demanded Anger.

"I reckon 'em did, but I warn't born then."

"Curgenven comes with the storm; I bring you sunshine. Trust me, and you shall keep your home, and I will stay for a time and work with you. Refuse, and you lose everything," said Anger finally.

"If you can hit wi' a sledge like as you hits wi' your words, you could smash all they rocks without tears and jumper," replied Bobby. "You ha' beat me every time, schulemaster. I wur a vule to sign vor him, I reckon, but I might be a bigger vule if I didn't sign vor you."

Thirza was not told this business. Her mind was sufficiently charged with cows, pigs, poultry, on the one side of the wall, and with pots and tables upon the other; she had nothing to do with things printed or with signatures, not even when, as in her husband's case, the signature was a mark which brought a cross upon their lives. She came from the animals outside to throw herself upon household articles, making the four rooms tremble as she changed their order to meet the requirements of the guest; picking up a bed as if it had been a heap of thistledown, and crushing it through the doorway until something gave, toiling with whole body from tongue to toes, more like an automaton whose motions were the result of mechanical laws than a human being acting with intelligence. Evidence to support this theory was forthcoming when evening came, and the schoolmaster gave instructions for the table to be cleared of its ever-present crockery, for the lamp to be placed thereon, and three chairs to be placed with decency around. Thriza gaped, for witchcraft was suggested. These preparations seemed terrible, not so much as a ceremony in honour of some unknown god, whose creed was the alphabet, but as a complete change in the ordinary routine of her existence.

"It is time for school," proclaimed the pedagogue.

Bobby was so impressed that he had gone into the shay to put on his best clothes.

"I did learn wance, but it never stayed wi' me," cried Thirza in defence. "I wur taught by an old master. He warn't like you, my dear; he wur white-headed, and he wore gurt golden spectacles. He told us as how we would ha' to work wi' our hands, so he said he wouldn't teach us much; and he wur right—he didn't. Us used to drap bumbledors down behind his collar," she observed with animation.

"I am going to make scholars of you both," said Anger.

"Bobby be one already. You can't teach me, sir. I ha' no mind vor learning. What would I do wi' it?"

"Read books and write letters."

"I ha' no time vor reading, and as vor that there writing, 'tis quickest to tell to volk than to send a letter what costs money. When it be dark I craves vor bed, and that's where I be going now," said Thirza.

At that moment Bobby appeared in black clothing, ready to be sacrificed to Minerva. "I be just agoing to finish off my education," he explained.

"Lor, Bobby, you don't need no more. You can talk down any man. The gentleman can't teach you nothing," said Thirza warmly.

"I ha' forgot things, and schulemaster be going to bring 'em back. I ha' talked too much, and I ain't never give my mind to reading and writing. Pitch yourself, mother, and hearken to schulemaster."

"I ha' got all the education I can do with; I never could sense that trade; and now I be agoing to bed," said Thirza. "Look ye, master! Could ye kill a pig?"

"Decidedly not," said Anger.

"Would ye know how many eggs to set under a broody hen?"

"I should judge by the size of the bird."

"Can you milk a cow?"

"I have nothing to do with such things," replied Anger.

"I ha' nought to do wi' your trade neither." And with this conquering blow Thirza went off to bed.

Bobby, although ready to learn, soon proved an awkward pupil, because he would insist upon the possession of an intellect many sizes too large.

"'Tis me," he exclaimed at once, when his name was written down and shown him; but when told to copy the same he asked for a harder task. Thereupon Anger directed him to write down the word Quoditch, but the result of much hard labour gave the impression of a thorn bush in black and white.

" 'Tis my style," he explained, in answer to criticism. "I goes in vor flourishes."

"You cannot write at all," said Anger. "I see we must begin with the alphabet. How many letters are there?"

"A goodish few," answered Bobby.

Anger explained each letter and its formation, while the pupil grew restless, and suggested he should read a little, explaining, "It ha' all come back to me now." So Anger wrote the simple sentence, "You are an idle man," and passed the paper across the table.

Bobby stared, sucked his instrument of writing, made finger-marks upon each word, and finally remarked that he agreed with the sentiment and would not mention it to anybody.

"What have I written?" asked the pedagogue.

"Us knows," said Bobby with the utmost caution. "Us won't talk about it."

"You are hopeless," cried Anger.

Then Bobby left his seat, and coming round the table whispered, "Tell ye how 'tis, schulemaster. Thirza ain't gone to bed. Her be listening, and her can hear every word us ses. Her fancies I be a wiser man than you. I'd be mighty pleased if you would say out loud, 'You ha' beat me, Bobby.' 'Twould please mother wonderful well, and 'twouldn't hurt you neither."

"What good will it do you?"

"Mother reckons I be the wonderfullest man living. She'll think no worse of you vor being second to me. I'll learn of you in secret, schulemaster. Mother won't listen after to-night when her be certain I be teaching you. I can hear she breathing by the keyhole, so I knows she'm there."

Anger did as he was asked, and so concluded the first lesson. When Bobby had retired, more of a conqueror than his wife, the lodger heard them for some moments talking and laughing with great contentment. Then he turned down the lamp and went outside, remembering how Lyson had advised him to prowl about Stiniel. No night could have been blacker. Anger returned for the lantern, which was one of the most prominent articles of furniture in the living-room, and while struggling to lift up the glass, its owner put forth his head and called, "Be you going out?"

"I am not ready for bed yet. It is not nine o'clock."

"By the sun 'tis midnight. You'm going vor a drink?"

"I am going a little way up the moor."

" 'Tis bravish cold."

"No worse than in my bedroom. If you have such a thing as a bottle, I should be glad of one in bed."

"Mother!" called Bobby excitedly, "schulemaster be craving vor a bottle."

With the lighted lantern swinging from his hand, Anger stumbled up the hill and reached the gate of Stiniel. The night was calm, but although frosty no stars were showing. He halted, unable to pass into that region of black evergreens showing a light, and lacking the courage to proceed without one, until he heard footsteps along the eccentric road. He listened, having been deceived before by ponies, and presently the moor-gate clanged, and the footsteps came on more quickly, hardly slackening when they began the steep ascent. Then Anger knew a man was walking up to Stiniel, and he could not be a villager because it was night time, and he could not be a stranger because he showed no light, yet knew the track well enough to keep clear of wayside rocks. This must be the creature which haunts me day and night, thought Anger.

Running along the turf a few yards downwards, he deposited the lantern near the hedge which was the highest boundary of Bobby's property, knowing the man must pass it and so become revealed; then swiftly climbed the bank opposite, mistaking furze for heather, clutching it and suffering for the error. Safe himself outside the circle of lantern-light, he looked down at Curgenven who hurried into it, then paused to look about with his big head wagging before aiming at the lantern one tremendous kick which scattered glass and light together; afterwards running on in the dark without a chuckle.

Waiting some minutes Anger followed, groping towards the hedge, passed into the forbidden garden, the gate being now wide open, and went on until a light fell across the mossy pathway, and in the midst of intense darkness appeared a small stage whereon actors played their parts in dumb-show.

He was looking into the window of the room generally occupied by Nicholas Vigar, who was present then, seated at the table in the attitude of a gambler about to deposit his last stake; while Curgenven stood by, stroking the old man's shoulder, and Mrs. Vigar was smiling opposite, like a natural woman. Petronel was not there. Anger drew closer, determined to miss nothing. He could see that Curgenven's lips were moving rapidly, but not a sound entered the garden. The lawyer held out his right hand to the weak farmer, who covered it with his, but without looking up or altering his attitude. Then Curgenven produced a document, unfolded it, smoothed it out upon the table; he turned to speak to Mrs. Vigar; she brought forward pen and ink. They hid the huddled figure as they fawned upon it.

All three looked up and the two faces visible to Anger became startled. He heard the sound of a door grating, and was forced to cry out when a figure in white stepped into the shaft of light. Petronel came to his side dressed like a bride.

"I heard Curgenven come into the house; I knew his footstep. Why are you here?" she said.

"I came to spy, and am getting more than I bargained for. Sweetheart, how beautiful you are in that ghostly dress."

"I was making it in readiness for the snow. Do you know what is going on in there?"

"Why, Curgenven is on his knees, pretending to humble himself before your father. Look at Curgenven in love! This is his passion. He is praying for you, my darling. See! he holds out his bloody cheque-book. 'Give me your daughter,' he is saying. 'I'll make a good provision for her. I will settle everything I have stolen upon her, I will steal all Youlstone, and give her a village as a wedding-gift.'"

"It is Stiniel he is after, and he'll get it too, if you don't settle with him," she said calmly.

"Is this the sale?"

"Of course it is. Look at them pushing the pen into his hand, and Mrs. Vigar with her arms round his neck kissing him!"

"He cannot sign. He will remember our bargain."

"They are too strong for him. He will sign to get rid of them. He believes Curgenven will beat you in the end. I suppose you do love me?" she said scornfully.

"You know I love you."

"If he gets Stiniel, you lose me. Father is holding the pen—he is giving way—Mrs. Vigar is guiding his hand—Curgenven is pointing. See how he smiles!"

"Let us go in," said Anger quietly.

"What for? To get our heads broken?"

"Then we are helpless."

"And father has signed," said Petronel, almost triumphantly. "Now let me see what you are made of."

"I can do nothing," declared Anger.

"Not even strike a little man for love of me! The night is very dark. Curgenven will walk back to Riversmeet with that deed in his pocket. If your mind cannot suggest the rest, my tongue will not."

"He would not see us, but then he is very strong," muttered Anger.

"I will help you. Wait for me upon Quoditch Pinch. I must take off this white dress."

Petronel slipped away, while Anger shivered among the cold and flesh-like shrubs. Rejoicings were taking place upon the lighted stage. Nicholas still sat in the attitude of despair, but Curgenven was hopping about the room, while Mrs. Vigar, a handsome if weird figure with her ravaged face and snow-white hair, clapped her hands for joy. The watcher drew back and groped towards the gate, keeping one hand before his face to ward off brambles. Reaching the brow of the hill he waited until heavy footsteps came near, followed by deep breathing and the question, "Can you see me?"

"Nobody could see a yard through this terrible darkness," he answered. "What have you done to yourself, child? You walk like a man."

"Put your arms round me," she said.

He did so and felt rough garments. Passing his hand higher, it touched dried clay upon her coat-sleeve, and feeling across her shoulder his fingers met a short iron bar.

"I am wearing father's boots and clothes," she said. "Curgenven has the nose of a dog; he would smell me out in the dark. You must do the rough work, for if I so much as gasp he will know me."

"Why have you brought that iron bar?"

"To get stones out of the hedge. I will do that, while you pile them across the path."

She groped about until her hands reached the rock she searched for, recognising it by its size and shape.

"This is where the Pinch plunges," she said. "The road is very narrow; only just wide enough for a cart to pass. Curgenven will come along at full swing, knowing every inch of the way. Stones a foot high the whole way across must catch him, and he will fall pretty heavily down the Pinch."

"He may be stunned!"

"All the better."

"He may break his neck."

"It is much too strong," she said carelessly. "Still we might give him something to fall on. Lower down, there is a hurdle stopping a gap. That will break his fall. There is no hurry," she called. "Curgenven will drink the health of all of us, and treat father to a song before he leaves."

She went off for the hurdle, while her accomplice, once the terror of burglars and now planning a highway robbery, lifted the iron bar and forced it into the hedge, finding the turf between two stones by the sense of touch. It was slow work on account of the darkness and the weight of the masses which had to be grubbed out, so that when Petronel returned dragging the hurdle, he had placed across the road no more than three stones. "You are no good in the dark," she said impatiently. "Give me the bar."

Soon the barrier was in position. They spread the hurdle, then stood beside the hedge waiting for the click of the gate which would proclaim the coming of Curgenven. The darkness was the same, but now they could feel a certain amount of breeze which suggested a clearing of the sky before long.

"You always turn up at the right time," she said. "When I wish for you, there you are!"

"My whole life with you is like a vision," he answered. "I feel that I cannot escape from the fate which brought me here."

"Do you want to escape?"

"I mean to say this: there is nothing to prevent us from leaving Youlstone to-night, and going away together to some place where we could forget Stiniel and live in perfect happiness; and yet we cannot do it. We are held here."

"Wherever we are, we must face the consequence of our actions," she said. "We cannot be free merely by going from one place to another."

"Is Curgenven brave?" he asked.

"He cannot look me in the face, but he has no fear of men; he will fight hard."

"I must see your foolish old father to-morrow," Anger went on. "I am staying at Quoditch now, so he can meet me at the boundary hedge. Tell him to look out for me in the morning."

"Why have you come to Quoditch?"

"They asked me to leave the inn. I am getting unpopular."

"There is the gate! Get ready."

Petronel left Anger's side and crossed the trackway, then whispered sharply, "Lie down. I seem to see you."

Again came the quick beat of footsteps, but now with a difference. Curgenven was elated, so he sang on the homeward way, believing he was the only man in the open air between that place and the road to Riversmeet. His voice sounded well, for it was deep and rich, and just then he had no part to play. As he hurried down, every word of his song rang out with a genuine sound:

> "An office, a house, and a pound a day;
> A mind free from care, and no debts to pay.
> Be true to your creed, and kind to the poor,
> And you will be happy for ever——"

The final syllable, 'more' was not uttered, for at the 'ever' he struck the barrier and went over, falling across the hurdle after a kind of leap; but he did not move again, for his head had struck the ground.

Petronel advanced from one side, Anger from the other, neither daring to breathe a word. They bent over the misshapen little body. Curgenven was breathing heavily, and even while they handled him the limbs began to move and one arm passed mechanically across his chest. Anger forced it aside, while Petronel unfastened the coat and drew from the breast-pocket all the documents it contained. These she handed to Anger, then they rose and ran a little way up the hill and waited.

"It was done very easily, but then he could not have missed those stones. What a noise he made in falling!" she said.

"I felt the shock like a blow," muttered Anger; and then asked, "What can we do if he is injured seriously?"

"He is only stunned. He broke the fall partly with his hands. They have suffered the most. Don't speak again; he may be listening," she murmured.

They waited for some time, hearing groans, and, presently, movements which were followed by some coherent noises. A few minutes later the dim light of a match shone out, but the watchers were far away in the darkness. Curgenven did not call out, nor did he return to Stiniel. He sat there and cursed, and at last some strength returning, he struggled to his feet, and the listeners heard him stumbling down the Quoditch Pinch.

"I told you no fall would ever break his neck," said Petronel.

"Can he walk home, or will he wake up the Billacotts? Shall I find him there when I return?" exclaimed Anger.

"He would get home to his own den if he was dying," she declared. "Is it likely he would show his wounded head and hands to the Billacotts, and tell them he had been beaten and robbed in his own parish of Youlstone? Go back and destroy that deed. I will send father down in the morning."

Anger made his way back slowly, getting many a shock before he reached the house. When safely inside he examined the stolen documents. First came the Stiniel deed, which he forced into the peat still glowing upon the hearth; then a mortgage, signed that day by one of the simpletons of Youlstone, and that too was destroyed; a few letters which testified that "Youlstone Limited" was being advertised; and a folded sheet of foolscap containing information of value, for it was a complete list of the properties mortgaged to the dwarf in Youlstone.

"I will send this to Woodland," said Anger, as he glanced uneasily at the door which was rattling in the breeze. "It will tell him just what he wants to know."

He went upstairs, feeling chilled and nervous. Immediately he came beneath the quaintly-shaped roof he smelt strong liquor; and going to the bed, which was clean if poorly furnished, he saw a bottle, not by any means the one he had asked for, but a black object uncorked and three parts filled with whisky, standing upon a chair, with a glass beside it. Ignorant Bobby Billacott had complied with the lodger's request to the best of his ability; he had been asked for a comfortable bottle, and had hastened to supply one. He must have groped his way without a lantern across the common to the inn after Anger had left the house; and the state of the bottle gave ample evidence that he had not failed to reward himself for the act of industry.

Before waking the next morning, after much tossing upon a mattress as uneven as the moorland, Anger was again troubled by his fancy. He seemed to be not asleep, but wandering, and in that state a figure hovered about his bed and asked, "What is your name?"

"I am John Anger," he answered.

"Your profession?" the voice continued.

"I have none."

"Then you must go on sleeping," the voice murmured.

CHAPTER XV

MANY KINDS OF PRESSURE

B EFORE the morning had decided upon its complexion for the day, Anger was walking through a world of hoar-frost. Passing along the track unseen, he cleared away all outward evidence of the man-trap, restoring the hurdle to its accustomed place in the gap, and rebuilding the hedge, somewhat roughly as the turves were themselves like stones. The iron bar he thrust through the gate of Stiniel, and hardly had he done so when Mrs. Vigar came round the bend, strolling as if it had been May and the frost which loaded down the rhododendrons had been white blossom.

"You are about early," she said pleasantly.

For a moment Anger was startled and could not find a word. She had not then the appearance of a violent woman, but he could not forget what had occurred and how she had acted the night before.

"I came yesterday to lodge with the Billacotts, so I am now your neighbour," he replied, and then went on more easily, "I see we have similar tastes. Like me, you enjoy a walk before breakfast."

"I had my cup of tea hours ago; somewhere about midnight, I fancy. Day and night are the like to me. I eat when I want food, and sleep when I can."

"This mountain air makes me sleep very well," said Anger.

"You don't look properly awake now. I reckon you are dreaming of my daughter," said Judith still more amiably.

"Why should I not, now that she is mine?" he asked her boldly.

"Did you come to Youlstone with the fancy of making love to the first girl who made eyes at you; without bothering your head as to who she was, or what her character might be?"

"Petronel made no advances. It was a long time before I could induce her to regard me as anything more than a stranger." Then

Anger plucked up his courage and added, "I know you object to me."

"I don't. I like young men," said Judith with great friendliness. "It's true we had a bit of a struggle when you came here the first time, but it was your own fault; besides, you found me in a bad temper. I had been locked up in that cellar all the morning."

"Who locked you in?" said Anger faintly.

"Your pretty sweetheart. Do you know what you are in for? Don't think you can master her, for she has the strength of a dozen men. Look here!" She held out a badly bruised right wrist, then came nearer and showed him her neck which was deeply marked with scratches. "There are some signs of my daughter's love," she added.

"I cannot believe you," he said manfully.

"Wait until she turns upon you then. You know I live here with my husband and daughter; you know that old fool wouldn't lay a finger on me; you don't suppose I scratch and bruise myself."

"I say nothing except that I am prepared to devote my whole life to Petronel," said Anger firmly. "My love for her is not an idle fancy, nor did I require to visit Youlstone for a wife. Hundreds of young women have passed me every day, but until I set eyes upon Petronel I had never known what I was made of."

"It was a bad day for you," she declared. "Well, you won't marry her, so you had best get back to your preaching. Her future is settled for, and you ain't in it."

"Petronel may choose for herself, and I will see that she does," said Anger warmly.

"If another likely young fellow came along to-day she would promise to marry him. She belongs to Curgenven."

"She hates him," Anger flashed out.

"What do you suppose she says about you?" cried Judith with her hoarse laugh. "How many pretty things has she whispered into your ear? We hear them in Stiniel: that 'lanky milksop of a priest,' that 'young monk who runs after women,' that 'humbug who throws over his religion for the first girl he meets.' These are not my words. I'm friendly to you, but I mean to keep you out of Stiniel."

It is true, thought Anger, Petronel rarely says kind things to me. But this woman is a liar.

"The girl wants a master, and she will get one in Curgenven," Judith ran on. "When she breaks out he will know the way to manage her, and if she tries to claw his neck she will split her nails. I have put up with her these last ten years. Even as a child of fifteen she would knock me about," cried the white woman passionately. "She is a fiend all the winter. Listen around here on the first wild night and you will hear her screaming. That's the sort of wife you want to have? Now what do you say?"

"Nothing," replied Anger.

"Do you still mean to marry her?"

He nodded carelessly.

"You reckon you can master her?"

"Not with the violence of an unnatural mother, but by a husband's love," he answered, and then made away towards Quoditch, hearing no sound except a laugh, looking back once to see Judith Vigar strolling along the mossy path as if the weather had been spring-like and she had no blood to freeze.

Returning with the battered lantern, he explained to Bobby that an accident had taken place the previous night; and the little farmer became warmly sympathetic.

"You took too many drops out of the bottle I fetched vor ye, and then you sat upon the old lantern. I ha' done the like myself."

Anger denied the charge in his usual headlong fashion, and went on to explain what manner of a bottle he had asked for, receiving the wise answer, "I ha' heard tell o' they, but they b'ain't bottles; they'm cloam jars. Only old women uses they. When a man be cold he warms his innards, and they warms his outwards, and they warms his bed. If you had asked for a grandmother's jar I'd ha' knowed, and I would ha' told ye us ain't got one. You was out a wonderful long time to-night," added Bobby curiously.

"I was not the only one. Do you know that Curgenven walks about here in the dark?"

"I ha' seen big footprints in the garden, but I never thought 'twas him along," said Bobby uncomfortably.

"He comes spying and peeping; waiting for a little moonlight to show him the place where he means to build an hotel. He has set his mind on Quoditch. He told me so himself; at least I fancy he did."

"Scat 'en and bust 'en!" cried Bobby.

"I have a particular reason for wishing to get you free from him at once. Will you come with me to Exeter to-day?"

"I'll come to-morrow," Bobby promised.

"I told you never to say that again. You have come near to ruining yourself with your to-morrows," said Anger sharply.

"To-morrow," repeated Bobby. "I'll lay all Quoditch to half a pint that I'm saying the right thing. Now I ha' beat you schulemaster, beat you proper."

"How have you beaten me?"

"This be Sunday."

"I did not know," said Anger with a start, moving towards the cottage, anxious to hide his earth-marked clothes and unclean hands. "There was nothing to remind me."

"I lay abed," said Bobby.

Nor was there anything in the living-room to suggest a day of rest. Thirza bustled about preparing breakfast, sandwiching the business between other duties, wearing a sack across her shoulders as she was continually running out. The place was filled with smoke; the internal arrangements touched a lower degree than simplicity and not far off beastliness; yet Anger was able to fit into these surroundings without disgust. It was no worse than drinking tea with some old charwoman in her back-basement; better, because the cleanest air in the country was bustling at the door; but there he had given pleasure to another, here he pleased himself; and Sunday was now to him a *dies non*.

"That bacon be home-secured," cried Thirza, who tacked on syllables or lopped them off in the ordinary course of ignorance, as she pointed to a reef of fat rising from red patches and yellow oils. "'Tis proper trade vor frosty weather. They eggs ha' gone abroad into the fat."

"To-morrow morning I am taking Bobby into Exeter. I should

like you to accompany us," said Anger, turning his eyes from the master who had a distressing trick of bringing his face into connection with his plate.

"Lor, sir, I never travels," cried Thirza. "I ha' the beasts to mind. They'd fret without me, and the fire would go out, and when I got home things would be all wice-wersy."

"A day's excursion would freshen you up," said Anger.

"The frost does that, sir. I get a bit tired like in the summer, but I be lusty again when cold weather comes along. You take Bobby, and I'll bide to home. Shall I fry another slice vor ye, sir? I see you likes a gude bit of home-secured bacon vor your breakfast."

"Mother means to say home-brewed," said Bobby apologetically.

"You gentlemen ha' got all the learning," said Thirza without envy. "You can get on with it while I does the work." Which saying from the lips of an intellectual woman might not have escaped a charge of irony.

The bells of Youlstone and a gleam of sunshine broke out together, while Anger went through the marshy ground which generations of Billacotts had not thought it worth their while to drain. Standing in the light, he awaited the coming of Nicholas from the dark; upon the Quoditch side of the hedge a few plants of barren strawberry were still in bloom; upon the Stiniel side long fronds of ladyfern decayed upon the moss. The gleam passed, the bells ceased, and as Nicholas did not come Anger climbed into the garden, ascended a few paces among mop-headed firs, pausing again when he saw the white walls of the house and heard a voice cry happily, "It's no use trying to escape. You cannot."

That is what I was saying to her last night, thought Anger.

Petronel and her father came down the bank at a headlong speed, strength dragging weakness by the hand; and it did appear to Anger as if she chose for him the roughest way, taking him over rocks and heaving roots, forcing him to make wild antics, for she could jump where he could only flounder. She held Nicholas tightly, so that he had either to keep up with her or fall; and his efforts to break her speed were so quaint that Anger laughed and brought them to a halt.

"Well, father-in-law," he cried, stepping out, "that was good exercise for a winter's morning."

"I have given him a good run, and he is awake now. He would never have come by himself," said Petronel, still with the light of mischief in her eyes.

"My bones will ache for days," growled Nicholas. "She is a wild maiden this morning. There's no holding her." Then he looked up and said crossly, "What are you doing on my property, sir?"

"He is a bit upset. His conscience worries him," said Petronel.

"I was trying to find you," explained Anger. "I am not damaging your crop of moss by trampling on it. You have broken your contract, Mr. Vigar. I know what you did last night, for I was trespassing then, spying upon a man whose promise is worthless, and I saw you with Curgenven selling your farm for nothing."

"He knows," said Petronel. "I made him listen before I made him run."

"It's no use talking, sir," said Nicholas sullenly. "Stiniel has gone and your hopes with it. I am satisfied with the price. It is better than any you can offer me, for I am to have Quoditch as a gift; I have an agreement to that effect signed and put away. By spring I shall have a farm in the sun, and Curgenven can live at Stiniel if he wants to."

"I see Petronel has not told you everything."

"I have left the best for you," she murmured.

"So you have been given Quoditch. What about Billacott?" asked Anger.

"Let him look to himself and pay his own debts. I have cleared off mine."

"What has come to him?" Anger murmured in amazement.

"Oh, he thinks it will be peace with mother now. He is still under the spell of Curgenven, but you can break that."

Nicholas would have escaped, but Petronel put out her strong arms and held him back.

"The bargaining is all over, child. Let me go," he said impatiently. "It is not safe to be talking here. Mrs. Vigar may be down upon us any moment."

"She and I have met already this morning; and I can understand the cause of her good temper," said Anger. "When you were bargaining last night, you forgot your daughter, and you forgot me," he said to Vigar strongly.

"It was the best thing I could have done for the maid," declared Nicholas. "If she marries Curgenven she will have Stiniel and Quoditch as well."

"With all the other lands of King Crookedback," added Anger.

"As for you, sir, you cannot marry. You are a priest. You are here for some purpose of your own. You are hiding from your friends. Go back to your monastery, sir."

"Take no notice of what he says," whispered Petronel. "He will come round like a lamb presently. Curgenven has beaten him; at least he supposes so, but he won't own to it. Now wake him up!"

"So you have sold Stiniel," said Anger to the farmer who would not look at him, "and you have been presented with the property of another man. Last night Petronel and I intercepted Curgenven, and deprived him of the deed you had just signed. We knocked the rascal down and robbed him. The deed is now destroyed, and Stiniel is as much yours to-day as it was yesterday."

"This is a made-up story," muttered Nicholas. "You rob Curgenven! No man would dare; and he is as strong as a giant."

"Ask your daughter," said Anger quietly.

"Ask Curgenven to produce the deed," she cried.

"One more thing," went on Anger. "Before you take a present from a man, be sure of the title you are getting. You suppose Billacott can never raise the money to pay his debts. You believe Curgenven can take Quoditch when he likes. But if he tries to meddle with those fields I'll make him smart for it. Quoditch is mine, Mr. Vigar. I have bought it for the sake of my friend Billacott, and to-morrow I am going to buy Stiniel for my wife."

Nicholas began to feel about him like a blind man. At last he looked up and began to smile. Then he put out his hand and mumbled, "You have done pretty well, sir. Curgenven spoke the truth when he said you were a Jesuit in disguise. What a tongue the man has! What a manner! Last night an angel would have trusted him. Yet you have beaten him, for the moment. I am your friend, sir; I always had a kindly feeling for you. Well, I am going now. I can breathe my own air again."

"You will come to Exeter in the morning and sign another deed," said Anger.

"I will see that he comes," cried Petronel.

"What shall I say to Mrs. Vigar?" mumbled Nicholas.

"Leave her to me," said the strong man. "When I am master she shall change her note."

It was scarcely noon when they left him, and Anger, returning across the marshes, discovered Bobby sketching on a sheet of paper, trying to copy his own signature which the master had written the night before.

"'Tis fearful how my hand shakes," he began. "He don't shake when I takes a mattock, but there b'ain't no dealing wi' this bit of pencil what ain't no heavier than a reed. Where he's wanted to go he never will, and where he ain't wanted to go he always do. Them old 'B's' be like bumbles in a garden, all places to wance and no fixing of 'em."

"Let me guide your hand," said Anger. "First a straight line, then a couple of loops, and the letter is made."

"Flourishes, schulemaster; I'll have a few o' they, if you please. I be main fond of flourishes. B'ain't he a proper 'B'? Seems almost as if us heard 'en buzzing."

The lesson continued and Bobby was soon enthralled by literature.

"If I'd known writing wur so easy, I'd ha' put my mind to it avore. This here shaking of my hand ain't nothing serious; it b'ain't old age, and it b'ain't affliction, and it b'ain't liquor, schulemaster. 'Tis ambition, I fancy. I wouldn't be certain it ain't genius."

"When you grow accustomed to holding a pen your hand will be as steady as mine. That is not a bad attempt. It is at least readable."

"Take your hand away and let a body write, will ye?" commanded Bobby. "I ha' got the letters fine. Little eye be a sort o' meat-hook wi' head of a door-nail atop; little ell be a loop and flourish to mun; little aye be a nought wi' a tail under; little see be another nought wi' a piece cut out on't; little nought be a nought; and little tea be a sort o' cross-mark."

"Write straight, Bobby. Your letters are like rungs of a ladder; and you must connect one with the other."

Bobby made a coupling between each character, and would endure no more criticism which was not flattering.

"I could sit here and sign my name till the cows comed home," he remarked with enthusiasm. "A 'B' here wi' flourishes, and another 'B' there wi' flourishes, and then two volks write their names to the side of mine to show as how I done it.

"Now that you can sign, only one witness will be required," said Anger; then, struck by a sudden idea, he drew up an agreement in most lay language, and urged Bobby to try his art again. But the little man grew distant and smoked at the words suspiciously.

"This is an undertaking that you will sell me Quoditch," explained Anger.

"What makes ye in such a cruel hurry?" demanded Bobby, looking down his nose.

"I have made a discovery since breakfast. Curgenven has given away your property—I won't say to whom. He might come here to-day, then I would show him this paper and warn him off."

Bobby stared up wildly and put a hand to his throat; while Anger merely pointed to what he had written and said, "Sign at once."

"How do you find out these things?" gasped the farmer.

"I walk about at night, when Curgenven does his work. Sign that paper, and then you can snap your fingers at him."

"I bought ye a bottle of whisky," muttered Bobby.

"And you opened it."

"I wur chilled when I got home. Night air be fearful poisonous. My hand be shaking worse than ever now."

"I understand you," said Anger; and he went for the bottle, helped Bobby generously, and the little man as liberally responded.

"If Curgenven wur to walk in," he announced presently, "I would sign my name, and wipe the pen across his mouth. You owes me three-and-sixpence vor that bottle. Will ye have a drop?"

"Thank you," said Anger drily. "But I do not drink spirits."

The paper was signed after a fashion, and Anger placed it in his pocket. The next business was to visit Woodland and to hand him part of the proceeds of the robbery, but Anger had not reckoned with the Sunday dinner, the feast of the week, which on that day was not ready until half-past two. Thirza was amazed to be told that time was of some value; while Bobby, who was prepared to spend a long hour gorging, stared in horror at the lodger's 'blasphemious' haste to leave the table. The little day was far spent before Anger escaped from Youlstone, and it was worn to a shadow by the time he reached the fields which sloped towards the vale of Riversmeet.

There approached a man, and a stranger, although Anger had a feeling they had met somehow before; while the same fancy connected that big body and white face with the webs of Curgenven. The incorruptible Wadge hesitated, lifted his hat, which was of a style worn by those whom all men respect, smiled in a loving fashion, and said, "I believe you are the Reverend Father Anger?"

"I prefer to be called Mr. Anger here," said the priest uneasily.

"I beg your pardon, sir. I am myself intimately connected with a type of religion, which may be called, without offence I hope, the grandchild of the church you have abandoned; a well-developed child, sir, which has broken free from the errors of its Anglican parent. If you have altered your views, sir, we shall be pleased to welcome you in Zion. All seats free, sir, and good sermons guaranteed."

"Thank you," said Anger stiffly, making a comparison between this form of welcome and Bobby's invitation to drink his own whisky. "But I am afraid your Zion is a long way from Youlstone."

"They are both set upon the hill-top, sir; the one actually, the other symbolically."

"Have you anything more to tell me?" asked Anger, anxious to stifle this patter.

"I was on my way to visit you, sir. Mr. Curgenven requested me to inform you it would give him great pleasure if you could make it convenient to call upon him and cheer him up. To-day he is confined to his bed as the result of an accident. He had the misfortune to stumble over a rock while walking in the dark and has wounded his head."

"Not seriously, I hope?"

"The wonderful brain is not affected, but as he is suffering from shock, doctor Palk will not allow him to go out. Sickness on a Sunday is a terrible calamity, sir. It deprives a man of his spiritual refreshment in God's house."

This fellow is certainly a rascal, thought Anger; then said, "If I have time, and those clouds yonder do not break, I will call on Mr. Curgenven. May I ask if you are employed in his office?"

"Mr. Curgenven honours me with a little work occasionally; some copying or surveying, sir. From my God I have inherited certain artistic powers—inherited I hope, sir, is not out of place. I illuminate texts of Scripture; I am not ashamed to say I frame and sell them, sir, but I do not forget to whom the ten per cent is due."

Anger drew out the post-card he had received the previous morning and presenting the address towards Wadge asked him, "Can you tell me whose handwriting that is? The post-mark, you see, is Riversmeet."

"I must admit, sir, the writing seems familiar, but I should be sorry to mention any name unless I felt certain I was right," said Wadge. "There are people in Riversmeet who have not found the Lord; I am speaking generally, sir. My mind has not fixed itself upon one sinner in particular."

"Yet you have some one in your mind?" suggested Anger.

"I should be extremely sorry, sir, even to mention the vicar of the parish, and I would not do so; but I would suggest the rascal has imitated his handwriting. Go to the church, sir, and compare that address with the written notices in the porch. I would not bring a charge against any man, and if the vicar were found guilty I would still shake him by the hand."

"Is he anti-Catholic?" asked Anger.

"I do not presume to offer my opinion, sir; but, according to the testimony of others, he is broad-minded where his own religion is concerned and narrow-minded as regards all others."

"I am obliged for your information," said Anger, as politely as he could, for the flabby mouth and puffy eyes repelled him. "I am also glad to have saved you the journey to Youlstone."

"I shall continue in the direction of the village," said Wadge. "The body is sane for the week's work—I am speaking personally, sir—but that is not sufficient. The mind must be in the same condition, and a walk where the mountains skip like rams and little hills like young sheep—they don't do it now, sir, but no doubt they did at one time—such a walk, I say, keeps the mind healthy. I am thankful to have met you, sir. May I shake you by the hand? Thank you, sir! You have done me good. God bless you, sir."

Wadge went on, murmuring to himself, "He will get a stronger post-card in the morning, God willing."

"He goes to Youlstone," was Anger's comment. "To Stiniel with a message for old Nicholas."

Woodland was not in his house, which connected with the Stores and was fitted up in a manner which suggested meanness; it being the tradesman's habit to walk on Sundays into lonely places. Leaving a message that he would return, Anger looked along the street, where not a living creature stirred from end to end, made a few paces irresolutely, then walked boldly to the door of the court of River Street, passed through, and pealed upon the bell. He was admitted by an aged dame, who pointed up a flight of steps and told him shortly, "Master be lying in the room up over."

The heat of a tremendous fire, a steam-like atmosphere, a vision of moisture on the roof and ivy trailing, were Anger's first impressions; afterwards he saw a bed, hardly larger than an infant's cot, and there a great head bandaged, while the room was filled, and the roar of the river conquered, by a great kind voice:

"My good friend, Anger! My dear old pal! Sit here, man, close to the bed and not too far from the fire. Lookye, my dear! What do ye think happened last night? I ran up to Stiniel, to have a chat with old Nick Vigar, and I tumbled over a great big stone set right in the middle of the track, and 'twas a wonder I didn't split my skull open. We little fellows get knocked over easy, but when we are short in the body we are long in the arms, and that's the way we save our heads. 'Twas one of Master Bobby's tricks, I fancy. A lazy little scoundrel, that Bobby. His way of mending roads is to roll big rocks upon the public highway. He did leave a lighted lantern, but I went and trod on it by accident. Now look at me, my dear! Lying abed all day for the first time in my life, forsaken by the world as you might say, for Palk has gone out chivying dear old Death from other bedsides, and my other old pal, Jimmy Woodland, gives me the cold east shoulder nowadays. Upon my soul, you, the visitor, are the only true sportsman of the lot, the only man who speaks as he feels, and has the pluck to obey his conscience and the decency to call upon a poor little chap who has his head squashed."

"Your tongue is as good as ever, Mr. Curgenven," said Anger, shrinking from those glowing eyes which had a different message.

"Don't give me any misters, you rascal. Call me toad, devil, or land-grabber, but don't mister me. You think I'm a land-grabber, don't ye now? What tales they put about in Youlstone! We all grab our bit of land when we die, and that's enough for me. You must have met old Wadge."

"A man with a flabby face stopped me."

"That's Wadge. A sanctimonious humbug, a pillar of Zion, and in private life the deuce of a bully. No sportsman! A crooked old Bible-spout. No offence, my dear. You are a man of the world since you came hunting along here, nosing down my girl, and carrying her off just as I was going to pounce. We hate one another sure enough, although we know a girl's not worth a quarrel. Riversmeet is full of wenches. What fun we had in our student days! Whether we are students at law, or budding clerks in holy orders, we defy Court and Church when we are twenty. We think nothing of holding up some country solicitor in the dark and taking a few deeds off him, but we never forgot to send back the deeds by registered post, and we generally had a good laugh with our victim afterwards; for if we were wild young devils we were honest ones. Find it hot, do ye? Push the window down a bit. I like the heat. I could sleep over a baker's oven."

"I can stand a dry heat, but this is damp," said Anger, glad to leave the bedside and hide his face.

"Forces the plants on the walls and roof. I like to lie in bed and see a bit of greenstuff. Lookye here, my dear! You and I are like politicians; we are bound to quarrel in public, but we are proper old pals in private. Up to Youlstone I'm going to call you an unfrocked priest, a corrupter of morals, and any other dirty name my tongue can get hold of; while you will call me a humpbacked son of Satan, a breaker-up of homes, a seducer of women, and so on. Outside this room we represent two different parties, but inside we are two good old sportsmen. Now, my dear, this is what I want to tell ye: I was robbed last night between Stiniel and Quoditch; I had some papers taken out of my pocket—'twas when I was lying stunned by the crack on my big-end—and Master Bobby Billacott was the man who took 'em. A dirty little coward, that Bobby."

"You are quite safe," said Anger. "He can neither read nor write."

"That's just it," cried Curgenven, feigning excitement. "He can't read my papers, but he can give them to somebody who has a bit of learning. You have made friends with him, and now you are lodging with him."

"Who told you that? I only went to Quoditch yesterday."

"My tame ring-ouzels bring me all the news. Bobby is sure to show you my papers, and I want you to grab 'em and send 'em down by post. One was a transfer of Stiniel from old Nick Vigar to myself; he owes me a bit of money, you see, and he reckons the easiest way to get clear is to pass over the property. Then there was a mortgage dated yesterday and signed just before I took my tumble; and there was a sheet of paper on which I had jotted down a list of my Youlstone loans. All these papers can be replaced easily enough, but it's a serious matter to know they are knocking about, for whatever Master Bobby gets hold of is sure to become public property. Will you get 'em back for me?"

"They may be destroyed," said Anger.

"Ah, well, that's likely. But Bobby would never make away with the list of mortgages. You know, of course, that nearly every bit of land in Youlstone is mortgaged to me. Ever since I started in practice my office has been besieged by farmers and moormen, all saying

the same thing, 'Give us a bit, master, and take the old land.' Now
I find myself properly slugged in Youlstone mire. I have advanced
hundreds of pounds, but I get practically no return, for these com-
moners can't keep the interest paid up, and most of 'em won't try.
I don't like the idea of taking possession, but if I don't I'm ruined.
Youlstone is forced upon me. What would you do with it?"

"Assign the mortgages," said Anger boldly.

"Ah, but I can't do that," cried Curgenven, foreseeing what
answer his opponent would have given to such a question as,
"To whom?" The spectre of Woodland leaning over the arm of
his chair, and staring of money, still remained. "I should lose half
my business. The people would say, 'You have thrown us over,
Curgenven.' I must either lose my capital, or take Youlstone; and
between you and me, old sportsman, I have decided to take it.
Lookye here!"

He grabbed a portfolio lying beside the bed, took out the proof
of an advertisement, and held it before Anger saying, "This will
soon appear in fifty newspapers. Listen, my dear! 'Discovery of a
moorland village, which lies hidden away among the mountains
like some old script in an Egyptian tomb. Scenery magnificent:
Devil's limekiln, Devil's throat, Devil's bellows, Devil's nose,
Devil's jump, and Devil everywhere'—that's my own suggestion.
'The last enchantment of the Middle Ages'—that's a quotation
from somebody. 'Astounding discovery by Jonathan Palk, M.D.
Is it Magic? Some potent quality in the air, which cures, in some
cases instantaneously, almost every disease which mankind can
suffer from. Staggering discovery recently made by a distinguished
Catholic priest, member of the Society of Jesus. His evidence
unimpeachable. A pool of water in a lonely glen, silent, remote,
o'erpressed by mystery. If the air should fail to cure disease,
the water cannot. The greatest wonder of all time. The pool of
Bethesda outdistanced. Great rush for land. Only a few plats left.
Come to the Air and Water. Apply at once to Jonathan Palk, M.D.,
Riversmeet. Do it to-day. To-morrow will be too late.'"

"I have not authorised the use of my name. Neither am I a
Jesuit," cried the bewildered Anger.

"Your name is not mentioned. You discovered the pool, and you must remain a priest for this occasion. This is advertising up-to-date, the only kind that fetches the public. The proprietor of a patent medicine would say no less in praise of his concoction, and the air of Youlstone is a bigger proposition than pills or tabloids. Now you see what use I am going to make of Youlstone, and you will be asking yourself where you come in. What do you say to a directorship?"

"I am no man of business."

"Be our chairman, and keep us straight," urged Curgenven.

"I am too ignorant. Besides I should not like to see Youlstone spoilt."

"It is as low down as it can be. We are going to lift it up, and make it a shelter of salvation for suffering souls—I might head the advertisement with that jingle. It's a proper scheme, my dear. There's a pot of gold in it."

"You will call in the mortgages before you publish the advertisement?"

"Why, certainly! I don't want to see a rich man, like old Jimmy Woodland, step in and outbid me. As I get possession of every piece of land, I shall fix a price upon it; and after the sale I shall divide the amount of purchase-money between the company and the late mortgagor. So nobody will suffer and everybody will benefit."

"That sounds fair," murmured Anger with a start.

"I think so. The land is worthless at present, like the work of an artist who has his reputation to make. We who make Youlstone famous are entitled to a half-share in the profits. You will keep the matter dark, my dear. Nobody knows of this except you and I, old Palk, and Jimmy, who won't come in and I will tell you why. He has made his fortune, good fellow that he is, but he don't like the idea of other men making theirs. He believes he has no pride, but for all that he loves to hear himself called the one rich man of Riversmeet. I told you he is dangerous, and so he is; our friend so long as we plod along, but dangerous, to you and to me, when we meddle with his monopoly. He don't trust me, Anger," said the lawyer with deep feeling. "He believes I am capable of low dealing—that's the tradesman's spirit in him. He thinks if the plan succeeds I shall grab the whole of the purchase-money, and not give a penny to my good neighbours. I couldn't do that even if I wanted to; for every transaction would go through the hands of Palk and yourself. Now then, old sport! Put in a thousand, and be one of us."

"I must have time to think about it," muttered Anger, wholly unable to say what was in his mind.

"Take the night, and come to me to-morrow. You might deliver a message for me to Bobby Billacott. Tell him if he dares play any other trick upon me, or if he makes public the contents of those papers he found on me last night—I shall know, for every man in Youlstone will be babbling like a poet; or if he opposes me in any way whatever, I'll show him no mercy, I will drive him out of the place and make him sorry he ever saw my hump. I don't call myself a vindictive man, but I am bound to protect my interests, and I am not going to lose my game to satisfy the pique of a rascal I have tried to benefit."

"I must be going. It is getting dark," said Anger feebly. "I hope you will be about again to-morrow."

"You are the best old fellow in the world to come here and cheer me up. Mind the stones as you go back. Don't you go falling over them like I did—and lookye here, my dear, take the maid and be happy, for I don't want her. We crooked little chaps were never meant for pretty wenches. Marry the maid, and God bless you both. I'll drink a glass at your wedding, I'll show you a country dance, I'll give you an acre or two up over Youlstone, and later on I'll be godfather to your children, hanged if I won't, for you and I are two good sportsmen and old pals."

With that voice roaring in his ears, Anger went out into the street which was deserted no longer, for townsfolk were crossing in currents on their way to various tabernacles. Woodland's house fronted a dark corner where boys and maidens were wont to meet and express approval for each other; Anger in his haste almost forced one such entwined couple off the doorstep. The shadow of

Curgenven's presence seemed to follow, interposing a hairy hand between his and the knocker.

The merchant was sitting with his boys, drinking tea after a ten-mile walk. He greeted Anger with effervescent warmth, and invited him to join them; and himself did all the talking until the guest made a sign towards the door.

"Certainly, sir. We will go and have a little chat," said Woodland briskly, laying down his saucer and replacing his cup upon it. "Mr. Anger comes on business, boys," he added, then followed the visitor in his self-reproachful way and ushered him towards the Stores.

"In the room we have just left there is always the danger of the housekeeper overhearing," he said. "That is why I bring you here. You heard me mention to the boys you come on business? That is enough for them. Unless you were seen entering my house, Curgenven will never hear of it."

He lighted a candle, and before the wick had finished spluttering heard all that Anger had to say, his head wagging and his hands folded across his stomach.

"It was very bold of you, sir, very bold indeed, to rob our friend," he said. "But I shall have to tell Mr. Lyson, as I tell you now, that I am unable to carry out my former plan. Briefly, sir, I find Mr. Curgenven too strong a foe. One moment, sir. There was something of a scene yesterday; I was hooted in the street; regular customers crossed the road. All the principal inhabitants had received post-cards, which pretended to expose the wickedness of my secret life. Fiction, sir, the usual style—it does not vary—and it is always more impressive than the fact."

"Why take notice of such things? I received a post-card too, and here it is. No doubt the handwriting is the same."

"No, sir. That is a different hand. These doses of poison may not trouble you, but they would destroy me in time. Anonymous letter-writing, sir, has now become something very like a recognised profession; it ruins many a man of business; breaks up homes, causes suicides. The ordinary bungler is easily detected; but the professional, the artist, is always safe from discovery, simply because he knows his business. You can fight a man who insults you, and shake him by the hand when all is over, but you cannot knock the stuffing out of shadows."

"We know Curgenven has sent these post-cards."

"But my business would be ruined if I brought the charge against him. No one would believe Curgenven was capable of playing so low a game, and he himself would weep with horror at the mere suggestion."

"What has made him suspect you?"

"Our eyes met at a public dinner, and that moment I was off my guard."

"I have bought Quoditch to-day, relying upon our understanding. Will you fail me?"

"Certainly not, sir. I am bound by every contract you have made, but I cannot continue. Through Palk I shall give a hint to Curgenven that I am passive in the matter of 'Youlstone Limited.' My boys have been talking to me seriously. Like me they were not meant for this shut-up business. It is true I have not failed, but I should have done still better in the air. They have set their minds upon the Colonies. Their imagination has been fired by accounts of the vast spaces still awaiting cultivation, and being ambitious lads they desire to acquire huge tracts of land and farm in the grand style. If I make no mistake, sir, Harry will be known one day as a wheat king, while James will reign in cattle; but each of them will require a large amount of capital to start with. Now you understand me, sir. The Stores are exceedingly prosperous at present, but if this crusade against me is to continue I may soon be doing a losing business."

"What about Youlstone?"

"It must fall into the hands of Curgenven. If I pledge my word not to interfere, I am powerless to act upon the day of sale. I owe a debt to Dartmoor, and would gladly repay it if I could. Business has developed in my mind while walking in its atmosphere. There is indeed marvellous air in Youlstone."

CHAPTER XVI

THE DELUGE

EVERY day was more or less of a holiday so far as Bobby and labour were concerned, but a day appointed for a trip to the city made the whole year memorable. Such an excursion would require far more energy than staying at home and doing a little carpentry at the gate, but then it was work of a congenial kind, and for that all lazy folk have stamina. At weird hours of the night Bobby was thumping like a watchman at the lodger's door, imploring him to rise, "Vor it be five miles to Riversmeet station, and us have only a few hours left." Near daybreak these disturbances increased in violence and occurred at intervals of two minutes, which enabled Bobby to run down into the living-room, there to assure Thirza it was far too late for breakfasting, then to reclimb the stairs with such pessimistic announcements as, "They trains won't wait vor we, schulemaster; if they sees us coming a mile away, they won't bide. I ha' hung the harness on old Pharisee and I ha' greased the wheels of the jingle. I misdoubts they wheels," he added on one occasion. At last Anger appeared, unmoved by all this clamour, and remarked that Nicholas Vigar was likely to accompany them.

"What you taking he vor?" asked Bobby jealously. "He b'ain't neighbourly and he'm cruel slow. Us'll never get away to-day, I knows us won't."

Anger did not reply, for just then the postman appeared, ill-tempered at being brought across the common merely to deliver an abusive post-card, which Thirza received and handed to the lodger, who tore the thing in half and flung the pieces on the fire; while Bobby hurried out to make sure of the time, returning with the depressing statement that the daylight was half an hour late and it was all up with everything.

"Eat your breakfast, Bobby man," Thirza implored.

"I can't spare the time," cried the restless little man. "Them old trains won't wait; not even half an hour. Schulemaster sots there, and eats bacon and drinks tea. 'Tis nought to he."

"Have some whisky, Bobby," said Anger mischievously.

"Well, schulemaster, that wouldn't waste no time, I reckon."

When later on the gate of Stiniel disgorged no Nicholas, the farmer of Quoditch became emotional. He ran up the Pinch, shouting for his neighbour, while Anger followed leisurely, desiring Bobby to be calm, and Thirza came out upon the road with a sandwich of bread and bacon and a worried countenance. This holiday-making was too much for her nerves and she was near the point of breaking down.

The cries took effect, for Nicholas appeared, alone, clad in his working garments, with his right arm in a sling. Bobby gasped in relief, and with amazement to see the old neighbour so ill-fitted for a jaunt, before hurrying down to bring forth the jingle and to inform Thirza they might do it yet.

"What is the matter with your arm?" asked Anger.

"Disabled by my daughter's orders," said Nicholas grimly. "Yesterday evening a man called Wadge came with a fresh deed from Curgenven. Petronel bandaged my right hand, put the arm in a sling, and told me to regard myself as suffering from blood-poisoning. So the deed went back unsigned."

"That means Curgenven may be here any moment, if he can leave his bed. Bobby is wise to hurry us off," Anger muttered.

"It's all right about the money?" hinted Nicholas sharply.

"Mr. Lyson will pay off Curgenven, and give you a cheque for the balance directly you have signed."

Nicholas gave a sprightly movement towards the rhododendrons, dived into them and produced a bag. "A few clothes," he explained. "If the business is settled to your satisfaction, I cannot return for some time. I have relations in Exeter, and will stay with them until the storm blows over. That crazy boy will look after the beasts, and he will do it better than I should, being fond of animals and one himself, I suppose. Petronel knows all about it."

"Where is she?"

"Watching Mrs. Vigar. My wife is not very well this morning."

"And Petronel is nursing her!"

"Watching her," growled Nicholas. "Let us be off."

"Come along, neighbour," shouted Bobby. "Us will get to the old train if the wheels don't fly abroad. What be doing wi' the bag?"

"Varmer be going to stand in market," suggested Thirza.

"That's right. Business as well as pleasure," said Nicholas.

"Woe unto ye, Pharisee," howled Bobby. "Push open the gate, mother."

The vehicle had been well-named jingle, for two wheels clinked, and two rattled, while all made fan-like motions as they revolved; but this state of decrepitude had been established for so long that it had become regarded as normal. The three men and a bag, huddled together like a group of statuary, reached Riversmeet without losing a wheel, attracting much attention as they jingled through the town and rattled into the yard of the inn where the vehicle was to wait until they returned. Monday was the day sacred in the business calendar of Riversmeet to pensiveness, and the sudden arrival of three countrymen stirred up the tranquil depths.

They made their way uphill to the station, Vigar's bag following in the omnibus, which, upon its arrival, was found to contain two passengers, one a commercial traveller, the other a small and smiling gentleman, who wore a large felt hat to conceal strips of plaster across his forehead. In a fine holiday humour he ran upon the platform, almost embraced the excursionists, and cried, "What, you rascals! So you mean to enjoy yourselves. Upon my soul, I am coming with you. We will frisk about for a day. Four good fellows are better company than three; when two quarrel there is no odd man out. Let me take the tickets. Upon my soul, I'll treat you all."

Bobby might look glum, Nicholas surly, and Anger might despair, for all three knew they could not hinder Curgenven from accompanying them, nor break away from him, nor explain the real object of the journey. The chattering lawyer pushed his three silent companions into a compartment and regaled them with anecdotes in broad dialect, ignoring matters of business, never glancing at Vigar's bandaged hand; Bobby was soon laughing, for he had come to enjoy himself, while Nicholas tacitly admitted Curgenven was an excellent companion, and even Anger had to smile at the merry little clown, who was telling them, "Never go for a day's pleasure without a lawyer. He can tell you just how far to go without getting into trouble; and if you do get into difficulties he is there to argue the law on your behalf. We countryfolk may be dull at home, but, my word, how we change when we find ourselves in town!"

When they reached Exeter the dwarf placed himself between Bobby and Nicholas, holding tightly an arm of each, and announced his intention of showing them the sights.

"No arm for you, my dear," he called to Anger. "I am guide here, and I promise you we will miss nothing. We will stand on the city walls—if we can find 'em—and go round the cathedral, and through the Guildhall and Museum, and as many churches as you have stomach for, and then we must pay a visit to the sewage farm which is one of the finest in the kingdom. Master Bobby don't want churches and ruins, I fancy. He's smelling for the latest thing in cook-shops."

So they went on, visiting one place after another, until the morning was gone, and still Anger could not hit upon a plan for releasing his two comrades. Not that Bobby desired his freedom, for Curgenven in that present mood was just the man for him; but Nicholas was getting weary, and said so.

"We will have something to eat," cried the lawyer.

"What about your bag?" asked Anger. "You did not claim it at the station."

"I forgot all about it. I'll come with you and see to it," said Nicholas.

"We will all go," said Curgenven merrily. "What are you doing with luggage, old neighbour?"

"I thought of staying the night," said Vigar.

"I'll stay with you. We will all stay, and go to the theatre, and carry Bobby home afterwards."

"It don't matter after all. The bag will be safe at the station. Nobody would steal my old rags," said Nicholas moodily.

"All hungry folks, this way," cried Curgenven, still hanging to Bobby and Nicholas, controlling all their movements. "A band plays in the restaurant over the way. Fair damsels shall charm us with harp and fiddle while we discuss a plateful of roast beef. Proper old sea-dogs, we three! Bobby with his nautical roll. Nicholas with his arm in a sling, and myself cut across the head. The shipmaster follows with an eye for foul weather."

That moment Anger saw his opportunity. Hesitating, until the others had advanced a few paces across the road, he went at the top of his speed to the court of the clicking typewriter. Passing through the office without a word to the clerks, he made for Lyson's private room, thumped the door, opened it, and came upon the old gentleman standing before the fire, with a glass of wine in one hand and a biscuit in the other.

"My dear sir!" gasped Lyson. "Why, it is Edward's old schoolfellow."

"Mr. Lyson! I have brought Nicholas Vigar to sign that deed, and another man whose property I have arranged to buy in Woodland's name," cried Anger. "Curgenven saw us pass through Riversmeet, joined us at the station, insisted upon coming with us, and now he has got hold of the two men, and hangs on to them, and won't let them go——"

"Slowly, please, slowly," interrupted Lyson. "I remember your story very well. Sit down. Help yourself to a glass of wine."

"What can we do?" Anger almost shouted, disregarding the invitation. "Curgenven has taken them both to a restaurant at the corner, and he won't leave them for an instant. You can't say anything to him—he is so devilishly friendly."

"These farmers are free agents," said the old gentleman. "We cannot bring them here against their will, and if they prefer to remain with Curgenven, who is to prevent them?"

"Billacott has forgotten what I brought him here for, while Vigar is far too nervous to mention it. They know that Curgenven would shrink from nothing to prevent them signing. He must be acting illegally by detaining them."

"I do not suppose Mr. Curgenven would do anything actually illegal in the streets of Exeter," said Lyson. "He is a clever man, and no doubt is playing his own game well; but you cannot go out and tell a policeman to remove him from his position between the men on the ground that he is exerting an undue influence over them."

"Cannot you order him to release them?"

"I will come with you to the restaurant," said Lyson. "You shall introduce me, and then, after exchanging a few compliments with Curgenven, I can tell the farmers I have something to say to them if they will be kind enough to wait upon me here. That is the utmost I can do."

He picked up his hat, and two minutes later they entered the restaurant to the sound of instruments of music; but the three holiday-makers were not there. In the endeavour to outwit Curgenven, Anger had actually played into his hands; and the merry little lawyer, who had towed his two victims in an opposite direction, would take good care they did not get into touch with the enemy again.

"He is too much for me," said Anger fiercely, as they went back into the stillness of the Close. "I bring these men to Exeter, and he goes off with them; and the scoundrel insisted upon paying my fare both ways."

"Then it would appear he has brought you," remarked Lyson.

"He will get Vigar's signature before the day is out; he will draw my secret out of Billacott," declared Anger. "He knows I never brought the man here just to give him a day's outing. Well, Bobby is a fool, and he deserves to lose his land."

"I understand Mr. Woodland does not propose bidding for these Youlstone properties," said Lyson. "It is just as well. He would only lose his money. These barren moorland fields are hardly worth a pound apiece."

"They may be worth hundreds some day."

"That time is far ahead. These schemes of development are generally fairy-tales with an unhappy ending for those who invest money in them. If Curgenven is a rogue—I don't say that he is— we have only to give him time, and he is sure to ruin himself. He will end by making himself an enemy of the public and having a quantity of unsaleable land upon his hands. Let the fox run on, you can follow at your leisure and come in at the death."

Anger wasted no time hunting about the city, but went to the station and returned to Riversmeet by the first train. The atmosphere increased in heaviness as he passed through the country, and while ascending to Youlstone he noticed a deathly stillness which exaggerated the smallest sound. Reaching the moor, the scene became wild and grand; clouds were hanging low upon Youlstone cleave, and between them granitic masses appeared as if suspended in the air; higher pressed a mist, tinged with colour which seemed unnatural, crossed through and through as it were with the glow reflected from deep blue lanterns carried in the sky by unseen hands.

"Savages would hide in their holes, believing their gods, or their devils, were descending upon them. Even I cannot escape a feeling of uneasiness," murmured Anger.

The blue light faded quickly, more clouds drifted down until the sky was filled and the whole moor darkened; but the silence remained, bringing a restless influence upon all things living. Anger heard a stampede of ponies among the rocks, and as he came up into the village cattle were lowing, horses plunging in their stables, and even the cocks and hens were chattering.

Thirza, hard at work piling faggots around her primitive fowl-house, stared up when she heard footsteps, and her simple face looked frightened as she called, "Where's Bobby to? Where's the old jingle, master?"

Anger told her how Curgenven had taken possession of his two companions, and added, "They will come by the next train."

"Not they," cried Thirza. "See what be coming down on us beyond!"

"What?"

"Aw, man, where be your eyes to? Snow be falling now up over. Us will be smothered avore morning."

Anger went into the house to escape her questions, and hardly had he reached shelter when the fall began, and the little room became dark, and all the fields seemed haunted. Flakes like curled feathers filled the air and settled upon ground which was dry with frost. The figure of Thirza, bustling from shed to byre, making preparations for a siege, with the everlasting sack around her shoulders, became white, then grey, and presently invisible.

She reappeared, stamping and spluttering, shook herself before fastening the door, with superstitious terror of some demon in the snow, then told the lodger almost sharply to light the lamp and be doing something.

"I will go up to Stiniel and tell them what has happened," he said.

"They won't get back to Youlstone, and that's a sure thing. They'll bide to Riversmeet. Us ain't had snow the like o' this vor thirty winters. I wur a young maid then, but I mind it well, vor us wur pretty nigh starved. Why didn't ye tell Curgenven to leave my master bide?"

"If Bobby chose to go off with him, how could I prevent it?" said Anger smartly.

"I b'ain't saying nought agin you. Bobby be led easy, I fancy, and if Curgenven tells 'en to do a thing he'm sure to do it," said Thirza more tranquilly.

"May I put this sack round my shoulders?" he asked.

"Take 'en and welcome. If you'm going up over, you'd best be quick about it."

There was no wind. The upland was then as calm as any valley, but darkness had settled, and the snow was more bewildering than a mist. Anger was forced to grope towards the hedge, then feel his way along it to the trackway. Once there it was impossible to go wrong. Snow, already heaped about the gate of Stiniel, made it hard to open, while, inside, the great shrubs were sprawling. No light shone from the house; Anger did not know he had reached it until his foot struck the porch. He knocked and the door was opened by Whippety, fantastically dressed, with a cat upon his shoulder and a lighted lantern in his hand.

"Go and tell Miss Vigar I am here," said Anger.

"Flowers! Pretty white flowers!" mumbled the imbecile, darting a finger at the flakes.

Anger pushed at the boy, who started aside, then shambled away without a sound. The uninvited guest entered, closing the door, waited in the dark for some moments, then called out. He seemed to hear a distant voice answering, and soon footsteps ascended towards him—certainly they were not descending—and a tired voice muttered, "So you have failed again. I was getting so tired of my own company I was just going to let her out."

"Petronel!" he whispered.

The girl gave a gasp.

"Sweetheart, the snow!"

"You glide into the house like a ghost. What have you done with father?"

"I will tell you nothing until we have a light. It has been a day of wretched disappointment, darling, and now I must cheer my eyes by looking at you."

"We do not want a light," she said, coming forward and holding his hands. "Use your imagination instead of your eyes. You know what I look like by this time. Now I am wearing old clothes, my hair is untidy, my face is covered with kitchen smuts. I am not fit to be seen. So the deed is signed and Stiniel is mine."

"It is not signed, and Curgenven has beaten me again."

For the second time he told the story, while Petronel listened, breathing fiercely.

"This snow you were waiting for has lost me Stiniel," she said. "I wished for an ordinary fall to whiten the ground, not this deluge. Father cannot get beyond Riversmeet, and Curgenven will never leave his side until he signs. Why didn't you wait at the station?"

"I could not have done anything. Curgenven would have dragged your father and Bobby to his house, and have slammed the door in my face. I have done my best, sweetheart."

"And lost," she muttered.

"Only Stiniel! What is that? Why do you cling to this dark and dreary house, little girl? It has brought you no happiness. Let me find you a better and brighter home. I have already begged you to give up Youlstone and to forget Stiniel. Will you not do so now?"

"I cannot," she said. "I am bound to this house, and if you are going to marry me you are bound too. Go to Riversmeet! Plough your way through the snow somehow, meet my father, and fight Curgenven for him."

"The roads are blocked already. It will not be easy to get down to Quoditch. What is wrong with you, my darling?"

"I am miserable. That is why I would not let you have a light. You might hate my face if you could see it now."

"Sweetheart, what are you wearing?" he cried. "Your clothes seem to be in rags—and your beautiful hair is down."

"Mrs. Vigar and I have been fighting," said the girl hoarsely.

"My poor little Petronel! I believe your wrists are bruised, and your face is scratched," he murmured, stroking her cheeks and throat with ardent fingers.

"I pushed her into the cellar and turned the key. You must have heard me come up. I thought you were father."

"You told me you were going to let her out."

"I should have opened the door if you had been father. Now she can stay."

"She makes no noise."

"She is tired out. My boy, do you still want to marry me? Do you still want to make me good?"

Anger's heart rejoiced at this, the first tenderness she had shown.

"More than ever when you speak to me so sweetly," he whispered. "The snow has come. I claim you by your promise."

"Would you fight through the snow with me now?"

"Yes, I would attempt the impossible."

"You are right," she said. "It is impossible to beat Curgenven. He is master of Stiniel now."

"But you are mine," cried Anger. "Stiniel is nothing to us. Let us escape, darling; when the snow thaws let us go away with it towards the sea, and put an ocean between ourselves and Curgenven."

"Let me go," she gasped. "I know of one way, but now—and since I have loved you—it seems terrible. Before it was natural. If you love me, you must help me."

"Once before you spoke like this," he murmured. "What holds you to Stiniel, darling?"

"I cannot speak yet. This snow stifles me. Go home now. I will get to you somehow in the morning. If you do not sleep to-night you will know I am also awake, thinking of you."

"I shall sleep, satisfied with the knowledge that you love me. Say you will escape with me?"

"To-morrow," she muttered.

"Let me light a lamp, and look at you—one glance."

"No, no; I could not bear you to see me in these rags. Go, before the snow gets any deeper. Good night, my darling, and God bless you."

"And you too, my own sweetheart. I have been longing for one sweet word from your dear lips, and now you have spoken it," said Anger fondly, while she gently urged him to the door.

While floundering over the Pinch, his feet stumbled at a stone which his own hands had placed there, the only one he had omitted to replace, and he fell heavily, bruising his hands. The influence of Curgenven had become so mighty in Youlstone that even the stones avenged him. Reaching the crazy cottage by the aid of lamplight streaming from the window, Anger discovered Thirza weeping for her husband, knowing him to be lost between the devil and the snow.

"If Bobby ha' got to Riversmeet, he'll come on. He'll never bide wi' Curgenven," she cried. "He'm on the road now, and he can't get forrard, and he can't get back."

Anger went to his room leaving the doleful woman to practise her gift of second-sight in secret.

All night the calm was as heavy as the snowfall which never ceased. When morning came with an unaccustomed glare, big flakes still drifted, while all the hills looked twice as great, sheds were hidden, and not even the strength of Thirza could force the door open.

"Us be buried alive," she shouted. "The like ha' never been knowed avore. Snow to the Pinches be twenty feet, and fifty feet, and a hundred feet, I reckon. It be all spread over the windows down under. How be it wi' you?"

"My window is just clear," replied Anger.

"Will ye jump out? You can't come to no harm. I ha' got a shovel handy; fetched 'en in avore dark. I'll drap him down to ye."

When Anger was dressed he forced open the window and committed his body to the great bank of snow which was firmer than he had expected. Sinking waist-deep, he received the shovel from Thirza, then struggled round to the front and began to dig. Half an hour later the door was clear, and Thirza reappeared with the mournful cry, "Postman won't never come this morning."

"Nor anybody else," gasped Anger, going inside to rest.

The morning was well advanced when a voice called from the snow, and hurrying outside Anger discovered Petronel, enveloped in a cloak, with a shawl about her head, and a couple of sieves tied firmly to her boots.

"I promised to come, and here I am," she said, "thanks to Whippety, who brought me these sieves and made me understand I was to walk on them. He has no brains, yet he manages these things better than we should. Where is Mrs. Billacott?"

"Milking the cows."

Petronel came into the living-room, threw off her cloak and shawl, and stood before him clothed in her white dress.

"While thinking last night I finished it," she said.

"And you wear it to tell me you are mine, that you will forget Stiniel, that you will escape with me from Youlstone?"

"Yes, I am yours, I will marry you as soon as you like, and I will go wherever you like to take me, and sometimes perhaps I will do as you bid me. The snow has come, I wear my white dress, and I am serious."

"Now Curgenven may do as he will with Youlstone," cried Anger. "For I have won the heart, the soul, the beauty, of the place."

The snow continued that day, and the night following; but on Wednesday came the thaw. No news arrived until Thursday morning: Bobby and Nicholas had been safe in the house of Curgenven, and that same evening they returned.

Leaving Bobby in the embrace of Thirza, Anger pursued Nicholas, asked his question, and received the answer he had looked for.

"I am the tenant of Stiniel now. I'll ask you not to come into the house again," said the old farmer in a surly fashion.

"May I ask what you have gained?" asked Anger boldly.

"A sum of money promised, freedom from persecution assured, and the friendship of Curgenven guaranteed."

"You may find his promise very much like your own," said Anger, as he turned to leave the shuffling old man.

Bobby lurched towards him in a tearful state immediately he was released from Thirza's mighty arms.

"Schulemaster," he muttered, forcing his pedagogue aside into a snow-drift. "I ha' done it; I ha' wrote my name at last, wrote him wi' flourishes, and I be ruined."

"As you deserve," said Anger.

"I told 'en I could write my name, and he wouldn't believe me. Cruel friendly he wur, pretty nigh kissed me, and give me the best of everything, he did, fine golden tobacco, and old brandy, schulemaster——"

"You fool!"

"Said I couldn't write my name, and so I done it to show 'en I wur a scholar, but I wur mazed wi' brandy, and then a man I hadn't seen avore come out from a corner, and said he had seen me do it, and wouldn't ha' believed if he hadn't seen me wi' his own eyes, and I'd done a gude bit o' business sure enough, and Curgenven wur laughing worse than ever, and got that kind he couldn't do enough vor me."

"So you signed away your house and farm," said Anger contemptuously.

"Told me next day, he did. Said I had pressed 'en to buy the place, and he had agreed agin his own wishes. I told 'en to give it back, and he said he couldn't, vor the deed was signed, and if he didn't take Quoditch he'd have to ask me vor the money back. Said he wur pinched vor money; laughing he wur, and squeezing of my hand like as if I wur a maiden."

"What did he give you?"

"Best brandy, schulemaster."

"What money, I mean?"

"Nought. Said he hadn't got none. Promised to give me a few pounds when he sold the place."

"Did you consent to the sale in presence of a witness?"

"Us wur talking and laughing a fearful lot, and I reckon I said yes to everything, but 'twas the brandy talking, and not me, schulemaster—gude liquor always ses yes; and the young fellow wur sitting in the corner, and I never knowed of it. What be the next best thing I can do?"

"Put your hands into your pockets and whistle," advised Anger.

Next morning the postman's holiday was over. He delivered for Anger the habitual post-card, which was never glanced at, together with a most kindly letter from Curgenven. Would the dear old sportsman mind clearing out of Quoditch at once, as he had bought the farm, and proposed pulling down the "hovel." There were some very decent lodgings in Riversmeet, and if the excellent friend would give consent he would run about and engage some rooms immediately. What a jolly good time they had enjoyed in Exeter! But why had the best fellow of the lot slipped away from him? He could not believe he was really inconveniencing his future partner by asking him to leave such a wretched hole as Youlstone—he meant Quoditch—but under the circumstances it was inevitable; and he remained for evermore his friend and brother, Curgenven.

CHAPTER XVII

WARNINGS

NINE o'clock—late night for Riversmeet—found Curgenven in his oven, which he called a den, a small but comfortable room. A huge fire of peat, coal, and logs nicely blended, and a padded chair, containing artful pockets, supplied the comforts; a desk beside the window, which jutted over the river, suggested mental energy; while a tall bookcase close behind gave the finishing touch of learning, although this narrow bookcase, standing in

deep shadow, was a fraud of painted wood. Had Curgenven been
hunted to his den, the pursuer would have found an empty room,
for the lawyer would have passed into his office by means of that
revolving bookcase which by then would have been turned back
into its usual position and fastened by a bolt.

"Here comes old Jonathan," chuckled the dwarf, as a bell
afar off jangled. "He is late to-night, but this is killing weather.
Pneumonia pinches the old folks and keeps him running."

"Gentleman to see ye, sir," croaked the aged housekeeper.

"Come along in, my Jo. Old Wadge! Good Lord!"

"Nobody about, sir. A good dark night, so I thought I might
drop in with great respect, and ask how things are going," said the
doorkeeper of Zion.

"Sit down, Wadge. Always glad to see an honest man. Any
good pushing the decanter your way?"

"Well, sir, if you would be so kind as to specify the contents,"
suggested Wadge obsequiously.

"Brandy, my dear! The heroic tipple. Pure juice of the grape.
Nature's sweet mother's milk."

"It is a sin, though I do not presume to judge my neighbours,
sir, to take strong liquor for the sake of bodily gratification,"
droned Wadge professionally. "But as a medicine, sir, as a panacea
for bodily ills, sir, brandy is like rain upon the parched soil. Strong
drink is raging, but then I have a slight chill upon me, sir; and I do
not forget the miracle of Cana."

"Help yourself," said Curgenven.

"I trust you are satisfied with my work, Mr. Curgenven," the
man went on earnestly, after swallowing a substantial dose, and
rubbing a little of the brandy upon his nostrils. "At first I feared
my little strokes of penmanship were likely to be disregarded. I
became somewhat extravagant, sir. It occurred to me sometimes I
might be running away with my pen."

"No offence, my dear, so long as the pen belongs to you,"
Curgenven chuckled.

"A slight lapse of the tongue, sir; this chill, I fear, develops into
influenza. Until to-day I was feeling somewhat downcast, sir, but

now that I know the Jesuit has left Youlstone my heart rejoices, and my spirit is strong to strike another blow for God and His Zion."

"Don't ye flatter yourself too much," said Curgenven smartly. "You have done your best, no doubt, but your literature never rooted the rascal out of Youlstone. To begin with, he goes to the inn and I have to tell the landlord to show him the way out. He passes on to Quoditch; I buy the place and ask him to move on. He runs round to every house in Youlstone looking for lodgings, but I have been over the ground before him. He actually had an idea of taking shelter in a ruin down Youlstone cleave, but when he gets to the place he finds the roof has been torn off and a side wall pushed over. These winter storms, Wadge! So he is compelled to take shelter in Riversmeet."

"I presume you wish to move him on, sir?"

"He must be cleared out of the district if you want to earn your money."

"I can do it, sir. I only wish to know if you approve of the extreme method?"

"You must be very careful, Wadge. Illegality is not to be contemplated, and your extreme methods go very near the wrong side of the line."

"Sir!" said the doorkeeper with holy indignation. "You would not cast a slur upon my character? Every man who knows me, sir—and every woman, sir—regards me as——"

"I know," interrupted Curgenven. "Your righteousness is a shining light. You live admired, and you will die respected. I cannot come up to you. I merely ask you to be careful."

"All things shall be done decently, sir. Ah, Mr. Curgenven, if I could only see you every Sunday, sir, morning and evening, seated in Zion, how full my heart would be; how thankfully I could sing!"

"It wouldn't do, my dear. I should be called a partisan. I have my business to think of and that compels me to be cosmopolitan in my religion. Zion is a poor place."

"But the joy of the whole earth, sir."

"In theory. Here comes old Jonathan," said Curgenven, as the bell jangled. "Good night, Wadge, and get to work as soon as possible."

"I will watch the Jesuit, sir, and directly the snow goes I will get to business."

The man went out, bestowing a blessing upon Palk as he passed the doctor in the passage; while Curgenven caressed his wounded forehead and murmured amiably, "I have everything local within my grasp. Youlstone, Spa of the West, is mine." Then he changed his note and shouted, "Jonathan, my love! What news?"

"This room is far too hot," began the doctor.

"For you, and no other man, I will open the window. Pitch in my own particular chair, while I stand before you as a fire-screen. The decanter is handy. What is the latest from the Stores?"

"Woodland repeats he will have nothing to do with the business," said Palk, half closing his eyes. "He has told me candidly he disliked the idea so much that he had serious thoughts of buying up the place himself with a view to restoring the properties to the commoners; but now he has given me his word he will not interfere. Woodland's word is as good as his bond."

"He's a queer old lad," said Curgenven. "This sort of thing ought to appeal mightily to his business instincts. Buying a whole village for a few hundreds, and selling it for twice as many thousands is an idea I should have expected him to revel in. But Jimmy has a difficulty with that selfish thing—his conscience."

"Where is the dishonesty?" said Palk in his heavy manner. "I cannot find it; and, as I told Woodland, I should be the last man to join in the scheme if there was anything wrong about it. We have to keep quiet, but secrecy is not dishonesty. If I make an important discovery in physics I am not going to tell everybody."

"Just so," said Curgenven. "Jimmy is jealous. If you and I were to die suddenly he would take up this Youlstone business with enthusiasm. A third share is no good to him."

"These people are going to sell their land at a fair price; we hope to resell at a profit," Palk went on. "If that is crooked dealing, where are we to find an honest man? We are gambling with our capital; we take the risk of losing every penny, and surely we are entitled to the chance of emerging with a fortune. Woodland's mind is disturbed by certain mortgages, which he understands you hold. I don't know why they should worry him, as it is part of a lawyer's business to accommodate his clients, and they may be supposed to know what they are doing when they borrow."

"Of course, there are mortgages, plenty of 'em—beastly things," growled Curgenven. "It is not divulging any professional secret to say I have lent money to the folks up over, and a rotten game it is. Nothing but worry—interest never coming in, capital unproductive. You know the way—pay to-morrow. No consideration for me whatever. They know I like 'em, they know I am easygoing, but not a man asks himself how I get a living. 'If I don't pay Curgenven, t'other fellow will,' is what they all say."

"And yet you propose to give them half the profits. It is too much," declared the doctor with more energy.

"Fair dealing," said Curgenven in a somewhat shocked voice. "I love the dear fools with all their faults. They are my neighbours, I am a member of every family circle—it is always the best chair and the fireside corner for old Curgenven—and I'll be generous with them, whatever happens. I have done some business already, Jonathan," he went on. "I have bought Stiniel and Quoditch. The best end of Youlstone is now the property of the company."

"Good!" exclaimed Palk. "I was afraid there might be trouble with Billacott."

"None whatever. He was anxious to sell, glad to get anything for his hovel and marshes. In addition I own two old farms at the top of Youlstone cleave; there are no houses, and the fields have been out of cultivation for years. Altogether we hold about twenty acres at present."

"And by spring we shall own the whole place."

"Before then; long before, my dear Jonathan. My attention has been called to the fact, or in other words I have myself discovered, that our little plot has sprung a leak. This dear young Jesuit friend of mine has meddled with the stop-cock. To earn his title to the enjoyment and benefit of Youlstone air, he conceived an idea of buying a property, and one thing leading to another, I suppose, his mind happened to land upon our track. To be perfectly frank with you, he went to Jimmy, and suggested that they should work out this plan of developing Youlstone."

"Now I understand Woodland's attitude. But what a shabby trick to play upon us!" cried the doctor.

"Not so shabby after all, when you remember Jimmy was not breaking confidence with us after young Anger had broken the idea to him," said Curgenven loyally. "He was acting merely as a man of business. Finding out by guesswork what was going on, I interviewed my young priest and invited him to join us. He has not given me a definite answer, and he never will. What can you expect from a jolly little Jesuit? But there is this danger, Jonathan: he may communicate with wealthy friends, telling them he knows of something good; quite right if he does; he would be a fool to lose so good a chance. But these friends would descend upon us at a critical moment."

"Or he may advise Youlstone people not to sell."

"In Youlstone the dear fellow may talk his face purple, for nobody would listen. He will never do that. It would be rather a mean trick, and he is one of the straightest fellows living. But you see, Jonathan, we must get to work at once. Little whispers make big scandals. This week and next I shall be busy; tongue by day, and pen at night. As for these mortgages, I can call them in at any time. Next month the sale, then the advertising. 'Tis a golden scheme! We are not offering drugs, nor puffing a brain-food. We are announcing the discovery of quintessential air and elixir vitæ. Drink, Jonathan! Next month!"

"And afterwards!" cried Palk, his dark face flushing.

All this time Anger was prowling about the streets of Riversmeet trying to arouse himself to action. His departure from Youlstone had not been dignified because everybody knew he was evicted by Curgenven's orders, and whole families had turned out to witness the exodus of the priest who had dared to meddle with local institutions. Anger was thinking little of the Billacotts, and caring nothing for the fate of Youlstone. His whole mind was set upon the problem of the flight. Petronel was ready to go away with him if he would allow her to fix the day, and would consent to emigrate without an hour's delay. He thoroughly understood the reason, but, if Curgenven chose to follow, how could they escape him, especially if he should clasp the girl by the arm and refuse to be parted from her until she had consented to return to Stiniel?"

"My difficulty is to communicate with Petronel," he muttered, while passing Curgenven's court. "If I walk through the village I am liable to be stoned, if I go to the house her father bars the way, and if I write her mother receives the letter."

Returning to his new lodgings, Anger found a figure waiting patiently at the garden gate; and as he would have passed in a voice called most pathetically, " 'Tis me, schulemaster!"

"Why, Bobby! What are you doing here this time of night?" asked Anger.

" 'Tis the only time I dares to walk abroad. I be a ruined man, and mother be a ruined woman. No ancestors of ours will ever till old Quoditch. I be ashamed to show my face in daylight."

Anger led the little man indoors, placed him by the fire, and scolded him for his folly until Bobby howled with useless penitence.

"Wit that be taught is wit that be bought, says 'em, an' it be true, I reckon. I ha' lost old Quoditch vor a sop o' brandy. My friend—I calls 'en my friend, though he'm my enemy really—ha' been too sharp vor me. You ha' taught me reading and writing, schulemaster—least I ses you ha' taught me, but I can't do neither yet. Would you kindly teach me how to be too sharp vor Curgenven?"

"Too late, Bobby. You cannot afford a law-suit with Curgenven; and if you could he would swear you were sober when you signed, and so would the man who witnessed your signature."

"There be that bit o' paper I signed vor ye," cried Bobby hopefully.

"It is of no use now. I cannot set it against Curgenven's deed. He is your master now."

"I b'ain't so certain," said Bobby cunningly. "Schulemaster, you'm religious, but I reckon you don't know religion through and through. You can teach me writing but you can't teach mother religion. When her was a maid," he went on in a whisper, "volks said vor certain her wur meant to be a wise one."

"I seem to have heard that expression before, but it conveys no meaning," Anger murmured.

"Her be making rags and images," whispered Bobby.

"What do you mean?"

"Her makes images and her puts rags round 'em, and her baptizes 'em wi' watter what ha' stood in munelight—'tis a bravish vull mune now—and her ses, 'I give ye the name o' Curgenven, and may what I does to you be done the like to he.' Then her takes one image and puts him in the fire, and her takes another and drowns him in the watter as 'twur, and her takes a third and buries him, and her takes the fourth and lays him out to freeze. Fire, watter, earth, and air, schulemaster; and Thirza ses one of 'em be sure to kill Curgenven."

"Nonsense," said Anger, but he shivered and his voice was solemn.

"I'll tell ye another thing," Bobby went on more cheerfully. "Nicholas Vigar come down to the hedge this forenoon and some words passed between us. He called you a proper scoundrel, vor you had told him you had bought Quoditch. He said you wanted to deceive 'en, and he reckoned Curgenven wur his best friend after all. Asked me to tell you if you ever comed over Stiniel he would take down his old gun."

"The man's a humbug," said Anger.

"He'm vulish," decided Bobby. "Don't ye get scared, schulemaster. His gun be nought but a bit of rusty iron. Keep out o' the village, vor Curgenven ha' sot the volk agin ye. If you comes to Quoditch, cross over Dartmoor. Us will be pleased to see ye. Us ain't beat yet. They rags and images ha' never been knowed to fail."

"One moment before you go," said Anger earnestly. "Get the men of Youlstone together, tell them how Curgenven has stolen Quoditch from you, and warn them he will do the same to every man who owes him money. Go to the vicar and tell him as well."

"Lord love ye, schulemaster, what will you be saying next!" cried Bobby. "Volks wouldn't listen; they would call me a mazehead if I said a word agin Curgenven. He ain't turned me out yet, you see, and if he did they'd reckon I deserved it. Mr. Hanson would listen, vor he'm a kind gentleman, and he'd say he wur cruel sorry, but it warn't no business of his, and avore I had got out of the door he'd ha' forgot all about it likely. There be only one thing what can give back Quoditch to me now; and that be religion, schulemaster."

Anger was still shivering at the sound of that word when Bobby went out into the moonlit night.

The snow had come, but not gone. Deep drifts were on the heights and white castles in the wood through which Anger walked next day hoping to receive a message. During summer the hut was reached easily by natural stepping-stones, but in winter and other times of flood the passage could only be made at a bend beneath the cliff, where the river flowed between two walls of rock, and as these were dangerous to jump on because slippery, Petronel kept a plank hidden away among the ferns. This plank was now missing, for the dwarf who haunted the wood and Anger's life, had made away with it.

The river was more than full; it reached the brink of the little chasm, white and boiling, thundering through with the dizzy speed of storm-wind. Anger hesitated; a slip on the edge, and his body would be flung upon dark boulders twenty feet below. He removed his boots, flung them across, then leaped and landed safely. The omen was good. If he could cross that chasm, why not others?

Reaching the hut he found a fire burning, and guessed by that sign Whippety was not far off. No doubt the boy's keen instinct had warned him somebody was approaching, and he had gone away to hide. The greater part of the fallen wall had been rebuilt; one coign half-placed gave evidence of sudden alarm and flight. Anger waited, and presently a jay fluttered to the hut; a few moments later the boy appeared, sucking his finger and lurching from side to side.

"Anything for me, Whippety?" called Anger gently.

The boy picked up a stone and flung it at him, making noises with his lips like a swarm of angry bees. Anger dodged the missile, and went towards the poor creature, who with signs of terror produced a scrap of paper from his rags and dropped it suddenly, then lurched away to continue his wall-building; while Anger snatched at the paper and warmed his eyes by reading:

"I don't know whether Whippety will give you this, but I have threatened to beat him if he does not. I do know that he won't let anybody take it from him. Life is now unbearable. My father and mother are almost friends; my power over him has gone. Come to my hut as often as you can, morning and afternoon. I can easily slip out, but Mrs. Vigar follows me like a dog. Don't give any answer to Whippety. Keep silent and wait for me."

That evening, while sitting in his lonely room wondering how he and Petronel could disguise themselves for the flight from Riversmeet, a pebble struck the window and looking out Anger perceived two figures in the lamplight, one tall and motionless, the other dwarfed and in perpetual motion. Passing a hand across his forehead and muttering, "Will this creature never let me rest?" Anger went to the door, and Curgenven immediately ran at him with ardour.

"Come out, old sport! Come for a frisk upon the moor. Here is Jonathan, the only possible doctor. He wants you to tell him about the magic water. Give each other both hands, my pretty fellows; let me join in. Here's a company, the three jolly bachelors, church, medicine, law. With a pound apiece in our pockets, and our brains pooled, we would stagger bigger towns than Riversmeet."

Anger did not say he was glad to see them, while Palk greeted him with a weary handshake, and Curgenven went rattling on, "'Tis a brave night for a walk; hard roads and a good round moon. I have a mind to tramp to this pool and have a drink. This water of life business is sure to take. The idea is as old as rain, but people never get tired of running after it. Offer 'em something original and they pass by."

"If the spring is medicinal, Mr. Anger may have made a great discovery," said Palk.

As he spoke an idea entered Anger's mind. That fatal walk to discover the waters of Nympha had led him to Youlstone. Another walk towards the pool, with Petronel, might lead them both to freedom. It would be safer to escape over the moor than by attempting to pass through Riversmeet. So he answered, "I will walk out if you like, and get you a sample of the water."

"I'll come with you," cried Curgenven.

"It would mean starting early and getting home late," said Anger despairingly.

"Just what I should enjoy. A long day on the moor with a good old pal. Let us go to-morrow."

"I believe Curgenven does half his work in the open air," said Palk.

"I cannot come this week. The snow has unsettled me," said Anger feebly.

"Liver, my dear. A good walk will shake it up. Name the day and you will always find me ready."

Anger said nothing to that, conscious he had already said too much.

"I am anxious to test this water," said Palk, the blind spider helping to spin a web he could not see. "An old moorman once told me he went sometimes when out of order to drink of a certain stream; but directly you ask these men direct questions they become mysterious. Possibly this pool may be the one he visited."

"It has been famous for some centuries, and was certainly made use of by the monks of Buckfast," said Anger.

"I knew you two would love each other; you are professional already," chuckled Curgenven. "But while you talk I freeze. Let us run about a bit and have some fun."

"I must ask you to excuse me. I have walked enough to-day," said Anger, fearful of some plot.

"I know Jonathan don't want to walk. If he had wings he would never use his legs. Go in with our holy monk of Buckfast and have out your chat, while I take a little frisk alone."

He went off with his hop and jump, which appeared to carry him up the hill without an effort, while Palk followed Anger into the house. Evidently this interview had been arranged, but the doctor did not appear able to strike his subject; and finding the silence of that sleepy face unbearable, Anger decided to satisfy his mind upon a matter which had haunted it for weeks. Unlocking a tin box, he produced the bone which he had taken from the heap inside the mine-shaft, and handed it to the doctor with the question, "Would you mind telling me what sort of a creature that belonged to?"

Palk brightened up at once and opened his eyes widely. Being a skilled anatomist one glance was enough. "It is the rib-bone of a small dog," he said.

A burden departed from the listener's mind, and the only suspicion he had dared to entertain for Petronel went with it as he explained, "I found a quantity of bones hidden away and wrapped in a woman's skirt. I was afraid they might be human."

"Did you find them near a village?" asked Palk.

"Quite close to a cottage," Anger prevaricated.

"It is the way some women bury their pets," said the doctor; and now that he was aroused continued:

"It is curious that you too should have entertained the idea of developing Youlstone village. You spoke to Woodland about it, I believe?"

"I did," replied Anger steadily, putting himself on guard.

"And he declined to invest his money. The lack of co-operation is a fatal defect in our business methods. People in these country towns will not trust each other. I hope you do not mind me asking questions?"

"Not at all," said Anger.

"Mr. Curgenven and I are deeply interested. It has always been his ambition to benefit Youlstone, a village he is exceedingly fond of, while I am anxious to get a better class of patients, and be given the opportunity of studying certain types of disease which never occur here. The scheme is a large one, and to tell the truth we are somewhat short of money—the usual difficulty. Would you consider again the question of joining us?"

"I am really a stranger," said Anger in a hesitating fashion. "Once I did think of making Youlstone my home, but now I have changed my mind. The winters are too fierce, and the evenings too long, while duty calls me back to the town. I cannot join you, doctor."

"I am sorry to hear that," said Palk, stroking his beard nervously. "Do not be offended, please, if I ask one more question. You are not thinking of opposing us?"

"I have lived here only a few weeks," said Anger with a smile, "but it has been long enough to show me that when a stranger opposes the inhabitants of a Dartmoor village his peace of mind is apt to be destroyed. I am not a land-agent; I will have nothing to do with the buying or selling of these moorland fields."

"Curgenven has been rather distressed," Palk went on. "He was afraid you might induce rich friends of your own to step in; of course, he admits you have a perfect right to do so. He would have asked you these questions himself, had he not taken such a liking to you——"

This is too thin, thought Anger.

"And he was so afraid of straining the friendship," went on the innocent man, "that I agreed to see you in his stead. He's a wonderfully good little fellow, but much too soft-hearted. These commoners play upon his affectionate nature, and do just what they like with him."

"He and I ought to change places. It seems to me Curgenven has a clear vocation," said Anger heedlessly.

"Certainly he would have succeeded as a divine. He has the manner, the eloquence, and I believe the character," said Palk quietly. A stick rattled against the gate, while Curgenven's laughter filled the road with merriment, and then his voice thundered into the room:

"Come forth, church and medicine! Come down to my den. 'Tis a searching wind up over, cold like criminal law. My bones fair ache with it. Hurry out, old sportsmen! We will make a merry night of it with punch and ballads."

"That's the man he is," said Palk admiringly. "Never downcast; the life and soul of the place. He has kept me hopeful these last twenty years."

"Come along, Anger, my dear. I want you to know me better," cried the deep voice with wonderful sincerity.

"Will you come?" said Palk.

"I am too tired," said Anger. "I should only make a silent third."

That night was a restless time; it seemed to Anger he was gradually getting more troubled in his sleep. In the morning he made the journey to the hut, and discovered Whippety putting the last touches to its roof; but there was no message for him. In the afternoon he went again, and when nearing a narrow bridge, crossing the river which separated him from the wood, he saw a man standing and looking down upon the torrent of melted snow. Anger came on, expecting the stranger to give way, but he continued to hold the foot-bridge, staring at Anger as if he had been a spirit.

"You are the man," he said. "But why have you changed your clothes?" Anger stared back, and saw the stranger shuddering. His face was thin, earnest, and deeply lined; his own clothes, evidently his best, were neat, his whole appearance suggested honest living; yet Anger was unable to free himself from suspicions of Curgenven.

"Were you waiting here for me?" he asked.

"I am sent by God," said the stranger with deep feeling. "We have never met in the flesh, yet you are the man I was to find upon this bridge. Yours is the face, but when you were shown to me, you were dressed as a minister of religion."

"I am a priest," said Anger with an effort.

"I do not know your name, and I need not tell you mine. We meet as spirits. I am a Cornishman, and my home is in St. Just. The night before last I seemed to be awakened by three knocks, and a voice said to me, 'Look!' I turned over and went to sleep again, but before my eyes a deep blue light was burning, and four faces seemed to pass me by. Then came darkness, and presently a picture formed of a cellar, not unlike many that I know of, and yet one my eyes had never seen before; for at one side, beneath a window, which admitted one faint gleam of light—it was cold, sir, freezing cold—I saw what might have been a child's garden, about the length and breadth of a child's bed, planted with ferns and such things as will live in the dark and damp. Beside it a young woman knelt. She was very handsome, and she wore a white dress, but one arm was bare, and I could see upon it a hand clutching a cross around which ran a scroll bearing the words, 'To the memory of my dear brother.'"

Anger was stiff and motionless. The stranger, rapt in his narrative, did not glance in his direction, but kept his eyes upon the rushing water.

"I began to be afraid. Some one seemed to be thinking against me and trying to prevent me from seeing. You were there, not as a man, nor as a spirit, but as a voice. I saw a woman with white hair close to the kneeling girl. Then the picture was blurred and I could not follow the movements. I called out, 'Light!' but you said, 'This is very bad. Don't look at it.' Then I saw the woman on her back and her eyes were rolling; her hands caught at the ferns upon the child's garden. There was a hammer near. I cried out, 'Don't touch that,' and you said, 'It is necessary.' Remember you were only a voice. The light became whiter. The woman was struggling and saying, 'It is neither one way, nor the other,' and you said, 'It must be one way,' but I had lost sight of the girl. The woman seemed to leap upon the floor. Something dark appeared to roll across the cellar, and the woman did not move again. I cried out, 'Are you all going?' and you said, 'Not together.' Then a feeble old man came up, and asked me if I had seen any one. You answered, 'This is nothing,' and the old man said, 'Those ferns grow nicely.' Then I saw you clearly. You were dressed as a clergyman, and you were kneeling in the place where I had first seen the girl, and you seemed to be praying over the child's garden."

Anger still stared; and, like the light in the dream, he was cold, freezing cold.

"I woke in a sweat," went on the monotonous voice. "Then I slept and dreamed again. Now I saw a railway station swept by cold wind. There was no sign of life about the place. I seemed to be standing on the platform, waiting for a train, but when it came in only one passenger left it, a man, myself. I called out, 'What is this place?' and I heard the echo of my voice for miles, but nobody answered. I kept on calling, until you came near, still as a voice, and said to me sullenly, but very distinctly, 'Riversmeet. You will be sorry if you stay here.' I walked on down a long pathway beside a hill, until I came to a river crossed by a narrow foot-bridge. You were standing on the bridge. Then I heard the three knocks again, and the first voice said, 'Go!' I awoke," continued the stranger, "but I could not settle to anything, so I walked to the station, took the first train to Plymouth and from there to Riversmeet. You are the man, sir, God has sent me here to warn. I do not ask your name. I see my words have moved you. May they help you. Now I must go if I am to get home to St. Just to-night."

CHAPTER XVIII

BROKEN SLUMBER

THE spell of the sleeping waters was wearing off, the time of awakening drew on; another visit to the pool of the Nymph would be necessary to prolong enchantment, yet Anger had no wish to renew a night which gave no rest; not even when the robust new body weakened and the feeble priest threatened to return. The countryman, who had risen from his bed in Wyld was now being reclaimed by the moor, and the pale-faced town was seeking its own again.

Headache, loss of appetite, fits of dizziness oppressed Anger; he walked with far less energy; it became increasingly difficult to control his mind; his memory played all manner of tricks. It was his custom each morning, before turning to more serious business, to plod along a road which led from his lodging to the moor, and in these expeditions he would often be accompanied by a kind of incubus, which was by no means horrifying as it took the form of an elderly gentleman, somewhat quaint and fussy, always wearing a tall silk-hat and blue spectacles. This comrade of the early walk was doubtless another visitor, spending a few weeks in Riversmeet for his health, and glad to exchange a few words with some other rambler. Anger had a distinct recollection one morning of driving his stick, with more precision than gentleness, into the ribs of the incubus to make sure he was in every sense a man of substance, when the fussy creature had the impudence to approach with the offer of an umbrella as it was raining.

Sunday morning the quaint old gentleman became so embarrassing with his eager questions that Anger turned from the haunted road and ran away. It so happened that he came out near the church, which stood apart from the chapel-sprinkled town upon a small hill; a cold and wind-swept building. Making himself a member of the congregation, he did his best to enter into the spirit of a service no warmer than the weather, but presently an announcement came sharply to his ears; banns were being published, and he heard two names, the only ones which mattered: Richard Curgenven and Petronel Vigar; and this was for the first time of asking.

Others were aroused beside himself. Anger became conscious of wonder upon surrounding faces; he saw smiles and shaking heads; he heard whisperings. The secret had been well kept, and this was the breaking of it.

"It is his last move," Anger muttered, as he escaped from the church. "His final proclamation. Now it is open war between us. If he comes with love again, I'll answer him with loathing."

A hasty meal, and then for the hut in the cleave. He had looked for this Sunday to bring forth sunshine. During the quietness of the afternoon Petronel would surely reach him, and name the day for flight from Youlstone, 'and so by the waters of Nympha, which be good for sickness,' to some tranquil and sheltered home.

The hand of the spoiler had done its work again, and now effectually. The hut was indeed a ruin almost level with the ground; the roof had been burnt, the primitive articles of furniture had been destroyed or scattered, the flat table-stones cast into the river, the hearthstone broken as if by lightning. Romance was gone, but love remained; for Petronel herself guarded the ruin, gazing upon the rain-soaked scene with watery eyes.

"See what you have done," she said in greeting.

"Do not reproach me, dearest," he cried, holding her tightly. "This is the place where my soul was born, it is the chapel of my heart; I worshipped every stone. But I can leave it gladly, as a ruined temple, now that I have you. I have waited dreary days looking for you, and spent nights longing for you. We are together again, and now we must stay together, and cling and love. My darling, I love you the more for all the lonely longing."

"If you had never come my hut would still be standing, and I should be stronger," she said. "You have taken so much out of me. I used to act without thinking; now I find myself saying, 'What would he do?' You have made me love, but you have weakened me."

"So sweet and grieved," he murmured, "but now too serious. I love your soft sad smile, my Petronel; I love your thoughtful eyes; but my heart is hurt to find you suffering. We have met to end it," he said strongly. "This is the first day of the last week of sorrow. We are young, and life is only beginning for you and me. We will leave a world of weeping and force ourselves into a world of laughter—the soft laughter, not of folly, but of two hearts happy."

"Find the way, and I'll come with you. But if we are to reach your place of refuge we shall have to hurry on the journey," she said languidly.

"Kiss me before I speak again."

She put her arms round his neck and kissed his forehead.

"Now with your heart."

Her arms became stronger as she kissed his mouth.

"Now with your soul."

She strained him to her until her small teeth cut his lips.

"How strong she is, my darling!" he cried gladly, for he had forgotten that the kiss of dedication should be given gently and lingered over; the kiss that bruised was carnal.

"Our hopes are not to be ruined like our temple," he cried. "I came to-day full of the certainty of seeing you at last. This morning I went to Riversmeet church, hoping for peace and finding a sword instead. Even there the man haunted me, and his hateful name was flung at me. Linked with the name of names—there, Petronel."

"I gave my permission," she said, smiling a little. "Do not draw back. You must know what happens to the suitor who will not take a negative; he gets paid with a blank promise."

"You have never promised to marry Curgenven—not been in his arms? Oh, Petronel!"

"The table was always between us, and Mrs. Vigar was present. He came yesterday, the little giant, laughing like a thunderstorm; I had never seen him so excited. There was nothing he would not give me; he would bind all the farms of Youlstone into one mort-gage and hang that round my neck. Quoditch would be a ring for my little finger. Fields, cottages, farms, beasts should go into the melting-pot and come out gold for me; nothing of silver. The days of Solomon should return when I was queen. This is some of his talk that I remember. Mrs. Vigar urged him on, while she stroked his hand and ogled him; and I said yes—not a word more—merely yes to everything; but if Mrs. Vigar and Curgenven had worked out those questions, they might find what one yes consented to another contradicted."

"But, darling," pleaded the puzzled lover. "Your consent——"

"Means nothing," she added. "By it I have disarmed Curgenven. I could not remain at Stiniel now. He never dreams I mean to run away. Mrs. Vigar knows I cannot go."

"Dearest, why make yourself a mystery to me?" he asked imploringly, feeling how cold she went, and thinking of that spirit-farmer on the foot-bridge. "We two are almost one. And yet you stand away."

She looked at him half-fondly, somewhat fearfully, then said in a low voice, "I am about to drive away the mists. Curgenven does not think of marrying me. He would no more take me as his wife than he would the moor; but he loves me, he has a feeling for me which you can never understand. He is my foster-father."

"Petronel!" cried Anger.

"Do you know you have never asked my age? I am only twenty-two; at least I do not think I can be more, but nobody will ever know where or when I was born, nor indeed how I ever came into this world. Eighteen years ago, on a bright spring morning—I can still remember the sunrise and the lovely colours of the clouds, I can see the little whortleberries in bloom, and the dewy gossamers upon the heather—I found myself toddling in Youlstone cleave, and—do not mind me speaking so simply—I was quite naked. A tiny child walking at dawn in the dew, as if the sun and earth were her parents, and she had just been born."

"Now I am dreaming again," murmured Anger.

"So I went on, keeping away from the sharp furze, and at last a dwarf came near. I went to him, and we seemed to meet quite naturally. He put out two long arms, just as if he had been expecting me, and lifted me upon his shoulders, and walked on with me. I rested easily upon his hump. And all the way across the lonely moor he laughed and talked, telling me stories about my little past—I have forgotten all that—calling me Little Queen and Princess Beauty, and kissing my hands which he held always near his mouth. At last we came to Youlstone, and he carried me into the first house, which, of course, was Stiniel, and gave me to the Vigars, and told them to take care of me, and if they should ever make me suffer——"

"They have made you suffer," cried the struggling Anger.

"Never mind about that now. I have disappointed him. I am a woman of strong mind instead of his pixy-maiden; but he loves me still, I am his religion; it was to see me that he haunted Stiniel. And now you understand why it is that I can rule Curgenven."

"I understand nothing. I think of you as a tiny child walking in the dew, alone, abandoned. Then Curgenven——"

"He is not my father," she cried quickly, anticipating his question. "He has sworn to me he is not. Nothing would delight him more than to be able to say that he was. I am the child of Dartmoor."

"Why does he entreat you to marry him? Why make it public that the marriage is to take place?"

"To separate me from you. He could not marry me, because I am the daughter of his imagination, and he cannot let me marry any man—why, I do not know. He hates you, and he must do so, because you will not give me up. I can rule him in every matter except this one; I must not marry. I must remain the innocent child walking in the dew of the morning fresh to him as a flower which has sprung up in the night. You never expected to find such feeling in Curgenven."

"Who brings the vilest charges against you."

"He speaks to you from his brain, not from his heart. Words are nothing to him if they can secure his purpose. He spoke the truth when he promised to give me all Youlstone if I would marry him—which means, as now you know, that I would not marry you, nor any man."

"Then, if I could give you up, Youlstone might yet be saved."

"How?" she asked; and he told her, but heedlessly, for his mind was upon other matters.

"Well, that is no affair of mine," was her reply.

"But your feelings towards him—they puzzle me. You have some regard for the dwarf who found you, sometimes you have seemed almost to defend him; but generally, and lately always, you have been as bitter against him as myself."

"Cannot your own heart answer that? You love me," she said, more sweetly than he had ever heard her speak. "You taught me to love you; I learnt my lesson. Does not a girl turn in fury against the man, whatever his relationship, who tells her the only thing in life worth winning is the one thing she must not have?"

"Darling," he murmured, "you are teaching me."

"I have affection for Curgenven, as my foster-father, the man who goes out to meet the dawn upon the moor and to seek inspiration from it, and to weep because he has fallen so low," she went on. "I do not notice then the crooked body, I forget the stormy and uncontrollable mind, I see only the splendid head and think of his wild love. But as a man of the world I loathe him."

"Why does Mrs. Vigar hate you? Why does she want you to marry Curgenven?"

"I am no relation of hers, but a miserable foundling, connected with some story of passion, not with a tale of mystery. She hates me for my wild moods; she hates me for what you would call my beauty; and above all she hates me because Curgenven loves me. There is another reason," she whispered, with a shiver. "You may never know of that. That woman!" she cried passionately. "Ah well, she shall know me soon. Some women, when they grow old, are jealous of their daughters," she went on quietly. "They envy the youth and beauty which they have lost themselves; and when a woman becomes jealous she goes mad. Mrs. Vigar has always loved Curgenven; when she was a girl, before Nicholas ever came near her, my discoverer was the idol of her heart. I suppose there was something in her that matched his crookedness. She tried her hardest to win him, but failed. Whippety is their son."

"Good heavens!" muttered Anger.

"Richard Blisland is his name. He looks like a boy, and I call him one, but he is thirty years old. He was brought up in a cottage, Curgenven paying for his keep—out of charity, he said—until the boy was sixteen, and then he was turned out like a pony upon the moor. Miss Blisland lost her home—she was an orphan living with grandparents—and as Curgenven would not marry her, she was forced to take Nicholas."

"And if you had married the father of this imbecile——" began Anger.

"Remember, I am no relation," she broke in hurriedly.

"Then she would have realised her ambition of living under the same roof with the man she loves."

"She knows Curgenven, and thinks she knows me," said Petronel. "Two strong natures, she reckoned, would be brought together, and neither would yield; and while my husband and I were wrangling she would be making love to him in the same old way. At last Nicholas and I would leave and go down to Quoditch, while she would remain at Stiniel with Curgenven. That was her plan, and it would have succeeded had it not been for my misty stranger."

"Then you would have married him, sweetheart?"

"I tell you he would not have married me; he could not. You will never understand Curgenven. When he ceases to be a man of the world, he becomes a poet, a sort of high-priest of the moor, the mysteries of which I represent to him."

"Then how would Mrs. Vigar's plan have succeeded?"

"As it is doing now—at least, as she believes it is. Curgenven gives out he is going to marry me, but the ceremony would not be performed here nor, as a matter of fact, in any other place. I consent to bear his name; he comes to live at Stiniel, but as my servant, not as my husband. I know he intends to live in Youlstone because he has told me so, and it is to suit his own purpose, in addition to defeating you, that he has bought Stiniel. He and I would soon be fighting; you see, I should oppose him in everything, and his nature cannot endure much of that. So Nicholas and I should go to Quoditch while he would remain at Stiniel."

"He has not bought Quoditch with that idea in his head," said Anger warmly.

"Perhaps not. But if I wanted Quoditch I should only have to ask for it."

"Will you, sweetheart? I should like the Billacotts to keep their home."

"You forget we are going to run away," she said rather crossly. "I will not ask a single favour, and why should I? The Billacotts are nothing to us. You do not realise, I suppose, that Curgenven will act like a madman when he loses me—and he will search all over the world for us?"

"I have given up trying to understand him," said Anger with a thrill of fear; then went on hurriedly: "What is the meaning of all this acting before Mrs. Vigar? Why is he so ready to obey her. Surely he cannot be afraid of such a woman?"

"Whippety is the cause," she answered. "Nobody knows he is their son except Nicholas and myself. I made the discovery by chance, when I caught him ill-treating the boy, and beat him for it. Yes, I did," she declared merrily. "He was like a dog, snapping at every one, but terribly afraid of his own mistress. Still he lost his temper—and he does that with nobody except me—and said he could do as he liked with his own son. Curgenven does not dare to oppose Mrs. Vigar, because he fears she may tell everybody the secret of the boy's birth, and that would harm him in Youlstone, and ruin him in Riversmeet. Curgenven, as a man of the world, will commit any act of villainy, but he must not be found out; he must appear respectable to the public at any cost."

"When we leave here, what will happen?" he asked fearfully.

Petronel looked down upon her hands, which were clasped in his, and shivered again.

"There will be a tempest, the like of which has never been known on Dartmoor," she said; and still he could not ask himself how it was a girl brought up in that mountain village could speak so well. "Curgenven will be raging, and acting foolishly, I hope, like a giant who has lost his only eye. All Youlstone will be shuddering, and Nicholas Vigar will be blundering about the dark bushes of Stiniel. We shall depart in a whirlwind, my boy, and you must pray that the echoes of the storm do not follow and reach us in our place of refuge. One more storm," she murmured, tightening her hold upon his hands. "Winter will rage again, breaking the tors, unroofing a few houses, and then it will be peace; and spring will come on, and we shall be calm. Then you will save me," she cried. "You will subdue my nature and supply what is lacking in me. Yours is a large soul, dearest, and you can spare me half."

"My darling, you and I are troubled by strange dreams. Have you too been drinking the waters of the Nymph?" he whispered.

She did not heed, or else refused to answer. Still in the same strained manner she continued: "If you love me, I must claim all you have; much more than home and comforts. Your life must protect me, your brain must scheme for me, your mind must fight for me, your spirit must enter me, and your tongue must plead for me."

"Shall I not be seconding myself?" he answered.

"After that night you will think the same of me as now?"

"What night?"

"The night of the last storm. You will take my hands, and say they are Petronel's? I have warned you that if you marry, you must take me. It is not too late to refuse; you may do so, and then I will go back."

"Go back!" he repeated.

"Into the cleave, alone, to be seen no more."

"Not alone, dearest, for I should be with you."

"You are saving me!" she cried, "I am almost free. I have won you, heart and soul, and now I shall not go back. Those people will have no claim upon me. You have broken the bond, which Curgenven could have broken had he been a man with a pure heart. You have trodden on the Springwort. Oh, if it had been you as a young boy who had come to meet me that May morning! Perhaps you did come, but we could not find each other; for we were all spirits that morning when the clouds were so lovely and the gossamers were shining on the grass. It was too soon then, so you waited. You came at last in the mist, and we shall take our flight in the wind. But it is the last storm, I promise, if you will not give way, if you never shrink from me. I will give you ever afterwards calm days."

"You give me love with words I cannot understand."

"My heart is my words. Look into my eyes."

He did so.

"You are always truthful. If you can find any ugly passion, anything but love, speak the truth now."

"They are eyes full of mystery and of longing, pure as the water below; the eyes of a child looking with wonder at the world. They have changed, and are now the eyes of a maid asking for faith. They change again. Ah, Petronel! they are the soft, strong, burning eyes of love. Now they are weary. Let me close them."

"We have been here too long," she murmured. "That wood is haunted by Curgenven. And yet if he had seen us like this, one in spirit, and almost one in body, all that is wild in him would have compelled him to show himself. I seem to hear him groaning and grinding his big teeth. We must part now; the day is almost over. Before I go——"

"Stay with me. Let us cling together," he cried passionately, the old devotion for mysteries thrilling his body. "It is near evening, and I fear the night. I would take you and kneel with you in some dim chapel before the image of the Queen of the world, and pray for her protection upon your life."

"Do not weaken me. Wait a few more days. The storm is coming. Watch yourself very carefully; see that you are not followed; keep well away from lonely places. When I send for you, come to Stiniel."

"How will you send?"

"You will hear the wind. That will be my message to you. Come when the wind is fiercest."

"Shall we escape by the moor, passing the sleeping waters? If we drink, another mist may spring up to hide us."

"Oh, no! We must travel at full speed. We shall be hunted. Dartmoor and Curgenven will try to hold me back; you must fight to carry me away. Let me go now. The wood is full of noises."

"Your wind."

"That is not my wind. It could not shake a rock," she answered scornfully. "Take your last look at the ruins of my hut. We meet at the gate of Stiniel when the storm is at its height. Do not come into the house or you will lose me."

She struggled free and seemed to glide away among the rocks, more like a spirit than a maid. Anger followed, but could not overtake her, though he could see her fine figure ahead ascending quickly, never glancing back, until the low drifting clouds received her out of his sight. Then he returned, leaped the chasm without pause or fear of slipping, and plunged into the crooked pathway of the wood, reeling from side to side, for his senses seemed to be forsaking him.

"I am not fully awake, neither am I sleeping," he muttered. "I do not know what I am; I cannot explain these phantoms which move about me. This is the hand she held. These trees are real, so are the rocks, and that river roaring yonder is no fancy. The Billacotts of Quoditch—surely they are made of flesh and blood. So are that weak fool Nicholas, his half-mad wife, Woodland the tradesman, Palk the doctor, even Whippety the imbecile; they are not types and symbols, but live creatures. I who move amongst them am the most unreal. What is Petronel? What is Curgenven? I love the one, I hate the other, as the spirit of romance and the power of evil. What has she been telling me? A wonderful story of the dawn; a promise to meet me in the wind at the gate of Stiniel. I remember nothing else; even her face has gone from me; I do not know the colour of her eyes. I see only that tiny child walking upon the dew holding up her arms to the dawn, and the dwarf coming towards her, lifting her upon his hump, carrying her away from the land of pure romance into the wicked world of human beings."

He went on heedlessly, slipping upon beds of slate, splashing through unenchanted pools, blundering against the trees; terrified at the prospect of an awakening to realities yet fiercer. Memory began to work again. He thought of the long illness which had changed his body; he remembered the nurse who had ministered to him at Wyld; above all, he was troubled by that fussy gentleman who insisted upon accompanying his early morning ramble. Why did the incubus display such friendship for a stranger who testified so plainly that his company was not welcome?

Anger was drawing near the gate of the wood. Beyond it were two rough trackways, one leading to the higher part of the town, the other working its way with endless windings towards the moor. As he advanced, the river roared upon his right, while to the left a cliff uprose, covered for the most part with oaks and dead bracken, but broken in one part by a disused stone quarry containing several feet of yellow water.

He passed this quarry, and was about to make the last bend before the gate when he heard a cry for help, and looking back in the dim evening light saw a young woman at the foot of the cliff, her body secured apparently between a rock and a brake of bramble, her feet in the yellow water. She was groaning as if in pain.

Anger hurried to her side, bent down to draw her from the perilous position—for her body was near the deeper water—but immediately he knelt she threw her arms about his neck, dragged him down, struggling and screaming madly; and while she clutched at and fought with him, a male voice answered, and a big figure came lumbering down the cliff, falling at last upon the combatants, and dragging Anger away with oaths and threats. The man was Wadge, but the young woman was a stranger. She lay there sobbing, while the two men stared at one another.

"Can it be you, sir? My God!" muttered Wadge. "Mr. Curgenven's dear friend, sir! This is awful. I would rather have cut off my hand, sir, than to have witnessed—— All right, my dear," he said to the screaming wench. "You are safe now, thank God. Oh, sir! what have you done?"

Anger perceived at once that he was trapped. That flabby-faced

man and the hysterical damsel were acting the parts which
Curgenven had assigned to them.

"I know now who you are and what you are," he said contemptuously. "You two are evil spirits."

"I am a plain man, sir. By chance I was walking upon the moor,
thinking myself alone, when I heard screams. I saw you, sir. You
were trying to overmaster this poor girl. A few more moments and
I might have been too late. I wish it had been any other man, sir;
I wish I had not seen you; but it was God's will that I should be a
witness, and now, sir, I must do my duty."

"Earn your money," said Anger bitterly, and with one glance
at the girl he walked away; but he was not to escape so easily, for
Wadge and his accomplice followed, keeping the same distance
between them, and while the one abused Anger violently, the
other with dignity and unction quoted texts of Scripture. They
passed a few strolling couples when nearing Riversmeet, and then
Wadge raised his voice to cry in holy tones:

"Take care, my good people. Keep away from the poor gentleman. A mad priest, neighbours! He is not responsible for his
actions, and I have just saved this young lady from him. I am afraid
we shall have to lock him up—unless he is clever enough to run
away."

CHAPTER XIX

A CALMER ATMOSPHERE

FIGURES were now seen dimly, and mist filled the room where
Anger sat shuddering, with a fierce humming in his ears as
if enemies were rejoicing behind the shadow. Only two characters were left in the drama of his life: Petronel and Curgenven.
Behind that haze, which threatened to bring up the storm, raged
the mighty dwarf, glaring at his caged victim whose hatred was
now swallowed up by terror; beyond, Petronel was beckoning
with fingers made of water. The fascination remained, and with

it the sense of impotence, an inability to escape from the crack of doom and to hide from those misty people. He was being separated from the star of good fortune by the planet of evil. The spirit of darkness fought against his for the full possession of the spirit of Dartmoor which had saved his life and was now about to claim his entire devotion.

"He will come," Anger muttered. "He is a creature of the night. I shall see his face against the window; I shall hear his fearful laughter."

He retired into a corner of the room and set his face towards the wall, while everything which had happened that day took a new form of terror. Even Petronel's story, told in the valley of rocks, lost its beauty now and was a tale of witchcraft. They had not passed into the land of old romance, into the place of truth where Nature's music was religious, and love was created without any straining of the soul; but they had gone into the darkest wood, among the rotten branches, across rings of fungi; and had embraced there within the shadow of the witch's castle. Yet it was not her story which aroused his terror. That was caused by the terribly carnal man and the shrieking wench, who were none other than the satellites of the power of darkness. They would have gone to their master, and he would waste no time.

Bells were still ringing across the valley of Riversmeet, and people, like conspirators, were passing down the dark side of the street on their way to church or chapels, when voices sounded near the window, and a bony hand rattled against the glass. Anger drew himself up and admitted two silent figures. They entered with him and stood for some moments without speaking. It was cunning of Curgenven, thought Anger, to have brought Palk with him.

"So you were waiting for me in the dark," said the lawyer without a laugh at last, but professionally solemn.

"There is enough light from the fire for us to see each other," replied Anger. "I know why you are here; I did expect you. This is a piece of villainy, Curgenven."

"I quite agree, although outside this room I am against you," the dwarf said briskly. "My dear Anger, the man who is cornered in this sort of way must either commit suicide or run. We are men of the world, and we know how often this sort of thing happens. Gangs of scoundrels keep these young women for purposes of blackmail, but we cannot expose them. Palk will tell you this case is serious."

"They came first to me," said the doctor simply.

"I am your friend, Anger, although in public I shall have to call you a scoundrel; I must do what I can for my client. We have come in secret to help you, to implore you to save yourself. It is impossible to think of defending the case. A man can do nothing in these matters. I should have to fight you, and even Palk would be required to give damning evidence against you. It is most unlucky that Wadge should have been a witness, for he is the most respectable man in Riversmeet and nobody would dream of doubting his word."

"This young woman is, I presume, his own daughter?" said Anger as bitterly as he could.

"Oh, no! His righteous soul in that case would have made your murder justifiable. Between ourselves, Anger, the man's a hypocrite, but he has never been found out, and personally I know nothing against him. The girl is a perfect stranger."

"Imported into Riversmeet for this occasion."

"Something of the sort. You know, my dear, you have made yourself unpopular. You are far too honest for these shuffling rascals."

"How much of the story do you believe?"

"As your friend, not a word; professionally I believe all of it. Is it likely that a girl would be walking in the wood alone upon a winter's evening without an object? She was there to trap you."

"And Wadge?"

"A man of the most unblemished character. The very soul of truth," said the lawyer scornfully. "You cannot show they are accomplices, and as a matter of fact I don't suppose they are. Wadge often goes for a ramble in that direction as a little exercise between his Sunday services, and he cannot find anybody quite respectable enough to accompany him. There is a conspiracy sure enough, but I doubt if Wadge is a party to it. You see, I am showing you my hand."

"It is very kind of you," Anger muttered, unable to speak his mind with that calm doctor in the room. "Your object in coming then was not to denounce me as a sinner?"

"Don't say that, my dear; it sounds like a reproof," cried Curgenven. "I could not have prevented this. You will never know how much I love you," he said in faltering tones. "I hoped you would settle here, and become my partner, and one of the directors of the new Youlstone; but now that is impossible. Palk and I have come to beg you to escape. I implore you to go, for my sake if not for your own. Think what it would mean to me to have to appear against a dear old pal."

"You mean to go in any case," said Palk. "Why not now instead of later?"

"This is Sunday evening," continued Curgenven in sharp business-like tones. "Streets are empty, chapels are full. The station is near; a train stops at nine o'clock. We cannot come to see you off, for professional reasons, but we can wish you God-speed here. Leave what you owe to your landlady and I will settle with her. You will write to me sometimes, my dear? I cannot lose you altogether. Some day you may need my assistance and be glad to work with me."

"You have made up your mind that I am going?"

"Because you must. This is not a matter you can play with. It means publicity, a terrible exposure, the ruin of your character—and you a priest."

"Curgenven is right. You must go," said Palk solemnly.

"As it is supposed I am a criminal, if a warrant should be issued for my arrest, how can I escape?"

"This is clearly a conspiracy to get you out of the place. I tell you frankly I believe the Vigars are at the bottom of it. If I am right, you will hear no more of this so long as you do not show yourself in Riversmeet or Youlstone. But if you insist upon staying, you must marry this girl."

"I will choose the lesser evil," said Anger, smiling a little at the lawyer's thoroughness, and perceiving that open warfare could not profit him. "My enemies have conquered," he went on. "They have expelled me from the village, and now they drive me from the town."

"It is a mistake to interfere with free people. Leave 'em their gods and their customs," said Curgenven still solemnly. "They merely tolerate Palk and myself because we are necessary. Jonathan, old Deathwatch, you and I will be two lone fellows now. Our good young priest must leave us."

Anger parted from Curgenven with the hope, but not the feeling, that they would never meet again. His own plan was a simple one; he would descend to Plymouth that night, seek out his old schoolfellow and win his blessing, as he had obtained his help in childhood; and then return to hide within striking distance of Youlstone. The parishioners of Wyld would receive him gladly, and there he could await the first mutterings of the storm which were to call him to the gate of Stiniel.

"I will at least be honest," he murmured, as the train carried him away from Riversmeet. "With these clothes I put on a new character. How can I disguise myself better than by putting on myself again?"

Early on Monday morning Anger hurried towards the slums along a dismal street which yet brought warmth to his heart, for he felt at home. Reaching the church he had entered once before, not then as a worshipper but as a wayfarer seeking rest, he found the same old man who had told him the vicar's name, and asked him where Mr. Lyson lived. Guided to a terrace of dark houses, not more than fifty yards away, Anger came to a door bearing the kindly words, Church House; knocked and asked if he could see the vicar.

"He is very busy this week," said a servant who looked like a sister of mercy. "A retreat is being held."

"Say an old schoolfellow asks to see him."

The woman soon returned and invited him to enter. Anger passed up a flight of stairs, hearing a subdued murmur of voices, and once, he thought, a distant muttering as of priests at their devotions. Then he looked up and saw a small room crowded with articles of religion: books with the sacred sign upon their covers, pictures of lily-carrying angels, crucifix and red lamp in one peaceful corner and underneath a prie-dieu; but here and there to show the priest's humanity were photographs of choristers, with crude little triumphs of the children's paint-box dedicated "to dear father." Slums were around, yet the odour of that room was pleasant.

With rustlings of a cassock, Lyson came extending both hands, and as Anger clutched them, forgetting he had not announced himself by name, the haze of wild Youlstone drifted from his eyes, and he exclaimed almost unconsciously, "How clean his face is!"

"You were at school with me!"

"I am Anger. You took me under your protection. You were strong while I was weak. We have not changed."

"Anger! Ah, how well I remember you. The little fellow who received more than his share of knocks," said Lyson, still holding his visitor's hands.

"You were the only one who helped me; and now that we are men I come to you for help again."

"I tried to see that you had fair play. You came to me one day and begged for leave off football, but I would not spare you, I refused to see the bruise upon your knee, I made you play. A little roughness at school prepares us for the world where the play is rougher. Stay with me, and let me help you if I can; but this is a busy time. The house is full of clergy, and almost every hour is as full as the house. A few more minutes and I must be in the church. Will you come, or would you rather wait for me here?"

"I will come," said Anger. "Last night I left Riversmeet with the determination of telling you my story. I have been staying the last few months in the Dartmoor village of Youlstone."

"Why then, you will see the vicar," exclaimed Lyson. "He is here, and is indeed conducting the retreat."

"Hanson in your house! I thought he had no life apart from science."

"He is a most excellent and earnest priest," said Lyson. "It is a terrible thing for a spiritually minded man to be placed in charge of a village. He cannot speak his message without offending the ears of his parishioners. It sometimes happens that he gives up in despair, withdraws himself from the community, and leads a life of study. Judge Hanson in my church, and not in Youlstone."

"I must say one thing before we go," said Anger, when Lyson would have left him. A moment he hesitated, then cried out boldly, "I, too, am a priest."

Lyson's face quivered. He said nothing, but put out his hands again and grasped those of his old schoolfellow strongly.

"Not of your Church. I put off my old garments because I put on a new body. I was not altogether false; I did not mean to deceive—but I have harmed myself."

"We will talk later on," Lyson murmured.

"I cannot go with you and your brothers as I am. Every word of that service, which has the same meaning for us both, would be a reproach."

Then Lyson broke in gently, "Come with me. We are much of the same build."

The others had gone into the church, and the introit was being sung, when Anger entered clad after the old style, feeling his fears recede as the protective atmosphere was wafted round his body from the altar where Hanson, the scholar of Youlstone, officiated so tenderly and solemnly. This was the greatest wonder. The man who knew nothing of his own parish was there chief priest. Not allowed to nurse the sacred flame at home, he sought the satisfaction of religion far away, and, in the church of a spiritually minded brother, became himself a mystic. When away from Fleet Street and the drawing-rooms of Kensington, he was present in his brother Lyson's church; but never in heart or spirit had he dwelt in Youlstone.

The service over, Anger waited until Lyson came to him, and they passed together into a chapel hung with blue and gold, pausing at Anger's request beneath the lamp. "I am now in my own Church of the Resurrection," he whispered. "Let me confess to you here."

And then he told the story of the banishment from London, the fight for his body in Wyld, the wandering in search of the waters of Nympha, the falling of mist, the coming to Youlstone, and all that had happened since that night. Last of all he spoke of the terror which had haunted him since Petronel had left him beside the ruins of her hut, and Curgenven had played his final move.

"I remember you, Anger, as a boy not like others," said Lyson presently. "You were always, I think, physically weak and extremely nervous. More than that, you were troubled by dreams and fancies which were not all fancy perhaps. Particularly I recall what happened after the death of poor little Chapman, who died of lockjaw following what appeared to be a slight injury to his foot. We were all affected by the tragedy, but none of us like you. One evening—it was summer time and broad daylight—you came to my study, and told me in the simplest possible fashion how you had just seen little Chapman, standing, you declared, in the boot-room, and worrying because some other boy had claimed his locker. I went with you, but could not see the figure which you persisted was still standing there looking at us sorrowfully. That incident made a great impression upon my mind; and now, after hearing your story, I am forced to the conclusion that these dreams and visions have not yet departed from you. Much of what you have told me appears incredible; I do not say your judgment is mistaken, but is it possible that your mind may have seen things wrongly? As a boy you were unlike others. You confess you have not changed."

"I have described to you my actual experiences in simple language," replied Anger.

"I believe you were mistaken about the ghost of Chapman. May you not be mistaken now?"

"It is true my mind has not changed, but I have another body. I am a different man from the poor thin creature who fled from London to save his life."

"A different man," repeated Lyson gently. "A worshipper of false gods, Anger."

"Did you say that? I am terrified now by every sound and vision. Your voice seemed to issue from myself."

"You are safe here," Lyson went on. "Our altar stands in a

sheltered place, not upon the crags of the mountain. We worship the protecting God, not those pagan deities of river and rock who claim from their creatures the sacrifice of blood. Let me retell your story. Not long ago you were an earnest priest, but something was wanting in you, some lesson had not been learnt, one side of your character remained undeveloped, and it pleased God to put you to the test by means of an illness which removed you from the narrowness of your life and brought you out into the open spaces of the world. Something was wanting, I say, to galvanise the sluggish spirit in you, to change the mechanism of your mind, to turn you into a strong man, with nostrils breathing the whole breath of life. You had walked always between stiff rubrics, looking in the wrong direction for your inspiration, seeking it from artificial flowers and indifferent images. You had not tested life, nor as you ministered did you ask the question, 'Who and what am I?' The purest water may run its course on mud, dear Anger. While you worked so well and faithfully nothing was revealed because your mind had not been opened and your soul was still in prison. So the message came, 'Go out upon the hills and find Me there.' You went and were healed; you felt the growth of knowledge and of consciousness, you felt also the wild freedom of the solitudes, you heard the rushing wind and saw the grandeur of the elements, and you said to yourself, 'These are the gods which have brought me out of sickness.' You looked at the wonders of creation and you called them deities; you worshipped the servants and forgot the Master; you put off the priest and became the savage, the creature untroubled by revelation, like the primitive goatherd tending his flock by day and creeping at night into his hut.

"Punishment followed," continued Lyson. "Instead of ascending towards happiness and light, you were descending into carelessness and darkness. You were drifting in unknown seas without a rudder. You had cut yourself free from the hearts of friends. In your loneliness you longed for love; you craved, like one of your own false gods, after human life; soft words, beauty, sympathy, companionship, appeared to you then the only gifts worth having. You sought for strength and beauty which were wild like the elements. You did not look for that perfect weakness and the submission of weakness which is one of God's best gifts in man or woman."

"It was my fate," cried Anger. "I was led to it through the mist. I could not escape."

"Do not talk to me of fate," said Lyson. "Every day I hear tales of that inevitable destiny to which in this place we give the name of weakness. Young men and women who have spoilt their lives bring their load of misery here, and tell me they are ruined by following the course appointed for them. Does a man who has made a great success of his life return thanks to the inevitable destiny which has made him prosperous? Not a bit of it. Nine men flatter themselves; the tenth thanks God. Yet every man who is a failure throws the blame on fate. Anger, there is one destiny for us all: it is our duty. If every man and woman did their best the final human issue would be happiness."

"How shall I free myself?" asked Anger.

"You wish to marry, yet you are priest of a church which forbids you matrimony. You must either remain a celibate or renounce your vows."

"I shall marry. That may not be my destiny, but it is my desire. I will free myself from what you call the path between stiff rubrics, and return to a Church which lets its priests go free. Our cloth and creed do not differ. A little matter of doctrine must not be allowed to spoil our lives," the sleeper murmured.

"I have no affection for the doctrines of your Church," said Lyson. "Neither do I like to see you change your views so readily."

"Will you advise me, then?"

"In such matters a man must advise himself. Build up your own character, Anger; choose the path which seems the best, only never speak to me of destiny. The man of God is not ruled by sun, moon, and stars. He does not yield to adverse influences, but sweeps them aside. Not many years ago Fate, as you call it, came to me and told me plainly that my religion was false, I was wasting my life and energy in ministering to others, I was not doing them any good, I was merely deceiving the people and myself, I was mad to fast and fight against sin, when in the next stage of existence I should find myself in exactly the same position as those who had given themselves up to pleasure. I took my destiny by the throat, as it were, and throttled it. No credit to me, for I hated the foul spectre. And afterwards my faith remained as clear as sunshine."

"You were always strong."

"We make our own strength; we are given our weakness, and it is enough to pull us down. Aim at something definite, Anger; it is the wobbler who goes down, not the lame man who limps on straight. Fix your eyes upon some spot in your spiritual landscape—the summit of Calvary to my mind is still the best—and proceed towards it, not in the rambling fashion of a Devonshire lane, but straight on, over the hedges of doubt, across the bogs of despondency, through the brakes of difficulties."

"Not alone."

"Well then, carry your passions with you, though I do not love the priest who is a bigamist; one bride, the Church, should be sufficient for him. But the passions are lawful. My Church in its broad-mindedness allows its ministers that liberty which removes temptation. Your Church binds the bodies of its priests and makes them burn. The garden upon the other side of the hedge is so much more desirable than our own. I am allowed to marry, yet I cannot regard myself free, for I am joined to my church and parish, and the thousands of poor folk who are my children. You are not allowed to marry, yet you determine to do so, and you have gone so far out of your way as to fix your mind upon a woman who must drag you down."

"No, Lyson, you must not say that—not here, beneath that picture which reminds me of her," said Anger earnestly. "Nobody has a good word for my Petronel."

"The opinions of others cannot be disregarded altogether," Lyson went on. "Do you love her simply because she is beautiful? This fatal trust in beauty makes many a man heathen; for the savage who worshipped the beauty of the sun, the Greeks who worshipped the beauty of art, and all the old pagan worshippers of Nature are allied in my mind with the modern Christian who

adores a woman for her beauty only. Let us have the truth, Anger:
the story of our redemption is not beautiful because it is charged
with all the fearful realism of a bloody agony. In this age of light-
hearted pleasures, when not to laugh is almost a sin, Christianity
becomes unpopular, I find, because it will not reject the stations
of the cross. A man who loves a woman for her beauty only, a
woman who is attracted to a man because of his strength, are no
better than earth worshippers. They would kneel before this altar
to be married, but never again. The only story I can tell them is too
depressing for these lovers. They would beg me to cheer them up,
to bring more happiness into their lives, to abolish Good Fridays,
and to be always a smiling optimist when in the pulpit. The realism
of the Christian faith is not for them."

"Do not suppose I am an unbeliever," said Anger deeply.

"What is it you love in this Miss Vigar if it is not her beauty?"

"She is strong," murmured Anger after a pause.

"Beauty and fierceness. How will she ever be a help to you? Can
you imagine her as the wife of a clergyman, the partner of a man
who fights with sin and goes into places of squalor to reclaim the
fallen? What is her religion? Will she not bring into your home the
gods of the mountain who have already proved too strong for you?
Have you found in this girl you propose to marry anything you
will cling to when her beauty fades?"

"Her love for me."

"That depends upon your own. And will yours last when her
wild nature urges her to resist—as it will—the course you have
marked out? One day, it may be, you will regard this Curgenven
as a friend who would have restrained you from an act of folly.
Which way are you going?"

"To my destiny. I remain a fatalist, dear Lyson. I will grow
strong enough to conquer myself, and to bring my wife to see
duty with my eyes, when I have returned with her to the old life
which was, I now perceive, a time of happiness. She will at least
destroy that restlessness derived from loneliness. If I have taken
the wrong direction, I have gone too far along it to turn back. I was
led through the mist to Youlstone and brought to Petronel that I

might help and save her from the misery of her life. It was my duty
to point out to her a better course; I had been brought there for
no other purpose. I was her friend, but she was lonely, so I became
her brother; but she was beautiful, so I became her lover; and now
that I love her I will be her husband. I have given my promise—I
won her in the passion of storms—and you would not have me
turn back now."

"If this story is not confused by the mists of your imagination, I
fear for you," said Lyson gently. "This Petronel of yours seems to be
a spirit formed before your eyes out of the wildness of Dartmoor
and your memory of Miss Wiggaton. Since drinking the waters of
Nympha you may have slept more soundly than you know of."

"That may be, but I am awake now."

"Take care you do not sleep again. Half-consciousness is often
worse than none. May you come safely out!"

"You will marry us," Anger exclaimed. "When we escape from
Youlstone, I shall bring Petronel here."

"I will serve you," said Lyson quietly; "if you must be bound to
the storm," he added.

Terror had departed from Anger when he left the Clergy House,
dressed again as a countryman, declining to stay a moment longer
than was necessary, because wind was blowing strongly from the
moor, and any hour the message of its fury might burst upon him.
The atmosphere of Lyson's church had made the visitor a stronger man; even the bodily weakness, which had been so distressing
those last few days, had gone from him. The determination to be
honest remained, so he entered a large shop, advanced towards the
tailoring department, and asked a salesman, who stepped towards
him, whether they kept ready-made clerical garments. "I am stock
size," he added in the jaunty fashion provoked by nervousness.

"We can get the garments for you, sir, if you could call again,"
stammered the man, amazement struggling with business
instincts, for this would-be purchaser of clerical raiment looked to
him more like a farmer.

"The High Church cut," directed Anger, in the same light-
hearted fashion.

"I will send out into the town at once. If it is impossible to get a new suit—I presume, sir, you may probably be requiring the clothes for a dramatic entertainment?"

"For a drama, certainly," Anger murmured uneasily, "I must have them to-day as I am leaving the town as soon as possible. I will call again in an hour's time."

"Thank you, sir. We will do our best."

Anger went out of the shop, pausing at the door a moment as he felt a sharp pain in his head. Presently he stepped into the street and making a clumsy movement collided against a middle-aged gentleman and a woman dressed as a nurse. While he apologised he recognised the visitor to Riversmeet who had insisted lately upon accompanying his morning rambles, still wearing the silk hat and absurd blue spectacles; while the woman at his side looked very like the nurse who had ministered to himself during the long period of illness and transition at South Wyld.

CHAPTER XX

THE PROMISED STORM

DURING the cross-moorland journey to Wyld that afternoon a lone farmer occupied the compartment with Anger; and, after the first stoppage, sought to make himself a man of the world by remarks about weather, soil, roots, and the state of his own health.

"I ha' been tortured with teethache," he explained, sounding the personal note strongly. "So I went into town this morning and saw a dentist, and I told 'en I lived in the cold country, and how the wind did whistle to be sure through my poor old hollow tooth, which was a tough one, I ses, fair riveted in my jaw, and I misdoubted whether any tool would lift him. The old chap took a sort of a side look and swore he wouldn't hurt me, but, lor' bless ye, I didn't believe a word he said. I don't know as if you'll believe me, mister, but be that as 'twill, it's the truth I be agoing to tell ye.

'Tis fair witchcraft what he done to me. He sits me in a chair what had a sort of a flying back to 'en, and screws my head up, without asking my permission, and he whips out a little tool, and, my dear life, mister, he took 'en abroad. The old man took my hollow tooth abroad, and never hurt me neither. I asked 'en how he done it, and he told me 'twas wi' science. Well, master, if I knew a bit of science I wouldn't till the land no longer. Some of us fellows in the country lives asleep, I fancy."

After the third stoppage the farmer gave practical proof that he did live in the country, and while he was snoring Anger seized the opportunity to unfasten a certain bundle which hitherto he had clung to jealously. Then and there he changed his clothes, without asking himself whether the action was not singular; and hardly had he done so when the train stopped again and the farmer, awakened by the jolt, gazed at his companion with evident approval, and began:

"I ha' been tortured wi' teethache, your reverence——"

"I have heard all that before," said Anger.

"Have ye though?" cried the farmer, looking frightened. "I'd like to know who told ye. When us started there was a young fellow sitting where you be, a fine set-up young fellow, but one of the idle ones, I fancy. He must ha' got out while I was resting. Did he tell you how the old man took my hollow tooth abroad?"

"Here are his clothes," said Anger.

"Well, I be dalled," the farmer muttered. "I fancy you knows a bit of science too, sir."

"I have made a change, you see. I should have asked your permission had you been awake," said Anger calmly.

"When us started you wur—well, sir, a hard-working farmer, I fancied, same as myself. Now you'm a parson. I won't go to sleep again," he said with determination.

"This is my first change, and my last," said Anger. "I had a good reason for wearing those clothes; I have a better one for putting them off. I shall not wear them any more."

"Good stuff too," said the farmer, leaning forward and fingering the fabric. "If you b'ain't wearing them again, your reverence, us might do a bit of business. Bide a bit until I count my money."

"Take the clothes and my good wishes with them. Keep your money to buy a book on scientific agriculture," said Anger kindly.

"Thank ye, your reverence. I'll wear the clothes, but I won't buy the book, vor I can't manage the words. I ha' been on the land too long. Lookye, master, I'll say nought. They won't get anything out of me," declared the farmer, making strange eyes by way of restoring confidence.

Darkness had fallen before the train reached the wayside station which was seven miles from the village of refuge. Once before Anger had alighted there, yet he did not recognise the place; moor surrounded it upon every side, a tempestuous sky swept overhead, no light of a house was showing. The scene had changed. He seemed to remember the covered station of a small country town, with a plantation of firs upon two sides, and a row of plain houses in the background. Since that illness, which had altered his own appearance, every place had changed in form and character.

The station-master informed him there was no chance of getting over to Wyld unless he could intercept the mailcart at the cross-roads beyond. Anger hurried in that direction, and when the lights appeared he waved his arm and called the driver to a halt.

"I ain't allowed to carry anyone, sir, but I'm always ready to oblige a parson. Jump up, sir," said the man.

Climbing upon the flat roof, Anger settled himself between two bags of literature, clinging to the iron rail and closing his eyes when the horse was given its head at the brow of a hill. They had hardly cleared a mile when the moon came out, and that part of the moorland belonging to Wyld parish, and so well named, appeared in sharp black outlines against a stormy sky.

"There was a village stood there once, sir," said the mailman, flicking his whip towards a space of enclosed fields. "Nothing be left now except a few heaps of stones. More than a hundred years ago, sir, so I'm told, a young fellow got into trouble wi' the folk, and one day they drove him up on Dartmoor, and as he didn't come home they reckoned he had got slugged in a bog. Forty years after an old man with a great big beard walks into the place, fair dropping money like rain, and he started to buy up the houses, and when the whole village belonged to him he told the folk his name and gave 'em all notice to clear out. Then he burnt the place, and what wouldn't burn he pulled down. That's the story, sir, but I don't know whether 'tis true or not."

"It is more likely the village was abandoned because of the storms. They must be very fierce across this upland," said Anger. "This old man with the beard was probably King Æolus."

"Nobody knows his name, sir," said the mailman. "But you'm right about the wind. I've known it so rough here I couldn't make way against it. See yonder hill, sir, just to the right of the firs? A hanging-post stood there once, and you can see the stone socket to this day. Tinners used to be strung up there, folks who didn't obey the laws of Parliament, not the one that sits in London, sir, but the one to Crockern Tor. Some were sent to Lydford castle, but plenty were hanged up on the moor. This part of the country used to make its own laws, but it was a nasty place to live in then I'm thinking."

"I have been along this road before; yet the surroundings are new to me," Anger murmured.

"I've often been asked whether I don't ever see ghosts along here," went on the mailman. "I've crossed this country vor years in all weathers, and heard the owls screaming, and seen the badgers running across the road, ah, and I've had many an old beetle in my eye; but I was only frightened once. 'Twas on a darkish night in summer, sir, and I was going round a bend yonder between a lot of old stones, when I heard a queer hopping sort of noise, and then a voice half singing and half crying. It made my blood run cold, I tell ye, and it scared the old horse so bad I could hardly hold him in. Well, sir, what do you think it was? I got down, and took one of the lamps, and began to look about me, feeling a bit wisht, I tell ye. All to once I heard a great big laugh, and out jumps Curgenven. You've tell heard of him, sir, surely?"

"Yes, I know him," muttered Anger.

"Well, sir, 'twas a bit of a shame to frighten me, and I can't understand him doing it, vor he'm the kindliest gentleman living, though I suppose he likes his joke. But what mazed me wur those cries of his. They wur awful, sir; just as if he was being tortured."

"Did he explain?"

"No, sir. There's only one funny story about Curgenven, and 'tis this: they say he loved a maiden, and her went out on Dartmoor one day, like this young fellow I was telling you about, and he never saw her again, nor nobody else neither; and they do say he goes out looking vor her, and calling after her. Perhaps he was looking vor her that night, but he must have wanted her cruel bad. All the same, sir, I don't believe the story. It ain't like Curgenven to crave vor maidens, and nobody can give the name of this one 'tis supposed he lost."

"This is a very long way from Riversmeet. What do you suppose brought him out here?" asked Anger.

"Curgenven be in all places to once, sir," said the mailman simply. "You can't go out on Dartmoor, whether 'tis north, south, east, or west, without running the chance of meeting him. I don't know how he gets about, vor he's only a little gentleman, but twenty miles seem no more to him than one would be to us. I fancy, sir, he must go with the wind," added the man with a chuckle.

"Have you seen him lately?"

"Not once this winter. But I heard something about him to-day. Maybe you know Youlstone, sir?"

"I have been there," said Anger.

"Well, sir, the place is going to be sold up, the whole village, like that one back beyond I was telling you of. People be telling about it all over Dartmoor, and they say Curgenven is pretty near off his head. Seems that he lent a bit of money to every Youlstone chap— they are an ignorant lot, and a queer lot; I don't suppose you'd find another village to match Youlstone anywhere. Yes, sir, he lent them money, and they signed mortgages on their property. One day Curgenven found he was short of money himself—this is what I've heard coming through the country this evening avore I met you—and he made over all these mortgages to another gentleman.

I don't know much about law, sir, but it seems he sort o' sold these mortgages vor ready money, see? Well, now, this gentleman, who is a bit of a rascal vor certain, calls in these mortgages sudden like, and as none of the folks can pay he means to take their land and clear 'em all out. Curgenven is half mazed, and they do say if he gets hold of this gentleman there'll be murder."

"Who is this man?" cried Anger.

"Don't know his name, sir. They say he's a priest; not a parson like yourself, but one o' these artful old toads of Catholics. Curgenven, being a religious man, trusted this priest—it was always the way of Curgenven to trust folk. He's too simple vor a lawyer, sir, and he can't look after his business, being half his time out on Dartmoor."

"Curgenven can buy up the land himself," Anger muttered, wondering when the dwarf would cease to haunt him.

"He ain't got the money, sir."

"When does the sale take place?"

"One day this week."

"It cannot be possible. A longer notice must be given."

"If it ain't possible, Curgenven will see to it. Youlstone be wonderful dear to him, and this priest won't get hold of the place without a lot of opposition."

Little more was said, as the sky soon clouded and a flurry of snow crossed the upland, which seemed to become more bleak as they neared Wyld common. Dark as it was, Anger thought he could find the way, since he had walked there a hundred times during the period of convalescence, and yet after leaving the mail-cart he did not know in which direction to turn. This was South Wyld, yet he could not discover the cottage where he had struggled back to life, while the broad village street was then a mountain trackway. He discovered a few squalid cottages nestling in a hollow beneath a canopy of peat-smoke, a very poor inn, not in the least like the old manor of the Wiggatons, and a few hungry-looking people clad in rags or sheepskins.

Shivering with cold, Anger made towards a flickering light, and stopped in front of the tumbling inn, noticing with amazement that the walls were propped up by wooden supports. Rough fellows were drinking and shouting. He entered, and a man, wearing a tattered apron, came up and asked his business.

"Is this South Wyld?" asked the wanderer.

"To be sure it is. Wyld in the cold country."

"I must have seen you before. Do you recognise me?"

"No, parson. You'm a stranger."

"I was here for many months, very ill most of the time. Where is Hillside Cottage?"

"Never heard of it."

"Where does Doctor Francis live?"

"Look here, parson, you'm a bit muddled. You have come to the wrong place."

"What is this village then? Who are these men?"

"'Tis South Wyld, I tell ye, and these fellows are drunkards. We'm all drunkards here. Have you come to preach the gospel to us?"

"I want shelter for the night."

"Show me your money, and I'll find ye a bed," said the landlord.

Anger passed the night in a room which admitted all the winds of Wyld, lying on a bed composed principally of sacks; not sleeping, but turning over in his mind Curgenven's conquering move. In the morning he paid his reckoning, and went out into the village, which had put on a new form with his own change of raiment. Civilisation had departed altogether. Wyld had reverted to its simple old-world character. The inhabitants appeared to be a race of swineherds. One, an old man, clad in a long black cloak with leggings of skin, agreed to drive him within a mile of Youlstone for a pint of old ale and the price of a sheep. Anger closed with this peculiar bargain, and they set off an hour before noon. The old man did not speak during the journey, which required three hours, for the horse was very slow. Midway the fine snow in the air was swept out of sight by wind, which, descending from the heights behind, soon raged with such violence as to drive the cart from side to side. The old man held the reins as a ferryman might have clutched the tiller, and sat like a figure carved in stone. Anger, rocking to and fro, in fierce excitement, began to sing, but the driver paid no heed. The storm was coming on, the great storm which was to end that stage of his existence. The sky was streaked with red and blue, clouds of a sulphurous colour swept revelling past, while the mad wind was hurling messages from Stiniel, incoherent sounds of happy meaning, forming in his mind the call, "Wait for me at the gate. Do not come into the house, or you will lose me."

The old man and his cart departed in a whirlwind, and, leaving the road, Anger took to the moor, letting the gale drive him across ridges and tussocks. He was about to enter Youlstone as he had done before, but not in a mist. Here were the bogs he had struggled through; and there the hill up the side of which he had scrambled; and beyond were the white and fearful walls of Stiniel. It was far too early to obey the message; nor could he venture into the church-town and run the risk of being stoned to death. All the people would be raging against him now that they believed him to be the breaker-up of their homes and the thief of their fields. Not a living creature could be seen; even the birds had been swept off the upland; and not a river could make its roar heard against the mightier element. Anger raced on, his feet touching the peat lightly. It was still early afternoon, but natural daylight had been gone some time, and the moorland appeared to be lit with deep blue candles. Yet the walls of Stiniel remained a ghastly white.

"I have friends even in Youlstone," cried Anger. "I will get some food in Quoditch, and hide there until the time comes. If I am seen at a distance I should not now be recognised. My cloth is my protection."

He passed Stiniel on the wings of the wind, descended the Pinch where Curgenven had fallen, plunged through the ruined gate, and reached the cottage. Bobby and Thirza were huddled over the fire. They appeared to fling themselves towards him when he entered.

"You see I have come back to you," cried Anger, as he swung back the door and bolted it.

"Schulemaster!" muttered Bobby. "No, it b'ain't he."

"You know me, Thirza?"

"Aw, sir, us knows ye. 'Tis the old master, Bobby."

The little farmer put out his dirty hand and wagged his head. "Too late," he said. "He can't help us now. Quoditch be gone, and all Youlstone be going fast; first one plat, then t'other. Us be all beggars now."

"Give me something to eat, Thirza."

"Don't ye go on, sir. They would tear you abroad. This be the day of the sale. Curgenven be here, going from one home to another, fair crying and howling."

"Us knows 'en," said Bobby. "The vules don't. You'm the priest what he ses be buying the village. Nothing don't work wi' he. Them old rags and images b'ain't no gude."

"They won't fail, Bobby, my dear. The day b'ain't over yet," cried Thirza.

"Could I make them believe, if I went up to the village and swore to them Curgenven is their enemy? He cannot lay his hands upon their homes so suddenly. Surely they would believe me," said Anger boldly.

"None of 'em would listen," said Bobby. "They'd knock ye down avore you could open your mouth. What Curgenven ses be the truth. What you ses be a lie."

"But if I take their part," cried Anger.

"They wouldn't let ye speak, I tell ye. You'm too late, schule-master. You come years too late. I'll never learn now," said Bobby miserably. "I'll be a vule to the end of my days."

"What be you saying, Bobby?" shouted Thirza.

"Keep quiet, woman. I thought I was a scholar till I met schule-master; but he beat me, same as Curgenven ha' beaten he. Well, us be ruined now, mother. Us will go out and try to learn a bit."

"I won't never leave Quoditch," shouted Thirza, spitting on her hands and glaring savagely. "I'll take that Curgenven, and I'll break 'en across my knee like any old rotten stick. The day b'ain't over, I tell ye. What be the wind sent here vor? B'ain't they old images working? The windy one be fair shaking his head and laughing. He knows a bit, I tell ye. He knows Curgenven won't never get home to-night. He knows us will bide in Quoditch."

"Bobby is right," said Anger. "The images are no good. Belief is the only thing that matters."

"You ses my religion b'ain't no gude," cried Thirza. "You believe in yours, master, and don't ye say a word agin mine. That old image out yonder—lookye there, Bobby!" she shouted furiously, as she stared from the window. "The wind ha' torn 'en abroad, torn his head off, I tell ye. Us be saved! Quoditch be ours again. Curgenven won't never set his foot in here as master, and if he do come he'll ha' lost that great big head."

"He'll be here avore dark. This is the only house he b'ain't come to yet," said Bobby, as he stumbled about the room. "He'm looking vor you, schulemaster. It b'ain't safe vor you to be here. Volks will come along with 'en, and us ha' got no place to hide ye in."

"I will go down Youlstone cleave and wait in the wood till evening," said Anger, rising. "Perhaps we shall not meet again. If you are turned out, and should you ever find yourselves in difficulties, ask for me at the church of Father Lyson in Plymouth. He will tell you where I can be found."

They parted, and Anger went out into the stormy solitude and climbed the hill which looked down upon Youlstone churchtown. That scene at least had not altered. He could see the tower of the church but he could hear no sound; none of the wailings of Curgenven and his children reached his ears because of the violence of the wind, greater then than before his visit to Quoditch. Looking into the opposite direction he caught one last glimpse of those white walls which appeared to tremble, while the windows were blind eyes straining to follow his course; but there was no motion of human life, no sudden appearance of a face, no brown hand waving from the upper casement. He went on, abandoning to Curgenven that haunted scene.

At least there would be shelter, he thought, at the bottom of the cleave; but this was another delusion, for the wind was screaming through the wood, the promised gale of Petronel, carrying her message into every part of the moor, hunting him down and yelling, as it seemed to him, the words of assignation which his own mind went on repeating. Oaks lay about uprooted; bushes had been swept by one element into the river, to be swept away by another; banks were breaking as if shattered by artillery; rocks, loosened by endless vibrations from their sockets of peat, bounded down the side of the cliff to leap the river boundary like young goats. The wood, so close in summer, now opened into vistas cut by storm, and along these narrow aisles dead leaves went whirling as if in some spiritual fury at their preacher's voice.

In the dim distance Anger saw Whippety sitting upon a rock, clapping his hands and laughing. The jay, settled upon his shoulder, looked a monstrous bird, its feathers puffed out by the wind and its big eyes staring.

Anger approached and stood in front of the boy who took no heed of him; the jay screamed, but did not move; and the leaves streaming past made a cloud between the boy who slept for life and the man who had a limit set to his deep slumber. The cliff rose over them, and where the rough pathway curved inwards to avoid a boulder, the soil, matted with roots, curled over, making a roof and shelter to the track for several yards. This mass of earth was moving, with every gust it rose and fell; and when Anger climbed up and went behind he perceived one long oak-root, tough sinew of a tree hard by, which prevented the fringe of stones and earth from toppling.

"Another hour and the darkness will be upon us," Anger muttered. "I will stay near these creatures and wait until then. The boy is an imbecile but he knows his own mind. Even the bird appears to be listening. They too can hear a message in this wind."

He went a few yards away and remained behind some holly-bushes, peering through the branches at the path below. It grew darker and wilder. Collecting a quantity of leaves, he knelt upon them. Once he stared out to see the boy and bird still upon the rock in the same attitude.

"I must be going," he murmured, as the sky began to take the colour of the sodden ground. "All the night I shall be flying through the storm with Petronel. To-morrow it will be calm. I shall be awake, and she will be saved. But if to-morrow is as far away as yesterday, there is a long dark journey waiting for us."

Conscious that Whippety was moving, Anger looked up to see the boy on his hands and knees, clearing the earth from that arm-like root. An instrument was gleaming in his right hand, and bending forward his arm set to work until the great fringe of soil began to topple. Surely a sane hour had come to him at last, for he stared across at Anger and clapped a hand upon his mouth.

"If I did shout, nobody above or below could hear," murmured Anger almost flippantly. "This is some fool's game, while I have the sanest work of life awaiting me. So the day of the great sale is over, and that little coward Woodland has not dared to interfere. All Youlstone belongs to Curgenven. He is now mingling his tears with those of the inhabitants, wringing his hairy hands, and cursing the cunning priest who has brought this misery upon them. Who could defeat such a man? The simple Billacotts make a doll of earth and rags," he said with foolish laughter; "they put it out into the wind, and when its head is blown off they thank their god for ridding them of the rascal."

Whippety had stepped back and was swaying from one foot to the other; while the eyes of boy and bird were directed downward. Anger again peered through the prickly leaves, and it seemed quite natural to behold the haunting dwarf, sauntering along the path, smiling to himself, indifferent to the tempest. On he came, stepping almost delicately, his big head thrown back, his face genial, his eyes kindly.

"That boy will get a beating. He is as powerless to harm Curgenven as Thirza Billacott with her rag-doll. I must not show myself, even if he does," Anger muttered, for Whippety was coming onward at a run, his face as white as the walls of Stiniel, leaves rustling past his head, the jay still settled upon his shoulder. He jumped upon the sagging roof, and with a crash all vanished—earth, stones, and roots—bearing down the boy and bird upon the path, and more, upon the body of the dwarf who, before that crash, was lord of Youlstone, master of Riversmeet, and living father of his murderer. He had hankered after the land and grabbed at it, and now he had it to his soul's content.

Anger fled, with one fearful glance at Whippety sitting upon that mighty heaped-up grave, sucking his thumb contentedly, and rushed through the wood, across the stepping-stones, up the side of the cleave, flung into sharp bushes by the wind or tossed in scorn upon the rocks. It went dark suddenly, but now there was no need for the night. The tyrant was dead and they were free. The Billacotts were safe in Quoditch, Youlstone people had their own again, the deed of Stiniel was so much waste paper. No enemy to fight against, no terror of conspiracy, no need for flight. Petronel and he could sleep in peace, and when it was known how Curgenven lay beneath his pyramid, the people might easily be shown how he had duped them.

Yet, it would be necessary to avoid the village, where the passions of the homeless were still at fever heat, so Anger made across the moor and over the rounded hill at the foot of which the bridge and Pinches nestled. The darkness was haunted by shouts of laughter and shapes of stone like headless men. There seemed to be nothing in the world but Curgenven's raging spirits.

Anger ran on, thrilled with another fear, remembering Petronel's wild words, her threats and warnings, her command to him not to enter the house until her work was accomplished and she should be ready to make the dash for freedom. Why had Petronel, while hating Stiniel, declared she could not leave it, herself and house must go together, and if they were separated some final act on her part would be necessary? What was the bond of terror which held her bound to Mrs. Vigar? Was it that which had to be broken before the flight?

"It is still early," he panted. "I may not be too late; I must not be too late. I am the only sane creature who knows that she is free. The foster-father, who loved her, is dead. The spirit of evil has been removed from our lives for ever. Nobody can tell her except myself. She must be saved. One more effort and I shall be at Stiniel for the last time, and then I shall see her coming out to meet me, sweet and pure as she was that May morning walking in childhood upon the dew, walking to me, her husband and priest, not to the dwarf and her evil fortune."

Even at a distance he could somehow hear that gate rattling

furiously and the black shrubs beating together. No break in the
clouds allowed a gleam of light to reach his world from others,
while the windows of Stiniel seemed darker than the hills. The
idea of space, empty of everything except the violence of storm,
remained as Anger flung himself down the last descent, and fell
against that gate.

"Not here," he gasped. "If I wait I may not save her. If I go to
the house I lose her. I will go—I must—to win her body and to save
her soul."

Again and again he grappled with the gate, but it would not
open, for iron bars seemed to be holding it fast, while sharp wire
ran along the top. He clambered upon the hedge, cast himself into
the shrubs, breaking branches, crashing through them into the ever
sunless garden, feeling clammy leaves wiping themselves like dead
men's fingers on his face. Snow was still lying there in heaps, and
the house looked made of it. Anger plunged to the door, opened
it at a touch, entered into darkness, very different from the night
upon the moor, for it was still and heavy like drapery, although the
roaring was in his ears, and the house shuddered, and slates were
being lifted from the roof.

The room upon the left was empty, but a small fire was burning,
giving out some light but no heat, more like a painted fire upon
a hearth of canvas. Stepping to the mantle, Anger removed the
miniature of little Petronel and clapped it into his pocket, saying
coolly, "We must not go without this," for the idea of flight was
still fixed firmly in his mind.

Still no footsteps descended the stairs, no light tread of Petronel,
no dreary shuffling of old Nicholas, crossed the passage; yet bodies
were in motion, crawling upon the ground somewhere and groaning, and there was a voice shivering in the accents of prayer. The
dwellers in that house seemed penitential, not passionate.

"I am waiting when I should be acting," Anger said. "Curgenven
is dead. His spirit is not master here."

Supporting himself against the wall, for his body had become
a burden suddenly, he descended the stone steps with a feeling
of annoyance, as if he had owned Stiniel and was vexed to find

the interior so ill-prepared for him, even cursing the cobwebs which brushed his face, and muttering with an oath, "This place is dripping with moisture." His mind was filled with blasphemous thoughts and hatreds. The steps were endless, winding like the thread of a screw, until he became dizzy and almost persuaded he was descending into the depths of the moorland. He grew more distressed, sharp pains of the head returned; he laughed in a foolish fashion, and wondered when he should see again the quaint gentleman in silk hat and blue spectacles, and if he would come to the wedding and ask tender questions concerning the bridegroom's health.

A light at last—that eternal blue lamp which had haunted him so long—and an open door. At last Anger saw Petronel in her white dress, the sleeves turned above her elbows, and towards him one fine brown arm upon which a sudden fierce light appeared to fall, showing him the hand clutching a cross and the scroll inscribed, "To the memory of my dear brother."

Her back was towards him for she was kneeling beside a bed of ferns, tearing them up and replacing them with flat stones, making the scrap of garden level with the cellar floor. The light about her throbbed as if some imp was trifling with the lamp.

"I wonder what she is doing there," said Anger impatiently. "Pulling up ferns and working like a mason in her wedding-dress. I wonder if she is getting ready to go."

A hand touched him, and he started round to see Nicholas standing upon the step above, his arms held out stiffly, his chest moving spasmodically.

"Quite wrong, sir. This is something bad, but you and I are powerless. I cannot look."

"He was not her brother," said Anger sharply.

"No, no. He will come back one day. I have often wondered why those ferns were planted in the cellar," said Nicholas.

Anger made a step forward, and saw Mrs. Vigar, hearing her groan at the same moment, for the woman was lying upon the floor, very close to Petronel, her hands and feet bound tightly.

"This will not do," he whispered.

"Don't tell her I am here," said Nicholas in the same hopeless fashion.

"Tell who?"

"Petronel."

"Mrs. Vigar is not her mother. Who has tied her up so cruelly?"

"You know."

"Which of them is the strongest?"

"That's a fool question."

"Why does she hate Mrs. Vigar?"

"She is fearful all winter," said Nicholas crossly.

"Will she hurt Mrs. Vigar?"

"I am going to keep my eyes shut. Don't interfere. She knows all the spells."

"She is good and beautiful," said Anger, going forward.

A wild sad cry broke upon his ears. It seemed to come from the tempest outside, but Petronel was looking at him, as beautiful as ever, her face without fierceness, full of desire and terrible anguish.

"So you have come," she said.

They seemed to be upon the moor, and the wind drove Anger onwards, while the blue light sank lower as if the supply of marsh-gas failed.

"Take it," said Petronel, without a sign of passion, but speaking tenderly and sorrowfully. "Now that you have come, you must do it." She forced something like a heavy cross into his hand, and said, "Three knocks will be enough."

"What am I to do?" he asked simply.

"Do what is in your mind. Oh, why could you not have waited for me at the gate?"

Anger raised his arm, shuddered, and cried, "I cannot move."

"You will find the strength now," she said sadly.

Anger struggled fearfully, then turned three times quickly, his right shoulder repelled as if someone had struck him from the front. He fell back gasping. A long body rolled in the dark across the floor and settled at his feet. Then the light became fierce and strong again.

"Are you all going?" called Nicholas, who seemed to be lying at the foot of the steps.

"That is like a woman's body," muttered Anger.

"It is," she said sadly.

"Curgenven is dead; he is cold, like the earth under which he lies. That is why I could not wait at the gate. I came to tell you."

Again he heard that wailing cry and found Petronel before him with her arms round his knees, gazing upwards with a face still pure and beautiful. "Too late," she sobbed. "Now I can only go with you to the moor. There you must leave me."

"What have you done? Are you not ready yet?" he asked impatiently.

"I had to free myself. If what I had done was not known to you, if I could have escaped the consequences of it, and come to your arms pure and sinless in your sight, you might have saved me. Bertram Vigar lies there; I killed him, not out of hatred, but because he was weak, while I am strong. Listen to the wind loosening the rocks! The storm must do the work for which it was created, but the spirit of the moor mourns over the destruction. I have mourned for the boy; I would have given up even your love if that could have restored him to life. This emblem on my arm is on my heart. Only Mrs. Vigar knew of it. That was her power over me. If I had left Stiniel she would have told Curgenven, and he would have brought me back, hating me at last. He told you I had killed Bertram, but he never believed it. He would shrink from no crime himself, yet he could not bear the thought of sin in me. I was purer to him than I have ever been to you."

"I will go. I am leaving something behind," moaned Anger.

Nicholas looked up and asked simply, "Are you going away?"

"To win my freedom Mrs. Vigar had to die. I have nothing to hide from you now. She was fierce, but I am fiercer; she was strong, but I am stronger. She was only a poor drunken woman. Now she has gone, and I must follow."

"Haven't you taken that thing away?" asked Nicholas crossly.

"It is yours to see to," said Petronel. "Ah, Mr. Vigar, there was no wild wind when you were born."

Anger put out his hands, appearing at that moment to see two faces, that of Petronel terribly sad, the other pale and solemn, reminding him of Mary, forcing the other sternly from his sight. This new face approached his shoulder, and its eyes seemed to melt in his.

"Are you angry with me?" he asked.

"No, no. I am sorry," answered the voice of Petronel.

"Are you going away?"

"Yes."

"What is that light?" he cried.

"Oh, that has nothing to do with me. It looks like a red lamp. This is mine—the blue one."

"Where is Mrs. Vigar? Is she asleep again?" called Nicholas.

"It is all over now," said Petronel.

"Who killed her?" cried Anger suddenly.

"You did. You gave her three blows on the head with that hammer. It was your desire to free me, and so you did it."

Anger cried out and struck his head against the wall. Petronel crossed in front of him, pointing upwards, and he turned, staggering, and blundered after her up the stone steps, across the dark hall of Stiniel, out of the porch, along the mossy pathway between the snow-heaps, and so from the gate which was then wide open. She took to the moor, a flickering figure in her white dress, and still he pursued up the steep trackway where she seemed only a few yards ahead, and upon the plateau where the bogs began; here she went away, but he followed, while many thoughts and words seemed to pass between them; and so to the great boulders strewn upon the hillside, where she became a dim receding figure, imploring him in cries of wild entreaty not to lag so far behind; and there he fell, for there was no more life left in him.

At last Anger revived. The wind had ceased, black clouds were racing off the sky, and the calm light of the sleeping moon fell upon his face, bathing it with caresses gentle as Petronel had been sometimes, white and cold like the figure which had gone beyond to be dissolved into the last storm-wrack of moor and mind.

CHAPTER XXI

THE LAST PHASE

THE sick body had been replaced by a strong one, the priest had made way for the lover, the Christian had been overwhelmed by paganism, and the new man had become a murderer. Such were the various changes through which Anger had passed since leaving his friends. Now he stood in the white light of the moon and the black coat of the priest, his mind still held in subjection by the profligate body which seemed bent upon its own destruction.

He was a criminal, therefore he became cunning. Flight would be necessary after all, although he had no companion for the journey; for he had the world against him, and not a friend would stand beside him now. First the enemy of Youlstone, then the haunted man of Riversmeet, and now the outlaw, with nothing remaining but the breath of life which had been borrowed from the storm and the blood of life lent to him by the spirit of the hills.

He was going away from Youlstone church-town, looking back, and trying to see through the mist of moonlight those terrible white walls surrounded by black shrubs, with the little tumbling cottage below where he had spent some pleasant hours; but not a vestige of that scene remained. At that hour the Billacotts were his only friends, and he longed to be with them, listening to the quaint nonsense of Bobby, and comforted by the kindness of Thirza. They seemed to be creatures more real than the others, and the humanity in himself clung to them. Yet they too were children of enchantment, borrowing no more from life than the rags and images of their religion, and they had followed Petronel into the waste places where the foot of man as a conscious being could not tread.

This was the cleave unchanged, and below the oaks were at

rest, and leaves had done whirling, while even that great heap of stones and earth, with the white-faced guardian and his bird sitting atop, were a part of slumber. The only wild and restless creature was himself. Yet there was a promise of life for him, because as he stumbled down and reached the ruins of the hut, he saw the moonlight striking between the trees and falling full upon the hearthstone, and he knew the spell was broken. The Princess Springwort was mightier than the spirit of winter—little primroses that night were showing buds and the honeysuckle was throbbing into leaf and ringing through the silence upward from the wood came the order of release:

"I salute thee, Nymph. When the moonbeams enter the hovel, and strike upon the hearthstone, let the sleeper go free. Upon that night, Nymph, at the appointed time."

Once more to the town of Riversmeet, not yet asleep, for it was still early. People were out now that the storm was over, trying to get rid of sixty minutes, useless to themselves. Going by some force of compulsion towards River Street, a great figure crossed before Anger, splashing up the mud, and the fugitive found himself in the presence of Wadge, who looked down at him with pitying eyes, half closed, and said benignly, "So you have come back. Ah, sir, how glad I should be to see you, were it not for your sin. Is it not foolish to be walking here, sir?"

"This is my last hour in Riversmeet," Anger mumbled, as he hurried on.

"It does me good to hear that, sir," said Wadge, following closely. "Still, I do not see how you can escape. Everybody knows you are a priest. Take off those clothes, sir, and disguise yourself as a countryman. When a man has his personal safety to think of, a little deception does no harm."

"I put off these clothes once. I never will do so again," cried Anger.

"Walk the shady side of the street then, sir. You will be safer there."

"I will walk in the light," said Anger.

"You are getting desperate, sir. That also is a sin. Are you going to see Curgenven? Remember how you have set yourself against him. Listen to me, sir. It is possible in this evil world to escape the direct consequences of sin by a payment of money. Give me a hundred pounds for Zion, and another hundred for the maiden. Then you shall hear no more of what happened last Sunday evening."

"Leave me!" cried Anger violently. "I know you now. I recognise in you the man whom Curgenven employed to ruin Woodland's business and to drive me away. You use religion as a cloak to hide your wickedness, I saw Curgenven going in the dark to Zion; I heard him speaking to you. My mind has been clouded over, but now it grows clear. One hour you are praying; the next taking blood-money. I heard your promise to resort to stronger methods. That young woman is your accomplice; Curgenven was your master. He is dead, and you can go to him."

Anger heard no sound, but looking out a moment later as he stood under the gateway of the court he saw the big figure gliding out of sight.

Curgenven's den was well lighted, and raging with heat. The river below was roaring more loudly than usual. Seated opposite each other were Palk and Woodland playing at chess. The combatants looked up when Anger entered, the doctor heavily, the storekeeper brightly.

"I thought you had left Riversmeet, but I suppose you cannot get on without Curgenven," said Palk carelessly.

"Good evening, Mr. Anger," said Woodland briskly. "I am very glad to see you again, but I should hardly have recognised you had we met outside. Clothes make such a difference! Besides, you seem to have lost flesh lately."

"You are waiting for Curgenven?" said Anger in a hollow voice.

"Yes, he is very late. It has been a busy day with him," said Woodland. "You are beaten, doctor. I have only to move my queen to this square. You may avert immediate disaster with your knight, but you cannot get away from my two bishops."

"It is your game," said Palk. "Now, had Curgenven been at my shoulder he would have found a move to beat you."

"What are you doing here, Woodland?" asked Anger sharply.

"Why, sir, it has been my custom for many years to spend one evening each week with Curgenven," the tradesman answered.

"Are you waiting here to celebrate the fall of Youlstone?"

"I am afraid I admire Curgenven. I say afraid, because I do not admire his methods, but then, sir, we must make the best of the world, and when Curgenven is successful I am always ready to congratulate him. Myself, I love a bold and daring scheme; and this capture of an entire village, with its subsequent conversion from a wild and uncivilised place into a modern spa, possesses a magnificence which appeals to my business instincts even if my conscience disapproves of the conqueror's methods. I sympathise with Youlstone folk, and if I could restore them to their homes I would certainly do so; but when Curgenven joins us as master of the village, I shall offer him my hand and my assistance."

"You were cold to us at first," said Palk. "You didn't like the idea of Curgenven and myself making a quick fortune, while you were buying for ninepence and selling for a shilling."

"I have not altered my opinions," said Woodland. "I merely accept the situation. I do my best for the weak side until it is hopelessly defeated. Then I cross over to save myself. I can still see that the victor does not go too far in his hour of triumph."

"You did not even make a fight," said Anger bitterly. "You had your chance to-day. Why were you not up in Youlstone bidding against Curgenven?"

"Because he knows we must hang together," murmured Palk.

"Stores will be required in the new Youlstone," went on Woodland amiably. "My boys would not let me forget that point. Had there been enmity between Curgenven and myself, he would have kept me out of Youlstone. Now that I am ready to assist him I can see new fields of enterprise opening before me. My fortune will increase! My boys will have their ambition realised!"

"Suppose Curgenven does not return?"

"Who could prevent him?" asked both the chess-players together.

"He went up to Youlstone to make people homeless, to deprive them of their land."

"Nothing of the kind," said Palk angrily. "He has gone to tell the people they will soon be a hundred times better off, and he will be telling them the truth."

"I will see to that," said Woodland firmly.

"What of the storm?" cried Anger.

"It was a big wind," said Woodland, "but not big enough to shake him. The stronger the storm the louder he laughs. There is never any keeping him indoors when the wind is fierce. He will say the moor is calling him and he will go out to laugh at the lightning and shout at the thunder. He would have been home before had it not been for the wind. He has gone up to fight against it."

"You did not feel it in this valley," Anger went on muttering. "It was terrible upon the upland. Houses have lost their roofs, people have been struck dead—one, I know, is lying now with her head battered. Curgenven would have come through the wood, and trees have been falling there."

"He is safe," said Palk with a growl.

"I looked down from the hill upon Youlstone; I saw only moon, mists, and ruins. There seemed to be no life left," cried Anger wildly. "Even the moorland was dead, for the spirit of beauty had gone from it; nothing was left but dead peat, dead rocks, where once I had found the origin of life. I was a dull fool; I caught hold of shadows and called them gods, I held a mist to my heart, I wasted my strength fighting the air. Now that the storm is past I awake and see myself, naked although clothed, claimed for ever by the false powers who forced their false life upon me. I cannot get back to the life of a man. I must go back to the Nymph and drown myself in her waters."

"Go to bed, sir, and get some sleep," said Palk, more sullenly.

"I have been sleeping all these months."

"Come out with me, sir, I will show you where to find Curgenven," said Woodland.

They went out, leaving the doctor nodding over the chess-board. The sky had changed during those few minutes and now the town was black and rain pelted. Without a word they passed along, and were about to turn into a narrow street when Anger perceived dim white boards gleaming beside the kerb, and before them a limbless bundle squatting in the mud, holding up an abject hat and a face as white as its own chalk pictures of snow and surf.

"It's very cold, gentlemen, very cold. They ain't lighted the lamps yet," cried a pitiful voice.

"A man," muttered Anger. "No arms, no legs; a man who makes pictures with his mouth."

"Do not give him money. He is a drunkard," Woodland whispered.

"He makes a living. What has the world done for him? May he not even have his vices?" said Anger, dropping money into the hat. "He is a better man than I am. He dares to lie in the mud and stare at the public. Where are you taking me? This is my farewell to Riversmeet, and yet I cannot get away from the place. I am in motion and in flight, but wherever I go the town follows, while Stiniel remains at my right hand."

"We enter here," said Woodland, going forward into a place of worship, lighted dimly, and guiding Anger through into a passage which led into a long low building with whitewashed walls. The atmosphere of the room was at freezing-point, and the breathing of those who were assembled upon cold benches made clouds of mist which hung between Anger's eyes and a platform whereon four men stood singing a grotesque quartette with tragic faces; while the huddled and shivering audience did not smile.

"What is this foolery?" asked Anger.

"A concert in aid of chapel funds. They will cheer up presently, when Curgenven appears. He tells them stories and makes them laugh," said Woodland.

"They will not be cheered to-night," Anger murmured.

The four men finished their painful task, and were followed by a young girl muffled in furs, whose voice was scarcely audible as she tried to sing about love and hearts estranged, being herself too young to know the meaning of such things. Badly as she sang, certain phrases touched Anger, and his own heart troubled him, for he remembered how grieved Mary had been to lose him; how true had been her foreboding that he would not return; how sweet and pure she had looked, yet how fierce at his trifling with her own best gift. Had she been singing songs of loneliness like this?

A pause followed, then whisperings, and a distant voice announced, "The next item on our programme is a recitation by Curgenven."

At last there came genuine applause, and in the midst of it Woodland exclaimed, "Now we shall see him. This is always his way. He does not appear until they call him."

The door had been thrown open, showing to Anger the long whitewashed passage lighted by one gas-jet, horribly cold and terribly empty. Somewhere a voice was shouting, "Curgenven!"

"He is playing with them," murmured Woodland. "We shall see him in one minute jumping along that passage."

Now men and women were standing and craning their necks towards that gleaming and frosty tunnel, while the voice still shouted, and another took up the cry at the door of the chapel, and a third called in the rain-beaten street, until all the town appeared to be ringing with the name of Curgenven, who never came without a merry voice and roar of laughter.

"A few tons of earth and a lunatic," Anger muttered, unable to remove his eyes from that passage. "What are they to a man who has just stolen a village and conquered its inhabitants?"

"He is coming. I heard his laugh outside," said Woodland, bringing out his snuff-tin.

"Curgenven! Come along, Curgenven!" called the laughing voices.

"Shut that door," Anger cried suddenly. "There is something in the passage. It keeps close to the wall."

"Nothing, sir. The shadow of the gas bracket."

"Something hairy—an animal."

"That was a mouse running back into the chapel," muttered Woodland.

"Keep it out!" shouted Anger.

"Only mice and spiders, neighbours. This gentleman was out upon Dartmoor during the storm," said Woodland aside to the waiting and wondering audience.

"Is there no other door?" cried Anger.

"Show him the way. Put him out!" said one or two voices. "That is the priest who assaults young women."

"Curgenven! Curgenven!" went up the shout beneath the dripping water-pipes.

"This way, sir. Follow me," said Woodland, drawing Anger on, and murmuring to right and left, "Don't be hard on him, neighbours. He is a good gentleman, but weak-minded. Go on with the programme. Curgenven will not be with you this evening. He is detained in Youlstone."

"If there is another white passage I cannot walk along it," cried Anger.

"There is no passage this way," replied Woodland.

They came out into a yard choked with refuse. Rain dripped upon them from the roof. Going to a door in the wall, Woodland shook it open and went on, but Anger did not follow the tradesman, who seemed bewildered and never turned his head as he hurried towards his house. Anger went in the opposite direction and coming out upon the uphill road which led towards the station, he ascended with a resolution to escape if flight was possible, and hide himself, and forget what he had been compelled to do and see that night.

"Curgenven is dead, but he haunts me still; I could not hide from his body, and where shall I go to escape his spirit?" he muttered to the black and streaming sky. "If I go upon the moor I shall meet him; I shall be seized and drawn into the mazes of their infernal dance—Curgenven and the old witch, myself and the young witch; I shall be delivered into the hands of evil spirits, the devil himself, the white-haired enchantress—I have not killed her, for she is immortal—the young one who twists her hair around our hearts. They are howling and whirling around Laughter Tor. Ah! here is something in the shape of a human being. What is the meaning of this wandering about on dirt and stones for fifty or seventy years?" he shouted. "Why do you go from one place to another? Wasn't the old life good enough for you? What is the time of night?"

"Nearly nine o'clock," said the wayfarer, answering the only question that reached his intelligence.

"Not midnight yet! It has been dark for a whole lifetime. Where is Curgenven?"

"At home, I suppose."

"Why, that's right. At home, baling out the pool of the Nymph with a limpet-shell. Did you hear the wind? That was Curgenven howling as he rushed over the moor, running in circles, leaping across the pool. By midnight he will reach Riversmeet. Perhaps he is here already making the people laugh. Go along home and tell nobody you have passed a madman. Those who cast their eyes on me will spoil their luck. I am on my way to the sea, to reap my harvest upon the shore, to gather together a truss of yellow-grains and to plait a rope of sand to bind it. When I have finished that task I shall be free."

He rushed on, crying in the wild fashion which had entered his being since leaving the hall of entertainment, "This is the progress of a fallen soul: in summer it sighs and sobs, in autumn it wails, and in winter it screams."

He came presently among houses and dimly remembered how in one of these he had lodged for a time. Up that road, now a shallow river, the fussy old fellow in silk hat and blue spectacles had every morning worried him with questions. Most of the houses were dark, but one was lighted brilliantly, although no lamp was visible in the room where a father and mother were playing with their children. As the barren and storm-driven priest stayed in the rain to watch, two merry youngsters dragged their creator to his knees, mounted his back, and used him like a beast of burden; while the mother looped ribbons round his neck to complete the subjugation; an aged lady, seated beside the fire in the calm and happy state of one whose work was finished, laughed at the sport; a pretty girl with fair hair flowing played music for these private revels; and the sound which reached Anger's ears was no longer that wild and terrible screaming of the wind, but the inno-cent laughter of children. It was the first glad sound since the fatal exodus—the laughter of children. It was the sound which baffled dark philosophy, confounded gloomy science, and restored religion—the laughter of children. By perfect simplicity a man could win his way to peace; by not struggling with matters which were too great for his mind; by thinking merely of those simple things which even a child could understand; by rejecting the complex and choosing the absolute; by giving and asking for simple love; by doing his best in some simple occupation, and making it simple if it seemed abstruse; by simply rearing children and playing with them, forgetting the complex nature of man and all the undiscovered qualities connecting his spirit with the elements; by going down upon hands and knees, even when grey-headed, allowing bit and bridle to be placed upon him and the children to ride upon his back. The issue would be laughter.

"This is the great lesson, and now I learn it—when too late," was Anger's bitter cry.

Somehow he found his way to the house where he had lodged, and there asked to be taken in for one more night. Going to the bedroom, he tore off his clothes, and his exhausted body sank to sleep. Yet partial consciousness remained, so that he could still hear the revelry upon Laughter Tor and the last echoes of that destroying wind—not then the music of the children—but presently another presence seemed to come near his bed, and the simple voice, which had spoken to him once before, asked the same quiet question:

"What is your name?"

"Father Jack," replied the struggler, remembering the lesson of simplicity, giving a truthful answer then.

"What is your profession?"

"I am a priest."

"You may awake," cried the voice, with the sound of children's laughter.

CHAPTER XXII

FROM MIST TO MIST

PAINFULLY awake Anger stepped out of bed, staggered, then fell back, his head throbbing; so that for a few minutes he lay without moving. The room was not entirely dark as the curtains had been left half-drawn, admitting sufficient light from a street-lamp.

"Last night I killed a woman," he whispered. "I was then half mad; now I am perfectly calm and sane—and a criminal. My victim's name was Judith Vigar. She lived in a house called Stiniel which stands near the village of Youlstone. I struck her three times with a hammer. To-morrow I shall be hunted for my life."

He shuddered fearfully, pressing both hands to his head, and by sheer strength of will, a virtue wanting in him until then, fought down a fit of nausea. Tortured by a storm of memories, he struggled upright, and when he had grown accustomed to that position crossed the room and poured out a glass of water, murmuring a prayer before he drank, and whispering, "Thank God! this is not the water of the Nymph."

No sound came from the house, nor from the empty street, but he could hear the shunting of trucks upon the railway. These noises reached his ears so distinctly that he was startled; the shout of a distant workman had in it more real vitality than the great laughter of Curgenven, while the breeze flapping the window-blind seemed pleasanter than the softest word of Petronel; but black and grim upon his brain lay the shadow of his crime.

"It is clear that I must escape from Riversmeet," he went on murmuring. "At the present I am thinking of my dear friends, my rector, my people. They must not know how Father Jack has fallen. When I am far away, I may think of duty towards my conscience. Less than two hours ago, it seems, I tried to escape but could not;

yet nobody prevented me. Now I have nothing to fight against except this weakness of my body."

With cautious movements he dressed, then taking his boots under his arm, opened the door, conscious of perspiration breaking upon his forehead. He saw another door half open and the light of a night-lamp stealing across the passage.

"God be merciful," he prayed. "Let me only get away from this town of Curgenven and of Wadge. Give me a little time to repent before I deliver myself up to receive the just punishment for my deeds."

Then he passed on more boldly, descended the stairs, unlocked the door, and fled out into the night.

Drawing on his boots, he went to the station, which was only a hundred yards away, and meeting a porter asked him when a train would be due. The man scratched his head and looked dumbfounded, then muttered, "I suppose it's all right, sir? Have you any luggage?"

"No, I took my things to Plymouth last Sunday night," replied Anger.

"Well, sir, the mail's just coming in," said the porter, looking still more perplexed. "In fact, here she comes."

Glancing at a clock, Anger noticed it was nearly midnight. Without staying to buy a ticket, he went as quickly as his feeble feet would carry him across the bridge and took a seat in the train which was timed to stop two minutes. Looking from the window, he saw the porter speaking with the station-master, pointing first at the train, and then towards the street which his questioner had lately quitted.

"They know," he said sadly, wiping his forehead. "That man— Nicholas Vigar is, I think, his name—must have rushed into the village after I left, and already a rumour has reached Riversmeet. I wonder they let me go, but it may not be their business to detain me."

The train moved on. Being alone in the compartment, Anger put a hand into his pocket to find his breviary, but it was not there. His fingers drew out a few dead oak-leaves.

"Memories," he murmured as he dropped them. "I must have placed them in my pocket as I placed Petronel in my heart; and now she is as they are."

Again he pressed his hands to his head and tried to bring back the past, not in the form which his memory represented, but as the actual drama of his life. It would not come. Curgenven and Petronel remained as he had seen them, as he had resisted the one and loved the other. That life in Youlstone was still too near him; he could not yet escape its influence.

"What I cannot make clear now, what I have forgotten, others will explain to me," he said. "Oh, Father Jack, the priest of poor strugglers, the friend of the Wiggatons and dear old Billacott, this is the end of your flight from home—a flight from justice. Where am I going?" he cried in sudden terror. "A message will be sent to the police of Plymouth. They will arrest me when I leave the train. Well, let it be so," he went on more calmly. "God's will be done. His law against murder must be enforced against a fallen priest. This is the hand! How often it has made the sign of the cross and given benediction; and last night it struck and killed a woman."

Nervous terror, heightened by the weak state of his head, became so great that when the train happened to be brought to a stop by signals outside Devonport, Anger let himself down upon the line, and, descending the embankment at a spot where a rough path was shown him by a street-lamp, escaped unseen. Not until the train moved on did the thought occur that he had travelled without paying his fare. He seemed condemned to act dishonestly in all his actions.

"I will make it right to-morrow," he said; but when he had climbed upon a car, and began to search in his pockets for money, he found only one shilling and two coppers.

Reaching Plymouth he stumbled so badly in attempting to alight that the conductor hurried forward to assist him. Anger thanked him gently, and added, "Can you tell me the way to Mr. Lyson's house? He is a well-known clergyman here?"

"I don't know the name, sir," came the answer. "Ask that policeman standing over there. He goes to church regular."

But the policeman, who was a singularly fine specimen of an intelligent man, shook his head at Anger's question. "You have made a mistake, sir. There is no Church of England clergyman named Lyson in the Three Towns," he said.

"I cannot be mistaken," replied Anger. "The Reverend Edward Lyson. He was a schoolfellow of mine. I was with him a few hours ago on Monday morning."

"This is Thursday night, sir," said the policeman, with a quick glance at his questioner's suffering face.

"Great heavens!" murmured Anger. "Have I slept two days and nights! Surely you know Father Lyson," he went on pitifully. "I cannot remember the name of his church, but I know it stands in the slums, and the Clergy House is about fifty yards away."

"Why, sir, I know every Church of England clergyman here, not only by name but personally. Perhaps you mean St. John's. That has a Clergy House quite near; but the vicar's name is Mr. Dinnicombe."

"Then I am lost!" said Anger.

"Are you here alone, sir?" asked the policeman, summing up the situation in his ready fashion, and arriving at the conclusion that this reverend gentleman, with unshaven chin and clothes tumbled on anyhow, required somebody to look after him.

"Alone! Yes, entirely," said Anger. "I have just reached Plymouth, and I defrauded the railway company by not paying my fare. I have practically no money. Can you tell me where I can get a bed for one shilling?"

"No place fit for you, sir."

Anger came nearer and held out his hand. "Take me," he said dreamily. "I will not resist. I may as well give myself up now as lie about some street till morning. Take me to the police-station. I have murdered a woman—in a Dartmoor village—a few hours ago. You say it was two days ago, but I must know best. They are looking for me now, and I must not put them to a lot of trouble. I am John Anger, the murderer of Mrs. Vigar. Perhaps you have heard about it. I am a thorough villain, but I do not know what made me so."

The policeman did not take the extended hand. He gave another glance at Anger's face, then said with an air of authority, "Wait here one moment, sir," and went at a quick stride across the road. A minute later he returned with a colleague, and said to Anger, "Now, sir, if you will come with me."

"I am ready," said Anger meekly.

They left the centre and passed along several streets, the kindly constable supporting and guiding the feeble young priest, who kept on murmuring in a heart-broken fashion until his protector could stand no more.

"Don't take on so badly, sir," he begged. "You haven't done anything. You are ill—that's what is the matter. Your head is full of queer ideas."

"I tell you I have murdered Mrs. Vigar of Stiniel. I struck her three times with a hammer during that awful storm. Everybody will know of it to-morrow. I hope you will be promoted for capturing me," he said kindly.

"Here we are," said the policeman, stopping at a door in a neat residential district.

"This is not the station!"

"No, sir, it is my home, and I'm going to give you in charge of my wife. She will look after you until we hear from your friends. Don't say a word, sir. You are in custody, remember."

Anger could not protest for long, as he was nearly fainting, but he broke down and shed tears of weakness at all the kindness which was lavished upon him in that humble home. Remembering his gold watch, he drew it out and forced it into the policeman's hand, but the good fellow merely passed it to his wife, and in due course it was ticking beneath Anger's pillow whereon his head presently reposed in the happiness of entire unconsciousness.

Waking when the morning was well advanced, still very weak but greatly refreshed, he insisted upon rising, and his first question was, "What is the news from Youlstone?"

"None, sir," said the smiling woman.

"Of course not," said Anger. "Nicholas Vigar is hushing it up. Where is your husband? Tell him I am ready to go to the police station."

"Won't you wait here, sir, and rest? My husband will tell them where you are. He is in bed now. He couldn't send a message off last night."

"I cannot stay here. I must get this awful business off my mind," said Anger restlessly. "I will go to the railway station, and I must find Lyson, and then I will say farewell to the world and go out of sight into a felon's cell."

"I will wake my husband," threatened the good woman. "He said I was not to let you go until he hears from your friends."

"I have no friends now. You must not disturb him. He has done too much for me already. I will go out."

"Shall I get somebody to go with you, sir?"

"Certainly not. I am strong enough to do my duty, but if I stay here and wait, I think I may go mad. Never shall I forget your kindness," said Anger warmly. "You have shown me perfect charity."

He went out, after making a note of the name and address of his kind protectors, and, inquiring the way to one of the railway stations with the ignorance of one who was visiting the western metropolis for the first time, entered the booking-office and said to the clerk, "Last night I defrauded the company by travelling from Riversmeet without a ticket. The train stopped outside Devonport and I got out because I am a criminal and I was then flying from justice. Now the police know where to find me. Will you tell me the amount of my debt and let me settle it?"

The clerk looked at the stranger in wonder; and being also an intelligent man he came to the same conclusion as the constable.

"What train did you come by, sir?" he asked.

"The midnight mail. The guard will tell you I got in at Riversmeet, but I am quite certain he did not see me get out."

"Well, sir, I must take your word for it, I suppose. The fare is two and threepence."

"Now that I come to think of it, the compartment I entered was second-class," said Anger.

"Three shillings," said the clerk.

But when Anger thrust a hand into his pocket, only the solitary shilling was forthcoming.

"I am sorry to be such a nuisance," he said with a sad smile. "The fact is I am not very well, and my memory has been playing strange tricks lately. I have only this shilling. Take it please, and I will bring you the rest in a very few minutes."

The clerk could only smile back. Taking the shilling, and watching the feeble figure move away, he remarked to an assistant, "That parson's not all there."

Anger had not far to go to find a pawnshop, next door to its ally the public-house. Although weak and nervous, he went in without the slightest hesitation because this was by no means a new experience, and that gold watch of his had often been put into pledge upon those occasions when he had been visiting in the slums and discovered himself without cash to relieve some urgent case. Well furnished with money, he returned to the station, and having eased his conscience in that direction, made towards the centre of the town with a very different object in view. Before surrendering his body, he had his spiritual needs to consider, and no priest, whatever church he might belong to, could minister to his necessities like dear old Lyson. Anger felt there would be no peace for him, until he had gone with the old schoolfellow into the cool shelter of his church, and had confessed, and had received absolution so far as that was lawful. The kind policeman had misunderstood his question, or perhaps he himself had put it wrongly. Some official at the post-office would give a better answer.

Yet it did appear at first as if Lyson was a singularly obscure individual, for the man whom Anger addressed at the post-office, although also highly intelligent, began with a shake of the head which promised badly.

"There are several Lysons," he said. "But I don't know the one you are looking for."

"Did you say a minister?" asked another intelligent man, who happened to pass that moment.

"Yes," said Anger eagerly.

"Wait a moment, and I'll give you his address. He hasn't been here more than a month or two."

That explains the policeman's ignorance, thought Anger, as he went back to the street, but not my forgetfulness. How was it I walked without any difficulty to Lyson's church on Monday and now I do not know which way to turn? It is no fancy that I knelt with him, confessed to him, and even wore his clothes. Yet they say this is Friday, when it should be Wednesday. Ah! surely I recognise this shop."

Acting upon the impulse, he walked in, passed into the tailoring department, and said to an assistant who came forward, "Allow me to ask you a somewhat peculiar question. Do you, or any of the others, recognise me?"

The answer from the intelligent faces all round was in the negative; and Anger went on, "I came here last Monday morning, wearing layman's clothes, and asked to be fitted with a ready-made suit of clericals. You would not have forgotten such an incident."

"Certainly not, sir," came the answer. "But I am afraid you have mistaken the shop. We do not supply ready-made clerical garments."

"And we have not received an order to supply any," added another.

"You will think me very stubborn, no doubt, but these are the clothes I bought from you," insisted Anger.

"Will you let me look at the coat? Allow me, sir," said a cutter, who was obviously the most intelligent of them all, approaching the peculiar visitor and turning back his collar. "This coat, sir," he went on decisively, "was made in the City of London by a well-known firm which does not turn out clothes except to order. Here is their name upon the tab."

Anger apologised for troubling them, so sincerely and sadly that the shopman perceived all was not well with him. Then he thanked them because they did not make fun of his misfortunes, and went his way.

"The policeman refused to arrest me because of my clothes; he took me home and was a Christian to me," he murmured. "Could he have been so kind had he believed my story? Yet it must have happened; it did happen. This arm is tingling still. My spirit is crushed beneath the weight of sin. My mind thrills with the horror of it. The policeman knew I could not escape. No doubt I am being shadowed now."

Following the directions given him at the post-office, his mind became more easy when the car reached an unsavoury district and the conductor told him he had reached his destination. This was slumland indeed, more foul even than his own, for no dark alleys of London could more than equal the darkest courts of Plymouth. Yet Anger smiled, for he felt always happy among the poor. But where was Lyson's Church of the Resurrection, and where the Clergy House? He saw a church, but it was cold, with, hard by, a chapel even colder. This was the district he had reached upon the first and second flights; but the living spirit of the slums was missing.

"Second turning to the right. Mr. Lyson lives at Number Twelve," was the information given Anger by a small shopkeeper.

He reached the street and stood aghast, seeing a narrow cul-de-sac, and upon each side a row of mean houses, all alike, all squalid, their windows choked with dingy curtains or filled with dusty plants. Certainly, number twelve was slightly different; its curtains were fresher, and between them and the window stood a table bearing a large Bible, which in its turn supported a full-rigged ship cunningly enclosed within a bottle. The door burst open while Anger stared, and a little general servant banged a mat against the railings. He beckoned to the child and said, "Mr. Lyson is not a Church of England clergyman?"

"Oh, no, sir. He's a Wesleyan minister," she answered.

"Tell him he ought not to keep that bottle upon his Bible," said Anger somewhat irritably, for his head was throbbing again, and the disappointment was hard to bear.

"I couldn't say such a thing, sir," said the child with dignity. "Mr. Lyson thinks a lot of that. He was a sailor avore he took to the ministry. He made that ship himself, missus told me."

Anger walked away, fully conscious now that some spirit of enchantment had been hanging over him since the arrival in Youlstone. As one delusion after another was shattered, he perceived it was a delusion. Lyson, his old schoolfellow, a man who undoubtedly did exist, became relegated, so far as Plymouth was concerned, to the land of imagination; but the terror and the crime remained. The village of Youlstone, the house of Stiniel, the haunting of Curgenven, the passion for Petronel—he shuddered at it now—the awful scene in the cellar, his own action there—these were not and could not be pictures and creations of a life in mist. He had clutched that hammer; he seemed to see the furrow of its handle ploughed upon his palm. He could see Petronel more clearly than upon those occasions when she had just departed from him; her every feature was burnt upon his memory; he could have taken a pencil and drawn her mouth and chin, as he could also have sworn to the exact attitude of Nicholas upon the steps, and have picked out the passionate face of his victim at a distance from among a thousand others. Although unable to dissolve the mystery which surrounded the disappearance of Lyson, his own visits to Plymouth, with the inability then to find the way about, his wearing of clothes made for him in London, and rejected after his illness because useless, the complete and savage change which had taken place in the village of South Wyld during his absence, he could not doubt that he had, acting under the pressure of a stronger mind, struck down the woman he had learnt to hate because he believed she tortured the woman whom he loved.

When Anger had passed the door, which he fully believed opened for him in one direction only, nobody showed any desire to rush forward and lay hands upon him. To his left was a barrack-like room where several constables waited for instructions; in an office upon the other side an inspector sat scribbling at a lofty desk. Anger approached him and made a few nervous sounds with his throat. The inspector looked up, started at the unkempt appearance of the visitor, then said cheerily, "Well, sir, have you lost a dog?"

"I have come to give myself up for the Youlstone murder," muttered Anger hoarsely.

"So you are the man," exclaimed the inspector, putting down his pen and sitting upright.

"Yes, I am the man," said Anger.

"I mean you are the clergyman who wanted to give himself up last night. The constable reported it when he went off duty. What is this fancy you have got into your head?"

"No fancy," said Anger. "Early on Tuesday evening, during a terrible storm, I murdered Mrs. Vigar in the cellar of Stiniel. Only this bare fact concerns you at present. I need not mention what happened during the tragedy or what led up to it. The same evening, as it was getting dark, Curgenven of Riversmeet was murdered in the wood of Youlstone cleave by a mad boy known as Whippety. With that tragedy I had nothing to do beyond being a witness, but it seems to me now I might have prevented it, only I did not wish to."

"Why, that's a queer story, sir," said the inspector cheerily. "How do you account for the fact that we have nothing but your own confession to rely on?"

"I can explain that. Mr. Vigar must have kept the matter secret. He may even have buried the body in that cellar. His own son lies there already, but he does not know of it," said Anger, shuddering so violently that he had to support his body against the desk.

"I am afraid you have not been quite up to the mark lately, sir. People have been looking after you? A little mental trouble perhaps?" suggested the inspector kindly.

"I was ill to the point of death last year," replied Anger. "But these last six months I have enjoyed perfect health. Certainly I shall not attempt to escape the just punishment for my crime by pleading insanity. I have lived alone and gone about as I wished. It is true I have suffered from delusions; for instance, I imagined an old schoolfellow was vicar of a church here, and I had been in the habit of visiting him. But the deaths of Curgenven and Mrs. Vigar are terrible realities."

"I am expecting a message from Riversmeet any moment. Unfortunately there is some trouble with the wire," said the inspector more briskly. "But, mark you, sir, this is Friday morning, and you tell me Mr. Curgenven was killed on Tuesday evening. We have received no information; neither have the newspapers."

"The body has not been discovered. I am the only man who

can point out where it lies, beneath tons of earth and stones in Youlstone wood."

"How about his disappearance?"

"Ah, yes!" exclaimed Anger hopefully.

"I know Mr. Curgenven well; he is often in Plymouth on business," the inspector went on. "Would you mind describing his personal appearance, sir?"

"Why, he is a dwarf, not five feet high," said Anger, seeing that figure more clearly than his questioner. "He is a humpback with enormous shoulders which I have often compared to mounds of earth, and a head much too large for such an insignificant body."

"That will do, sir," said the other with a laugh. "Don't you think you had better go to some hotel and rest until we hear from your friends? You are not in a fit state to go about by yourself. You might murder somebody else, you know."

"I hope you are not laughing at me," said Anger quietly.

"No, no, sir. But you must get rid of these ideas, and believe what I tell you. Last night I looked up Youlstone in the directory, and I could not find any house called Stiniel, nor is there any mention of Vigars actually in the village, although there are several in the parish."

At that, Anger turned aside impatiently and murmured to himself, "All these people are playing with me."

He declined to leave the police station, declaring it was not right that such a villain as himself should be set at liberty, so the inspector ushered him into a room where he could be alone, and supplied him with newspapers which contained many worldly horrors, but no reference whatever to any local tragedy; but it was not long before the examining officer returned rustling with telegrams, and then Anger started up to hear his fate.

"Well, sir, we know all about you now. Last night it appears you slipped away from your friends, who are in a great state about you."

"My friends!" cried Anger. "They hate me in Riversmeet and Youlstone. They drove me out. My only friends are the Billacotts."

"And they are the people who are looking for you. Just glance at this," said the inspector holding out a telegram.

Anger took it and read, "Take care of him. He has no money and may not be responsible for his actions. Keep him safe until I come, or send him under protection to Riversmeet. Wire me train. Billacott."

"Bobby has profited by my teaching," Anger murmured. "He wants me to come back because Curgenven is dead and Youlstone believes in me at last."

"You see you are wanted," said the inspector, "but not for murder."

"Whose hand struck Mrs. Vigar if it was not mine?" cried Anger.

"That is all fancy, sir, from start to finish. No murder has been committed in Youlstone, and, as I told you, there are not any people called Vigar in the village. Directly I set eyes upon you I guessed what was wrong, but I was bound to make inquiries for your own sake. The only crime you have committed is to run away from your friends."

"Innocent—innocent," whispered Anger, and he repeated the blessed word a dozen times. "Then I am free," he went on. "You cannot detain me."

"Not unless you consent to stay here until your friends come for you."

"Bobby and Thirza," said Anger, laughing outright. "Excellent people though they are, I will not wait for them. I need no protection, inspector. I am strong already, my head is better, the pain is leaving me. See! I can stand up now without trembling. I did not kill Mrs. Vigar, neither did I love Petronel," he murmured. "Yet I have killed some living creature, and I love a woman. I have been a priest, and a priest I remain; but now I am a man as well."

Declining to remain in the police-station now that his character was cleared, and equally firm with a refusal of any guardianship, Anger hurried out to mix with his fellow-creatures and to feel the sun of liberty. "Now that I can hold up my head, I will go back to Youlstone," he said, as he tramped the street with such strange motions that people turned to look at him. On this occasion he was being shadowed, as the inspector had felt it his duty to instruct a man to keep his eye upon the bewildered priest, but Anger knew nothing of that.

"I shall find out what has happened to me," he ran on. "Bobby should be able to tell me the truth, and if he cannot I will go to the man whom I thought was Nicholas Vigar, and get him to explain the mystery."

A voice called to him in that town where he was a stranger, and Anger starting round, still clinging stubbornly to the name of Lyson, perceived a smiling middle-aged gentleman hastening across the road. A very hearty-looking man, somewhat below the average height, strong and broad at the shoulders, clean-shaven, of a ruddy countenance, with a pair of bright blue eyes, and an exceedingly large mouth which looked made for laughter. His clothes were a shade too large for him; so was the hat which had slipped well down over his forehead. A quantity of blue papers protruded from the side pocket of his overcoat. Anger stood perplexed as this entire stranger advanced towards him with the smiling features of a friend.

"My word! this is a surprise," cried the merry gentleman, holding out both hands to Anger and almost shaking the senses out of his frail body. "Father Jack running about Plymouth with nobody to look after him, all on his own! It is great, it is splendid, it is magnificent, and I hope it is wise. You have had a rotten time, a regular stinking bad time, and I am jolly glad to think it is all over, and you will soon be one of us, tramping old Dartmoor, hunting the otter, and going to find the sleeping water, eh? There will be no holding dear old Bobby Billacott when he is certain you are yourself again."

"I have just received a message from him. Now I am going back," was all that Anger could say.

"I saw him this morning," continued the merry gentleman. "He was swearing at the fool of a porter who let you run away, and in a terrible stew about you, declaring you didn't know what you were doing, and you were certain to wander on Dartmoor again and get lost in a mist; but I told him you would be all right, and I promised to look out for you, though I never expected to see you at this hour of the day. I thought the police might have nabbed you last night. Funny idea, eh? The celebrated Father Jack being run in by the police because he was found wandering in the streets without any visible means of supporting his existence. Seriously though, I am right glad to find you—just as you should be, you know. We must have a little dinner to celebrate the waking up—just you, and good old Bobby, and yours truly."

And the merry gentleman laughed tremendously.

"You must pardon me," said Anger faintly, "but I do not know you."

"Of course you don't. What am I thinking about? We have met plenty of times, and I can't say we have always been the best of friends. One afternoon, when we were out on the moor, you just pitched into me. My word! you did! That little girl, Petronel, Father Jack? Eh, Father Jack, you rascal? Ah, well, it's all over now, thank heaven."

"Still, you do not tell me your name," cried the harassed Anger.

"I am the good old sportsman of Riversmeet—Curgenven."

CHAPTER XXIII

CLOUDS PASSING

CONFUSION returned when Anger escaped from the rattling tongue of the man who had haunted his life, who was certainly alive, and by no means a humpbacked dwarf, but a jolly countryman full of worldly slang, loving a day's sport, and no stranger to good living. His breezy talk brought back the fog. What was the little dirty farmer, Bobby Billacott, that he should wait at the station to meet Anger and be invited to make a third at the lawyer's table? And as he did exist, what had happened to the Vigars? Why should Quoditch survive when Stiniel had been wiped out?

Settled upon the journey which was to finish his wanderings—having paid his fare and behaving on this occasion like a normal being—Anger turned the light of his mind full along those highways of the past, and presently discovered some of the darkness giving way. Undoubtedly he had become much stronger since leaving the police-station; his body remained feeble, there were sharp pains in his head, but the weight was off his soul. The meeting with Curgenven had stimulated thought, so that he was able to perceive that his existence since leaving Wyld to search for the pool of the Nymph had been passed under the shadow of some mental and moral affliction. The cause and the precise moment of its commencement he had yet to learn. The feeling of consternation which came to him was owing to an inspiration of his newly awakened mind, assuring him that during a long period of partial consciousness his personality had been not only sane in many respects but actually more complex than it had ever been in time of health. He had been, in fact, not one man, but three separate and distinct beings: the God-fearing and charitable priest, the passionate and unmoral countryman, and the wandering spirit. It was then, when these three persons were joined together and made one by the restoration of a normal condition, that Anger was able dimly to remember the conference between Curgenven, Palk, and Woodland in the lawyer's office, with those other situations at which he had not been present as a bodily entity. One personality had been hovering near the scene, but it had failed to record its impressions upon the others. He had not been shown those things a knowledge of which would have benefited him, such as the deceitfulness of Petronel, and the storekeeper's love of wealth, stronger at last than his devotion to honesty. He had been left to follow the path chosen by a man who had become careless of morality, until crushed by fate, which the Lyson of his fancy had called the false god created by a failure to bear the blame of his own neglect of duty.

The train stopped at every station. When more than half the journey had been covered, Anger's nervousness returned, so that the prospect of getting out at Riversmeet, facing a sympathetic but staring crowd, and hearing the rough welcome of Bobby Billacott, became a positive terror. After all, he knew nothing about the town; it might be a large place, possibly that was market-day, probably the meddlesome police had sent a message intimating the time of his arrival. A number of people might be collecting at the station to have a good look at him. Anger hit upon a scheme for evading such an ordeal, after searching in his pockets and discovering he had sufficient money for his purpose. Then he fell again into musing:

"Who has been maintaining me all these weeks, first at the Youlstone inn, then at Quoditch, finally in Riversmeet lodgings? Somebody must have been looking after me, and yet I have been hiding from my dear good friends in London—why I cannot imagine. Is it possible that I wrote to my banker for a supply of money? Well, a letter will settle that part of the mystery. But these clothes!" he exclaimed, half fiercely. "My mind does not help me there. Assuredly I was in my right mind the day I walked out from Wyld, and certainly I was not wearing clerical garments. Why, I remember I had increased in size enormously, and these things had been thrown aside as useless. Now I am wearing them and they fit me perfectly—the very clothes I was in when I left London. Ah, Dartmoor! Dartmoor!" he murmured, sadly shaking his head at the rivers and cleaves and black rock-masses. "What have you been doing with my body?"

At the last station before Riversmeet Anger left the train, and going to the inn hard by, came to an arrangement with the landlord for a conveyance to Youlstone.

"It's nearer by road than rail," he was told by the driver, "though 'tis rough going up over Dartmoor. Be you the gentleman what's going to take the funeral?"

"What funeral?" asked Anger with a start, adding quickly, "I am a stranger and a visitor."

"Mrs. Runnal's, who died a bit sudden like on Tuesday evening. Well-known folk in Youlstone, sir. If you know the place, they live in the big white house just across the common. They do say, sir, she died a bit queer. She was too fond of the drink vor certain, and she and the old man didn't exactly get along very nice."

"How did she die? I mean who—what killed her?" asked Anger, his voice so troubled and his manner so frightened that the driver stole a glance at him.

"Well, sir, Doctor Palk, he ses she died natural."

"So there is a Doctor Palk," murmured Anger.

"'Twas a fit what took her, he ses. And of course it wasn't for the coroner to go against his evidence."

"Who is the coroner?"

"Mr. Curgenven."

"I shall never get rid of him," was Anger's inward comment.

"But there's a tale going about Youlstone of a glass what was found in her room with stuff in it a bit stronger than whisky—rat poison, sir. Doctor Palk and Mr. Curgenven are both kind gentlemen, and they had an understanding, I reckon. They didn't want to be hard on old Bill Runnal, vor, what with one thing and t'other, he's had a lot of trouble; so they ses 'Death from natural causes,' and has done with it."

"You are sure Runnal is the name—not Vigar?" asked Anger, wandering again in mist-land.

Again the driver looked at his passenger, this time uneasily, for the question seemed to him a queer one.

"Runnal—that's the name. I'm a Vigar, sir," he answered. "There's a lot of that name hereabouts. About a hundred years ago a young chap called Vigar got married, and he had a big family of sons; and when they married they all had a lot of sons."

"What is the name of the house?"

"That one down under, sir?"

"The house where the Runnals live."

"I fancy it be called Landend, but I ain't quite certain."

"What does the family consist of?"

"I b'ain't quite sure of that neither. I fancy there's a son who went off to be a sailor, and there may be a maiden or two. I haven't been up to Youlstone vor a gude many years."

After that Anger became silent, as all answers to his questions merely involved him in storm clouds. Obviously he had been the spectator of some human drama played upon the stage of Youlstone, but he could not have been a leading actor. No effort of his mind was able to guide him through the labyrinth of names. Apparently Curgenven, Palk, the Billacotts, and Quoditch remained "true to name" like plants grown from honest seed; while the Vigars and Stiniel had disappeared. Lyson, who no doubt existed somewhere as a hard-working parish priest, had been nothing more than an apparition, while Petronel became a moor-myth; and yet Curgenven in his new form had certainly alluded to her.

Weakness closed his eyes, and despite the jolting of the cart he slept a little until the driver pulled respectfully at his arm and asked for instructions, as Youlstone was in sight. Then Anger shook off his drowsiness and looked up. They were leaving a narrow lane, and he saw in front a few acres of flat moorland; beyond, a compact village, and in the background a chain of ragged tors. It was the place he had known, yet not the same. The mountains were not fierce enough; the village looked too peaceful.

"I will get out here," he said nervously, wondering who would be the first to recognise him, and what his reception would be.

While settling with the driver he heard a bell tolling for the funeral, and when left alone upon the road he distinguished among the sycamores the tower which he had looked upon so often during his stay at the inn. "Now let me cross the barrier which has existed between imagination and reality," he murmured, and walked on boldly towards the cottages.

A man approached with a dog, looking for his cows as it was near milking time; seeing Anger, he stopped and loitered, pretending to be searching for his beasts, while keeping his best eye for the priest, whom he seemed to recognise, although with some symptoms of astonishment, as if he had not expected ever to see again the enemy of Youlstone. He did not hold his stick in a threatening fashion, nor did he bend to pick up a stone; but he smiled in quite a friendly way, lifted a battered hat, and gently hoped the gentleman was himself again.

"You do know me, then," said Anger happily.

"Yes, sir, surely. I ha' seen you plenty of times, when you was up to the hotel."

"I was not so well then?" Anger suggested, anxious for information concerning his own past.

"No, sir, I reckon."

"What did you suppose was the matter with me?"

"You passed me often," repeated the man evasively. "I never noticed anything wrong with ye, sir."

"You knew I was not quite responsible for my actions?"

"The old gentleman did say you was a bit mazed like, sir."

"What old gentleman? You do not mean Curgenven?"

"Well, sir, I have seen you with him. I mean the old gentleman, your father, sir, and the lady who was with you."

"My poor head!" murmured Anger. "Where am I being led to now?" Then he said to the respectable but not very communicative commoner, "Have you ever seen me with a young and handsome lady? You must not mind my asking you these questions, as I have only just awoke, recovered—I really do not know what to call it— and I am completely in the dark as to what has been going on. A young lady with dark hair and beautiful eyes. Have you seen me with her?"

"Yes, sir, surely; but her warn't here long," came the stupefying answer.

"Do you know her name? Was it Miss Vigar?"

"No, sir," said the man, becoming less reserved and chuckling a little. "Landlord got telling me and a few others, when us wur sitting in the bar-room, how you did call the young lady Miss Vigar, and her didn't like it much."

"What was her name?" cried Anger.

"'Twas some such name as Wiggaton, I fancy."

"Great heavens! Mary here! Mary was Petronel!" gasped Anger. "Never mind what I say," he went on with a smile. "You know I have been off my head completely. Did Curgenven—no, I must not ask such questions. Thank you very much for telling me. But one moment—my head is whirling. What is the bell tolling for?"

"'Tis the funeral of Mrs. Runnal, sir."

"Who lived at Stiniel?"

"To Landend, sir. I be just agoing vor the cows, and then——"

"You wish to attend the funeral, and I am detaining you. Just tell me—which is the way to Quoditch?"

"Why, sir, there b'ain't no such place here, sir."

"No Quoditch! But this is Youlstone."

"That's right, sir."

"Then where do the Billacotts live—Bobby and Thirza?"

The answer was the same. Lazy little Bobby and hard-working Thirza lived in the land of fancy.

Anger went on with staggering movements, unable to get clear of the slumber, or to discover one body of reality, muttering, "Did I see the man who called himself Curgenven? Did he refer to dear old Bobby Billacott? Am I conscious now, or still asleep?"

He went towards the village street so slowly that the commoner had time to collect and number his beasts, and, having left the dog to drive them home, to reach the churchyard and take counsel with others before the lone wandering figure came in sight. Soon a youngster upon a stout moorland pony was racing downhill to Riversmeet charged with a message which concerned that figure.

A crowd in black stood near the wall of the churchyard which seemed to Anger full to overflowing. There was a murmuring at his approach, some hats were raised, some sympathetic glances given, and the people gave way to let him advance. Standing beside the open gate, he could hear the deep voice of the vicar reciting the prayer of committal, he could see that short bearded clergyman who was so utterly unlike the Hanson of his fancy; and he could see also, with a fearful sensation of being compelled to be present at his victim's funeral, Nicholas Vigar, Bertram Vigar, and Petronel, whose names in that hour of reality were William Runnal senior and junior, and simple Emily, who was a red-faced country maiden not blessed with beauty. And these had been the actors in his subhuman tragedy. That old man bending at the grave was not much like the weak and cunning Nicholas; yet the hard-handed farmer played that part in Anger's mind. The tall young man, dressed as a sailor, was, in the way of Nature, many years from death; but to the watcher his body appeared spiritual. The girl alone could not stand surrounded by illusion, for Petronel survived the storm and lived as the real person, with sweetness for passion and goodness for deceit; and Mary was her name. Not last in order of emotion came a feeling of thankfulness that he had been spared a glance at that body; it might have been white-haired.

Before the last words were uttered Anger passed away and found himself soon upon the well-remembered strip of winding road leading across the common. The air was calm, as if the hush in the churchyard had stilled the elements. Not a living creature came in view. Anger went on, and presently the peaceful corner opened before his eyes, and he saw the gorge with its zigzag road, the cottage of the Billacotts, the house of Stiniel. Both were white, and the one above was certainly in shadow, but not beneath that horror of darkness with which his fancy had environed it, although in position and general appearance it was not unlike "the house of Stiniel." Anger saw the Pinches, which had become much less steep, the corner where he had helped to throw Curgenven, and the bridge which had shrunk into a culvert; but he did not see "Quoditch." A triangular field, covered with coarse grass and reeds, occupied the spot where his imagination had placed the tumbling cottage. The home of the mythical Billacotts had been shifted from left to right; it stood upon the narrow road, built back into the slope of the moor, and although much in need of painting and restoring it was by no means in a ruinous condition.

It was a pleasant, actually an idyllic, place, appealing to the happy memories of Piping Pan rather than to the mutterings of the tragic muse. It seemed to Anger then the land of toys. The cottage was very like a doll's house; trees in front were tiny and mop-headed, and swayed from side to side as if rocking upon discs; along the side of the gorge little red and white cows were feeding; the copse below the home of the Runnals consisted of diminutive and moss-like larches; the bustling stream, before plunging beneath the culvert, crossed a stone-paved gully across the granite floor of a ridiculous court beside the Noah's Ark cottage, supplying the inhabitants, whoever they might be, with sparkling water. And in this place of beauty one of Anger's personalities had been tossed about by the moorland spirit, now gentle, now fierce; and here he had been haunted by the all-pervading influence of Curgenven.

"It is true that the shadow of the hill must fall always across Stiniel," said Anger, "but that does not make the house fearful. I am sure it has no secret cellar. While Quoditch is a place of sunshine. Now I perceive that my mind was morbid. It placed the cottage there among the bogs; while it made the Billacotts swamp-dwellers, not hard people of the rocks."

He went on, still in some fear at walking through that haunted region, hearing voices at the back of the cottage, perceiving a rough linhay open to the trackway, and within it a cart bearing the names, "W. Cutland, Farbetter." While struggling again with his memory, a man appeared, tall, clumsy, and decidedly dirty, with a woman who was short and dark. They stared at Anger with eyes of wonder, and both of them looked exceedingly uncomfortable.

"Is your name Cutland?" asked the man who felt himself a stranger there.

The farmer only laughed, but the woman answered, "Yes, sir," and added, "I'm glad to see you so much better."

"What do you call this place?"

"Farbetter, sir."

"I thought it was Quoditch," said Anger, becoming strange in his manner for his strength was giving out. "I called you the Billacotts, and that house, I fancied, was known as Stiniel. You have seen me here before?"

"You stopped wi' us, sir," replied the woman.

"You called me Bobby Billacott," cried the man gleefully. "Told me to put up a new gate and build up the hedges. Proper old dump, you wur."

"Be quiet, Bill," whispered Mrs. Cutland.

"Yes, I was a dump," said Anger. "You called me schoolmaster, and I insisted upon giving you lessons."

Seeing a surly look on Cutland's face, he realised that the man was indeed illiterate, and ashamed of it, but he could not admit his ignorance, nor allow a stranger to dwell upon it. "The first time I met you," Anger hurried on, "I have an idea you told me this was a far better place than Youlstone village."

"Likely I did," said Cutland.

"And its name is actually Farbetter."

"It ha' been called that time out of mind," said Mrs. Cutland. "They ses, sir, when folk to Youlstone got telling theirs was a gude place, the folk here answered 'em and said theirs was 'far better.' Runnal's ha' been called Landend only these last twenty years."

"A vule of a name, I calls it," added Cutland.

"Please to step inside, sir, and take a cup of tea, will ye?" invited the woman; and Anger accepted gladly, for his head was feeling light again.

He went into a dark and smoky kitchen, wholly unlike the living room of Quoditch, while Mrs. Cutland whispered excitedly to her husband, and sent him off at a heavy trot across the common.

"I'm ashamed to ask ye to sit in here, sir, but 'tis a bit cold in the parlour," she said apologetically. "You mind the house well enough, I fancy?"

"Did I ever lodge here?" asked the unbelieving Anger.

"Yes, sir; you and the lady."

"What lady? Not Miss Wiggaton!"

"No, sir; the other lady. You came in here, sir, from the inn, as that wasn't to your liking. All the bedrooms look over the churchyard, and Doctor Palk said that wasn't gude vor ye."

"Another lady! These endless names! What was hers?"

"Miss Davidson, sir."

"Why, she was my nurse at Wyld.—Make the tea strong, Mrs. Cutland.—How long did I stay here?"

"Nearly two weeks, sir. Then as you didn't seem to be getting on fast enough Doctor Palk said they had best take you to Riversmeet. He fancied Youlstone might be a bit too high up vor ye."

"Was there a great snowfall?"

"Yes, sir. Us had plenty of snow."

"Did I ever get out of my bedroom window?"

"You tried to, sir, but Bill wur handy, and he wouldn't let ye."

"Did I ever go to Exeter?"

"Yes, sir. They took ye there to see a doctor."

Anger drank his tea, but it did not refresh his mind. Stupor was creeping over him again, and terrified by the thought of returning to the fatal sleep before learning the cause of it, he said quickly and as earnestly as he could, "Mrs. Cutland, I beg you to tell me how I came to Youlstone, and what has been the matter with me all these weeks. I know nothing. I left Riversmeet the night before last—in fear. I have not been back there. I have been as it were out of the world, and I have been shown visions of the elements as men and women."

"Well, sir, you wur a bit mazed like when you come to," said Mrs. Cutland with great hesitation, selecting words from her limited vocabulary carefully, and afraid of saying too much. "Perhaps the gentleman had better tell you, sir. If he don't come vor ye, Bill will drive ye into Riversmeet."

"Go on," he cried. "I may not be able to hear you soon. You may turn into Thirza Billacott before my eyes."

"They thought you was dead, sir, when they brought you in," she stammered.

"Who brought me in? I walked to Youlstone in a mist."

"Mr. Curgenven found ye, sir. 'Twas next day. Bill said it wur the bravest mist us had seen vor years. When you came to, sir, you wur that strange in the head you didn't seem to see things same as other folk."

"This cannot be true," said Anger faintly. "I remember being lost and wandering upon the moor until dark. Then I came to the hut—I saw Whippety—I met Petronel. Tell me, is there an imbecile boy here?"

"Yes, sir, young David Gagg. He wur born mazed, but he's a quiet lad and don't do no harm to any one, so they lets 'en bide wi' his folks. You can see the boy any time you'm passing through the village."

Anger scarcely heard what she was saying. He had asked too much from his body since awakening, and the strain upon his mind had not been relaxed till then. He was conscious that Mrs. Cutland was placing a cushion behind his head; he knew it was dark outside; he could hear the murmur of water beneath the culvert. A lamp was lighted, making the kitchen peaceful and homelike in spite of the poor furniture and cold, whitewashed walls. He murmured, "Kind people! Good people!" and placed his hand upon Mrs. Cutland's hard fingers to testify his gratitude. Once he whispered with a sense of new knowledge, "Mary," and repeated the name many times as if afraid he might forget it. When wheels sounded upon the winding road above, and the moor gate banged, and Mrs. Cutland hurried to the door, he tried to turn towards those sounds and to exclaim, "I am innocent; I did not kill Mrs. Vigar. I killed something in myself. Tell Mary that."

The kitchen seemed to be full of light, with confused figures and buzzing voices. There was the dark toil-marked face of William Cutland, and here the grave, bearded Dr. Palk, not bothering his head about "Youlstone Limited," but full of anxiety for his patient; and this quaint figure, stumbling forward with arms extended, always odd, always full of kindness and devotion, wearing those well-remembered shabby clothes, the ruffled silk hat so out of place there, and blue spectacles slipping down its nose exposing weak and watery eyes, this figure beyond all question, and outside all mist, was the head of "Winnacott, Billacott, and Wiggaton," crying to the priest who was both father and son:

"Ah, Father Jack, dear Father Jack! Thank God I have found you. Thank God you are yourself again."

CHAPTER XXIV

ALL CLEAR

SOME anxious days followed, during which the wanderer hovered between darkness and light, his mind still a prey to images of storm and mist. He returned at last to the world of sympathetic and simple faces to find himself in the same lodgings near the station of Riversmeet, attended by the nurse from South Wyld and the faithful bachelor who had a woman's heart. Awaking from a healthy sleep, untroubled by roaming fancies, he found himself united in his own house, one man again, and still a priest; lifting up his eyes no longer to the hills with their stone altars but to the sheltered tabernacle of his religion.

"My fault, and mine alone," declared old Billacott. "From first to last I have been your evil spirit. Friend Wiggaton shall bear part of the responsibility of sending you to Wyld, but no more. It was I who ordered you out of London, and sent you to the parish of my ancestors."

"What nonsense!" said Anger. "Dear Mr. Billacott, you have saved my life and reason; you have been the guardian angel of my wanderings. Why, you tried to prevent me leaving London. It was only when Mr. Wiggaton took me to the doctor, and then insisted upon my going away at once, that you gave way."

"I do not talk nonsense," said Billacott, as he walked up and down the room, rubbing his hands and ducking his body in sheer delight. "I have always been more rascal than fool, as befits a successful merchant of the City of London. Usually I speak the truth, and on this occasion I am speaking it with emphasis. I have acted like an unmitigated scoundrel. You are not to become excited, and if you interrupt me with anything more than monosyllables of acquiescence I will summon from the misty moor Vigars, Lysons, and a whole company of Dartmoor spirits, and instruct them to leap upon you. That beastly household book of mine has been the cause of your mental trouble, and here is the rogue who read you extracts from it."

"Wrong again; I will prove it presently."

"Your proof!" cried the merchant, snapping his fingers. "I sent you to Wyld with your head stuffed full of Vigars and Billacotts, and water of the Nymph. Upon recovering health and strength, the first thing you did was to follow my instructions and search for this pool."

"I found it," said Anger, "but I lost myself."

"You were caught by the mist of the century, and you wandered through it until your strength gave out. The next day you were discovered, unconscious, apparently dead, by that jolly little rogue Curgenven."

"And he haunted me ever afterwards as the enemy of mankind."

"Your best friend. I represent the enemy of mankind," declared Billacott; and added more seriously, "Do you remember creeping into a hole upon the side of the hill not half a mile from Youlstone?"

"I have no recollection at all," said Anger. "It seems to me now I was on the point of giving up several times, but when I came down the cleave and found the wood I became stronger. And that was the first part of a life I never lived! Is there a wood? Is there a ruined hut beside the river?"

"You shall see them soon," promised Billacott. "Not for the first time, of course, as you and I have been there often, although you were not then our Father Jack. It was owing to Curgenven's prompt action that you defeated my villainy and are alive now. They carried you to the Youlstone Inn, Palk was sent for, but you remained in a state of coma for some days. Then you woke up, but not as yourself," added Billacott, his voice shaking a little.

"What was I?" Anger murmured.

"My dear Father Jack," said the merchant, seating himself upon the bed and holding the patient's hands, "you must allow me to make the hackneyed statement that we human beings are complex creatures. As a general thing we are commonplace, and then we appear to live in a commonplace world. Sometimes we become abnormal, and then our surroundings take upon themselves the same complexion. Send an ordinary humdrum individual like myself out for a stroll with a man who is a great genius; I notice only what is commonplace, my companion sees what is exceptional. The man of genius is abnormal to me, and most likely I am the same to him."

"I am a very ordinary individual," said Anger.

"But that is exactly what you are not. You happen to be a man of extraordinary psychological development, and such men, I am told, are always morbid, or are at least compelled to pass through periods of acute morbidity. You are also an extremely nervous man. When you recovered from the state of coma, your mind was to a certain extent diseased, so that you could not recognise your friends, while you regarded all strangers as abnormal beings. In the first place your entire system was altered by the course of treatment you underwent at Wyld; then you suffered the shock of exposure upon the moor. Your brain was charged with memories of my household book, and as a result the Cutlands of Farbetter and the Runnals of Landend became to you the Billacotts of Quoditch and the Vigars of Stiniel. Later on, when you came to yourself at the inn, your brain was further troubled by glancing through the *Tragedy of the Cenci*, Miss Davidson having unfortunately left the book beside your bed. The rum part about it is that the names of Quoditch and Stiniel actually occur in my household book, but I feel quite certain I never read them out to you."

"Say at once that I have been a maniac," cried Anger.

"You did not behave like one. Your mind was not as it is now, of course, but the alienist whom I sent for agreed with Palk that you did not exhibit any of the usual signs of insanity. On the contrary, you were perfectly calm except when you supposed some great elemental change was about to happen, while your conversation was often extraordinarily brilliant. You were, in short, a man of genius, Father Jack, although you did see things wrongly. You were constantly declaring that a wonderful change had taken place, and you were no longer a priest, but——"

"A savage!"

"Well, a primitive type of man. It was a tragedy of clothes. The only real trouble we had with you was the desire to change your coat. Sometimes you would ask for clericals only to declare when we brought them that you could not put them on because Petronel might not like to see you in them, or Curgenven might be stimulated to renew his attacks."

"It was a tragedy," Anger murmured. "And the first act was played in Wyld, for when I was conscious I chose to wear layman's clothes. And yet, when I came to myself in this room, and escaped, believing I had murdered Mrs. Vigar, I was wearing the clothes I had discarded at Wyld, and they fitted me. They were the clothes I had worn when leaving London, the clothes of my ministration, the clothes of my old body, which I had been forced to lay aside because after treatment they were of no use to me. Explain that."

"The old body has been restored to you," answered Billacott gently.

"Give me a glass," cried Anger.

Billacott brought a mirror, and looking into it Anger saw no longer the bronzed and lusty face, the lips full of blood, the manly chest and heaving shoulders. The face before him was again thin and much lined, with tight-lipped mouth, and below were the shrunken chest and bony shoulders. The lusty countryman had disappeared with those sixty pounds of flesh. John Anger, priest of the slums, was back again. But the bright eyes remained; they had not been removed by this last change, although careless no longer, for they had become the windows of a soul which was open and had learnt to know itself.

"Do not be afraid, Father Jack," said Billacott tenderly. "The old trouble is gone, and you are healed. You were forced to borrow those sixty pounds of flesh from old Dartmoor, and now you have repaid them. They have done their work, and they can go."

"The same man, but one who has learnt his lesson," Anger murmured. "The same old body, but with light and understanding added to it. I thank God for the restoration, not the god of the mountain, Mr. Billacott—I did turn aside to worship him—but the only Creator Who has given me back the body and the clothes I worked in."

"That is the voice! You have come back; you are my little priest again," cried Billacott.

"How did you come to hear of my condition?"

"The day after Curgenven found you we knew all about it. When you walked away from Wyld, to find the water, you did not go alone; a link of the chain which connected you with the old life was hidden in your pocket. Don't give any credit to me, Father Jack. I still avow myself your bitterest enemy; I let you go, I drove you out into the wilderness; but somebody else held on to you and called you back. Do you wonder who that person was? I must tell you, I suppose; one must speak the truth sometimes. It was to Miss Mary Wiggaton that Curgenven's letter was addressed."

"Mary, my friend, my comrade, now my saviour," Anger whispered. Then he cried, "What was the link I carried with me?"

"A letter," said Billacott.

"Ah, now I do remember. It came that morning, together with

an appeal from members of the congregation. They wanted me to return. I should have sat down at once to answer Mary's letter, but instead of that I went out to drink the sleeping water. How is she, Mr. Billacott? How was Mary looking when last you saw her?"

"She was well enough. Just the same outspoken child, the same dear nuisance," said the merchant, trying to speak sharply.

"Is she happy? I thought she was too pale when I parted from her. She has not been doing too much for my poor people?"

"How could the girl dare to be anything but happy, with a good home and the best parents in the world? A little London pallor is a sign of good health, if anything," said Billacott uncomfortably.

"And she has actually been nursing me!"

"She did come for a few days to relieve Miss Davidson, who had taken a chill. She insisted on it—you know her way."

"I do remember Mary," said Anger simply.

"You must rest," ordered the merchant, returning to his fussy manner. "Excitement and energy are forbidden for the present. Plenty of healthy sleep is what you most require. Obey orders, Father Jack, or I'll send for Curgenven."

"I saw him in Plymouth," cried Anger. "He accosted me, but, of course, I did not recognise him, and he puzzled my mind still more by referring to you as Bobby Billacott."

"By that title of disrespectful levity you often called me; and the merry little lawyer had the audacity to imitate you," replied the merchant.

"Did I really walk about with him and with you? Was I ever alone with Mary without recognising her? I saw you often, Mr. Billacott, and you appeared to me as a perfect stranger. You were always wearing blue spectacles."

"We had a big snowfall followed by sunshine, and my eyes became so weak that Palk recommended me to wear blue glasses," explained Billacott. "It is quite true that you walked about like any ordinary person, and nobody would have taken you for an invalid, as you could walk any of us off our legs. It is a pity we didn't bring you down from Youlstone before, because Riversmeet suited you far better. Directly we removed you from the heights to the valley you recovered rapidly. What none of us could understand was your extraordinary fear and hatred of Curgenven."

"You know a great part of my story, which I still believe was not all fancy. Some time I will tell you the rest," said Anger. "Then you will understand. One question you have not answered—that which concerns Mary and myself."

"You mean to bother me," said Billacott, going to the window. Standing there, he went on without turning, "Before I answer, will you tell me who was Petronel? She was something more to you than the lady-help of my long-gone ancestor Hugh Billacott."

There was a pause before Anger answered, "She must have appeared to me as a spirit while I was lying in unconsciousness upon the moor. It was then I supposed myself accepting her hospitality in the hut beside the river. She was very beautiful, but fierce as beautiful. I felt she was no stranger, I had seen her in a different form, and had fallen in love with her. Do not be horrified, Mr. Billacott. I believe I had fallen in love with the spirit of Dartmoor, which had breathed into my body the breath of new life; and when I met Petronel I recognised her as the woman I loved, not as the spirit of Dartmoor personified; very beautiful, tender, and woman-like upon some days, and equally unattractive, pitiless, and fiend-like upon others. I was compelled to follow her, to do her bidding, even when she placed a hammer in my hand and told me to kill a fellow-creature."

"Thank you," said Billacott, still without turning. "I think it may be my duty to answer your question fully. I am very sorry Molly ever came here, but since she did come, and you certainly did not recognise her as Mary Wiggaton, a complete answer may save her from embarrassment when next you meet. I will ask you to banish this mythical Petronel from your mind altogether, and look here, Father Jack," he stammered with great earnestness, "you are my priest, and the priest of others. You must never mention that name of Petronel to Mary."

"I have spoken to others," said Anger in a low voice. "I know I called her Petronel."

"Shall I go on?" asked Billacott hurriedly, "or shall I keep silent for ever?"

"Tell me all," cried the man Anger. "If you remain silent I shall be compelled to ask Mary herself."

"You know the child loves you," whispered Billacott. "She cannot hide it—she never would try hard enough—and perhaps you did go about with her more than was necessary. We cannot shut our eyes upon the facts of existence, though I have tried to; I am only an old bachelor, a selfish brute, but I look upon the young Wiggatons as my children. It is wicked of Mary. She is a bad child—worse than I thought—but she loves you, and that's the beastly fact."

"Are you certain? How do you know?" cried Anger simply.

"My dear Father Jack, Molly is the sort of girl who publishes her emotions. Let me finish. You called her Petronel—and more, far more. Do you understand me? You called her by other names, you made violent love to her, you—you kissed her, and she let you; she couldn't help it, she gave way, being a silly, weak, foolish, and rather sinful child, and she loves you, Father Jack; I came upon you; I had to tear her from your arms."

Billacott rubbed his eyes furiously, then hurried from the room. Had he ventured to look round he would have seen the face of his little priest glowing and its eyes shining yet more; for the healthy mind had been restored with good things added, and the body was growing strong in every sense, and the lesson had been learnt.

Anger said nothing that day, but slept well. The next he was allowed to leave his bed, and the day being fine Palk recommended a drive. Seeing the doctor for the first time clearly, the patient's nervousness returned, for he could not help recalling certain incidents in connection with "Youlstone Limited," and Palk had not greatly changed. He was the same shy heavy-eyed man, a recluse although his active life was spent in visiting sick folk, and a fast friend of Curgenven's; but, as Anger was to learn, this doctor was no money-lover, his only ambition was to acquire more knowledge, and that heaviness of the eyes, which looked like torpidity of mind, was actually due to midnight studies after the long day's round.

"He was a character in my drama," said Anger when Palk had

departed. "He appeared to me as a satellite of Curgenven's, almost as death, a creature without much principle. His simple manner and sleepy face gave me the impression of callousness; but it seems I was only able to judge by the outward appearance. As we drive through Riversmeet this afternoon I mean to look out for Woodland and Wadge," he went on eagerly. "And then we must go up to Youlstone."

"I am worried and depressed to-day," said the merchant.

"You are worrying about business," replied Anger gently. "You have always been the soul of kindness to me, dear Mr. Billacott, but now that I am out of danger you must not give me all your time. Won't you go home tomorrow and tell them all how well I am?"

"I am going soon. I do not worry about business. Nothing can shake 'Winnacott, Billacott, and Wiggaton,' except the joint failure of the Bank of England and the Church of Rome. You will take great care of yourself, Father Jack?" said Billacott imploringly.

"I will never go out alone upon the moor with a mist blowing up," Anger promised.

"I am afraid of another kind of mist. Plague the dear girl! Why can't she love him as I love her?" Billacott murmured to himself; and then to his companion, "You cannot stay in Riversmeet. There is no church. And Palk declares you must rest in idleness for at least six months."

"I was thinking of that last night. My duty has been neglected for nearly a year," said Anger sadly. "I have it in my mind to go back to South Wyld, directly Palk will let me."

"That will be better. Riversmeet and Youlstone may give you the horrors. Later on I will join you, and you shall show me the tombstones of my ancestors."

"The Wiggatons must come too. I am longing to show Mary the old manor house," cried Anger happily.

"Oh, Father Jack!" exclaimed the merchant. "I'm an old fool, of course, and perhaps, without offence, with great respect, you may very nearly be a young one. There! don't listen to me. Only for heaven's sake keep miles away from that beastly mud-hole."

"As I remember the pool, it was clear and sparkling. I shall certainly go to it again, and I will take Mary there. Every one of you shall drink the water, but you must not sleep afterwards as I did. Ah, Mr. Billacott, do not be depressed, for I am happy."

"There is a change, but you don't notice it yet," muttered Billacott heavily.

"I do know of the change," said Anger. "I am a young man, and I am being shown the way. When you hear of my adventures among the elements you will understand how I have been taught and why I am changed."

"Tell nobody. Forget all about it," implored Billacott. "It is a phase of your life you must not think of."

"I shall tell Mary."

"Father Jack, you must not. Remember Petronel!" cried the merchant in an agitated fashion.

"I do remember her. You must also remember one thing, Mr. Billacott: I came to Dartmoor a priest, and I hope to leave it a man as well."

With an effort Billacott restrained his tongue, mindful that Anger was not in a fit state to hear reproaches. The merchant was very jealous of his religion. He did not like to think of Anger as a man, for that suggested worldliness, and his little priest was a spiritual being. Consoled by the idea that his companion's body was not yet entirely released from the tempestuous atmosphere which had tossed it about between Youlstone and Plymouth, he answered simply, "Do not tell me your story now. We might become a little excited. Wait until we start upon our drive."

There was more bustle than usual in Riversmeet, as a sale of ponies was taking place, blocking the one street, so that, when the carriage drove through, Anger could see only a more or less familiar scene occupied by strangers.

"Not fiends, not lost spirits, but homely men and women," he exclaimed thankfully. "When I walked here, it seemed to me that every human body possessed an enormous influence upon myself, and that influence was derived from the elements. I saw men and women as mere bodies, which could not cast a shadow, passing through a scene without a background. It is strange that I found so little good and so much evil."

"There is your enemy!" exclaimed Billacott, with a spacious movement of his arm; and Anger turning saw at the corner of River Street the cheery Curgenven waving his stick at them. He put up his hand somewhat stiffly, for there was still in his mind some terror of the man who under a different shape had haunted his existence. Then the carriage went on, and the crowd of those who dealt in ponies passed down the road and hid that genial figure from his sight.

They went up to Youlstone, and Anger was astonished to find the village easy to get at from Riversmeet, and the roadway to it something more than a stony trackway. He had commenced the history of his adventures, but when the carriage turned into a well-made if narrow lane at a corner where a signpost stood bearing an inscription which looked like "I'm Youlstone," the painter having represented the one mile in the form of the first personal pronoun, he broke off and said, "I thought the village was still a long way off, but now that the enchantment has been removed things are changed. You must know, Mr. Billacott, I have been all my life a great reader of mystical romances. The stories which above all others have impressed themselves upon my fancy are those of the *Arabian Nights*, more especially the story of the Fisherman; that, when I was a boy, had an almost painful effect upon me. You may remember that when the sultan proposed returning to his own country, after avenging the King of the Black Isles and removing the enchantment from the pond and fishes, he discovered that a year's journey lay before him, although he had reached the pool among the mountains after four hours' travelling. It took me four hours to reach Dartmoor from London. It may take me a year to go back. I do remember, however, that the sultan had a very happy journey."

The merchant roused himself—driving always made him sleepy—and began to give a little good advice. "You have far too retentive a memory," he declared, "and that is a plague to a man of a nervous temperament. Somehow he always manages to remember those things which are bad for him. You know I regard you as one of the best men living," he hurried on, "and I am persuaded you would not think about anything vicious, but these wild stories, Father Jack, may play the deuce when the mind becomes unsettled. I was altogether to blame for introducing the Vigars; I ushered them into your presence and called out their names; but Petronel might have been an ordinary country girl had it not been for the mystical romances. You were a practical man at home, outside your study; but directly you come here, you surround yourself with jinn and fairies. I don't want to hear any more of your story," he added decidedly.

"It is getting dim already. Still, we must draw to the conclusion," said Anger. "I have never been a practical man," he went on sadly. "While I walked in the streets, and even when I ministered at the altar, there was a sense of enchantment about me. Nothing seemed quite real except the tragedy of certain lives. I was tormented often by a sinful fancy that the people whom I served were far below me—I do not mean morally—but they were mortals, while I was a spirit—not necessarily good—destined to live in this world for ever. I actually asked myself if the time would come when I should be able to work miracles: strike the liar dumb, pass about invisibly, make myself master of the world. It was a form of madness, I suppose. May it pass with all my weakness."

"It will. You will beat the devil and all his works," murmured Billacott.

"Ah, but I never beat Curgenven," said Anger; and he went on with his story.

Little was left by the time they reached Youlstone village, which then appeared in its true form as one of the most peaceful places in existence. Looking down the short and irregular street, Anger found it hard to occupy the place with the creatures of his fancy. No doubt there was drunkenness, and a certain amount of laxity in other matters, but it was easy to ascertain that no tragedy, other than a suicide, had been placed on record there for years, nor had any inhabitant been brought before the magistrates upon a charge more serious than driving at night without a lighted lamp.

No doubt the people had given themselves up to Nonconformity, and the learned vicar, being in the wrong place if indeed spiritually minded, had been forced to let them go, and was occupying his leisure writing theories concerning the Ice Age. No doubt a little restlessness was making itself felt owing to a change in social conditions, and certain men were asking themselves what was the fair reward of labour when they saw so many visitors from the rich and villa-sprinkled southern coast, who appeared to pass their time in idleness, whose hands and foreheads had never blistered and perspired save in the way of pleasure. But these things were below the surface. It was the calm prospect of a village which, outwardly at least, had altered very little, either for better or for worse, since the last echoes of the trumpets of civil war had died away behind those grey granitic masses. The atmosphere of the mystical romances did surround Youlstone upon three sides; but at the fourth side, which was open to valley, market-town, and railway, the waves of modern life and modern thought swept in. There was danger for Youlstone from that side. Lawlessness might rise upon the wave to banish peacefulness and a healthy communism.

"I'll give you a Quoditch for your Stiniel," said Billacott at last, in a more cheery fashion.

"Why, that is a fair bargain, but a bad compliment," replied Anger. "You will exchange fancies, and give nothing in exchange for nothing."

"Quoditch, you thought, was the home of the Billacotts, and of that family I am the head. Suppose I retired from business, and came here to live, among people whose language I can hardly understand, without a church or a congenial companion, with nothing to occupy my days. After a few months my Quoditch would become a reality which I should be very glad to escape from. Therefore my Quoditch is an idle fancy, and that is a thing which is best forgotten."

"But the actual name of Quoditch is Farbetter."

"Work and energy up to the last," cried Billacott. "Life among the people you understand, near your own church, and among your friends. That is far better."

"My Stiniel has become Landend. What do you make of that?" said Anger.

"The end of the mystical romances. The beginning of your matter-of-fact household book," replied Billacott.

"The first page is written. Come down with me into the cleave, and I will read you extracts from it."

They returned to the carriage after taking a last look at Youlstone, and drove along the lane as far as the stile, where Anger in the course of his first flight had met the boy playing with a skull. They climbed over it, came out upon the cleave and began to descend, Billacott clutching his companion's arm and imploring him to proceed with caution. "This is too much for you," he panted. "I should have brought Miss Davidson. She has more control over you than I have."

"Nobody would prevent me from taking this walk; not even Curgenven," said Anger.

They descended towards the shelter of the budding oaks, until they heard the gentle roar of the river and caught a glimpse of ruins choked with brambles. Billacott was now picking primroses eagerly, declaring he should send them to his dear lady, while Anger was lost in wonder at the beauty of the glen, and murmuring, "The spirit of enchantment is here, but the spell is holy. That wood, which was once occupied by witches and devils, is now filled with fairy-blossoms. This is the place," he called, "and down there are the ruins of the college where I received my education."

They clambered round, and stood at last upon the turf beside giant furze and alders hanging over the river, and looked upon that pile of mossy stones which no hand of mortals had meddled with for centuries. The greater part of one side-wall, and a portion of chimney, remained, but there was no roofing, and no hearthstone for the moon to strike upon.

"And yet I learnt, I grew up, I discovered my vocation, here," said Anger.

"You must not get sentimental, my dear Father Jack. Frankly, I do not like your ruins. They are damp and unpleasant; while the whole of the nook is too much out of the sun."

"Stay a few minutes, while I finish my story here. Let us walk up and down this piece of turf, arm in arm, just as we used to walk from the church to your office. That's the old style, but now the positions are reversed; you are the father, I am the son. I am about to make my last confession; but before I talk in the true, let me whisper out the false. I have now come to the meeting with the mystical Cornishman upon the bridge, which lies at the other end of this wood, a mile from here; it may be less now that the place is not enchanted."

"More mysteries. I would rather you spoke about realities," said Billacott.

"I am going to; I brought you here for no other purpose. This is the place I came to surrounded by mist in every sense, and I shall leave it soon for sunshine. The fancies of the past, Mr. Billacott, become the facts of the future."

Anger continued his story, only breaking it to ask if he had actually gone to Plymouth before the last awakening; and Billacott answered, "Once I took you into Exeter, and it is true Curgenven accompanied us upon business of his own. Twice we went to Plymouth, and upon the second occasion Miss Davidson went with us. You were often wishing to go there, and I supposed it was because the place reminded you of London and your duty."

"The horror of the final tragedy was only necessary to show me the end of a man who allows himself to be led by elemental forces," Anger continued. "I resigned my body to the moor, I gave my spirit to the whirlwind, and so when I awoke in my right mind I believed I was a murderer."

Then he described the storm, the death of the dwarf, the hurried action in the cellar of Stiniel, and the flight of Petronel towards the upland; while Billacott caressed his face with the bunch of primroses and muttered, "Your spirits are somehow human. They could not bleed, but they could weep."

"Petronel seemed always pathetic, even when she was fierce," said Anger.

"Ah, well, there's always a note of sorrow in the wind," said Billacott.

"Now for the future," cried Anger, tightening his hold upon the merchant's arm.

"Wait for it. Rest a few weeks. Don't make any plans yet," implored Billacott.

But Anger would not wait, for, like a husbandman with the home field waiting to be tilled, he felt that an hour's delay might bring the clouds along. So he opened the household book of his mind, and read the promised extracts, which dealt with the future and were modern, although they had something to do with Hugh Billacott of the past and Petronel his lady-help; while the kind merchant listened, and answered with the same affection, although his quaint face towards the close became more creased and anxious. Presently there fell a silence between them; they took another turn beside the ruined hut. The air was warm, the sky serene, and all Nature was at peace. Anger could not conceal his joy at the recovery of his freedom, although one thin layer of sorrow was spread over his mind by the thought that he was about to take an everlasting leave of one form of duty. While the merchant was sorrowful to know that another work was being planned by the ardent spirit at his side; yet he too could rejoice at the knowledge that the second book would deal with history, not with myth.

At last he murmured gently, "You know I love you both."

"The story of love," said Anger, "is the story of simplification of character."

CHAPTER XXV

THE LIVING PRESENT

AFTER that Billacott went home, and Anger became again subjected to the hauntings of Curgenven. Palk, in a lenient mood, permitted his rapidly-improving patient to receive visitors, and from that hour the lawyer saw to it that his enemy of mistland should not remain in loneliness. The little man was marvellously ubiquitous; out for a ride almost before daylight; humming about Riversmeet like a bombardier beetle during the morning;

in and out of Dartmoor villages, the friend of every family, settling disputes, attending weddings and funerals, most of the afternoon; arranging entertainments, presiding at them, performing
at them, compelling the success of charity bazaars after dark; and
in a mysterious fashion attending to a very large business without
a partner.

He would shout beneath Anger's window at six o'clock in the
morning, run up for a chat at noon, rattle his stick against the
railings about bedtime. He sent up his gardener with flowers, his
coachman with the dog-cart, his bailiff with a dish of trout; and he
was always praying "the dear old sportsman" to come and spend
an evening, and to dine, and almost to live, with him.

By this time Anger had seen Woodland rubbing his hands contentedly at the door of the Stores; and had indeed spoken with
him, but had gone away in disappointment, for the successful
man, although superior to his brother tradesmen, was not capable
of speaking or of thinking like the enchanted Woodland. Also
Anger had seen Wadge walking in his own oils along the streets
of Riversmeet, humbling himself exceedingly before every man
better than a pauper. No enchantment had been able to alter his
character. The certainly popular Curgenven was possibly the soul
of honour, but the respected Wadge was, without any doubt whatever, a scoundrel, a breaker-up of homes, a destroyer of reputa-
tions, the blackmailer and anonymous letter-writer of the town.
With a thrill Anger recognised that nobody except himself knew
what this man was capable of.

While sitting with Curgenven in his den, the window of which
did indeed project above the river, he turned the conversation
towards these men who had played their important parts in his
cloudland drama.

"I know very little of Woodland, though he and I have lived here
all our lives, and we pass each other every day," said Curgenven, as
he attended to his guest, anticipating his wants after the manner
of a born host. "He has always kept to himself. A great reader, I
believe, but no talker. He has been in my office on business a few
times, but never once inside this room."

"Not even in connection with 'Youlstone Limited'?" suggested Anger slyly.

"Eh? I want to hear all about 'Youlstone Limited.' They tell me you were always babbling of green fields," cried the lawyer.

"You shall answer my question first. What is your opinion of Woodland?"

"Why, he is the sort of man that nobody does form an opinion upon. He supplies us with the necessities of life, and takes our money with a smile. Ask him for a subscription, and out it comes. Ask him a question, and you will get a very careful answer. He has never shown any peculiarity, he has no political bias, no social inclinations, no religion apparently, no ambition beyond money-getting. You cannot discuss his character; you might as well attempt to form an opinion upon the moral qualities of a minting-machine."

"He has a very decided character; and I found it out," said Anger. "He may be too fond of his money, but I doubt if he loves it much more than his books."

"You make me nervous, Father Jack. That extraordinary mind of yours permitted nothing to escape it," said the lawyer.

"What do you know of Wadge?"

"Nothing to his credit beyond incessant praying in public. A bad Cornishman, a loathsome brute; hated and feared by all decent people; the sight of him induces nausea. It's a wonder to me how he gets a living."

"By blackmailing," said Anger heedlessly.

"What!" cried Curgenven, jumping in his chair. "Upon my soul you must be careful, or you really will make yourself unpopular. You must know I have suspected something of the sort," he went on, lowering his voice. "There has been a plague of anonymous letters the last few years, and there have also been one or two ugly cases of blackmail. I will say no more; I shall remember, though. My word, Father Jack, what a dangerous man you are! I feel almost tempted to offer you a partnership."

"In an office which has moss upon its walls and ivy trailing along the ceiling," said Anger pleasantly.

"Ah, now that you make malicious statements, I can deal with you," cried Curgenven, laughing in a fashion which recalled the past.

"Let me ask another question, but do not answer if it would mean divulging any professional secret," Anger went on. "What has been the home life of the Runnals—the people whom I called the Vigars of Stiniel—during these past months?"

"You push me on thin ice," said Curgenven, shaking his head.

"Listen to my experiences with these people," said Anger, and he proceeded to tell all he could remember of the Vigar family.

"This beats everything I have ever heard of," muttered the lawyer, when Anger had finished. "How can I keep anything from you, when you know more about the Runnals than I do myself? Yes, it is true there were wild scenes at Landend during the winter, for the woman was always in liquor and often little better than a lunatic. She hated her husband, and beat her daughter—the poor wench took it like a martyr—and it is true she tried to make the old fellow sell the farm so that she would be supplied with more money to buy whisky. I wonder what did go on up there towards the end! These people are so beastly proud there's no getting the truth out of them. They would put up with anything rather than face publicity."

"There was the glass containing rat-poison," whispered Anger. "Do you suppose this girl Emily——?"

"Hush, Father Jack! Don't say another word. The tragedy is finished, the woman has been buried, poor old Runnal is at peace. Let us leave it there. Just a little drop, a sprinkling of mountain dew, to keep me company? Palk is not here to wag his beard at ye."

"I never drink spirits," said Anger hurriedly.

"Well then, tell me more of the adventures; something in lighter vein. Bring me into the picture, as you promised, and let me see myself as the mystic saw me."

"You know I hated you."

"Because I made love to your girl. My word, Father Jack! You and I fighting tooth and nail over dumpy little Emily Runnal!"

"It was a struggle between us for the possession of the spirit of Dartmoor; or, at least, of a form which expressed health, strength, and happiness to me."

"You cursed me beautifully," cried Curgenven. "I took you out for a walk, as Billacott had letters to write, and Miss Davidson was not well; and when we got up upon the moor you went for me."

"You had your revenge later on, when I broke up the Court of Lomyns' Furze," said Anger.

"So that didn't escape you either!"

"You don't tell me that orgie actually took place," exclaimed Anger; and he went on hurriedly to give his version of the incident.

Curgenven sat for a few moments with hands upon his knees, staring at the fire. Presently he put up his head and said without a trace of his usual liveliness, "Father Jack, this passes everything! The Court of Lomyns' Furze was established more than two centuries ago, and was held exactly as you have described it until the commencement of the Victorian period. Youlstone was a very rough place then, but although the commoners were careless drunkards it was not difficult to persuade the majority that such barbarous customs must be put a stop to. The Court is held now after this manner: an inch of candle is lighted, then the competitors for the field begin to bid; and the man who has named the biggest sum by the time the candle burns out is declared the tenant; the money goes to charity. I believe nobody except myself, and possibly an old man who lives in Youlstone parish, knows how the Court was held originally. The tradition has died out because the people did not care to talk about it."

"That is another matter which we need not go into," said Anger nervously. "It was a fearful scene, and you were sitting at the end of the table with your eyes glowing like live coals."

"I seem to have been the devil himself," said Curgenven.

"You were," replied Anger simply, and he fully described the plots and counter-plots in connection with Youlstone Limited.

"And now I must go," he continued. "It is nearly ten o'clock, and I promised Palk to be in bed by that time. This is my last week in Riversmeet, and I cannot say I shall be sorry to leave it. If I stayed I might actually become as hated as I thought I was. I am dangerous, as you say; I have found out too much."

Curgenven's manner had changed. There was no laughter

in him as he went with his guest to the door, and shut him out abruptly, almost fiercely. Then he returned to his den, glad to be alone, for his body was trembling and his merry red face had turned to no colour.

"Those Youlstone mortgages," he muttered. "Those fields for a few sovereigns—I have only done the same as others—and he saw me as Old Nick."

Next morning there came to Anger joy in an envelope and enchantment upon notepaper. The inspirer was Billacott; the writer his dear lady. The whole cloud of Wiggatons was about to descend upon Riversmeet and to burst in loving-kindness upon Father Jack. The junior partner needed a change, as he had been forced to work at full pressure during the long absence of that excellent man who had himself ordered the holiday, going a little way against his conscience and the whole way with his heart.

"We come to Riversmeet to pack you up," wrote Mrs. Wiggaton. "And then for Wyld, to see the old manor and to go a-picnicking beside the sleeping water."

"And after Wyld, gentleness," Anger murmured in perfect peace. "I see here the heart of Billacott, who loves us both, who loves everybody. He has persuaded himself that happiness comes before a matter of doubtful doctrine. The dear old man's an angel."

He had already acquired the habit of writing to Mary every day; and he proceeded to answer Mrs. Wiggaton's letter, which had been dictated by Billacott, in the roundabout fashion of writing to her daughter, yet somewhat differently, and after this fashion: Tell your mother this, and your father that; give this message to dear Mr. Billacott—a few lines only—and now, dear Mary, the rest of the letter is for you.

For two whole days Curgenven was silent and simmering in his own thoughts; upon the third, while Anger was waiting, half on tiptoe, with heart beating rapidly, for the arrival of the Wiggatons, the lawyer came without a shout, and when alone with the young priest, who had now become his haunter, said in a jerky fashion:

"I have been thinking over what you told me, Father Jack. When you are settled in your new parish, write to me, will you? If

there is anything you want—a club for the lads, or a new chancel—
just talk about it. I am going up to Youlstone now; I have some
land there, and you have given me the idea of making it over to the
village—for the common use. What think you of the plan?"

"It is a very good one," said Anger, taking the lawyer's hand,
and still holding it while he murmured, "Only this was wanting to
make me forget."

"One more thing," said Curgenven, beginning to laugh in his
usual merry fashion. "It was popular belief, I flatter myself, which
forced you to regard me as an understudy of the personage who,
according to Milton, 'swindges the scaly horror of his folded tail.'
Here is a small memento of your stay here. If you have no fancy
to keep the thing, hurl it into the river. At all events I will have it in
my house no longer."

He handed to Anger a piece of iron which at a glance might
have been taken for a horseshoe, although it was not of that shape
and was considerably less in size.

"Here is also a copy of a local newspaper, dated February 23rd,
one thousand eight hundred and fifty-five," Curgenven went on.
"The one explains the other. Fifty years ago, if you had asked a
Devonshire schoolchild, 'What do you know of the devil?' you
would probably have received the answer, 'Please, sir, he lives to
Youlstone.' That is the popular belief to which I referred. The
newspaper will tell you about the apparition which in the year I
have mentioned disturbed the life of Dartmoor and east Devon.
It was during the night of Thursday the eighth of February that
remarkable footprints were left upon the snow, beginning at
Youlstone and passing along the estuary of the Exe, and so to the
sea. The size of each footprint was four by two and three-quarter
inches, but instead of progressing as any animal would have done,
namely feet right and left, foot followed foot in a single line, the
distance between each tread being eight inches. The visitor left his
print in each courtyard and garden throughout the country, and
upon each house in the towns, through which he passed; going
over roofs, hayricks, and high walls without disturbing the snow,
locked gates being no hindrance to him. These footprints actually

appeared within culverts too low to admit even a small dog, while every one of them removed the snow cleanly as if it had been branded with a hot iron; and everywhere the snow was ruffled behind as by a tail. Although most of the savants in the country offered explanations to allay the panic, no satisfactory solution was ever given. My father took an impression of one of these footprints and had it cast in iron. It came to me as an heirloom, and now I pass it on to you."

"Thank you," said Anger quietly. "I will keep it."

Even the elements were at rest, and the sky was kind, as Anger went towards the station, forgetting Curgenven, and thinking of the mythical Bobby's words of greeting, "What are you bringing me: Rain? Snow? Wind?" And he had answered, "I hope to bring you sunshine." Now Mary would be crossing the boundary of Youlstone parish, and he need not ask what she brought; not rain, snow, nor wind; but that serene and happy atmosphere he himself had wished to bring to Youlstone.

During those almost tempestuous moments when the Wiggatons burst into arrival, Anger remained calm, for the sunshine was upon him. Mary was not the same, because of the change in himself; she seemed stronger because he had grown strong; so much more beautiful because his own character was formed; so marvellously human because he had humanised himself. Yet he could hear, far away, the last sobbing echo of the tempest, as he looked into her eyes, which were those he had seen in the hut at Stiniel, and within the wood, but now without fierceness or passion; and upon the dark hair which was also part of his romance; and upon the graceful figure which he had thought was lost to him for ever. Around them surged young Wiggatons, their cheeks blown out with laughter like wind-spirits, all impatient to sweep across the moor and tumble their bodies into every nook; and behind were the authors of this happy band of noisy pilgrims.

"Mr. Wiggaton, how glad I am to see you!" said Anger, his voice choked with love. "Dear Mrs. Wiggaton, you seem to bring your home with you."

"We are all awake now that we breathe our native air," declared the merchant. "Directly the train entered Devonshire, I took a deep breath and felt alive again. Unfortunately we had to wait an hour among the ruins of Exeter. I spent it sitting in the waiting-room with my eyes shut."

"Oh, what a whopper!" cried one of the younger children. "Don't you believe a word of it, Father Jack. Dad took us out into the town and showed us everything."

"And if I had encouraged his fit of sentimentality, he would have gone upon his knees and kissed the ground," added Mrs. Wiggaton.

"I do not argue with members of my own family," said Wiggaton stiffly. "To be loyal to our country when we return to it is only decent."

No more than twenty-four hours were to be spent in Riversmeet, and in that short time there was much to be done. Tea being over, the congregation dispersed, old and young instinctively avoiding Father Jack and Mary, who had always gone about together and were not likely to alter their custom then. They soon found themselves upon the track which descended towards the foot-bridge across the river, to the wood and the ruined hut which was to be rebuilt as a temple during this last walk through that region of the mist. The evenings were getting long, so they were not pressed for time; but neither feared the darkness, for the struggle was over, and the night of enchantment—which was merely the passing out of youth into the full state of manhood—would weave no more dark spells. Instead of the destructive storm-wind came the revelation of the wind-flower; it was spring and the wood was white with swaying blossoms; and all the wide prospect had been purged of the dark witch, the dwarf her son, and the elf-maiden alluring youths astray. The chains of winter had been shattered; the growth followed. It was their birthday. Over the hills came the golden-haired son of Kalew bearing the miracle of his harp, and striking upon it to change coldness into warmth, making the dullest creature dance with the joy of living which thrills in spring or never. The wind was not always destructive; at one time it was dark and terrible, howling for victims; at another a restorer of life, a gentle spirit of the garden, a herald of the resurrection. Buds broke, creation shook off the mystic sleep; even the lowest animals thought of mates when the magic harp was ringing to the dawn.

No more the dull sleep of fancy, dimly lighted by the blue lamp of the marshes, but the white light of living reality and the red lamp of religion. For as sleep is the most remarkable change to which the human body can be subject, so is the awakening of life at spring the greatest miracle which can happen upon earth. Hearts must be stirred then, and minds forced open to be taught, as the Lord of Life descends with a message and a call. The gates of the Garden which contains the two immortal trees are thrown open, and all may enter to wander and to search; like the few faithful who came at break of day to the empty tomb, and, while questioning the gardener, found their God; but hearts must be pure while the gardener passes through, and that magic harp is ringing to the sun.

"And here we make our future," said Anger, after assisting Mary tenderly across the stepping-stones, retaining her hand when they had crossed, and were standing beside the ruins of the tinners' shelter which had been to him the hut of Petronel. "I awoke with it half formed, and here, in this place sacred to you and to me, it shall take a shape which cannot be altered while heaven is kind and we are strong. You know that I am about to follow the example of others, far better and wiser than myself, who have not been ashamed to be called perverts when their humanity has been awakened by the call of love. It is not a sin to change from a former position of belief when by continuing in it I should commit a crime against my conscience which is speaking to me now more clearly than it has ever done, making me remember my faults at last."

"I was afraid, so terribly afraid, that you would not recover," whispered Mary.

"I knew so very little in that past life," Anger went on resolutely. "A heaviness was upon my soul; I could not think. Every action of my life was mechanical. Then I came here, my whole body was changed, and I received to a certain extent a new mind also. Thoughts came to me, and courage to express them. Dear Mary, I grew careless, and indifferent to my duty. I went too far out of the way, but that was because I saw, or thought I could see, the faults in my religion."

Mary said nothing; she was prepared. But still, as a companion she moved a little nearer, and as a comrade pressed his hand.

"Then it seemed to me I met Lyson. No doubt my old school-fellow lives and works as a priest, but where I do not know. Mr. Billacott suggested at once that the advice and warning, which I believed came from his lips, really proceeded out of my own mind. All the more reason then for my change of creed. He was the pattern of the perfect priest, such as I shall aim at, not the Roman priest, who, however English he may be, must remain an alien, since he acknowledges as his head a foreigner, and must abide by his decrees however arbitrary, even if they bid him resist the laws of his own country and fight against his king. The English priest of Rome works in a narrow field so far as his own country is concerned; the members of my congregation, as you know, were chiefly Irish and Italian; he is unable to play the patriot, or to reach the sympathies of our liberty-loving people. I saw in my imagination the old and young of our own land flocking into Lyson's church; I perceived the Englishman may now be a priest and father of his people; and he is free, he may work untrammelled, and teach the doctrines which he believes are true. The decree of infallibility was always my stumbling-block; now it is something more. When I was shown Lyson in his beautiful church, I envied him, and my ambition was to be as good and free. No mysticism is here, Mary."

"It is simplicity," she murmured happily.

"I made the same remark to Mr. Billacott, standing in the same place, and he answered, 'Love urges you to take this step, which seems to me a fearful one. I would rather see you a layman of my church than a priest of any other. Your Lyson was not a married man.' I told him it was love. I told him I had lost something during that tremendous change which visited every part of my being during the terrible, yet helpful, winter months. But I had gained far more than I lost. I had learnt that it is a man's duty to work out his salvation by love alone, by love which helps him in his work, by love which leads him higher. If he can work it out through love for religion unaided—good. If he cannot, he must either love a woman or be lost. I see now those things, those simplest things which, when I worked in London, were beyond my mind. I know that I gave myself to you, dear Mary, and I permitted, encouraged, even implored, you to give yourself to me. Yet when you replied, with all the sweetness and goodness of your nature, I drew back because I remained complex and could not simplify myself. I had your companionship daily but was too weak to know I had a human heart. It was when I came away, and received for the first time strength, that I missed something which my religion had not given and could not give. I lacked what had become necessary, the presence of Mary, the voice of my companion, the help of my comrade. And now I have brought you here, to the place where I loved the spirit of the moor as the girl Petronel, because she had your eyes, and your hair, and your figure, although none of your goodness. I confess that it is my love for you that compels me to become, in the sight of my old rector and Mr. Billacott, our dearest friend, a pervert. For I am a man now; I was a weak boy in London, and like a boy did as I was told by my masters, and had not the courage to put questions to my heart and mind. You and I, dear Mary, walked together through that narrow life unlawfully. Still together, in some such parish and such church as Lyson's, we may continue our work, united no more in fancy, but in the reality of the fullest life, in the eternal verity of love. Mary, my saviour!" cried Anger, drawing her closely to him, "I am awake!"

THE END

www.ingramcontent.com/pod-product-compliance
Lightning Source LLC
Chambersburg PA
CBHW011344010726
47493CB00011B/2938